HERE COME

A block and a half. [...] *forever.* There it was, though—the empty lot, complete with snow-covered two-rut road, diving straight into the black heart of an overgrown woods.

These places never look so ominous in the daylight.

Minerva stamped her feet to warm them; stared down that overgrown maw of a tunnel.

Light from the flashlight illuminated no more than ten feet into the gloom. The beam seemed dim to her; she smacked the base of the flashlight once with the flat of her hand, but it didn't help.

In the stygian blackness, something terrible waited for her. Something straight out of her worst nightmares.

And that something had her kids.

"All right!" she said into the wind. "Give them back to me now and I won't come after you."

The wind whistled and howled. It made voices—but the voices said nothing she could understand.

"Give them back or I'm coming in!" she yelled. "You don't want me to come in."

But the invisible thing that waited evidently did. . . .

HOLLY LISLE

MINERVA WAKES

A Baen Books Original

Baen Publishing Enterprises
P.O. Box 1403
Riverdale, N.Y. 10471

ISBN: 0-671-72202-6

Cover art by Clyde Caldwell

First printing, January 1994

Distributed by
SIMON & SCHUSTER
1230 Avenue of the Americas
New York, N.Y. 10020

Typeset by Windhaven Press, Auburn, N.H.
Printed in the United States of America

In Memory of Susan Woodward

ACKNOWLEDGEMENTS

Thanks to my children, Mark and Becky
Deaton, who acted as technical advisors
on the kid portions of the book;

To Michael MacWatkins, the Crazy Celt,
who gave Jamie his personality;

To Chris, who went over every
word of this after me and helped me
put everything together;

To Schrodinger's Petshop—
world's best writing and critiquing group;

And especially to my editor,
Toni Weisskopf—who has been patient,
and terrific, and who made me
do this right in spite of myself.

CHAPTER 1

"No! Please don't shoot!" The hospital's data processing director groveled in the aisle. "I'll never do it again, I promise! Just let me live—" Mrs. Mindley was on her knees, begging and sobbing. Minerva had waited a long time to see her like that.

"Too late, you inconsiderate cow—you've blocked the aisle one time too many. Now you die!" The machine gun in Minerva's hands jumped and snarled, and Minerva gleefully splattered bits of Mrs. Mindley over the entire soup section.

Minerva Kiakra's lips curled into a tight smile as she imagined that scene. It beat reality. Reality was that Mrs. Mindley's shopping cart angled across most of the Soup/Sauce/Pasta aisle, allowing no passage, while Mrs. Mindley's wide-load rear end blocked the rest. The woman bent over the display of Tomato and Rice soup, carefully choosing cans—Minerva was unable to determine the method the other woman was using to establish can ripeness, but three out of every four of the little suckers were obviously failing some sort of test.

The Chicken and Noodle soup was tantalizingly within view, and completely out of reach.

"***Chicken and Noodle soup—6 cans!!!" Darryl had marked on the shopping list.

1

Minerva stared at the list, and gritted her teeth, and waited.

But patience wasn't going to work. Minerva suspected malice in Mrs. Mindley's glacial slowness. She was going to have to be direct. Toughness was what the situation called for, she decided.

She cleared her throat. "Excuse me, Mrs. Mindley, but I'm in a hurry."

The woman didn't even look up. She just waved her hand in one of those dismissive "wait a minute" gestures that meant she'd move when she was damned good and ready, and not before.

Minerva raised her voice a notch. "Mrs. Mindley, I need to get past you."

Her voice sounded contemptible and pleading in her own ears. She could imagine how it sounded to Mrs. Mindley— and sure enough, the woman continued to ignore her.

Minerva watched her knuckles whiten on the cart handle. "My baby-sitter needs to get home, and she can't leave until I get there."

The other woman glared up at her and, with a vicious snort, moved her cart just enough that Minerva could squeeze by if she dragged her left shoulder along the shelves on the opposite side. Naturally, doing that meant all the boxes of macaroni and spaghetti stacked on those shelves toppled to the floor. They rattled loudly behind her, and Minerva cringed—but the baby-sitter really was in a hurry, and the weather was building toward a North Carolina ice storm that was going to lock everyone in for a week or better. She was miserably short of time. So, feeling guilty, she left the boxes on the floor, and, as she'd expected, she heard the old bat snort again.

"The nerve of *some people*."

Minerva's imagination created a fantasy shopping cart for her that featured twin-mounted submachine guns on the front end and a flamethrower at ankle height, and pleased herself by mentally frying Mrs. Mindley to a cinder after gunning her down. That would teach the old harridan to block the aisle. Or to drop a stack of reports on Minerva's desk and demand that she handle them because they dealt with data problems in the Administrative, not Data Processing, Department.

Feeling better, Minerva returned to shopping. "Six cans of Chicken Noodle, some Chicken and Stars for the kids, and some asparagus soup for me . . ." she muttered. Then she checked the price on the asparagus soup and put it back. It was a luxury that would have to wait until another time. She'd have Chicken and Stars with the kids.

She snarled and grumbled her way down the aisles, checking off Darryl's special items with an extra dash of venom; Darryl was going on his biennial health kick, which Minerva knew from experience would last exactly five days and would drive the rest of the family nuts in the process. She also knew from experience that it was easier to give in to his nonsensical demands than to fight them.

"Wheat germ. Ri-i-i-i-ight. He's going to sprinkle it on a huge serving of ice cream and claim it's a health treat. And I'll end up sneaking it into casseroles and homemade cookies for a year to get rid of it." Nevertheless, she did find some wheat germ and tossed it into the cart.

"Sunflower seeds." She just rolled her eyes and sighed.

She brushed her bangs out of her face and surveyed the list critically. Thank God she was almost done. The cart would give a junk-food junkie nightmares—it was full of whole-wheat crackers and bean sprouts, exotic vegetables and strange fruits, and chicken and fish and expensive lean ground beef. And this mess, most of which she and the kids would eat after Darryl got bored playing fitness expert, was going to cost twice the usual weekly amount.

She cruised into the cereal aisle in a foul temper.

****WHEATIES!!!—BIG BOX!!!* the list demanded.

That was the last of her beloved spouse's special items.

Wheaties, for chrissakes, she thought. *Ugh! Not even I like them.*

She marched the entire length of the aisle, looking for Wheaties. There weren't any.

"Oh, damn," she muttered. Darryl would throw a royal tantrum. She turned around and looked back the way she had come. There, at the very opposite end of the row, on the very top shelf, a single box of Wheaties sat in lonely splendor.

She sighed and backtracked, carefully not looking at the box. If she looked at it, some other shopper was sure to notice the direction of her glance and decide to beat her to it. Grocery shopping was a vicious, competitive event even in good weather. Right before an ice storm, when "Snowbound Panic" took over, it became truly bloodthirsty.

However, this time her strategy worked. The box was still there when she shoved her cart in front of it and reached up.

Her reflexes were a little off. It had been an awful day, which was segueing into an awful evening. Edgy as she was, her reach for the Wheaties was more of a desperate grab. The box was hers—until she fumbled it away with one clumsy move . . . and saw it grabbed in midair by another shopper.

Like a wild thing, she faced the devious thief, teeth bared, warning growl readied in the back of her throat—

The growl stopped, strangled, halfway to delivery.

A dragon stared back at her out of serene amber eyes.

It looks real, Minerva thought. *What sort of promotion is FoodLion having that uses a dragon? Dragon Days? They're going to give some old lady a heart attack with that thing. Or me. They may give* me *a heart attack.*

The vertical slits in the dragon's amber eyes dilated, and it cocked its head to one side, staring at her as if it found her as peculiar-looking as she found it.

It had a bony, oversized snout full of curved ivory teeth the size of ten-penny nails. Its delicately scaled blue hide shimmered with rainbow iridescence. The pale, glossy wings of flesh around its face and down its neck flexed and spread with a slow, steady rhythm; its long, thick tail trailed around the corner, while two membranous pale blue wings unfurled slightly as she glared at it.

That's real, she thought with growing wonder. *No one makes costumes that perfect.*

Other shoppers hurried past. They pushed their carts by without paying attention to either the dragon or Minerva, but Minerva noticed that they detoured around the space the dragon occupied and kept their eyes averted.

There is something standing there. It isn't just a figment of my imagination. Could it, perhaps, be a woman—and I'm just seeing a dragon?

That's it. I'm hallucinating. I've cracked up. I'm about to get into a fight with Mrs. Mindley over Darryl's fucking Wheaties, and my mind has turned her into a dragon.

The dragon clutched the box against its belly scales with one wickedly taloned hand and grinned at Minerva, exposing even more teeth. It definitely had a Mrs. Mindley-ish smile. Then the dragon dropped the box into its own shopping cart.

A vision of Darryl deprived of Wheaties danced in front of Minerva's eyes. Darryl's voice, whining, "Is it such a problem for you if I ask you to get me a few simple things? Can't you even take the time to do a little favor for me, when you know I'm trying to take care of myself?" droned through her memory.

"NO!" Minerva yelled, willing to face down a woman who made her job hell, or even a real dragon, to avoid that self-pitying whine. She grabbed at the cereal box.

Opalescent blue-green fingers gripped viselike around her wrist, and a sub-bass voice rumbled in her ear, "MINE."

As abruptly as that, she found herself sitting on a bruised rump on the cold tile floor, staring up at the dragon's receding sapphire-blue back as it strolled casually down the aisle.

That, lady, is one hell of a muscular hallucination, she told herself.

The dragon and its shopping cart made two stops. *It's getting Pop Tarts and Instant Breakfast,* Minerva noted, bemused. Then it turned the corner, and disappeared.

Taking the Wheaties with it.

"Darryl, there was this dragon in the supermarket today, and it snatched the only box of Wheaties out of my hand and wouldn't give it back," Minerva imagined herself saying. *Right. Darryl will love that. I could save myself a lot of time by going to the Emergency Room and telling them the same thing. They could check me into a padded room in a hurry.*

A padded room seemed like a nice idea. It would be a quiet room, with people to take care of her, round-the-clock tranquilizers, no responsibilities, no hassles, no chores. It was obviously something she needed, something she'd been building up for.

Well, fighting with a dragon in the supermarket over a box of cereal no one in my house likes is definitely stupid. And probably crazy. So is sitting in the aisle, waiting to get run over by a crazed shopper.

She got up, dusted off the back of her slacks, and began shoving the cart toward the dairy section.

But, delightful as a stay in a sanitarium would probably be . . . we don't have the time or the money for me to lose my mind this month.

She took a deep breath, and let it out slowly.

You're going to have to be okay, Minerva, she told herself. *You don't have any choice.*

The checkout lines stretched endlessly. The weather service was calling for four inches of snow and freezing rain by morning. They might be wrong; they were often enough, after all. But everyone in town was stocking up on staples, just in case. Checkout line camaraderie was high. Neighbors and strangers alike chatted about the impending storm, about their snow tires or newly bought tire chains, about their kids and their kids' sleds that would probably only get one use this winter. Minerva submerged herself in the chatter and felt better.

Outside, pushing the cart across the parking lot, freezing as the wet, cold wind bit through her ski jacket and gabardine slacks, Minerva managed to put the dragon incident out of her mind.

Jamie is having a spelling test tomorrow—fifty words. Did we have fifty words at a time in fourth grade? I can't remember.

She shoved paper bags into the back of the station wagon, wedging them in against each other so they wouldn't tip and dump groceries all over the car.

And work is going to be hell tomorrow. The visit by Joint Commission means a ton of extra paperwork. God, but I

hate JCAH visits. I'll have to start on revisions of the organi-
zation charts and Mr. Asher's presentation for the trustees
first thing in the morning, or I'll be buried in paper by next
week.

She slammed down the hatch, and pulled her keys out of
her ski jacket. There was a shrill squeal of tires on cold pavement from across the parking lot, and she glanced over.

A red sports car. Mazda Miata? Yeah, a Miata. Even own-
ing one of those things, and red at that, is begging for killer
insurance premiums—and then to drive the way that idiot is
driving— She shook her head, bewildered.

There had been a time in her life when she'd dreamt of
red sports cars. It was hard to remember what that was like,
wanting a racy, sexy little convertible two-seater to show off
in—and to hell with the practicality. Remembering that was
almost like trying to remember fourth grade. She'd been a
different person both times.

She stared at her white LTD wagon with loathing. For
just a second, she could almost reach into her past to touch
the Minerva who'd wanted that red two-seater—but reality
reminded her that a cute little car wouldn't carry her own
three kids and several of their closest friends, or all the groceries, or half the PTA moms. A Mazda Miata was not a
mommy car.

Reality reminded Minerva that she was a mommy.

She backed out of her parking space, wormed her way
into the solid block of cars trying to get out of the lot, and
inched forward.

There was another screech of tires, and the sleek red
Miata skidded over the grass to the right of the drive, and
nosed back in, right in front of her.

She stared at the license plate, which read "FLAMER."

I'll remember that all right, she thought.

The bumper-sticker was even worse. "I ♥ VIRGINS," it
declared. The most obnoxious thing about the little red car
was the yellow diamond stuck to the darkly tinted rear window, though. *That* told the world, "Living Legend On
Board."

"What an asshole," she muttered.

As if the little convertible's driver had heard her, the dark-tinted window on its driver's side rolled down.

The blue dragon leaned its head out of the window and grinned its cocky grin at her. Then, as the line of traffic surged forward, the dragon gunned the engine and roared out into the river of cars.

Minerva floored her own gas pedal and shot after it in desperate pursuit.

Thirty-five miles per hour through here, Minerva, her reality-based self growled. *A ticket will raise your insurance.*

Goddamned dragon driving a goddamned Mazda Miata at fifty, and I'm going to catch it and find out why! the rest of her growled back. *Or die trying.*

There were, surprisingly, no police cars in sight. She and the dragon made it through the center of town without injury, and headed toward suburban streets, and her house. The dragon kept to the main highway. Minerva stuck to the dragon. The LTD's speedometer crept to the eighty-miles-per-hour mark, and then past it. Minerva didn't care.

One street from her house, the dragon slowed enough to hang a rubber-burning right. Minerva followed suit, then gunned after it, accelerating into the curve and giving the car a little extra gas to cut down the fishtailing as she pulled the car straight and closed on her target.

The dragon dove into another right, with Minerva moving in fast.

Then the Miata slowed way down and turned right again onto an incredibly overgrown dirt road in the middle of what Minerva would have sworn was a vacant lot the last time she looked. She stopped. The little sports car's red taillights flickered down the tunnel-like gloom. She watched them dim, then vanish.

She started to swing her car onto the side road—the compulsion to follow that dragon was overwhelming.

But—

But the ice cream in the back of the car would melt, and Carol needed her costume started. *But* the baby-sitter needed to get home, and Jamie had a test he would need help studying for. *But* a storm was coming, and it was time for supper, and—

As if to add emphasis to the real world, the first light flakes of snow drifted through the beams of her headlights and across her windshield. Feeling that adventure was passing her by, she nosed the station wagon onto the dirt road and executed a neat three-point turn.

Home, she told herself. *Go home right this minute like the responsible adult you are, and no more dragons in Mazdas. No matter what it might have meant.*

Minerva had second thoughts the whole last block and a half to home.

Barney met her at the door, full of four-year-old angst.

"They won't let me play," he wailed. "They said I'm a little boy. I'm not. I'm a big boy, and I can play, too!"

Carol and Jamie looked up from Chutes and Ladders, and Jamie said, "Un-UH! You can't count and you cheat on the chutes!"

Carol added her own five-year-old wisdom. "When you get bigger, you'll be able to play. Right, Mommy?"

Seventeen-year-old Louise had her jacket on, and her books piled in her backpack, and revulsion in her eyes. "You promised you'd get here half an hour ago, Mrs. Kiakra. I'm going to be late for my date."

"Going to be an ice storm tonight, Louise. You might have to cancel. But I'm sorry I'm late. The supermarket was a zoo." She handed Louise her cash, and watched her baby-sitter flounce out the door without so much as a "thanks."

"You ought to be used to zoos," she heard the girl mutter.

I love you too, dear, Minerva thought.

The phone rang.

She ran for it. "Kiakra Demolitions," she said. She usually got a kick out of saying that, but this time she just hoped the ritual family greeting would fend off whichever siding sales-man, encyclopedia vendor, or purveyor of time-share condos at Myrtle Beach happened to be calling. But it wasn't a member of North Carolina's three great growth industries on the line.

It was Darryl, saying that he was going to be late. Would

Minerva mind keeping supper in the oven for him, he'd be there when he could?

Minerva stared at the groceries, sitting in their bags silently thawing, at Carol and Jamie squabbling and pouting over their game, at Barney crashing his cars into the base of the television set, at Murp sharpening his claws on the table leg—and she assured her husband that she wouldn't mind. She tried to ignore the strained quality of her voice as she said it. She hoped she gave him a headache when she slammed the phone down.

"We interrupt your regularly scheduled program to take you live to the home of Mr. and Mrs. Darryl Kiakra, where Mrs. Kiakra has just been led from the house, bound in a straightjacket.

"Inside the house is the scene of recent horrible slaughter. The bodies of Mr. Darryl Kiakra; a young woman identified as Louise Simmons, the Kiakra's baby-sitter; and a large orange tabby have been found chopped into tiny little pieces.

"Neighbors say that Mrs. Kiakra, who has confessed to slicing up her spouse, the baby-sitter, and the cat with a cheese grater, has always been a fine neighbor. 'She was always right friendly. Real quiet. Real nice,' says one source who asks not to be identified. 'Them's the ones you have to worry about.'

"Mrs. Kiakra's children have been located at a friend's house, where they say their mother only told them she was tired before she sent them off to visit. They all three agree that 'her eyes were real funny when she looked at us, though.' "

Minerva leaned on the counter and rested her head in her arms. Weird, violent fantasies, and images of dragons and fighting kids and Darryl-the-wonder-spouse and her stupid job and her boring life all crowded together, and she scrunched her eyes closed and wished them all away.

When she reopened them, hoping for a miracle, nothing had changed.

She sighed, screamed at the kids to quit fighting, hissed at Murp—and began unloading groceries.

Barney quit playing with his cars and wandered over. He hugged Minerva's leg.

"Hi," he said.

"Hi, yourself."

She stopped what she was doing for a moment and picked him up and squeezed him tightly.

"I love you, Mommy," he told her.

She sighed, and smiled. "I love you, too, punkin."

She put him down. He watched her a moment longer, an intent expression on his little face. "I will miss you when you're gone," he informed her.

She nodded, a bit puzzled. Of all her kids, Barney was the one who spent the most time out in left field. He was famous for his cryptic remarks. He probably just meant he missed her when she went shopping or somesuch—but she wasn't about to ask. Barney's answers to questions tended to be even weirder than his out-of-the-air comments.

She gave him a tired smile. "Go play, sweetheart, and let me get done here."

He nodded and wandered back out to the living room.

Darryl Kiakra scrunched lower in the folding chair and tried to block out Geoff Forest's nasal voice. Geoff stood at the podium in front of the creative development staff, exhorting them to greater deeds— *Same shit, different day,* Darryl thought.

The girl in the chair in front of him had pretty hair. It was long and thick and wavy—glossy chestnut-brown with bright red-and-gold highlights that didn't come out of a bottle. He imagined what all that hair would feel like, then extended his daydream to include the entire girl. She also, he noted, had superior legs. She crossed them and uncrossed them and wriggled impatiently in her seat in a way that Darryl found quite entertaining. Considerably more entertaining than the next installment in Geoff's endless series of pointless meetings.

Everyone stood. A beat behind them, Darryl stood too.

The stand-up, sit-down crap was part of Geoff's "show-me-you're-with-me" style of management, and Darryl detested the whole process. He had, however, learned that if he bucked the flow, he got singled out as a purveyor of low morale and earned a "non-team player" label.

"That's great," Geoff said, and granted his thralls a long look at his horsy smile. "Now, everyone who thinks we can meet the next quarter goals for new accounts—sit back down."

Everyone sat. The girl in front of Darryl covertly flipped the boss the bird.

Darryl decided he liked her.

There were a few more "gosh-gee-whiz" questions from the kiss-up contingent, and Geoff outlined his idea of reasonable goals for the next week—Darryl decided the man must have been doing drugs to come up with such off-the-wall projections. Then the meeting came to an end. Darryl thought if he hurried, he might make it home in time to eat supper before the food got so dried out it lost all taste.

But the girl with the nice legs and the nice hair came up to him and smiled. She had a nice smile, too.

"You're Darryl Kiakra, aren't you?"

He nodded.

"You were on the team that developed the new Hearth-Home campaign, weren't you? The one that's up for a Cleo?" Her eyes were full of admiration.

Pretty eyes, he thought. *Bright green. Contact lenses? Probably.* He smiled. "I was. Junior member of the team, but certainly on it. Why do you ask?"

She looked down at her feet, then back up at him. "I'm new. I thought maybe you could tell me how you did it—how you came up with such a terrific campaign." Her voice implied that, junior member or not, she knew he was the idea man—that HearthHome was *his* success.

He could go home right then, he thought. Home to Minerva, who bitched about the kids and her job; who didn't look at him with admiration in her eyes anymore, but instead with something approaching disgust. He could go home and listen to her tell him that he had a fulfilling, creative job, while she was being stifled by all her responsibilities—as if his sixty-hour weeks that paid for most of the house and most of the food and most of everything else were totally divorced from responsibility; as if writing commercials for dog food and dishwasher detergent and the detestable HearthHome cookies was the same as selling his plays would have been.

Yeah, he could go home, where he was the thirty-one-year-old producer of paychecks, the person whose thrillingly creative career didn't pay enough to free Minerva from the drudgery of her own job. He could listen to her talk about painting, and he could see in her face the certainty that if he were a better provider, she would be a professional artist by now.

He could listen to the kids fight, and hear Minerva complain about how he didn't ever want to *talk* about their relationship. Darryl hated the word "relationship." When Minerva used it, it meant fun and spontaneity—and sex—were out of the question for the evening. The conversation would be about her growth as a person and his not-growth as a person and how she wished he would read one damned self-improvement book or another and change. After all, she'd changed, hadn't she?

Yes, she has, he thought, *and it hasn't been an improvement.*

Or he could stay late at work, skip supper, and tell this young girl with the bright green eyes what a clever fellow he was. Hell, with an ice storm coming, maybe he could play his cards really right and spend the whole night with the girl, the two of them huddled in his cubicle of an office for warmth while the weather raged around them. Maybe they could find some creative ways to keep warm.

He'd never cheated on Minerva. He'd never wanted to before. But she wasn't really Minerva anymore, he thought—not in the important ways. She wasn't the girl he'd married. She was a stranger he didn't understand and didn't like very much.

He gave the gold band on his left hand a momentary glance, twisted it nervously with his thumb, and took a deep breath.

"I have a file in my office on HearthHome," he said. "I can show you some of our sketches and preliminary work, and tell you how we turned those into the final Hearth-Home campaign. Would that help?"

She looked at him, radiating awe and respect. "Thank you, Darryl. It really would."

"Great then." He glanced at her and frowned just a little. "By the way, what's your name?"

Barney listened while Mommy finished singing bedtime songs. She tucked in Jamie first, then headed for his bed.

"Mom!" Jamie yelled. "Don't step on Waterloo!"

She looked at the hundreds of tiny plastic soldiers littering the floor around Jamie's bed. "Waterloo?"

"I figured out a way for Napoleon to win it—I think," Jamie said. "But I have to finish trying all the stuff tomorrow."

"Waterloo." Mommy sighed, and stepped carefully around the battlefield. "All right. I won't bump anything."

She sat down on the side of Barney's bed. He smiled at her.

"G'night, punkin. Have sweet dreams."

He hugged her. She smelled nice, he thought. "Seymour got a new fire truck," he told her. Seymour had played with his new truck all day at preschool—and hadn't shared. It was big and red, and it would have sprayed real water if Mrs. Allen had let Seymour fill the tank. But she hadn't. Nevertheless, Barney was in love. "Can I have one, too?"

"You always want what everybody else has—doesn't he, Mom?" Jamie opened his big mouth. Barney wanted to punch him.

"That's enough, Jamie." Mommy gave his stupid brother a hard look, and he shut up. She looked down at Barney, and shook her head, and brushed his hair off his forehead with her hand. "We'll talk about the truck later, Barney. Right now, it's time to go to sleep."

"Okay. Will we get to play in the snow tomorrow?"

She nodded. "If there's enough, and it isn't too wet, I'll let you go play in it."

Barney snuggled under the covers, and Mommy handed him Brown Bear. He whispered, "Don't forget to tell the monsters to go away."

She sighed. Mommy *always* sighed. "What have I told you about the monsters?"

He frowned at her. "You said there aren't any monsters." Barney added, "But, Mommy, there are. Under the bed. Really."

She looked under his bed. "Nope. No monsters." She kissed him on the forehead, and said, "You only dream them. Just remember—you can make a magic sword in your dreams and chase the monsters with that." She smiled at him. "And once you chase them away, you won't ever be afraid of them again."

Barney nodded solemnly. All the kids in preschool agreed parents were pretty stupid about monsters. But there wasn't much he could do about his mother.

The monsters were another matter.

She blew him and his butthead brother a kiss, and turned out the light. Barney heard her walk across the hall to Carol's room and start to sing again.

"Only sissies are scared of monsters." Jamie propped himself on one elbow and looked over at his brother. "You're such a sissy."

Barney lay in the bed and studied his brother. He could feel the monsters waiting in the darkness around them; could hear them licking their lips and scratching their itches and waiting. Just waiting. Waiting was what monsters were best at.

The feel of monster was worse than usual, Barney decided. Closer, and hungrier. He was going to have to do the Turtle Shield. But first he had to take care of his butthead brother.

"That's okay," he told Jamie. "All the monsters are under your bed tonight." He rolled over with his back to his brother and dug himself deeper beneath the covers.

"They are not!" Jamie whispered.

Barney lay very still and smiled.

"They ARE NOT!" Jamie yelled.

"Jamie! Leave your brother alone and go to sleep!" Mommy yelled from Carol's room.

Barney's smile grew bigger. He could always get Jamie in trouble that way.

"They are not, poopface!" Jamie whispered again.

Jamie gave up when Barney pretended to be asleep. After a while, Barney could hear his brother's steady breathing. He waited a few minutes longer—just to make sure. He didn't want Jamie to catch him.

But finally he was sure his big brother really was asleep. Then he sat up and rummaged under his blankets until he found all four of his Teenage Mutant Ninja Turtles.

He put their weapons in their hands, posed them for fighting, then set Michelangelo, holding his nunchuks, on one side of the head of the bed. He liked Michelangelo best.

"Magic, magic Michelangelo," he whispered,

"Keep the monsters all away.

"Ooola-boola-boola-boo!

"Cowabunga!"

He crept down to the foot of the bed and eased the sai-wielding Raphael over the edge to the floor. Barney made magic signs with his fingers at the dark shape and whispered, "Ooola-boola-boola-boo! Cowabunga!"

Next came Leonardo, and then Donatello.

The Turtle Shield was in place. Barney could almost see it glowing in the dark. No ordinary monster would dare cross the Turtle Shield. He could still hear the slimy, scaly, awful creatures rustling around the room, whispering and laughing nasty laughs to each other. He wasn't worried.

If they got hungry, they could eat his brother.

Murp padded into the room and jumped on the bed. "Mrrrrrp?" he asked.

Barney moved over so the cat could have half his pillow. Murp was big enough he would have covered the whole thing if Barney had been willing to give it up. Barney wasn't, though, and the cat was willing to share.

The two of them snuggled in together. The monsters receded a bit. Monsters were afraid of cats.

With the cat curled next to his cheek and the Turtles keeping watch, Barney drifted off to sleep.

Murp woke Barney up by standing on his chest and staring into his face. Barney pushed the cat off him and sat up. He could hear the wind howling outside. The storm was scary—but he knew that wasn't the reason Murp was growling with his fur all sticking out.

There was something in the house. Not the usual monsters. This time it was something even worse.

He clutched Murp tightly with one hand and with the other, pulled the blankets up around the two of them.

"Jamie," he whispered.

Jamie didn't move. Mommy always said Jamie slept like a rock—and usually that was fine with Barney, who didn't. But not when there was something big and awful coming to get them.

"Jamie," he whispered louder. He was really, really scared. He could hear hissing outside. There were *big* monsters hunting through the storm.

The thing in the house was too big for the Turtle Shield, Barney thought. But Batman was in the closet. He lived there when he wasn't beating bad guys. All Barney had to do was get from the bed to the closet without the little monsters getting him, and he'd be safe.

He had to save Jamie, too, though—if he could. He whispered urgently, "Jamie—*wake up!*" His brother didn't wake up. Barney threw his pillow. It missed and fell onto the floor, into monster territory. No chance of getting *that* back. Barney took a deep breath, reached down, and grabbed Michelangelo. He threw the Turtle and hit Jamie squarely on the side of the face.

Jamie grunted and rolled over without waking up.

Barney wanted to cry. His brother was a butthead—but he was also his brother. Clutching the cat, he took a deep breath, then jumped to the floor and ran to Jamie's bed. Barney climbed onto the mattress as fast as he could and tucked his feet under him to keep them out of the reach of monsters. "Jamie! Jamie! Wake up! Really bad monsters are in the house!" He shook his brother with the hand that wasn't holding the cat. "Come on! We gotta hide in the closet. Batman will fight the monsters."

This time Jamie opened his eyes. "Don't be stupid. I'm not gonna hide in the closet. *You* hide in the closet if you want to." He pulled the covers over his head.

"I'm scared." Barney held Murp tighter.

"Nothing's going to get you. Go back to sleep."

Barney eyed the dark expanse of floor between Jamie's bed and the closet. He was going to have to go alone. He tightened his grip on Murp, who protested by struggling.

One, he thought. *Two. Three . . .*

He ran for the closet, as fast as his legs would go.

CHAPTER 2

Everything was darkness, void, enveloping emptiness. The void was self-aware, hungry, angry—evil. It wanted to devour Minerva but something was holding it back.

She tried to escape, and couldn't. She could think of the motions required to run, but she discovered that no matter how hard she tried, she could not make her body respond. I don't *have a body, she realized.* The monster can't figure out how to get at me because I don't have a body. But that's only slowing it down. It won't give up until it has completely destroyed me.

The malignant intelligence became angrier, and suddenly she was surrounded by a terrifying hissing that came from everywhere and nowhere, and a circle of radiance surrounded her. She was in the spotlight—and the light gave her form. She looked down and found that she once again had a body with arms and legs—arms and legs that were shackled to something outside of the cage of light.

Dark, foaming water rushed around her feet and rose with supernatural speed. She struggled, but her bonds were unbreakable. The water climbed from her knees to her waist to her shoulders to her nose and mouth. She began to drown in the dark and swirling currents. She fought for breath, and cried out, and kicked—

And woke up.

For a long moment, she could do nothing but clutch the

covers and shake, suppressing screams. She stared at the ceiling, feeling the lingering residue of helpless terror and the presence of immense evil. She began counting her breaths, exerting effort to slow them down. And gradually, the nightmare's grip on her loosened. Minerva's pulse rate dropped fractionally.

It was just another bad dream, Min, she told herself. *Get a grip.*

The hissing sound continued, though, challenging Minerva's thin veneer of control. She fought to identify the sound—and when she did, felt embarrassed by the silliness of her dark terrors.

That's nothing but the ice storm—freezing rain on the glass and the roof—

So she heard the ice storm and incorporated it into her dream, creating quite a nasty nightmare out of totally mundane stuff.

But . . .

The terror of drowning refused to be subdued by logic. With a start, she realized her face was wet. So was her pillow. And the choking sensation was still there.

She sat up, wiping at her face with the back of her hand. The taste of salt tears was at the corner of her mouth.

Christ, I've been crying in my sleep again. I am going nuts.

She sagged back onto her pillow and looked over at Darryl's side of the bed. He wasn't there. She sat up and rubbed at her eyes. *He might be downstairs watching late-night TV,* she thought. *Or he might have gotten snowed in at work.*

It was almost a relief to find his side of the bed empty.

When did I last love him? she wondered. *I did, once. I know it. I remember thinking the day began with his first kiss; thinking the world would end without it. I remember when just looking at him made me happy. I remember feeling warm when he smiled at me. I remember feeling loved. When did all of that change?*

There wasn't any sharp line where she could say, "This is when I quit loving Darryl." She stared at the ceiling some more, and thought about it, and decided instead that not loving him had been the result of a series of disappointments, a series of little betrayals and failures. There were all the nights he'd wanted to watch football instead of making love; all the days when he'd stayed over at work because he was in the middle of some exciting project or other rather than doing something with her and the kids; all the times he'd told her he'd help her with something, and had then forgotten. There were the times when he'd said he didn't want to do a load of laundry because he always had trouble with the clothes tangling—as if she didn't—or that he didn't want to scrub down the shower because she did it better. There was the way he let her work to put him through college, then said that they couldn't afford for her to finish her education—not with a house and three kids and bills.

Not loving Darryl wasn't the result of some huge disaster in their relationship, she realized. It was the fact that they really didn't have much of a relationship—three children and eleven years of marriage notwithstanding.

She held her left hand out in front of her and stared at the wedding band on her ring-finger. Even in the dark she could make out the intricate interweavings of the pattern. The old man at the Renaissance Faire all those years ago had insisted those rings would bind the young lovers soul-to-soul, "across the worlds and through all time"—and Minerva and Darryl, charmed by the fairy tale, had bought them.

And like all fairy tales, that one was just so much bullshit, Minerva thought.

She crawled out from beneath the covers, and her bare skin prickled with the chill. She grabbed the bathrobe that was draped over the bedpost and wrapped the thick, warm terrycloth around her. Then she tiptoed to the window.

Outside, the streetlight illuminated falling flakes of snow and the gleam of drops of freezing rain, and within the circle of its light, a glittering, surreal world of eerie, alien shapes was born—a magical kingdom of diamond-crusted trees and glass-frosted houses. She pulled her glasses off the night-stand and put them on. The scene became clearer, but lost none of its magical quality.

The world outside was incredibly beautiful. A poem she'd written years ago, in the days when she still believed she could be an artist, drifted through her memory, and staring into the snowstorm, she whispered it.

"Another world is mine, that none else see,
Cast from a softer, stranger, sweeter mold,
Created by some laughing god for me
Alone—its colors bright, its textures bold,
Impressionistic sweeps. I look at trees
Like Renoirs, vivid splashes tossed against
The towering, thundering, watercolor seas
Of sky. New-washed, chalk-drawn—my world—unfenced,
Unlined, unsigned, it bears no scars of men.
Its velvet folk, androgynous, unflawed,
Move with a boneless grace from home to glen.
I stand and watch in joyous wonder, awed.
    I need no spacebound ship, no mystic passes
    To reach my world. I just take off my glasses."

As she recited the last line of her poem, she slipped her glasses off and stared at the blurry, fuzzy wonderland outside her window one more time, and wished with all her heart that the real world could be so beautiful, so peaceful—so perfect.

No school tomorrow, she thought, and put her glasses on again with a sigh. All three kids would be home and in her hair, fighting with each other, whining to go outside, whining to come back inside, bored out of their skulls. If Darryl was home, he would prop himself in front of the television and watch game shows and ESPN and cable movies all day. He'd yell at the kids to be quiet and to play in their rooms, and criticize her for not making them behave. All four of them would leave messes, and she would either nag at them all day to clean their messes up, or save a lot of trouble and just do it herself.

She shivered again, this time not entirely from the cold.

Is this what life is supposed to be? Isn't there something more? Something important that I'm supposed to do?

All her life, she'd waited for the moment to come to her, for a neon sign to light up, for someone to tell her— *Now, Minerva. Now is the time for you do something wonderful. Now is the time for you to save the world. This is what you have to do.* But the sign never came, and no one ever told her what she should do to save the world.

That's just real life, I guess. In real life, married mommies don't count for much in the scheme of things. We don't affect politics, or history, or art, or religion—we don't change the world. We just get married, have our children, bring them up, watch them leave—then we grow old, and die.

Minerva rolled the smooth chintz of the curtain between her fingers, and watched the snow and ice accumulate on the walk beneath her window.

In the scheme of things, she wasn't too badly off. Darryl didn't drink, he didn't beat her, he kept a job and paid the biggest part of the bills. She was employable, even if she didn't like her job very much, she lived in a nice house, had decent neighbors, and great kids— Minerva smiled when she thought of Barney and Carol and Jamie. She really did have wonderful children, without any temporizing. Plenty of women were married to men they didn't love anymore. Those women didn't mope around with pity-poor-me expressions on their faces, did they?

Is there something wrong with me for not being happy? God knows there are plenty of people worse off than I am. Why can't I be satisfied, when I have it so good?

She shrugged. She didn't feel like going back to bed. The nightmare, whatever it had been, was still waiting in the back of her mind. She could feel it.

The green glow of the alarm clock's digital face read "4:23 A.M." It reflected in the full-length mirror on the other side of the room—and as she watched, the light reflected in the mirror changed from green to blue.

That's odd. I wonder what makes it look like that.

She glanced at the clock. Its numbers were still green.

A rifleshot crack from nearby plunged the world into darkness. "Aw, shit!" That was the sound of a branch burdened by too much ice taking out a power line. Great. Now she was alone with the kids in an ice storm—in the cold and the dark. Better and better. She swore again softly and stared out the window into total darkness.

But when she moved, she could see her own shadow on the wall, outlined in blue. *What—?* she wondered. She turned to look in the mirror again—

She stared, unable to breathe, pulse racing. The blue glow had spread—had grown from a hazy pinpoint to a rippling, luminous sheet that filled the mirror. The nightmare feeling grabbed Minerva again, and she backed away. The glowing blue oval of light broke free from the mirror frame and floated over to her, its shape shifting like a column of smoke in a breeze. She kept backing until she felt the cold window glass behind her; kept pushing even then until the bare skin of her neck pressed hard against the icy pane. The blue light kept coming. It brushed against her skin—cold, oh God, it was cold—and then it sizzled and whipped away from her—and shriveled up and vanished.

Released from its spell, she pressed her hand to her mouth and muffled her scream.

Oh God, omigod, ohgod-ohgod!

What had it been? A ghost? A hallucination? Another incident like the dragon in the grocery store? She made herself take a deep breath. She smoothed the heavy terry robe beneath her fingers. She walked toward the mirror.

A muffled crash came from Carol's room. Minerva froze. Carol shrieked—then something cut her piercing little-girl voice off in mid-yell. Minerva heard a soft popping noise.

"NO!" Minerva yelled.

Bathrobe flapping, she raced out of the bedroom and down the hall toward her daughter's room.

Darryl lay on the couch in the lounge with Cindy Morris spooned against his chest. Her hair fanned out over his left arm. Beneath his right hand, he could feel the steady rise and fall of her chest as she slept. He could see the two of them, reflected in the mirror on the other side of the lounge, burnished by the warm glow of the candles they'd found before the electricity went out. He wasn't happy with what he saw.

The sex had been good—*but then, the worst I ever had was good,* he thought, repeating an old line. It had been exciting enough for him; just the fact that he'd never done anything like that before—the fact that Cindy wasn't Minerva—made the whole experience a forbidden thrill. And Cindy couldn't be much over twenty-one. Her body was young and tight and voluptuous in all the right places. She didn't have Minerva's experience, or Minerva's enthusiasm, or Minerva's wild imagination; *but then,* he thought, *she doesn't have Minerva's brains, either.* Cindy didn't know how to do any of the really neat stuff Minerva liked, and the girl acted embarrassed and awkward when he tried to show her.

However, you don't expect the first time with a stranger to be as good as any time with somebody you've been practicing with for eleven years, either, do you?

You asshole.

He stared at himself in the mirror across the room. His eyes were holes of darker black carved into the shadowed planes of his face. He looked guilty as hell.

He twisted absently at his wedding band with his left thumb and rolled it around and around. The ring seemed heavy on his hand. He imagined it growing bigger with its disapproval. Minerva was at home with the kids—probably in the cold and the dark, without electric. He ought to be there with her. Instead, he was with a naked bimbo on a cheap Naugahyde couch that was getting colder by the minute, a long way from home, feeling like a shit—a feeling he had to admit he'd earned.

Cindy shivered and woke up, and ground her muscular little ass into his groin. "Hey, there," she murmured. "You awake?"

"Yeah," he said. "I'm awake."

"Oh, good. Let's get warm again." She slid one of her cold hands behind her and between his legs, and arched her back like a cat so that her breasts jutted out.

"Good idea," he said, and firmly removed her hand from

between his legs, and pushed her far enough away from himself so that he could sit up.

She sat up and glared at him. "What's the matter with you?"

"I'm cold, and I'm going to get warm." He rummaged around on the floor, found his shorts, and pulled them on. He found one sock and put that on, too.

"C'mon—let's screw some more," Cindy said. Her eyes seemed even greener in candlelight. Those eyes watched him, alert and not anywhere as sweet and innocent at that moment as they'd seemed earlier.

He raised an eyebrow. "Charming invitation," he drawled. "But I don't think so. I have to get home."

"Home?!" She laughed. Her face was the perfect picture of disbelief. "You've got to be kidding. There must be two feet of snow and ice out there by now."

"Yeah, well—" He found his other sock and put it on, and located his sweater. He shrugged. "I'll manage. I don't want to leave my wife and kids there alone."

"Your *wife*! And your *kids*!" She narrowed her eyes. "What an interesting time to be remembering *them*."

"No shit," he muttered. "But you knew I was married. I saw you looking at my wedding band." He pulled the sweater over his head. His shoes lay by the mirror. He walked over to them, caught a glimpse of the blizzard raging on the other side of the windows in the hallway, and shivered. The shiver was not entirely from the cold.

He bent down to pick up the shoe, and glanced up into the mirror. She was staring at him, her shadow-distorted face bearing little resemblance to the girl he'd met—but it was dark in the room, he thought. Her eyes followed his every move. The green of them seemed to glow in the candlelight. Her expression was unreadable.

"Yes. I saw your ring. I thought it was cool—all those swirls and stuff. Kind of pretty." Her voice sounded childish and sweet—and it didn't match her eyes. Her stare burned into his imagination. It seemed dangerous somehow. "Let me see it while you put your shoes on," she said. She smiled.

There was something compelling about her voice. Darryl

started to pull the ring off and show it to her. Then he stopped. "I never take it off," he said.

One shoe was on. He reached for the other.

"Aw, c'mon, baby. Let me see it."

The timbre of her voice changed—or was that his imagination? She was beginning to frighten him. He watched her reflection in the mirror. He would have sworn her eyes were actually glowing—like car headlights—and not merely reflecting the candlelight. It was the weirdest damned trick of the light he'd ever seen, and unnerving as hell. He forced himself to look away from the mirror and concentrate on dressing.

A nervous sixth sense made him look up.

The mirror wasn't showing Cindy anymore. She had been replaced by a glimmer of brilliant blue. The glimmer spread to cover the entire mirror, and he heard Cindy start to laugh.

"We'll have all the time in the world now, babe," she said.

He turned to look at her, to ask her what she meant by that.

She was stalking out the lobby door.

Good, he thought. He hoped she'd stay gone.

Movement in the mirror caught his attention. The blue glow was still there, but other things were visible as well. The things he could see didn't make any sense—they were not reflections of the lounge. He was looking *through* the mirror at what seemed to be the mirror in his bedroom back home—lit by blue light. The view shifted crazily, and he was staring out the window into darkness and snow that lashed against the glass. Another dizzy shift, and he could see the front of a bathrobe—his bathrobe—as if he were wearing it and looking down at it. Bare feet—*Minerva's* bare feet. The floor and the feet dropped away, and he could see the mirror again, and something blue coming out of it. *A ghost,* he thought. The shifting, glowing wraith blew toward him— *Not me,* he suddenly realized. *Minerva! It's coming after Minerva!*

She was backing up—he could tell by the way the room shifted, by the way she was looking around for some path of escape. And the blue thing was moving forward inexorably. It reached out and touched her, and he shouted, "NO!"

The ghost whipped away from her and seemed to shrivel. It pulled in on itself, wrapped its tatters of light into a tiny ball—and then it vanished. Minerva's eyes showed him the darkened mirror, the pitch-darkness of the room.

She's safe. His heart pounded in his throat. He could hear his blood rushing in his ears.

This is craziness, he thought, staring at the mirror in the lounge. *I can't be seeing Minerva attacked by ghosts at home.* He looked away from the mirror, then looked back. All the things he couldn't possibly be seeing were still right there.

Not good, he thought.

Then his view jerked crazily again as Minerva spun toward the door and started running. She raced out of their dark bedroom and into the puddled light of the hallway. The dim glow of the emergency night-lights plugged into the low wall sockets bounced around the bottom of the lounge mirror. The scene in the mirror rolled and swung—it reminded him of watching pictures taken by a handheld camera in a home movie—hard on the stomach of the observer, and not very illuminating. He wished he could *hear.*

Minerva slowed, and he got a quick glimpse of her hand shoving Carol's door wide open. His daughter's room, also lit by the soft yellow glow of an emergency night-light, was empty. Carol's blanket was thrown to one side of her bed, and her teddy bear was halfway across the room.

Minerva ran to the bed—through her eyes, he caught the sensation of flinging himself to the floor and staring under the bed. The space was full of naked Barbies and broken crayons and rumpled shirts and pants and socks rolled inside out. Minerva's hand shot out and pawed through the mess. Then, inexplicably, she stopped and looked around.

Good, he thought. *Minerva heard her. Carol must have been down the hall in the bathroom or something.*

But Minerva was up and running again. She flew across the hall and burst into Jamie and Barney's room.

The tattered blue ghost hovered at the foot of Jamie's

bed. It cast long, flickering shadows—shadows that made Darryl think, for a moment, that both boys might still be safe under the lumpy piles of their covers. But as the light moved away from Minerva, the shadow shapes changed, and he could see clearly that both boys were gone.

No, Darryl thought. *This can't be real. It isn't real.*

Minerva covered her face with her hands, and for an instant Darryl couldn't see anything. But she pulled them away again and her head jerked toward the closet. The slatted closet doors flew open, and Barney, with Murp incongruously tucked under his arm like a football, exploded out of the dark space—running toward Minerva.

The blue light intercepted the little boy, and swallowed him and the cat. Then it shot toward the bedroom window and blasted through it, leaving shards of glass in its wake.

And then the mirror went dark. He stared at it, and the only thing that looked back was his own face, shadowed by candlelight and twisted with fear.

That cannot possibly have happened, he told himself. *I'll call home*— But he couldn't call home. The office phone lines had gone out shortly after the power.

This is my guilt talking, he said. *This is my conscience telling me that because I screwed around on my wife, the world will now come to an end.*

He stared at the mirror, which stubbornly remained nothing but a mirror. *I wish to hell it had shown me the home movies* before *I screwed around on Minerva instead of after. Then I wouldn't have anything to feel guilty about—and I'd be home.*

He had to get home. Once there, once he could convince himself that everyone was safe and that everything was all right, he would come to terms with his conscience. He would never, never, ever, stray again. *That* he was sure of.

The blizzard outside seemed to be getting worse instead of blowing itself out. Cindy had apparently gone, taking every trace of her existence with her. He supposed she'd gotten in her car and left. She might have gone to whatever part of the building she worked in. He didn't care. He didn't think she'd be back—but he wasn't going to wait around to find out.

His ancient Chevy Nova waited in the parking lot. The storm had buried it under a thick, hard shell of ice. He chipped at the ice with his pocket comb, seeing his hot breath puff out in front of him; he swore and wished he'd thought to wear a heavier jacket or gloves or a hat. Stinging sleet blew down the back of his neck and sandblasted his face.

Time slipped into high gear around him; his body felt as if it had been dunked in icy molasses and strapped all over into weights. *Faster, faster,* he kept thinking, and every time he did, seemed to move slower and slower. The windshield was still caked in ice—but he had a clear circle. He would drive with the windows down, he decided, so he could see out. Not good, but it would have to do. He chipped the ice away from the door handle, fought the door open. The inside of the car was freezing—but at least he was out of the wind and the sleet. He turned the key in the ignition. The motor turned over once, sputtered—died. He tried again. Same response.

"Crank, damn you," he muttered. Tried again. The motor whined, caught, rumbled to sullen life. The heater blasted frozen air into the interior.

He backed cautiously and felt bald tires slipping on the shield of ice-sheeted snow that coated the parking lot. He prayed to a distant and dubious god, to the storm itself, to the very idea of home and safety. He prayed that his world would still be intact when he got there, and shivered with the cold and the fear that a moment of childish lust and the desire to get even with Minerva might have destroyed everything.

He eased out of the parking lot, and nearly got himself creamed by a bright red Mazda Miata that came out of nowhere, headlights off until after it was right on top of him. The driver laid on his obnoxious toy horn, skidded around the Nova, throwing snow behind his ridiculous little tires, and vanished almost immediately down a pitch-dark side street.

The Miata's bumper sticker stuck in Darryl's unhappily circling thoughts long after the car itself was out of sight:

"I ♥ VIRGINS."

"Not me, pal," he muttered into the frozen air. "Not me."

It was a dark and stormy night, he thought with some bitterness, and eased his way down the dark, silent, snow-shrouded street, crawling—wind-blasted and guilt-ridden—toward home.

The ghost tore through houses and forests, through the bitter, angry storm and then beyond it. It dumped Barney, his brother, his sister, and the irate Murp in the exact center of a dimly lit room, then dissolved into the floor. Murp slunk around the room, hackles raised, growling.

The three children looked at each other.

Barney frowned at Jamie, and said, "I told you so, butt-head."

"I didn't know there were really monsters," Jamie said.

Carol gave her older brother a disdainful look. "Of course there are monsters. That was a really scary one."

None of the children had any clothes on.

"Gross," Jamie said, and looked around desperately for something to wear.

Barney looked, too. On a small rug next to the door, someone had laid out three outfits—pullover tunics and baggy pants and curly-toed boots . . . and even underwear and socks.

"Somebody knew we were comin'," Jamie said. He grabbed the largest set of clothes and started tugging things on. "We gotta get out of here. Before they come back."

Barney nodded, and began to dress, too. He fumbled with the unfamiliar clothes, not certain how they went on. He had no doubt that the house was full of other monsters, monsters who would be coming to the room shortly. He could feel them, somewhere down below, moving around, thinking dark, scary monster-thoughts.

Carol was the first one dressed. She stood and looked solemnly at her brothers. Then she made the secret sign. "I am Carolissia, Queen of Butterfly World."

Jamie snorted. "We don't have time to play that stupid game."

Barney glared at his brother. Jamie was getting to be no good at adventures. Didn't he know they could do more things when they were the Kings and the Queen? Barney stood, and made his own secret sign. "I am Barnissius, King of Dinosauria."

"Oh, grow up, will you?" Jamie turned his back on the two of them and crossed his arms over his chest. "Pretending to be a stupid king isn't going to get you out of here."

"King Jamisor does not believe in his magic powers," Queen Carolissia intoned, her pug nose tipped at a haughty angle. "If he does not help us, we will have to leave him."

"King Jamisor did not believe in monsters," King Barnissius added. "He is a poopyhead."

Jamie turned around and glared at Barney. "Real kings don't call each other 'poopyhead.' "

"Poopyhead," Barney said.

"Skunkbreath."

"Buttface."

"Turdmouth."

Queen Carolissia pointed one regal finger at each of the two prospective kings. "Stop it, or I won't tell you the secret mission."

Barney and Jamie stopped. Carol was the one who always made up the secret mission—they were kings in charge of trapping tigers and spying and capturing the enemy, but Queen Carolissia was the one who invented the secret plans.

"Okay." King Barnissius stopped calling names and looked at Her Majesty. "What's the plan?"

"King Jamisor hasn't given the secret sign. Maybe he is a pretend king."

King Jamisor sighed. "Do you really have a plan?"

The Queen rolled her eyes. "Of course," she said.

King Jamisor stood, and made the sign. "I am King Jamisor of The Worlds Beyond the Sea."

All three royals bowed to each other.

Carol beckoned them all closer. "Let's climb out the window if we can," she said. "We can tie the sheets together to get down."

Barney was impressed. Queen Carolissia always had really good plans.

The three children tiptoed to the huge window and looked out into the night. Murp jumped onto the windowsill and looked out with them.

They were a long way up. People tiny as ants scurried around on the ground far below. Barney backed away from the window. He wasn't scared of very much—but he didn't like heights.

The Queen's expression became thoughtful as she studied the ground far below. "Ooooh!" she whispered. After an instant, in her royal voice, she said, "I shall think of a new plan." She stood, eyes squinched closed, fists knotted at her sides.

"King Jamisor," she said at last, "will spy out the door and tell us what he sees."

Jamisor nodded, and crept to the door. Murp seemed to think this was a new sort of game. He prowled beside the King. Jamie tried to open the door. "It's locked," he said.

The Queen stamped her foot. "Stupid, stupid, stupid!" Right then, King Barnissius thought, the Queen didn't look very Queenish. Instead, she looked an awful lot like Carol when Mommy wouldn't let her do what she wanted.

King Jamisor took charge. He looked at the younger two, and spread his legs and stuck his hands on his hips. "We're going to have to build a trap," he said. "Find stuff we can use. I want string, and heavy stuff."

"Why?" Barney asked.

"Going to make an ambush." King Jamisor, also known as Secret Agent Jeevus, was the master of ambushes. Both Barney and Carol, in their alternate guises as Secret Agents Equator and Renskie, had fallen into his traps.

King Jamisor pushed one of the heavy, oddly angled chairs toward the door.

Queen Carolissia found a small, heavy stone statue, and gave it to her brother. King Barnissius located the curtain cord. "I found string," he said, "but I can't cut it."

The Queen came over to look. "Yes," she said, and nodded, "this is excellent string. I shall bite it into pieces."

She pulled the curtain cord down as far as it would go, then climbed up onto the windowsill, so she could chew off a longer piece.

"Mom says you're not supposed to chew string and stuff with your teeth," Jamie said from the other side of the room.

"You got any scissors?"

"Nope."

"Then just shut up." She gave him the killer-sister look, and as an afterthought, added, "Buttface."

King Barnissius watched the other royals squabbling among themselves, but he didn't descend into the fray. He had something more important to do.

He pulled the sheets off the high bed and started twisting them. The Queen finished chewing through her string and took it to King Jamisor, who set up his booby trap. Then Carol came over to Barney.

"Watcha doin'?"

Barney didn't say anything. He thought it ought to be obvious what he was doing.

Carol, after a moment's thought, began to help him twist the cloth.

"It's ready," King Jamisor announced, and hopped off the chair. He pushed the seat back against the wall, then studied his handiwork critically, tipping his head at an angle and closing one eye.

"That statue is gonna hurt," Carol remarked.

Jamie had balanced it precariously on the edge of the doorsill. He'd tied one end of the curtain cord around its middle and the other to the door latch.

"It's supposed to hurt."

Queen Carolissia looked doubtful. "If it hurts too much, whoever comes through that door is going to be really mad at us."

"That's what we need these for." King Barnissius dragged over the first of his homemade ropes and presented them to

King Jamisor with a bow. "To tie them up when we catch them," he said.

"Good work, King Barnissius!"

"So when are they going to come up here?" the Queen wanted to know.

Both older children looked at Barney.

He knew what they expected. He took a deep breath and closed his eyes. His thoughts ranged through the lower reaches of their prison, and he sensed the life that inhabited the enormous castle. There was not one person awake in the place—excepting the three children. But the minds were quiet, full of sad dreams and worries. In all the floors beneath them, the monsters slept.

CHAPTER 3

Minerva opened her eyes and stared up into darkness. She was freezing. Snowflakes and sleet pelted her face and arms and legs and blew down the open neck of Darryl's terry robe. Wind howled around the room, and papers snapped in little gusts and eddies—snow and sleet piled around her.

But I'm lying on carpet.

Everything was incredibly dark, and very blurry. Minerva sat up, took off her glasses, cleaned them on the inside hem of the robe, and put them back on. Everything was still dark, but now it was recognizable.

I'm in the boys' room, she thought.

Minerva recalled bits and pieces of how she came to be there. She didn't like what she recalled.

I fainted?! She stood up and brushed snowflakes and bits of broken glass off the bathrobe. She was disgusted with herself. *I've never fainted before in my life.*

Minerva wrapped her arms around herself and shivered and tried to remember. *There was the blue light, and Carol screamed, and I ran to her room but she was gone—ran to the boys' room . . . Jamie was gone, but Barney came flying out of the closet screaming "Mommymommy!"—the ghost-thing got him.*

Her stomach churned. *No. That can't be. Things like that don't happen.*

But the window was blown out. Not in. Out.

They're okay. They have to be okay. They're my kids.

"Jamie?" Minerva yelled. "Barney? Come out! Come here, guys! Where are you?"

She looked for the boys, under the beds, in the closet— she called their names but got no answer. Her sons were gone. She went into the hall and closed the door behind her. She stood and called their names again. Nothing. Checking, still not able to believe what she remembered had really happened, she went to Carol's room.

Carol was gone, too.

She stood at the doorway and listened.

The house held within itself the deadness of absolute abandonment—always before in the middle of the night, she'd been able to hear the children breathing, though the sound was subtle and not one she thought about. She would note subconsciously the rustle of sheets as the kids rolled over, the soft thud of Murp's paws hitting the carpeted floor or his quiet footsteps padding softly down the hall. The normal sounds of an occupied house were tiny when present. They roared in their absence with the hollowness of eternity.

This is all a nightmare, she told herself. *It isn't happening. It can't be happening.* She stepped into Carol's room. She looked down at the rumpled blankets of Carol's bed, at the indented pillow. She reached down and touched the hollow her daughter's head had left, picked the pillow up and pressed her face into the hollowed spot and breathed in Carol's scent—soap and sunlight and little-girl sweetness.

Minerva pulled her face from the pillow and felt a tight lump burning in the back of her throat—imminent tears. "Give them back, dammit!" Minerva screamed into the stillness. The house echoed her shout, then returned to waiting silence. The grandfather clock in the greatroom ticked— metronome-steady, surreally loud. Snow and sleet hissed against the glass. In the whole house, no one breathed save her.

Alone—a suddenly childless mother. It was too much for her.

She flung herself across Carol's bed and sobbed. Rocking

back and forth, freezing, teeth chattering, she cried until her ribs ached. "I want my kids back! I want them *back*, dammit!"

Her sobs died down to sniffles. She curled into a tight ball, staring at the night-light, hiccupping, with her nose stuffy and her eyes swollen.

"It was the dragon," she whispered. "The dragon in Food-Lion. It wanted me to go after it. If I'd followed it, the kids would still be safe."

Maybe she could still go after it. The dragon had wanted her. The light, too, had come after her first, and had only swallowed the kids when it couldn't get her. She knew where the path was, that overgrown trail the dragon had vanished into like a rabbit down a hole. If the dragon wanted her, if the light wanted her—even if they were one and the same—they could have her. She would go down that path, and by so doing, trade herself for her children. She hugged the pillow tighter. The tears came again; their wet heat soaked her cheeks.

My life for their safety. Just let them come back home, you bastards, she thought. *You can do whatever you want with me.*

Nothing changed. The house remained empty and cold. The grandfather clock downstairs began to bong—slow, steady tolling of the time, a soft and mournful dirge. *One*, it said. *Two. Three. Four. Five.*

"Where are you, Darryl? Why weren't you here when I needed you?" She glared into the darkness. *Why aren't you here when I need you now?*

Damn Darryl. She would go out into the night. *She* would face the terrible storm and the dragon and the ghostly blue light and God only knew what else. But she was going to get her kids back.

She went downstairs. In the laundry room, she rummaged through the dryer and pulled out insulated underwear and a pair of heavy, quilt-lined corduroy jeans and unfolded her bulkiest hand-knit wool sweater from the top of the washing machine. She dressed in the dark. In the kitchen, she located the flashlight and the biggest kitchen knife they owned. She stared for a moment at the phone—

the urge to call Darryl's office or her parents' house or the police was almost overwhelming. She wanted just to hear someone's voice—to get some small reassurance that she was not alone in the world.

She moved toward the phone-stand—and the hair on her arms stood up. The blackness in that corner of the room seemed darker than it had any right to be. She imagined she could feel something waiting with breath held for her to step across an unseen line—she could almost hear ghostly whispers, beckoning her near.

She was being stupid. She didn't care. *Too much in one night*, she thought, and did not brave the phone. She took the flashlight and the kitchen knife and fled. Minerva wished right then that she and Darryl had a gun. But the knife would have to do.

Parka on, knife in her coat pocket, she stepped out into the bitter blackness of early morning. No one was visible outside, either. She left the front door unlocked and trudged down the stairs. The wind blew like the end of the world— intensely cold and miserably wet. The darkness seemed to devour her as she stepped carefully away from the house. Her boots crunched on the mixed ice and snow, and her nose began to run. *No sense,* she thought, *taking the damned station wagon for the short distance I'm going. I'd probably just slide it into a ditch, anyway, and I don't think it would fit down that path.* She jingled the keys in her pocket and left the hated LTD behind.

It's only a block and a half, she thought.

Halfway to the empty lot, she began to wonder if she'd made a mistake. She looked up at the sky and shivered. *God, but it's dark!* she thought. *And scary.* The streetlights would have been some help in the near-blizzard—the flashlight simply wasn't enough. She watched the little puddle of bobbing light she made, feeling the weight of the storm and the night all around her. The eyes of the darkness seemed to watch her—she felt their gaze fixed on her back.

Wretched, wretched storm.

She trudged through the mess of slush and ice; her boots slipped from time to time as they hit spots where the asphalt was uniformly glazed. As long as she could walk on the grassy shoulder, the going wasn't quite so bad.

Gusts of wind buffeted her and shoved her from side to side. She slipped once, fell into the ditch, and the knife in her pocket jabbed into her hip. Swearing, she pulled the point loose. *Not deep—sure as hell painful, though.*

Wet snow and crystals of ice lashed her cheeks and stung her eyes. Her hands inside her knitted mittens felt frozen. She jammed the flashlight under her arm and pressed the arm tight against her side—her hands had grown too numb to hold it.

There were no cars at all—nobody up, no lights on in the houses she passed. Minerva felt like the last living person on earth.

A block and a half. Seems like it took forever. There it was, though—the empty lot, complete with snow-covered two-rut road diving straight into the black heart of an overgrown woods.

These places never look so goddamned ominous in the daylight.

She stamped her feet to warm them; stared down that overgrown maw of a tunnel.

Light from the flashlight illuminated no more than ten feet into the gloom. The beam seemed dim to her; she smacked the base of the flashlight once with the flat of her hand, but it didn't help.

In the stygian blackness, something terrible waited for her. Something straight out of her worst nightmares.

And that something had her kids.

"All right!" she said into the wind. "Give them back to me now and I won't come after you."

The wind whistled and howled. It made voices—but the voices said nothing she could understand.

"Give them back or I'm coming in!" she yelled. "You don't want me to come in."

But the invisible thing that waited evidently did.

She stepped onto the road. Immediately, the canopy of pines and evergreen hollies overhead cut the wind and blocked some of the snow and sleet. The blanket of snow was smoother where the road lay—a narrow ribbon of white between the overarching trees. Even out of the wind, the woods were colder than Viking hell, Minerva thought. She jammed her mittened hands into the pockets of her nylon, polyester-stuffed parka, and plodded along with the flashlight pressed between her elbow and her waist.

She paced along her rut, darting her flashlight from right to left and back, looking for some sign of the Miata. She walked for what she guessed would be the length of the empty lot, but the path went onward, and the woods showed no evidence of thinning. She walked on, doggedly. She lost all sense of time, and the cut on her hip began to throb. Her legs grew tired. The woods stretched out on all sides, devoid of people or houses.

How much longer does this road go on? she wondered. *Stonebridge should be over to my right, and the Loch Lomond development should be to my left. There should be houses and streets all over the place.*

The trees crowded closer. The path became a single rut. There was no way the Miata could have gone down the path—but there was nowhere else it could have gone. The impossible had ceased to faze Minerva. She kept stubbornly on.

The cold ate into her, and her lungs burned from the freezing air. Ice-covered branches slapped her cheeks, and their bony-fingered assaults stung like hornets. Needles of white-hot pain stabbed her fingers and feet.

Suddenly the burning sensation grew overwhelming. It enveloped her body, and she bent over, gasping for breath while invisible needles ran through her from all sides. Dizziness overtook her, and her ears roared, drowning all other sounds. She felt suddenly light and disconnected—almost as if she would faint again. She collapsed—but could not feel herself hit the ground.

After an instant, though, the pain vanished, and the sense of strangeness passed. She stood and took a step.

Funny, she thought. *I'm not at all cold anymore.*

A warm, gentle breeze blew past her and caressed her skin, and she stared down at her body with horror. Her clothes were gone; she was completely naked. She realized at the same moment that her glasses were gone, too; the outlines of the trees around her had become blurry and indistinct. Her flashlight and her knife were gone. So was the snow. The leaves beneath her bare feet crunched.

Minerva screamed. She dropped to her knees and began feeling around for her clothes or her glasses—for anything.

Rational thought returned in tiny pieces, and she forced herself to sit, and breath slowly, and collect herself. Panicked, she would be useless to her children.

The air smelled of autumn—the tang of cider-apples fermenting on the ground somewhere nearby; tannin; earth damp from recent rains; freshly fallen leaves. She didn't understand what had happened—but she would have to keep a grip on herself and pretend she did. Feign sanity.

Losing her clothes wasn't as bad as losing her glasses, she decided. She *had* to have those. If she couldn't see, she would be helpless.

Knowing perfectly well she was being illogical—that if her clothes had just vanished, the glasses would have, too—she still got back on her knees, calmly this time, and started digging through the dry leaves. She *would* find her glasses, she decided. She just would.

She could almost see them half-covered by leaves, could almost feel the cold metal frames under her fingertips. They were as real in her mind as twenty years of desperately nearsighted dependence could make them—and suddenly her fingers brushed icy metal and snow-covered glass, and there they were, under her hand.

Better not to ask too many questions, she thought, and put them on.

She stood, and pulled her shoulders back and lifted her chin. The dragon, the ghost light—they were playing games with her—changing things. She wouldn't let it stop her.

"You can't scare me," she whispered. Then louder, "I said, you can't scare me. You have my kids. I want them back!"

She started walking again, determination undiminished in

spite of her fear. She noted her hip didn't hurt anymore, and she had no cut where the knife had gone in. It didn't matter. She didn't care what happened to her, she thought. Only finding Jamie and Carol and Barney mattered.

She arrived abruptly at a clearing. The sky along the horizon wore the first pale flush of coming dawn—there was enough light that Minerva could see she was at the top of a huge, dome-shaped hill. Meadowland spread in front of her, golden grasses bent and rippled like waves in the ocean. A string of little moons hung across the waist of the world like brightly colored jewels strung on an invisible chain.

The horizon pinked up, and from all around her, meadow birds began cheeping and singing. The path continued in front of her, along the ridge to the next hill over. Huge standing stones circled the top of that hill like a heavy crown. She walked toward them, a few tentative steps at a time. Nervously, she looked behind herself, and got a nasty shock.

The path behind her was gone.

So were the woods.

The sun was coming up when Darryl pulled into the drive. The world glared ice-white and dawn-pink—blinding, beautiful, wickedly cold. The walk up to the house was a solid sheet of glaring white, marred by two sets of footprints, both almost completely filled with snow.

He got out of the Nova, blowing steam into the frigid air, and crunched up the walk.

The front door was unlocked.

He swallowed uneasiness. *Maybe Minerva is already up,* he thought, and went in.

The house was still. He stood in the foyer, holding his breath, listening. *Maybe the kids are still asleep,* he told himself.

"Minerva!" he yelled. "I'm home!"

No answer.

"Minerva! I'm home! Is everything all right?"

Still no answer.

Darryl closed his eyes. *Please,* he thought. *Please just be pissed off at me. Please don't be gone.*

He walked to the stairs and up them. They creaked beneath his weight, incredibly loud in the silence. The grandfather clock bonged once, and he looked at his watch. Six-thirty.

He thought about calling out to the kids, then decided against it. *They're still asleep,* he told himself. *If I wake them up early, Minerva will kill me. There's no way she'll believe I'm freaked out because of something I thought I saw in a mirror.*

He reached the top of the stairs, turned, walked slowly along the landing. He peeked into Carol's door. Her bed was empty.

He opened the boys' door, and a blast of icy air hit him. The window was out—looked to him almost as if it had been exploded from the inside. He clenched his fists. Tears burned his eyes and rolled down his cheeks.

Real, he thought. *It was all real. Something got them— something took them away—*

He heard a noise coming from his and Minerva's bedroom. Someone walking around, sitting on the bed, squeaking the bedsprings. *Oh God,* he thought, as relief rushed over him, so intense it made him queasy. *They're all in our room. Of course. The kids got scared because the power went off—because a tree limb or something knocked out the window. They're all in our room—*

He took a deep breath, and sighed, and laughed softly. *Panic, why don't you, Darryl?*

"Minerva!" he called, and left the boys' room, and closed the door behind him. "Why didn't you answer me?" He went down the hall, his stomach still tied in knots from anxiety, and walked into his bedroom.

He immediately backed out, slammed the door, and stood in the hall for a moment, hyperventilating. *I didn't see anything,* he told himself. *Everything is okay, and when I walk back in there, Minerva and the kids will be fine.*

He opened the door just a crack, and peeked in.

A vivid blue dragon curled up on his bed, eating Wheaties

out of a box and reading a book. It had a can of Budweiser clutched in one huge forefoot. The dragon grinned at him.

"Hi!" it said, in a very deep, gravelly voice. "Want some Wheaties? Or a beer?"

Darryl slammed the door again. He leaned against the wall and slid down into a crouch, and rested his face in his hands. *There is not a dragon in my bedroom,* he told himself. *There isn't.* He said it out loud. "There is not a dragon in my bedroom."

"There was the last time *I* looked," the incredibly deep voice rumbled from the other side of the door.

Darryl pressed his face against his thighs and wrapped his arms around his legs. *There's a dragon in my bedroom—I don't even like having to get rid of* mice!

He took a deep breath and straightened. He was going to have to get rid of it. He couldn't leave it in there. What if it had hurt Minerva, or the kids? He stood and thought for a moment.

How the hell do you get a dragon out of your bedroom? Darryl suspected this wasn't the sort of thing you could call Terminex for. He used an old golf club on mice—but that wasn't going to work here. First, mice weren't likely to turn around and charbroil you when you swung at them—and second, the golf club was in the bedroom, under the bed.

I don't have a gun, I don't have a sword, I don't have a suit of armor. Modern man, Darryl decided, was remarkably unprepared for fighting dragons.

The dragon didn't look all that threatening, really, he thought. *It had really sharp teeth, and it was big, but— It was sitting in there drinking beer. I mean, unless it turns out to be a nasty drunk, maybe there won't be a problem.*

He stuck his head in the door again.

The dragon pulled a handful of Wheaties out of the box, tossed them down its huge maw, and chased the cereal with a dollop of beer.

"That wife of yours is a major babe," the dragon offered. "I *love* babes."

Darryl stepped into the room, caution forgotten. He

was instantly angry. "How do you know my wife?" he demanded.

"Met her at the grocery store. We were both shopping and we, ah, ran into each other. I'll bet she's hot, huh?" The mythical beast stared heavenward and sighed gustily. He started to sing.

> *"The lovely lady sang so sweet,*
> *Upon her harp, she PLUCKED.*
> *The dragon's lust grew great and strong,*
> *His heart thundered and BUCKED.*
> *When she was through, he took her home,*
> *And all night long the-e-e-e-ey—*
> > *WE-R-R-R-RRE—*
> > > *Anatomically incompatible,*
> > > *His was flyable, her just SAT-able.*
> > > *True love di-i-i-ied, 'cause nothing FIT!*
> > > *That's the long—and—SHORT of it!"*

Darryl leaned against the doorframe and tried to talk sense to himself. The dragon was a manifestation of his guilt. Had to be. His subconscious had to be finding *something* deeply significant in a randy blue—*blue?!*—mythological beast that made lewd remarks about his wife and sang dirty ditties.

"I love that song," the psychological manifestation said. "It's sort of the dragon national anthem." He erupted into the second verse.

> *"They tried their best to make it work,*
> *With effort pure and TRUE!*
> *They used appliances and gels,*
> *And lathered up with GOO!*
> *'Twas all for naught, though—sad to tell.*
> *They simply couldn't—*
> > *THE-E-E-E-EY—WE-R-R-R-RRE—"*

He launched into the chorus again, and Darryl closed his eyes. *So let's do a brief comparison here. Is a dragon singing*

*on my bed better or worse than seeing my wife in the mirror
at work? Sanity-wise, that is?*

The dragon began the third verse.

> *"The dragon ceased his striving, but*
> *Alas, it was too LATE!*
> *They buried her while he bemoaned*
> *The fickleness of FATE!—"*

Darryl gathered his courage and located his voice. "Excuse
me," he squeaked to the blue hallucination. "But would you
please go away?"

The dragon stopped its racket long enough to stare at
him. "—Eh? Oh, not right now. I'm singing. I wrote this
song, you know."

> *"Dead not for love but just because*
> *They could not FOR—*
>   *THE-E-E-E-EY WE-R-R-R-RRE—"*

"I know you're singing," Darryl interrupted. "I want you
to stop."

"I'm almost done. But the bridge is the best part. Here,
listen."

> *"The moral of this sad lament,*
> *Avoid the clench of FATE!*
> *Make sure the plumbing measures up,*
> *Before you copuLATE!*
>   *THE-E-E-E-EY WE-R-R-R-RRE—"*

The dragon waggled the spiny rilles over his eye-ridges
when he sang that last part. Darryl found the effect
disconcerting.

"Very nice," he interrupted again. His voice was coming
back stronger. He didn't sound like such a wimp anymore.
He still felt like a wimp. *Oh well,* he thought. *Can't have
everything.* "Did you eat my wife?" he asked.

The dragon stopped singing. He cocked his head to one

side and looked thoughtfully up at the ceiling. "No, unfortunately. She didn't ask me to. Of course, we were in the supermarket at the time." He fixed a hopeful gaze on Darryl. "Do you think she might?"

Darryl looked at the dragon with disbelief. "NO! Did you eat my children?"

"I get the feeling we aren't talking about the same thing here. Kids aren't my thing—" The dragon huffed and pouted. "And I *never* munch babes. For the record, I am an omnivore. Mostly, I require the same sorts of nourishment you do—by the way, these Wheaties taste like straw. You actually eat this stuff?"

"No," Darryl said. "I hate Wheaties. So if you didn't eat my wife and my kids, what did you do with them?"

"What did *I* do with them?! What did *I* do with—*I* didn't do *anything* with them!" The blue rilles around the dragon's face stood out like fans—the long, delicate spines quivered. The dragon's pupils dilated and contracted rapidly, and he puffed out a thin tendril of smoke. "I'm just here to keep you company so you won't be alone, bud, and to protect you from the Weirds. *I* wasn't out till all hours of the morning boffing the office bimbo, was I? *I'm* the good guy in this little morality play."

"How'd you know about that?" Darryl asked, then decided he didn't want to know. "Look," he said, "I didn't mean to offend you. You know where they are, though? My family, I mean."

"Sure." The dragon finished the Budweiser with one long gulp and crushed the can into a metal sphere the size of a marble. He flicked that across the room into the trash can, where it rattled noisily. He grinned. "Two points." He immediately popped the top on another beer, sipped appreciatively, and leaned back on the bed. "Hey, I just had a great idea. I have this way-cool car and the afternoon off. And babes just love my wheels. Let's go cruise chicks."

"Let's not. I want to find my wife."

"Find her? She isn't lost. Look—she's right there." The dragon pointed at the full-length mirror.

Darryl looked in the mirror. He couldn't see Minerva.

What he could see was a replica of Stonehenge, fixed up like new. Then the view tilted crazily, and he could see what seemed to be Minerva's own view of her body—stark naked. The curves were familiar, and he recognized the mole on her right breast.

The dragon whistled appreciatively. "Ooomph! You got some babe there, pal. She could scratch my scales any day."

Darryl glared, but decided not to comment on the dragon's rudeness. "What about my kids, then? Where are they?"

The dragon nodded sagely. "You have a problem there, all right. The Weirds have them. They intend to use them for bait to catch you and the tomato, I imagine."

Darryl let out his breath in a short *whoosh*. "And if, ah— the *Weirds*?—the Weirds catch us?"

"Then they reduce you to your component atoms and destroy the atoms." The dragon slurped his beer, then arched an eye-ridge and popped the can into his mouth. He crunched vigorously, swallowed once, then sighed. "Hell, I didn't know these were so tasty. I would have been eating them and tossing the Wheaties."

Things weren't coming together the way Darryl would have liked. Instead of making progressively more sense, events seemed to be making progressively less. Not only did he have a lecherous, beer-swilling dragon lounging on his bed, but the kids were gone and Minerva was back in the mirror, and something wanted him dead.

"Can you take me to Minerva?" he asked the dragon.

"Nope."

"Can you help me get my kids back?"

"Not right this minute. But I can give you a beer. You look like you could use one." The dragon grinned again.

There were some creatures that should never smile, Darryl thought. Dragons fit into that category. Entirely too many teeth. He took a deep breath and turned his back on the bouncing reflection of the spruced-up Stonehenge. He didn't have any idea what to do next. Getting stupendously, overwhelmingly drunk, though, seemed like a promising start.

"Right," he said. "Give me a beer."

✤   ✤   ✤

A thump followed by a loud crash brought all three children awake and off the floor.

The ambush had worked. Its victim lay sprawled on the
stone floor, with a thin trickle of blood oozing from the cut
on her forehead.

Jamie, Carol, and Barney grabbed hold of the makeshift
rope and edged warily up to the fallen figure. Murp skulked
along just behind them, hackles raised.

"What *is* it?" Carol asked.

Barney couldn't even imagine. He was certain that the
creature was one of the monsters he'd sensed. She was a girl
monster, though—and even with the example of his sister to
the contrary, he'd never really considered that monsters
might come in boys and girls.

Her eyes were closed, her mouth partway open. She had
long, sharp teeth. Not like Dracula's, he thought. More like
Murp's—but bigger. Her ears stuck out, curly and furry at the
edges like the flowers his mother called cockscombs. Her hair
was kind of brushy and stuck up. It was plain old brown, except
for a black stripe that ran right down the middle. Her hands
were big, and her fingers had sharp claws at the ends of them.

Jamie took a walking stick he found propped up against
one wall and poked her with it. She didn't move.

"Maybe she's dead," he said, sounding both scared and a
little bit hopeful.

Carol said, "No, she isn't. She's still breathing."

Jamie studied the fallen monster, then nodded. "Yes, she
is. You're right. Should we leave her here like this, or should
we tie her up?"

"Tie her up," Carol said.

Barney nodded. "Before she wakes up."

Jamie nodded again, looking thoughtful. "Yeah. I think so,
too."

They took the twisted sheet, pulled her hands behind her,
wrapped the sheet around both wrists a number of times,
then tied one huge knot.

"Feet, too?" Carol had the other sheet ready.

"Feet, too."

All three of them worked at tying her feet.

When they were done, Jamie studied the unconscious monster, then pulled a huge dagger out of the sheath she wore on her belt. He grinned at his brother and sister, and raised the knife skyward with both hands. "Heeeee-yah!" he whispered, and tucked the knife into his belt.

Secret Agents Jeevus, Renskie, and Equator did high-fives.

"Now what do we do?" Renskie asked.

Secret Agent Jeevus crossed his arms over his chest. "We have two choices. We can try to escape, or we can fight."

"Fight?" Carol looked horrified. "We're kids! They're monsters!"

"Yeah, but if we run, we have to get past the castle defenses. If we fight, we might win."

Equator hooked his thumbs under his tunic into the top of his pants. "If we lose, they might eat us."

Secret Agent Jeevus frowned. "Then we'd better not lose. Look." He hunkered down and stared into the eyes of his two cohorts. "This place is made to be defended—and we are in the best location to launch a counterattack. The very best place to attack is from behind."

"We don't have any guns."

"We don't need them. We're in a castle keep." Jamie traced an imaginary diagram on the stone floor with his finger. "We're at the top of a hill. If you look out the window, you can see the wall of the inner bailey below, and outside of that, the wall of the outer bailey. Look out the door, Renskie—but be careful. Tell me what you see."

Carol went over and peeked out the door, then closed it behind her. She reported back. "Just stairs, sir. They go around and around and around—with a big hole in the middle."

"Perfect. If more monsters come after us, we can drop stuff on their heads."

On the floor beside them, their captive groaned softly and opened her eyes. She looked up at the three children, her expression bewildered. She tried to get up, and discovered her hands and feet tied together. "Wha—?!" The monster twisted around, fighting to free herself.

Jamie grabbed up the walking stick again and brandished it over her head. "Don't move or you're a goner," he growled. Then he looked at his brother and sister. "The President has asked us to inter . . . um—interrogate this prisoner. Secret Agent Renskie, take your position."

Carol frowned, her face questioning. Jamie pointed behind the monster. Carol nodded. She glared fiercely at the creature on the floor and walked around behind it.

"Don't move." She made her voice as tough as she could.

Barney looked at his older brother. "You have to hold the secret weapon, Secret Agent Equator," the unflappable Jeevus said.

Barney picked up the cat, and Jeevus nodded gravely.

"Very good, Equator."

Then Jeevus spoke into the air. "Yes, Mr. President," he said solemnly. "We'll get her to confess, sir." He saluted, and Equator, who was trying to keep the "secret weapon" from struggling too much, saluted too.

Jeevus, still clutching the stick, knelt just out of the monster's range and took a deep breath. Then he said, "Give me your name, rank, and serial number, monster. The Geneva convention prohibits torture, but we will do what we have to do to complete our mission."

"Are you children crazy?" the monster asked.

"We are not children," Jeevus said, and narrowed his eyes in an impressively spylike manner. Equator liked the expression well enough he tried it out himself. "We have captured you, and you will tell us what we want to know."

"Are you going to untie me?"

"We make no promises, monster. But if you cooperate, we will . . . um . . . we will take that into account."

Barney recognized the lines from the cartoon "Dan Steed, Kid Detective." After Dan Steed said that, the bad guy, who'd been holding a kid and her father prisoner until they told him where to find the buried treasure, had sneered, and said "I'll never tell you nothin', you rotten kid."

But this captive just sighed. "Right," she said. "My name is Ergrawll. My personal identification credit number is 505-2-10347-21. I don't have a serial number, so that will just have to do. My rank is Childsitter, First Class." She pulled her lips back in a terrible smile that showed all of her teeth to best advantage. "And as your Childsitter, I have to tell you—you're in big trouble."

Jeevus laughed coldly. "So your name is Ergrawll, is it? Hah! A likely story," he sneered.

Equator thought his big brother's answer that time was pretty good, too. He imitated the sneer and the cold laugh, and said, "Yeah. A likely story."

Renskie maintained her fierce silence.

"Now we want the truth. What is the secret password? Where have you hidden the treasure? How many of you are there? Who is your leader? Why do you want to take over the world?" Jeevus glowered down at the prisoner and tapped his foot.

Dan Steed always tapped his foot.

"Those are silly questions—and my head hurts. Untie me." The monster glared at Jeevus.

Jeevus glared back. "Right, then. Renskie—torture the prisoner."

Renskie looked panicked. She shrugged at her older brother and spread her arms wide. "How?" she mouthed.

Jeevus rolled his eyes and sighed. "Do I have to do everything?" He walked around the downed monster, being careful to keep his distance. When he drew even with her rump, he lifted his stick.

Thwack! Jeevus smacked her once with the stick. "What is the password?" *Thwack!* "Where are the secret passages?" He lifted the stick a third time, and brought it down with an especially vigorous stroke. "Who is your leader, and where is he hiding?"

"Little boy," the monster said, and her eyes glowed incredibly green, "I'm about to get angry. You wouldn't like me when I'm angry."

Barney froze. Those words were straight out of *The Incredible Hulk*. Of course, the Incredible Hulk started out as David Banner—who was a wimp. Secret Agent Equator thought hard. After David Banner was a wimp, though, he *became* the Hulk, who was great if he was on your side . . . but not too good if he was coming after you.

Jamie gave the monster another smack on the rear.

The monster looked really angry.

Murp, in Barney's arms, hissed. The monster was not a wimp like David Banner. Did that mean she would become something worse than the Hulk? He shivered and stared at her. Barney had known some bad feelings in his short life— the one he got at that moment made the rest of them seem like nothing.

The monster started to shift and twist—Barney was pretty sure she was going to turn into the Hulk, sort of, but really bad. He dropped the cat and picked up the heaviest thing he could find that he could pick up—a stone doorstop—and dropped it on her head.

The prisoner's face slammed into the floor, and her eyes closed.

"Shit!" Jamie yelled. "What did you do that for, poop-face?! She was gonna talk."

"She was *gonna* turn into the Hulk, moron."

Jamie put his hands on his hips. "Yeah, right. Asshole."

Carol's mouth dropped open. She stared at Jamie. "Awww—I'm telling. Mom is gonna kill you when she finds out you said that, Jamie."

Jamie's cheeks turned red, and he glared at his sister. "How's she gonna find out, huh, shrimp? *You* better not tell."

Barney was unruffled by his brother's insults. "I told you about the ghost, didn't I? If you hid in the closet with Batman and me, it wouldn't have got you."

Jamie shut up.

Barney loved it when Jamie shut up.

Carol, however, gave Barney a disbelieving look, then turned to Jamie, the former enemy. "He thinks Batman lives in your closet?"

"He thinks a lot of things," Jamie muttered. The older boy shrugged. "He was right about the ghost coming for us, though. And it didn't touch him till after he came out of the closet."

Jamie knelt beside the still form of the monster. "She's going to be trouble when she wakes up. We need to lock her in here and find someplace else for us."

Barney picked up Murp and asked Jamie, "Do you think she was really our baby-sitter?"

Jamie frowned. "Probably not. But if she was, she couldn't have been much worse than Louise Simmons."

All three children lifted first and fourth fingers and touched their noses, a gesture Jamie once told them was supposed to ward off evil. Most of the kids in the neighborhood did it every time they saw Louise—it made her crazy, which was why they did it. Not even Barney really believed that she was going to turn into a witch on her eighteenth birthday and eat the neighborhood children. At least, he didn't believe it very much.

"Grab her legs," Jamie said.

Barney and Carol grabbed the monster's legs and started tugging; Jamie pulled on her arms. The stone floor was smooth—they slid her away from the door without too much difficulty.

"Get the bedspread."

The two smaller children dragged it over, and all three of them spread it out on the floor, then rolled her up in it like a mummy.

"That ought to slow her down." Jamie's voice changed—suddenly he was Jeevus again, brushing imaginary lint off his shirt and plotting the overthrow of monsters.

"Now, men," he told them, "we reconnoiter the lower regions of the castle. Keep quiet, keep close to me, and watch out for booby traps and ambushes."

Renskie and Equator lined up behind him. Equator carried the secret weapon, who had calmed down.

They skulked out the door onto the landing. A massive stone staircase curved around and down—it had no railing and the center was a straight drop to the ground. Barney made the mistake of looking, then backed against the wall so fast he slammed his head on the stone. Jeevus was still staring down over the edge.

"Man—if we only had supplies, we could hold this place forever." They closed the door to the tower room, then all three of them together dropped the big wooden bar into the brackets set in the stone.

"Onward," Secret Agent Jeevus said, his whisper sounding small and scared in the dark, echoey tower.

"Onward," Secret Agent Renskie repeated.

"Onward," Secret Agent Equator said, and clutched the cat tighter.

CHAPTER 4

Minerva stared at the string of gemlike moons strung across the sky and wrapped her arms around herself. She shivered violently, but this time not from cold. Wherever she was felt infinitely far from home. Her way back had vanished, and her children were nowhere in sight.

She walked into the circle of standing stones and brushed her fingers over the nearest menhir. The coarse rock felt very solid and very real. She braced herself and pushed as hard as she could, and the standing stone didn't topple or vanish.

Minerva shoved her glasses up her nose and studied the henge. She licked her lips thoughtfully.

"Okay," she said. Her voice shook, and her hands trembled. "Okay. Okay. I understand this. The kids vanished into another universe." Her rational mind scoffed—*Another universe. Really, Minerva, don't be ridiculous.* But the animal brain was not to be denied its truth. "When I followed the dragon, I came through after them," she whispered. "It's like Alice through the looking glass—but no. Not really. She was just dreaming."

"True—and you aren't," said a masculine voice from just behind her.

Minerva jumped and shrieked and turned, pretty much in a single action—and the speaker stepped away from the menhir that had hidden him.

59

Her first sight of him left Minerva speechless—and frantically aware of her nakedness. She tried to cover herself with her hands. She didn't have enough hands. "Oh, God!" she wailed, and looked for someplace to hide from the stranger—the creature. He—the creature was definitely male—was more terrifying to her than the dragon had been—for where the dragon had been a monster, this . . . this *thing* . . . was somewhat human. *Enough to make him frightening,* she thought. *Not enough to make him safe.*

From the tips of his pointed ears to his sharply cloven hooves, he was a rich cinnamon-brown. He stood upright on two slender goatish legs—broad-shouldered, lean—

Well-hung, her startled subconscious whispered.

Lean, she told herself nervously. His features were sharp, his point-tipped ears swiveled slightly to follow sounds, his four-fingered hands were long and fine-boned and heavy-nailed. He wore a knife belt and carried a duffel bag slung over one shoulder and a wooden flute in one hand.

"Hello, Minerva Kiakra. My name is Talleos," he said. "I'm here to help you." He grinned at her—he had broad, square teeth, very white, in a smile that curled devilishly. Eyebrow arched, he murmured, "I *knew* I got the better end of the deal." His gaze wandered up and down her body with overt appreciation and his voice oozed sexiness.

Minerva could have died of embarrassment for being caught without clothes on. She was furious that the creature dared leer at her. But mostly she was frightened. This Talleos-creature knew who she was. By name. He'd been expecting her arrival—he knew enough about what had happened to her that he knew to wait for her near the circle of standing stones. That meant the magic that brought her there—the magic that stole her children from their beds in the middle of the night—was no surprise to him. Her fear became anger. She stared at him and clenched her hands into fists. "Do you know where my kids are?" she asked.

Talleos nodded. "Of course I do. That's why I'm here."

Smug bastard. That's why he's here, all right. She flexed her knees and watched him; studied his arrogant, amused face and his confident stance. *He's so sure of his ransom—or whatever his game is!*

Fury gripped her, and something snapped inside Minerva, and she screamed. She went straight for him—straight for his eyes with her fingers bent into talons; straight for his throat with her lips pulled back from her teeth. "Give them back, you sonuvabitch!" she shrieked. "Give me back my kids."

Minerva hit him—hard. The creature tumbled backward and Minerva landed on top of him. She gouged at his eyes with her thumbs. She bit at his throat. He howled and grabbed her wrists and managed to pull her hands away from his face. His hooves slashed very close to her head—connected solidly with her ribs. Spurred by pain, she kneed him in the groin, and he screamed and rolled into a little knot.

"Give them *back* right *now!*" she screeched. "*Right now*—or I'll kill you! So help me God, I will." She grabbed two fistfuls of hair, crawled up, jammed her knee against his throat and pressed. She was shaking with fury. Her voice quavered and her heartbeat pounded in her ears. "Right now—or I'll break your damn neck."

"I don't—have them!" he wheezed. His voice squeaked. Tears ran from the corners of his eyes. He lay tucked into a fetal position with his hooves wrapped nearly around his ears. He tried to struggle out from under her knee, and she tightened her grip and pressed harder.

"Who does?"

"Look, I can tell you all of this—" He squirmed, and she increased pressure. "But you have to let me go," he gasped. "I came to help you."

"The hell you say."

"It's—truth. By all the gods—I swear it." His face turned increasingly dusky.

Truth. Hah! she thought. Terror and adrenaline made her crazy. She wanted to hurt him, wanted with everything in her to rip the strange creature to shreds. But if he was telling the truth, and she hurt him, he might not help her. If she killed him, of course, he couldn't. If, however, he was lying . . .

She gritted her teeth until her jaws ached. *If he's lying, I'll kill him later.* She let go of his hair and eased the pressure off his neck.

Her palms sweated, and she panted. She had the horrible urge to burst into tears. *Nerves. Or fear. Or shock,* she thought. *Or all of the above.*

"I'm going to let you go," she told him. "For your sake, you'd better be able to help me."

He rolled away from her, twisted into a knot, and rocked back and forth.

She wanted answers. "Well—?"

"Let me die in peace, won't you?" His voice was a hoarse croak.

"No! I have to find my kids!" She could hear the edge of hysteria in her words. She didn't care. "Help me now. I have to get them back."

"Get the bag. Stuff in it's for you." He didn't make any move to get up—just kept rocking back and forth.

She picked up the bulky broadcloth bag from where he'd dropped it and undid the laces. It was full of clothing. She pulled the items out; they were foreign—peasanty-looking garb in loud primary colors. Vivid grass-green leather pants; cobalt-blue shirt covered with hand-embroidered flowers; lemon-yellow vest; purple boots; a scarlet tam with jaunty feathered cockade. She found white linen bloomers and a rather coarse camisole that, she supposed, would serve as underwear. She also found a utilitarian black leather knife belt, complete with sheathed silver knife.

"What the hell?" she asked him. "Stuff looks like it was designed by Barbarians of Hollywood, with colors by Crayola." She wasn't going to look the proverbial gift horse in the mouth, though. Hastily, she threw the clothes on.

He didn't look at her—didn't say anything. He was still writhing.

"You're honestly here to help me?" Dressed, she felt less vulnerable. She sat crosslegged, elbows propped on her thighs, playing absently with the little silver knife. She watched Talleos rolling in the tall grass sucking air like a carp on land. She began to feel a little sorry for him.

"Much to my regret," the creature groaned.

"I'm sorry. I thought you were responsible for kidnapping my kids." She tipped her head to one side and stared off into space. *I don't actually know that he isn't, even yet.* "If you were responsible for it, I'd kill you," she added, just so there wouldn't be any misunderstandings.

"I figured that out." He sat up with apparent difficulty, wincing as he did. "Where'd you learn to fight like that?"

She shrugged. "I have a brother."

He raised an eyebrow—the only part of him that still seemed to be working. "Have? Lucky fellow—I'm surprised he survived childhood."

Minerva laughed in spite of herself. "That's where I learned most of it. I also took a self-defense course my freshman year of college, but I never used that. It all came back, though, when I thought you were hiding Jamie and Carol and Barney."

"Thus proving the oldest law of survival." He didn't say anything else.

Curious, Minerva asked, "Which is—?"

"Never screw with the mommy."

She grinned. She was amazed how calm she was beginning to feel. She could think clearly again—even plan. Clobbering Talleos had proven therapeutic. She felt in control of the situation for the moment—though she suspected the feeling was illusory.

"You're a satyr, aren't you?" she asked Talleos. He'd finally struggled to his feet and was hobbling around, groaning. He was taller and thinner than the statues of satyrs the ancient Greeks had carved, and he didn't have horns—but the similarities were pronounced.

He gave her a dark look. "Certainly not. I'm a *cheymat.*"

"What's the difference?"

He posed, displaying his . . . attributes . . . to their most obvious advantage. "The differences are *immense.*"

She rolled her eyes. "Never mind." Satyrs—ugh! He could call himself a cheymat if he wanted to, but he was blood kin to those randy party gods, whether he wanted to admit the relationship or not. She stood, sheathed the knife, and picked the red tam off the grass. "What do I have to do to get the kids back?"

"Your kids are safe for the time being. The person you need to be concerned about is you. I'm here to keep the Weirds from destroying you."

And I took you out in one round? Oh, great. How reassuring. She didn't voice her doubts, though.

"Somebody wants to destroy me?" she asked.

"You and your husband, actually. The Weirds stole your children so you and your husband would go charging after them. I suppose they expected you to call the police on your telephone. Very bright of you to stay away from those, by the way. The Weirds planted their gate on your home phones. If either of you had touched one, you would have both been sucked straight into the Conclave chambers, and the Weirds would have annihilated you."

Talleos stopped talking. He cocked an ear in the direction of the path, and his head snapped around. He stared down the base of the next hill over, where the path wound around out of sight.

"Shit," he whispered and snatched up the empty duffle bag. "Up. Start skipping around the stones," he ordered. "And laugh like hell. Act like you're having a wonderful time." He put the wood flute to his lips and began to dance around the stones as well, piping a wild, alien jig.

Minerva's fear returned in an overwhelming rush. She didn't ask questions. She pasted a phony smile on her face and leapt to her feet and began skipping and dancing.

"Laugh," Talleos whispered tersely as he passed her. He glared at her and kept piping.

Minerva laughed and stamped and whirled. As she came around one of the stones, she saw a handful of dark shapes on the path at the base of the hill, staring up at her. Her stomach knotted in fear. She skipped faster, and laughed more merrily, though her laughter rang falsely in her own ears.

Talleos circled her again. He muttered, "On the far side of the henge, skip straight down over the hill—and giggle. Soon as we're out of sight, run like hell."

Minerva, still laughing with phony wild abandon, nodded.

She and Talleos skipped another daisy chain around the stones. On the far side, Talleos yelled, "Ho, wench! Let us sport us while we may! Ho! Ho! Ho!"

He bounded in her direction, and she squealed and giggled loudly and skipped down out of sight. When they dropped below the crest of the hill, Talleos passed her, springing at a tremendous pace. Those goat legs could move. She fled after him.

They ran through scrubby brush and tall grasses, racing as if devils were riding fiery horses in their wake.

Never know, Minerva thought. *Maybe they are.*

They ran until they were gasping for breath. Finally Talleos flung himself flat in the tall grass.

Minerva followed suit. "What—was all—that about?"

"Later—" he wheezed. "It's—complicated."

They lay hidden in the field, catching their breath. Minerva thought Talleos was remarkably out of shape for a woodland creature, but she didn't comment on that.

"We're going to stay here for a while," Talleos whispered. "If we don't move, they'll never spot us."

The dry grass beneath her made her itch, but she was too scared even to move enough to scratch. She desperately wanted to understand what was happening. She wanted to believe there was something she could do to make things right. "You started to tell me about the . . . um, Weirds?"

"Weirds. Most powerful magicians on Eyrith."

"Right. Magicians." She remembered those dark shapes at the base of the hill and shivered. "Why would the . . . Weirds . . . cross universes or dimensions or whatever to try to kill Darryl and me? We aren't anybody special."

Lying beside her, Talleos nodded vigorously. "That's why."

"What?" Minerva frowned, not understanding.

"You're supposed to be the Weavers of the universes. When you and your fiancé bought your wedding rings, you got them from an old guy at a festival, right?"

Minerva closed her eyes. *Events from so long ago,* she thought. "Ren Faire. Right. He told us this fairy tale about the rings being magical—he said they would 'bind us across

the . . . universes . . . and through . . . time . . .' " She ground
to a stop and stared over at the cheymat. "Oh, God. It wasn't
a fairy tale, though, was it?"

"No—it was real."

"Oh, God," she whispered. "I always *thought* there was
something I was supposed to do, you know? I always
believed my life was supposed to be more than a boring
nine-to-five job and kids and a house in the suburbs." She
nodded. "A quest. Saving the universe." She held her hands
in front of her and stared at the woven gold ring that
gleamed in the morning sunlight.

She pursed her lips and nodded again, sharply. "Yeah.
That's all right, then. Whatever it is, I can handle it." She
looked over at Talleos and gave him a brave smile. "This is
what I've been waiting for. This is what I was born for."

Talleos stared at her, disbelief written on his face. "That's
quite commendable," he said in a faint voice. "Really, I am
amazed—and quite impressed. Especially considering the
circumstances."

She didn't like the sound of his voice when he said that.
"Circumstances?"

"Yeah." Talleos took a deep breath. "You see, the old guy
sold the rings to the wrong two people."

It hit her like a slap in the face. "The wrong people?"
Her voice sounded petulant to her own ears. "How can
that be?"

Talleos shrugged. "Shit happens." He pulled a long stem
of grass and shredded it absently. "The old guy was in a
hurry—the Unweaver was after him. You two showed up at
about the right time, you looked about right—so he gave you
the rings and ran like hell. Half an hour later the right people showed up at the appointed place—"

"That seems like a sloppy way to determine the fate of the
universe," Minerva interrupted.

"We all can potentially live forever. Knowing that, how
would you feel about your own immediate and eternal
annihilation?"

Minerva didn't even have to ponder that. "Not good," she
said.

"The idea didn't thrill the old guy, either. And that was what would have happened if the Unweaver caught him."

"How do you *know* we're the wrong people?"

"The universes are falling apart. You've gotta be."

"I see," Minerva said. "What about Darryl and me, then? Can't we do whatever it was the real Weavers were supposed to have done?"

Talleos sighed. He rolled over on his side and propped himself on one elbow. His right hoof tapped out a regular pattern on the grass. "That's the heart of the matter. You aren't cut out for the part. If you were, everyone is pretty sure you would have shown some sign of it by now. And as far as the Weirds are concerned, the universes can't wait any longer to find out. You are a nice lady, I'm sure—and damned attractive—but you're ordinary. There is nothing *special* about you—*nothing* that anyone can see as potential. The Weirds of the Conclave want to destroy you and your husband so that they can give the rings to someone with a chance of repairing the damage. An infinite number of universes are at stake. If someone isn't found who can keep the Unweaver in check, he'll unravel everything back to chaos."

"So *they* made a mistake, and they're going to destroy *us*? That's not fair."

"And life is?"

Minerva twisted the ring on her finger and stared off into space. People were trying to kill her and her husband. They had kidnapped her children. She was stuck in some alternate world where dragons and cheymats belonged—a world where she didn't belong. And it was all for nothing. She wasn't anyone special. She really *didn't* matter. All her secret desires and grand dreams of making a difference came down, at last, to the simple fact that, whoever it was that the universe needed to save it, it wasn't her.

She pulled the ring off her finger. She held it in the palm of her hand, offering it to Talleos. "Take this," she said. "Tell me how to get back to my own world, and I'll get the other ring from Darryl—you can have that, too. We won't fight over this," she told him softly. "No one has to kill us. If we aren't good enough, take these, and find someone who is. All I want is to get my kids back before I go."

Talleos took the ring, then carefully placed it back on her finger. "I couldn't take it even if I wanted to. The metal ring is only an outward symbol of the power you now contain. That power is linked to you for eternity and binds your soul to your husband's, making the two of you halves of one greater being, until time ceases to exist. If you only had whatever rare spark of greatness it takes to use that power, Minerva, you could create a galaxy with the flick of your fingers, form planets out of nothing, create life."

Talleos pulled several grass stalks and twisted them together so tightly the crushed stalks stained his fingers. His eyebrows lowered. "Only one way exists to separate a Weaver from a Weaver's ring—and that is to destroy the Weaver. Not to kill—for dying is only moving from one plane of existence to another, after all—but to annihilate. To take the Weaver's power from you, you would have to be Unwoven, and the very matter of your soul destroyed so that not even the smallest particle of that matter remained."

"Oh." Minerva clasped her hands in front of her. She looked up at Talleos and chewed nervously on the side of her lip. "So the situation is thus—" She held up her hand, fingers spread. "The guys in white hats want Darryl and me out of the way because we're the reason the universes are falling apart. The guy in the black hat doesn't care, because we're no threat to him, but he's the one who's trying to destroy everything in the first place—so what he wants, I don't want. Darryl and I can't just give the rings to someone who can use them—they're stuck to us. And we're not able to use them." She ticked the points off on her fingers, then stared at her hand with distaste. "Not good. Not good at all. I don't see where there's a happy ending in this for me, that's for sure."

She sighed. "So, where do you fit in all of this? If you don't want me dead, you must be working with the black hats."

He frowned at her. "Where is it written that there can

only be two sides to any issue?" He flopped back in the grass. "In rescuing the two of you, my dear, Birkwelch and I are merely displaying enlightened self-interest. We don't want to see the universe end—not a chance. And we're going to do everything we can to teach the two of you to use whatever puny talents you possess."

"Birkwelch?"

"Big blue dragon. You met him?"

"Oh. Yes. We met. Sonovabitch took my Wheaties." Minerva was surprised at how angry she still was about that. "Why are you willing to help us?"

His eyes widened and he gave her an ingenuous smile. "Because we're great guys."

The warning bell started ringing wildly in her mind. She didn't believe that line for a minute. "What happens if we fail?" she asked, and studied him with narrowed eyes.

He arched one eyebrow and shrugged. "Then we go back to the first two options. The good guys win, and you die—or the bad guy wins . . . and you die. So you don't have a lot of options, huh?"

He sat up and peeked over the waving grasses, and said brightly, "Enough of that. We're all clear—so let's *move*."

He took off toward a narrow copse of dark and twisted trees at the edge of the field. Afraid to be left behind, she jumped up and ran after him.

The Unweaver stepped out of swirling mists and green-lit fog—black-cloaked, tremendously tall, his robe billowing around him like the spreading wings of night. His face, if he had a face, was hidden within the deep recesses of his hood. He spoke, and his tones were unearthly—menacing—sepulchral. "Why have you called me forth, puny human?"

Minerva faced him—short, unimposing, and definitely outclassed. Who, me? Call *you*? Definitely a wrong number, fella, *she thought.*

But she heard her voice squeaking, "I am the universes' champion, and I challenge you to battle."

"Battle?" he asked. "To the death?"

She thought, Honestly, I'd rather play poker for tiddly-winks—and the winner gets to confine the loser to a really huge shopping mall forever.

But her stupid, big mouth was going on without her. "Not to the death. To the utter destruction, to the complete annihilation, to total abrogation, to nullification, to absolute nonexistence throughout eternity—you universe-sucking abomination!"

The universe-sucking abomination started to laugh—a very large, hollow, scary laugh.

Minerva thought, That's pretty much the way I see it, too. *She pulled a magic wand out of somewhere, and started waving it around and uttering incantations. She looked silly, she thought.*

The Unweaver just stood and watched her. She got to the end of her song-and-dance routine, and wound up with her big double whammy, and shot it off at the unmoving form.

Nothing happened.

The Unweaver continued to stand and watch her. His laughter crescendoed around her, growing louder and more terrible. Then, without doing anything that she could see, he promptly stomped her flat.

Minerva caught up to Talleos, where he stood waiting under the first sheltering branches of the little trees. She was breathing hard, and she had a stitch in her left side that stabbed and burned with every inhalation.

"For the record," she told him between gasps, "'the very existence of the universes depends upon you—and you're a screw-up,'—is not the best thing anybody—ever said to me on—a Tuesday morning."

"For the record, that isn't exactly what I said."

Minerva gave him a sidelong glance. "It's what you—meant, isn't it?"

"Well—yes."

"Then my comment stands."

Darryl had been drinking beer with a dragon long enough, he decided. He'd heard the whole save-the-world story, and it was crap. All of it. This dragon was a hallucination—had to be. In spite of the fact that he really could see it, it just wasn't there. He was a little off the edge—no doubt about it. But he'd bet anything that as long as he realized it, he wasn't beyond hope. All he had to do was convince his subconscious to sober up. *Inform the apparition that it isn't real. That will do it.* He stood up and weaved his way toward the connecting bathroom. When he reached the door, he leaned against it and turned back toward the dragon. He pointed a finger and said, "When I get back out here, I want you gone."

He avoided looking in the mirror the whole time he was in the bathroom. *Think things will be back to normal. Believe it. Make yourself believe it.*

The dragon was still on the bed when he went back to the bedroom.

The dragon gave him a hurt look. "Don't you like me?"

"I don't believe in you. It's bullshit. All bullshit." Darryl slipped the ring off his finger. "There is nothing— *nothing*— special about this ring." He threw it at Birkwelch.

The braided circle of yellow gold flew across the room, smacked him on the nose, bounced off the ceiling, landed on the very edge of the mattress, fell onto the floor, and finally rolled across the carpet. It came to rest at Darryl's feet. He looked down at it lying there. *Coincidence.* He shrugged and turned his attention back to the dragon. "It's— just—a—stupid—ring."

Birkwelch sighed—smoke swirled from his nose and mouth, and Darryl thought he might have seen just the slightest flicker of flame. "Fine. It's all fake. So where are your children? Why is your wife in the mirror instead of here?"

"I don't have all the answers," Darryl said. "I can't explain why I think I'm seeing the things I am. Guilt probably—" He ran his fingers back through his hair. "*I—don't—know.*" He ground the words out with as much force as he could muster. "But I do know there is a sensible explanation somewhere. In the meantime, I want you gone. As long as you're here, I'm going to keep thinking I've lost my mind."

The wedding band floated up from the floor, hovered for a moment in front of his face, then slipped itself back on his finger.

Darryl would have reacted in exactly the same manner if a snake had materialized out of thin air and slithered into his jockey shorts. He jumped straight up, screamed, and immediately began a wild attempt to remove the offending item.

No dice. It was stuck on his finger as if it had been welded there. He yelled. He swore. He pled. He tugged at the ring until the finger swelled and turned a nasty shade of red. He slammed his fist against the doorframe, then howled with pain.

Downstairs, the phone began to ring.

"Got it," the dragon yelled, and leapt for stairs.

"It's *my* phone!" Darryl snarled, and tried to shove him out of the way.

Birkwelch grabbed Darryl by his shirtfront and lifted him off the floor. "Yes," the dragon said, suddenly menacing. "But *I've* got it."

Birkwelch dropped him and ran like hell. Darryl followed. He got to the kitchen half a step behind the dragon—fast enough to see the bright blue apparition pick up the phone—

Fast enough to see the explosion that occurred when he did. Smoke billowed out all around Birkwelch, and black lightning crackled, and the air suddenly reeked of ozone.

The dragon cocked an eye-ridge at him. The expression said, *See, asshole. Aren't you glad you didn't get that?* He smiled and handed the smoking receiver to Darryl. "It's for you," he said. "The hospital."

Oh, God—she's at work, Darryl thought, and felt sudden relief. Other explanations could come later—

He let out a deep breath, and shouted into the receiver, "Minerva, what are you doing at the hospital? Are the kids at the sitters? I've been worried out of my mind—"

"Mr. Kiakra—this is Ilene McDougald in the emergency room. There's been an accident. We need you to come to the hospital."

Darryl knew Ilene's voice. She was an ER nurse, and one of Minerva's friends. She sounded rushed and frantic.

"What kind of accident?" he asked.

"We don't know what happened. The ambulance just came in— Please call your family though—" Someone in the background yelled for Ilene to hurry, that they were calling a code.

"It's bad, isn't it?" He could feel that it was from her voice, but he wanted confirmation.

"I don't know—" The voice in the background shouted for her again. "I've got to run, Darryl. Be careful driving," she added. "The roads are awful."

He hung up, feeling suddenly very sober. He stared at the telephone, then quickly dialed his folks' number. He passed the little information he had on to them, and then to Minerva's family. Then he ran for the door.

He stopped on the way to grab the station wagon keys— the LTD was a heavier vehicle and it had new tires on it—but the keys were gone. He didn't know where the spare set was. *Odd. Minerva always hangs her keys on the board.*

She hadn't though. He took his car.

One of the boys must have been hurt when the window blew out, he thought. Minerva must have called an ambulance to come to the house to get them. It had to have been pretty bad—she hadn't been able to break away to call him— But what could have taken them so long to arrive?

It only registered with Darryl halfway to the hospital that the dragon had disappeared after the phone call. *So now I'm sane again, huh?* he thought. *Damned good thing.* He wished he hadn't drunk so much beer. It was the sort of thing his father would notice at eight-thirty on a Tuesday morning.

He got to the ER before any of the relatives and ran through the automatic doors reserved for ambulances. He caught a glimpse of Ilene as she ran from one cubicle into another. The ER was packed, and people kept running past him. He didn't see anyone else he recognized.

He stood there in the doorway for a moment, and Ilene

hurried past—her face pale and drawn. Behind her, someone yelled, "Another amp of epi, goddammit—and push it!"

"I'm going to let you wait in the nurses' lounge." Ilene rested her hand on his arm. "I'll send your family in when they get here—we'll be with you as soon as we can. We're still working on her."

"Ilene—I need you in here!" the voice yelled. Then—"That did nothing! Fuck it! Defibrillate at three-sixty!"

Ilene pointed to a doorway. "Go in there. I'll be with you as soon as I can." Her voice shook slightly—her eyes were red-rimmed and bright with unshed tears.

He nodded, and walked slowly to the door she'd indicated. He felt queasy and helpless, and lost. The noises of the ER—the beeps and rattles and high-pitched whines, the shouting voices, the cries of babies in some of the cubicles and the groans of adults in others were overwhelming. The smells were awful—disinfectant, urine, sweat and feces and fear. Patients in blue gowns sat propped in wheelchairs. Somewhere, someone was vomiting noisily. Out of sight, a woman wept—hopeless, grieving sobs.

Darryl stepped through the door into the nurses' lounge and closed it behind him. That door provided an insufficient barrier between him and the pain of the rest of the world. *We're still working on her,* Ilene had said. *Her . . . Carol?* He stared into the nurses' lounge mirror—and saw a woods, bounding and bouncing, with a goat-legged man just ahead of the runner through whose eyes he saw. *Minerva. Running. So I'm still crazy after all.*

The ER was swamped, nurses and doctors and technicians thundered past at high speed, shouting arcane commands, terrible things were happening. He wanted someone to come talk to him—to tell him what was going on. But they were still working on her. His little girl. The lump in his throat made it hard to swallow. He sat down in one of the ugly blue-vinyl-and-stainless-steel chairs and stared at the half-eaten Hardee's biscuits that littered the round table. Someone had been reading *Cosmopolitan,* someone else a book with a dragon on the cover. He was frightened and restless. He picked up the book, thinking that the dragon didn't look like Birkwelch at all—*Slay and Rescue*, he read. *By John Moore*. He didn't know the author, didn't recognize the book. But he wasn't into that kind of stuff, anyway. He put the book back down and stood and began to pace. *Things must have been pretty peaceful this morning, if they had time to read, time to get biscuits. They didn't have time to finish them, though,* he noted, and the sick feeling in his stomach got worse. He twisted the ring on his finger.

Maybe it isn't all that bad, he hoped. *A broken arm— or—or something.* But the nurses didn't have any other families waiting apart in the privacy of their lounge. *Oh, God, Mom—Dad—hurry, hurry, hurry up!*

Minerva's folks opened the door and came in. They both looked pale and scared.

"Brian—Laura—" He nodded to both of them.

They gave him questioning looks.

"They're still working on her—Carol, I think. No one has even had the time to tell me." He shook his head slowly.

Laura said, "We passed your parents out in the parking lot. They were just pulling in." She stood there, looking at the disarray in the lounge. Then she clasped her hands together, took a deep, resolute breath, and sat down. His father-in-law sat beside her, and rested a hand on her arm.

His own folks walked in, his mother leaning on his father, chattering at an incredible rate—inane stuff. The roads. The ice. The cold. So many trees down in the neighborhood.

So she was scared, too. Normally, his mother was the quietest person on earth.

He hugged her and his father, and told them what he'd been told.

His father sniffed his breath and frowned. "Why don't you know what's going on?" he asked with that hard-eyed look Darryl remembered from his childhood.

Darryl felt the bottom fall out of his stomach—but he didn't have to come up with a lie.

Ilene McDougald walked in, followed by the doctor. *Mike Frankel,* Darryl realized. Mike and Darryl and Minerva had gone to school together—they hadn't been friends really, but acquaintances anyway. Mike had gone on to medical school and had come back home to practice. Everyone said good things about him. He nodded to Darryl, but didn't smile.

Mike looked around the lounge, found a chair, and sat down. Clasped his hands. Unclasped them. Leaned forward, resting his elbows on his knees. Took a deep breath, and let it out.

Hurry up, hurry up, hurry up! Darryl's insides screamed. "I'm sorry. I have bad news."

Well, yes. They knew that—that was the reason he and his relatives had come racing from all over town. How bad; who did it involve—those were the things Darryl needed to know.

The doctor said, "Minerva's had an accident."

Minerva? Darryl's racing thoughts screeched to a halt, stricken dumb. *Minerva?* He hadn't really even considered that something might have happened to her. He'd been sure she was all right—because of the things he'd seen in the mirror. Somehow he thought that meant the accident couldn't involve her.

Minerva's mother said, "What kind of accident? Is she going to be okay?"

Mike looked down at his hands, then up and around the room at all of them. He looked shaken, Darryl thought. He remembered suddenly that Minerva and Mike had dated briefly one year. "I don't really know what happened," the doctor said. His eyes were unfocused, looking someplace far away from the ER and its horrors. "It doesn't seem to make any sense. Some kids were out playing in the snow this morning. They went into a wooded lot in the neighborhood, saw something bright, and ran over to investigate. They found Minerva lying there in the snow and leaves. They were bright kids—two stayed with her and the other two ran for help."

"How is she?" Minerva's father asked. He was hanging onto his wife's hand so hard his knuckles were white.

Mike Frankel swallowed hard. He pressed his lips together. "She didn't make it. I'm very sorry."

"She's dead?" Darryl gasped. "Omigod, she can't be!" He closed his eyes. His guilt pressed on his chest with an elephant's weight, so that he almost couldn't breathe. "She can't be dead. This has to be some sort of mistake."

Laura had her face pressed into Brian's chest. She was sobbing. His own mother came over and put her arms around him. "Oh, Darryl—oh, poor Darryl," she whispered, and stroked his hair. "Oh, Darryl, I'm so sorry."

"She's not dead, Mom," he said. The tears streamed down his cheeks and ran off the tip of his nose. The hair on the back of his neck and on his arms stood up. He couldn't comprehend the possibility of Minerva dead. That very moment, he could see through her eyes—she was right there in the nurses' mirror, and she was running. "It has to be some sort of mistake—it can't be her."

He shrugged free of his mother and wiped his eyes on the back of his sleeve. "I want to go in and see her," he said to the doctor.

Mike nodded. Ilene stood. "We'll both go in with all of you," she said.

"I want to go in by myself first." Everyone looked at him. "Alone. Okay?"

"Darryl, I don't think that's a good idea." His mother was looking at him with worried eyes.

"Mom, I have to see her first. I have to be sure it's really her."

The rest of them kept their seats. Darryl stood. Ilene waited for him, then led him into one of the ER cubicles that had a curtain pulled around it.

It was a rainbow-striped curtain, he noted. Rainbow. Symbol of hope. How could anything bad happen behind a curtain like that?

"I'll be right out here if you want me," Ilene said.

He went around it, came in at the head of the stretcher. The first thing he noticed was a bright splash of purple in the wire basket under the stretcher. Gaudy, awful, loud purple—the infamous tacky purple parka he'd hated ever since the day she'd bought it. He knew that coat, and recognized the sweater and the boots that were with it. He looked at the still form—the brown hair wet and mussed; the shape of the head narrow, familiar; the curved and rounded body under the sheet the right shape and size.

He walked around the stretcher, and for a moment he felt a rush of hope. He had been right. That couldn't be Minerva. The woman on the stretcher was too pale, waxy and bluish—her face was slack and unfamiliar. She didn't even look like Minerva. How could they have thought—?

He reached out and touched one hand that rested at her side on top of the sheet—and stiffened. The body's hand didn't feel real; it felt like soft, cold, damp rubber stretched over something hard. Minerva's hands were warm and strong and lively.

But the freckles were her freckles. The short, sharp nose was her nose. The pale, pale lips were still round and full, their shape undeniable, familiar. It was her. She always had looked odd to him without her glasses, and her glasses were gone.

It really was her.

He brushed her bangs back off her forehead. Cold, wet, rubbery skin—so hard to believe it was the same skin he'd touched with such passion for so long. Oh, God, it really was her. What was he going to do?

He reached out and took both of her hands in his own. He couldn't see; his eyes were too full of tears. All he could do was feel—and the hands belonged to a stranger. He felt as if he were going to choke, or stop breathing and die right there. He wished he would.

Her hands felt wrong—wrong in some way other than the cold, other than the stiffness. Something was missing.

He wiped away his tears and stared at her hands.

Her ring was gone.

What? he thought. Minerva never removed her ring. Neither did he. *The ER people? Did they take it off, maybe put it with her glasses?*

"Ilene," he said. His voice came out in a croak. "What did you folks do with her glasses and her wedding band?"

Ilene came in. "She wasn't wearing either of them."

Darryl froze, and stared at the body on the stretcher. The very air in the tiny cubicle seemed to roar in his ears.

His mind grabbed onto that fact, swallowed it readily, accepted it completely. No glasses—and she was almost blind without her glasses. No ring. And Minerva *never* took off her ring.

He started to laugh, softly at first—but then louder, and giddily. "It looks like her," he said. "My God, it looks like her. But it isn't her." He felt dizzy with relief, felt he'd been pulled back from the edge of some unfathomable abyss. He smiled at the ER nurse. "It really isn't." He smiled so broadly his face felt as though it would split. "Oh, it isn't her, it isn't her!" Ilene stared at him as though he'd just lost his mind. He spread his hand out. "Don't you see? It can't be her. She *never* took her wedding band off. Never."

He started to laugh again, the relief was so great. Minerva was okay—still lost in the mirror, but okay. This body was—somebody else.

"Doctor Frankel!" Ilene called, and backed out of the cubicle. "Doctor Frankel! I need you in here stat!"

And Mike came running, and Ilene came racing back with a needle, and a couple of big guys held him still while she gave him a shot of something, though he protested when they did. They walked him into a private room and put him on a stretcher, and his mother and father came and sat in the room with him and talked to him. Meaningless gibberish. Silly stuff.

Minerva dead. Silly. Silly. Minerva wasn't dead. She just wasn't here.

After a while, everything went dark, and he slept.

Secret Agents Jeevus, Renskie, and Equator crept down the steep stone stairs to the first landing below the tower.

"These stairs are just what we need," Jeevus whispered. "They're designed to be easily defended."

All three children paused on the landing. Agent Jeevus lay on his belly and scooted to the very edge of the stairs. He looked down for a long time, then scooted back again and stood up.

"This is bad, men," he said, and crossed his arms over his chest. "There are a bunch of them down there. All monsters like the one we got. It's going to take a lot of ammunition to beat them."

"We don't have any ammunition." Carol crossed her arms, too. "I think we should just run away."

"Heck, I don't even think we can get out of here right now. This place is full of monsters. We're going to have to beat them just to get to the door."

Barney said, "I think we should sur—um, sur— . . . give up."

"Surrender? You want us to surrender! Never!" Jeevus whispered. "Only sissies quit." He glared down at Barney.

"Well, I want to go home," Barney said. "Maybe the monsters will let us go home."

"Ninny! They'll eat us." Secret Agent Renskie rolled her eyes, then glared at her brother.

"I don't think so," Barney said. He didn't want to be a secret agent anymore. The game was no fun. The stairs scared him, the monsters scared him, and he wanted his mother and father . . . and breakfast. He was hungry.

Murp, tired of being held, yowled once, and Jeevus paled. "Keep him quiet!" he whispered. "If they find out we're here, they'll come up the stairs and eat us—and we haven't even had the chance to set our booby traps yet."

Just like his butthead brother to think anyone could make Murp be quiet, Barney thought. "Okay. *You* hold him, stupid. Maybe he'll be quiet for you." Barney held out Murp toward Jamie. The cat sensed impending freedom and squirmed out of Barney's hands—then darted out of Jamie's reach and down the stairs. He disappeared from view.

Jamie stared down the stairs after the vanished Murp. "Shit!" he whispered. "You let him get away, you moron! You were supposed to take care of him."

Barney wanted to cry. He started to go after the cat, but his brother grabbed him.

Jamie looked like Barney felt. "You can't go after him. They might get you." Jamie closed his eyes and rested his head against the stone wall. "Oh, boy! I hope they don't eat him."

Barney realized his big brother was scared, too. In a funny way, knowing that made him feel better.

Jamie pointed to the huge wooden door that led off the landing. "We need to go in there, and see if we can find any stuff for weapons. Maybe Murp will come back." He didn't sound very sure.

Carol whispered, "What if someone is in there?"

Jamie chewed on his bottom lip and frowned. "That would be bad," he said.

Carol put her hands on her hips. "I *guess*! So what are we going to do?"

Barney closed his eyes and took a deep breath. He could feel nothing but emptiness from the other side of the door. Wherever the monsters in the castle were, they weren't in there. He decided if Jamie could be brave when he was scared, then Secret Agent Equator could be, too. "We can go in there," Secret Agent Equator said, and pushed on the door. "It's okay."

The door didn't budge. He pushed harder. The door was really big and really heavy.

Jamie and Carol pushed with him. Suddenly, something behind the door gave way, and it slid open, screaming on its hinges like the ghosts in Barney's nightmares.

"Oh, man," Jamie whispered. "They're going to hear us for sure."

Carol stared through the opening, and groaned. "It looks like your room," she said.

Jamie looked over her shoulder, then at her. He gave her a puzzled frown. "No, it doesn't."

"Yes, it does. It's a dump." Carol stepped through the doorway, and Jamie and Barney followed.

The place *was* a dump, Barney decided—but a really neat one. Huge trunks sat along one wall, some with the lids open to reveal hats and clothes and stacks of paper. Silly-looking suits of armor took up one corner of the huge room, moldy boots and high-backed saddles and piles of books cluttered the floor. Several mop buckets sat just inside the door—full of slimy green water and with the mops propped beside them.

Jamie ran to a huge mound of rusted metal and started pulling spiky objects out of it one by one. "Wow! These are caltrops," he whispered, and held up one of the small, sharp weapons to show Barney.

"What's it for?"

"Armies put them in fields and on roads and stuff so the bad guys' horses can step on 'em. But," he grinned up at Barney, "we can throw 'em down the steps."

"Wow!" Barney was impressed. "Doesn't it hurt the horses when they step on them, though?"

Jamie nodded. "I guess so."

"I don't like that very much."

Carol wandered over, swathed in ropes of big, gaudy glass beads. "No one should hurt horses. I won't use those."

Jamie sighed with exasperation. "We aren't gonna hurt horses. Jeez! We're gonna hurt monsters." He frowned at Carol. "Unless you'd rather get eaten. Or chopped up into little pieces or something."

Carol sucked in her bottom lip. "No."

"Okay, then. I promise we won't use the caltrops on horses."

"Okay."

"You need to take those beads off," he said. "They'll slow you down if you have to run."

Now it was Carol's turn to look annoyed. "That isn't what they're for."

"Oh, no. Of course not. So what are they for?" Jamie rolled his eyes and muttered, "Girls."

Barney felt something moving in the stairwell; sensed curiosity and concern. He tapped his brother on the arm. "They're coming."

Jamie's face went ghost-white. "We can't let them get above us," he whispered. "We've got to attack now!"

He ran for the door, carrying as many caltrops as he could, and flung them down the stairs. The clattered and bounced. Below, a gruff voice yelled, "Hey, watch it with that garbage. You might hurt somebody!"

Barney imitated his brother.

Carol didn't. Instead, she took one of the necklaces, bit

the string apart, and stripped the beads off with one hand. The round beads rolled and bounded around the stairwell, clattering as they fell. Below, the children heard a scream, followed by a heavy thud.

Jamie stared at Carol, amazement clear on his face. "All right!" he yelled. "Yes-s-s-s!" He pumped the air with his fist, and tossed a few more caltrops.

"Stop that immediately," the voice yelled. Barney ran back into the supply room and grabbed the first thing he could find—a bolt of cloth. He dragged it out and shoved it to the open center of the stairs, then out into the void. He didn't dare watch it fall.

Jamie and Carol, meanwhile, pushed the first of the trunks out of the storage room. It crashed down the stone stairs, making a tremendous racket and scattering debris in all directions.

"Fly up the middle," one of the monsters yelled.

Barney grabbed three caltrops and, as soon as he heard the beating of wings, threw them into the center of the stairwell.

There was another scream, and a solid thunk. "Great Karras! Don't fly! Don't fly!" a monster voice screamed. "Try something else."

The castle below the children grew quiet.

Jamie, Carol, and Barney stood on the landing, breathing heavily. Jamie mumbled something too softly for Barney to hear. Then he said, "They're going to do something else." He turned to Barney. "Can you tell what?"

Barney held still and listened to the whispery feelings that touched his mind. He clenched his fists tightly and sucked in his breath. After an instant, he nodded. "They're going to fly again in just a second, when they think they can catch us by surprise."

"Do we have any more caltrops?"

Barney shook his head from side to side. "I couldn't find any more. Maybe we could shove another box down on them."

Jamie nodded. His face grew stern, and he tapped his foot. "All right. Agent Renskie, Agent Equator—shove a box over the side as soon as you can get it there. I have another idea."

Equator and Renskie chose a trunk with lots of little, hard things in it, and started shoving that through the maze of junk toward the stairwell. Agent Jeevus, meanwhile, dragged a chain to the edge of the landing, then a couple of loose pieces of armor. Then, both buckets of slimy cleaning water. Jamie's weapons didn't make a very impressive pile, Barney thought.

Barney suddenly realized he and Carol weren't going to get to the edge in time. "They're ready now, Jamie!" he yelled.

Below, Barney heard the leathery flap of wings.

"Keep coming, men," Jamie shouted back. "I'll take care of 'em! Chain!" he screamed, and shoved it over the edge.

The chain made a long, slithering rattle as it fell. Below, the monsters yelled and shouted instructions. The chain hit the ground noisily—then Barney heard the wings again.

"Shrapnel!" Jamie screamed, and kicked the pieces of armor over the edge.

Barney heard thuds and screams from what sounded like direct hits. He and Carol were almost out of the room with their box. They kept pushing. Jamie crouched on the edge, hands gripping the edges of the bucket.

The sounds of flapping wings came up the stairwell for the third time, and Jamie shrieked, "Boiling oil!"

He dumped both buckets, and below, several voices screamed. Barney heard glass breaking.

"Psych!" Jamie yelled.

Carol laughed. "Got 'em! Got 'em! Way to go, Jamie!"

Carol and Barney maneuvered the trunk onto the landing, while Jamie did a little victory dance. "Suckers!" he shouted down into the stairwell.

The trunk sat, poised on the lip of the abyss.

"Don't shove it over yet," Jamie told Carol and Barney. "Save it for the next attack. Get ready—"

Both Carol and Barney braced against the trunk, waiting for Jamie's signal. *We're gonna win,* Barney thought. *We're gonna beat the monsters.*

Below, everything was silent.

Without warning, big claw-tipped hands lifted Barney into the air from behind. Identical sets picked up Jamie and Carol.

"No!" Jamie yelled. "They flanked us! They flanked us!"

Barney shrieked and kicked and tried to bite.

The monster who'd captured him growled, "That will be quite enough of that."

CHAPTER 5

Minerva and Talleos kept themselves out of sight. They went through the endless meadows crouched over, until Minerva's lower back burned with pain. They ducked into every available stand of trees. And they ran north—steadily north.

Minerva kept seeing those still forms silhouetted on the path—watching her. In her mind's eye, they grew hideous. Their cloaks whipped around their legs, their hands twisted into talons, and from empty eye-sockets in hideous faces, eerie ruby light burned.

She wished to hell she'd never read Tolkien.

Talleos' response to her few attempted questions was to press a finger to his lips.

It was a long, exhausting, frightening day.

At twilight, when Talleos led her into a dark woods, she was ready to drop. She was hungry and thirsty, and she longed for a place to sleep, or even something soft to sit on for just a while. In the gloom, she saw the bulk of darker gloom—a building of some sort, squat and dire and silent. Talleos motioned her to be still, then crept around it and out of her sight. She clenched the hilt of the little silver knife that hung at her hip and pressed her back against the biggest tree she could find. Whatever came after her, she was going to be ready.

She waited. No sound of Talleos. No sign of him. Things

cracked and crunched around her. Leaves rustled. A night bird screeched right behind her and she nearly jumped out of her skin. The damp night air brushed the hairs at the back of her neck, familiar as a lover. She shuddered.

They're out there, she though. _Those things, those Watchers—they're out there looking for me. Oh, God, what if they find me?_

She was scared. She wanted to be home, safe, with her kids and her husband. She wanted someone to tell her everything would be okay.

Suddenly, cold, bony fingers gripped her shoulder.

She whipped around toward her attacker, swinging the knife up underhanded, putting all her strength into the tip. She knew that the wraith or whatever had come to get her wouldn't be stopped by such a tiny weapon—

Talleos shrieked and leapt back before the knife connected. "Gods on hot rocks, Minerva!" he yelped. "What are you trying to do—kill me?"

Minerva was shaking. Her heart pounded in her throat, and her pulse roared in her ears. "Why the hell did you sneak up on me?" she snarled. "You damn near gave me a heart attack."

"Yeah? Well, you just returned the favor," Talleos muttered. "I was checking out the house to make sure we didn't have any unwanted company. We don't—" He glared at her. "Unless I decide you're unwanted company. If you think you can refrain from skewering me, I'll let you go inside."

"You mean we get to rest now?" Minerva whispered. "Oh, how wonderful."

She followed the cheymat along the tiny flagstone path to his house. It was a big cabin built of rough, hand-hewn logs, chinked with what looked like a mixture of moss and clay—the windows were small and covered with oilskin.

Primitive, Minerva thought. _But I don't care. If I have to sleep on animal skins tonight and kill my breakfast in the morning, that will be just fine. At least I'll get to sleep and eat._

Talleos ushered her through the door and closed it behind him. Then he switched on the light.

"What?" She stared around the entryway in shock. *Foyer,* she thought, and rubbed her eyes to make sure she was seeing it right. *Straight out of the pages of* House Beautiful. *Featured in Robin Leach's "Lifestyles of the Well-Hooved and Famous."*

The walls were creamy white plaster, the hardwood floor gleamed warm honey-gold. The electric lights were tastefully set in hand-hammered brass sconces—they filled the entryway with cozy yellow light. The big, thick throw rugs looked like Aubusson to her.

"Hungry?" Talleos asked.

"Ah—er—"

"C'mon," the cheymat said. "Let's get something to eat. He trotted off to her right, through a bookshelf-walled sitting room, a charming breakfast nook, and then into a kitchen her mother, God's gift to cooking, would gladly have killed for.

"Wow," Minerva whispered.

"You like?" Talleos grinned, looking tremendously pleased. "I got a really good architect." He trotted to a polished oak door and pulled it open. A light flicked on inside.

Architect? What kind of wild woodland creature hires an architect? she wondered. And then she saw where the wild woodland creature was leading her. "Wow!" she murmured. "A walk-in refrigerator! Neat!"

"Nice, huh?" the cheymat asked. "The other door is the freezer. I have a huge pantry, too. I'm so far from the main drag out here, it's a pain in the ass to go shopping. Besides, the groupies make it almost impossible for me to shop. So I stock up about six months at a time."

"This isn't quite what I expected," Minerva remarked.

Talleos came out of the fridge, arms loaded with sandwich fixings and canned beer. He kicked the door closed with one hoof. "Yeah. I could tell. The outside of the house has to meet standards set by the Winterkinn Woods Property Association. They determine acceptable styles, window coverings, stuff like that. We have to keep all our power lines buried. No external antennas—lots of rules. Inside, we can do whatever we want."

"Property Association? That sounds so—suburban."

"Nah. Worse than the suburbs. This is a hot tourist spot." Talleos started slathering knifefuls of green stuff out of a jar onto one slab of bread. He grinned at her. "Fix yourself a sandwich. The stuff in the bright red pack is imitation kaldebeast—low salt, low fat. The sausage is Summer Cherkie. The really dark meat is roast fowks—top grade."

Minerva looked at the packages—they looked like standard grocery-store fare from home until she picked one up. Then she discovered she couldn't read a word on the package. The alphabet was swoopy and loaded with curlicues and little stars and dots. She rubbed her eyes, hoping that would bring things into focus. It didn't.

"—and the beer is Tothfi Premium Dark Lager," he continued. She realized she'd missed part of what he'd said. "Huudegelf Tothfi, the local brewer, makes it. It goes great with the shoodlaf cheese." The cheese he pointed to was a pale powder-blue through and through.

"*Shoodlaf* cheese," Minerva whispered. She picked up a blunt-tipped knife and began loading things onto a slice of bread. "What does this stuff taste like, anyway?" she asked, piling on slices of the meat he'd identified as "imitation kaldebeast."

Talleos winked at her. "Chicken. Everything foreign tastes like chicken, doesn't it? Never mind—you'll like it. Trust me."

They took their sandwiches, some bright yellow fruits he identified as *bose*, and their beer, and went into the book-lined sitting room. Talleos took a seat on the couch and patted the space next to him. Minerva sat in the chair furthest across the room.

"You said something about tourists—" She took a bite of the sandwich. It tasted nothing like chicken, but was still good.

"Oh, yes. Tourists. The curse of my existence. The Winterkinn National Heritage Preserve runs from south of Hallyehenge—where you came through today—to north of the Green Mountains. It's sort of a reservation for us magical types—the few dragons and cheymats and nillries and whatnot who managed to survive the Magic Drought all got corralled over here about—oh—seventy-five, eighty years ago. The government paid each qualified individual a stipend to stay in the Preserve, so that the rest of Eyrith's population could come point their fingers at us and say "Golly, Thubert, a real cheymat. Just imagine, there used to be millions of those randy suckers."

He pinched his nose when he imitated the tourist, and made his eyes round and his jaw slack.

Minerva, who was swallowing a gulp of lager, laughed at the effect and got beer up her nose. She coughed and sputtered, and her eyes watered. "Must be a heckuva stipend," she finally managed to say.

"Why would you say that? Oh—the house?"

She nodded. "Pretty nice for government issue."

"Nah. I made a killing in the stock market."

Minerva closed her eyes and rubbed the bridge of her nose with her fingers. *Just imagine what it was like when there were millions of them,* she thought. *But maybe he's exaggerating.* Hoping for the best, she asked if there really had been millions.

Talleos cocked an eyebrow and sipped his beer. "Not of me personally. The universe has never been that lucky."

"Hah!"

He shrugged. "All right. Once we were common. Well, not *common.* We've always been spectacular. But *plentiful.* Before my time, of course. But cheymat history does speak of how easy it once was to get laid on Jolfing night."

"Jolfing night?"

"The spiritual equivalent of your Friday."

"Oh." The bose was delicious—just a little sour, with a great citrusy bite. Minerva leaned back in the chair, resting her head against the soft, deep cushioning. Right at that moment, it was hard to believe anything was wrong in the universe. The rich, bitter lager spread its glow through her veins, and her full day of hard exercise mixed with the soft crackling of the fire in the fireplace made her sleepy.

But there were things wrong. Her kids—she would have given anything to know that they were safe. And the people who were out to get her. And those dark shapes at the bottom of the hill—

Talleos was sipping his lager, eyes closed.

She had to know. "Those things watching us this morning—what were they? Ring Wraiths?"

Talleos gasped and beer foam sprayed out his mouth and nose.

She smiled slowly. Revenge, even unintended revenge, was a wonderful thing.

When he got his breath back, he looked at her incredulously. "Ring Wraiths? Karras! What do you think this is—a set from *Lord Of The Rings*?" He shook his head, disbelief apparent.

Minerva took a big bite of the sandwich and shrugged. "Okay," she said through a mouthful of the stuff that didn't taste like chicken. "So they weren't Ring Wraiths. What were they? They sure put the fear of God in you."

"Worse than Ring Wraiths." Talleos propped his hooves on his coffee table and stretched out. "They were tourists. If we hadn't done that dance and then run like hell, they would have been after me for my autograph. They won't interrupt a performance, but they would have wanted pictures—they would have asked me a whole lot of stupid questions about how I thought the death of magic was going to affect life in Eyrith and whether I had any kids." Talleos snarled and bit into his sandwich as if he wished *it* were tourists.

Minerva looked at the pale meat in hers and frowned. She couldn't swear that it wasn't. "*Do* you have any kids?"

"Hell," he snarled, "I can't even find a female cheymat. Why do you think I'm committing treason and risking my life to help you? Because I'm such a great guy? Unh-unh." He shook his head. "If the magic doesn't come back, you're looking at the last of the cheymats."

"You're almost extinct?"

"Yeah, well—" He shrugged and drained his lager. "We all have our problems."

"Darryl—Darryl—wake up."

Someone was shaking his shoulder. Sounded like his

mother—but his mother hadn't woken him up in years. The fuzzy edges of what must have been a nightmare clouded his thinking. He opened his eyes. He was in his room—the room at Mom and Dad's. His senior picture was framed on the wall, his Voice of Democracy plaque hung next to it. The curtains were the same gruesome green they'd always been.

He sat up and rubbed his eyes. Something awful had happened—or had he dreamed it. His wife—a dream? He looked at his left hand. The wedding band was there, braided gold that gleamed dully even in the dim light. Not a dream.

"Darryl, who's watching the children?" His mother was beside him, face worried. "We checked with the little girl who usually babysits for you, but she doesn't have them."

Oh, Jesus. The kids. He'd seen the blue light swallow Barney—he had to assume it had gotten Jamie and Carol, too. Where were they? He didn't know—he couldn't say. But if he went home, maybe—

Or was the vision a sign of insanity? Minerva was dead. Gone. What had happened to his kids?

"I don't know, Mom. I—got snowed in at work last night. When I got home this morning, Minerva and the kids were gone." He thought a moment. His version of the truth wasn't going to go over too well. He came up with a better version. "When I got home this morning, the window in the boys' room was out. From the storm, I suppose. The power was out, the phone lines were down—so I figured she'd taken the kids over to her folks' house because it was so cold. Then the hospital called and I just wasn't thinking at all."

His mother went white. "But Laura called me to see how the kids where holding up. She thought they were here." There was a long silence. Then his mom whispered, "They're missing?"

Darryl nodded slowly. His thoughts seemed to crawl at a snail's pace—some side effect of the shot they'd given him at the hospital, he imagined. *Missing. My kids are missing. And my wife is dead.* A lump grew in his throat. He wouldn't let himself cry. He wouldn't.

He shook his head back and forth as if that would clear his muzzy thinking. "I don't know what to do."

His mother put her hands on her hips. "I do. The police have been trying to figure out what happened to Minerva— I'll tell them about the children, too." She hurried out of the room.

He nodded. Yes. Of course. The police. Why hadn't he thought of that? Probably because he knew his kids weren't anywhere the police could go.

"You know, the yokels in the local constabulary are going to find your alibi just fascinating," a sub-bass voice rumbled behind him. He jumped and jerked around in the bed. Birkwelch leaned against the wall next to Darryl's old school desk, grinning.

"Jesus Christ!" Darryl made shooing motions. "Get out of here before somebody sees you."

The dragon crossed his stocky arms over his chest. He chuckled—the sound was almost identical to the garbage disposal in Darryl's kitchen sink. "They can't see or hear me. Only you can. You're wearing the ring, so you can perceive alternate realities."

"And I can't get rid of the ring." Darryl kept his voice down and one ear trained on the hallway. It wouldn't do to get caught talking to the walls.

"Nope. But be glad of that. Without the ring, you couldn't get Minerva back."

Darryl felt hope blaze in his chest—and gutter out. "Minerva's dead," he whispered. "Gone. There is no going back from that."

The dragon clucked his tongue. "Well, in a sense, she's dead—if you want to look at it that way. *I* certainly wouldn't. And in a way, you're correct. There is no going back—but there is always moving ahead."

"*In a sense*, she's dead?!" In spite of himself, Darryl's voice rose. "You can't be dead in a sense. Dead is dead. She's dead! She's gone!" His voice dropped again, and he gripped the bedspread. "Gone. I'll never get to see her again."

From down the hall, Darryl's mother called. "Darryl? Is everything all right?"

No, Mom, he thought. *The world came to an end and didn't take me with it.* "I'm sorry, Mom," he yelled. "I'm having trouble dealing with things right now. I'll be okay."

The dragon laughed. "And you know so much about life and death? You didn't even know there were dragons. Just think of all the other things you don't know."

Darryl scooted to the edge of the bed and stood. The room made slow, dizzying spirals around him, then settled down and satisfied itself with merely rocking back and forth. "There are no dragons," he muttered. He turned his back on the one that stood in his bedroom. He wasn't going to humor figments of his imagination anymore.

"*Oh.* Oh, *thanks.* No *dragons.* And what am *I*—a Canada moose?"

"Canada goose," Darryl corrected. Then he remembered he wasn't speaking to the nonexistent monster. He wobbled down the hall to the bathroom.

He looked in the mirror when he was washing his hands. He wished he hadn't.

He didn't see his face. What he did see was that same damned goat-man from earlier, with a big glass stein of dark beer clutched in one malformed hand, and a plate with a half-eaten sandwich propped on his lap. The satyr lounged on a couch, talking.

The view shifted. An identical glass of beer welled up in his field of vision, then moved back out of sight. A hand reached up to rub the bridge of the nose and removed the glasses. Minerva's glasses. The left hand wore a ring—but everything was blurry without the glasses. He waited. The glasses went back on again, and the view cleared. He caught another glimpse of the ring—just a brief one in passing. It was identical to his own, on a hand he would have recognized if he had to pick it from a million others.

Minerva was still on the other side of the mirror. If the dragon was telling the truth, she was alive somewhere. If the dragon was telling the truth, there was a chance he could save his kids—and the universe, too, now that he thought about it. If, of course, there *was* no dragon, he was certifiable. Nuttier than a fruitcake. In serious shit.

Okay, Darryl, ol' buddy. Let's look at this logically. You can hang onto your sanity, refuse to admit you can see your dead wife in mirrors and hear dragons talking to you. You can be nice and sensible and you can attend your wife's funeral, and kiss your kids goodbye forever and that will be that. Or you can embrace the madness. Pretend the dragon and the mirrors and all that shit is real. And maybe—just maybe—you can get them back.

He gripped the edges of the sink and stared at his wife's hands on the other side of the mirror.

No contest, Kiakra. No contest at all. His mouth started to stretch into a grin. He squinched his eyes shut, and the grin got bigger. *LET'S—GO—CRAZY!*

He had to get home. Miracles might be waiting to happen, but they weren't going to happen in his parents' house, in his old bedroom with the ugly green curtains. God knew, they never had before.

He burst out of the bathroom in high gear. The dragon's head snapped up, and his eyes widened.

"Go get in the car," Darryl told Birkwelch. "I'll be out in a minute."

Birkwelch tipped his head to one side, then smiled his alligator smile. "Well, all *right!* Way to go, Darryl!"

Darryl's parents were sitting in the kitchen, drinking coffee. His mother jumped out of her seat and hugged him before he even got through the door. His dad stood up and patted him on the back.

His mother was still wired. Too much coffee, Darryl decided. In pretty much one big gasp she said, "Let-me-get-you-something-to-eat-do-you-feel-like-food-oh-we-have-some-leftover-turkey-and-some-tuna-casserole-I've-called-the-police-and-Stanley's-flying-in-from-Massachusetts-to-see-you." She looked at him expectantly, waiting for an answer.

"Mom—Dad—" He looked into those familiar faces, the faces of people who loved him. Darryl ran out of words.

What do I tell them? That I don't need comforting because she's only gone, not dead, and besides, if I did need comforting, I'd rather be comforted by Birkwelch the socially unacceptable dragon than Stanley my asshole brother? That I've got to magically get my dead wife and my missing kids back? I don't think so.

Both parents were looking at him. He took a deep breath. "I'm going home. I need to be alone for a while."

His mother looked into his eyes with that intense mother look, then nodded. "Of course, dear. We'll be over to check on you—if you need anything, just call."

Just call. The mother mantra. And his dad, walking with him out to the car, totally ignoring Birkwelch in the passenger seat and draped half into the back of the Nova; his dad telling him life has meaning, and time heals all wounds, and have faith, his kids will show up and they'll be fine, just fine.

Just call. Mom words, because only moms can make everything better.

And later, when he'd been home for a while, he thought about calling—but what was he going to say? *Mom—the police have invaded my house. They're crawling all over the place, giving me fishy looks and asking me where I was and why do I think Minerva went out in the cold and died. I see my dead wife in a mirror, and I'm supposed to save the universe, and Mom, I want to go back to being a kid again. I want to go back to my life before I forgot what mattered, before I lost my dreams and became a nobody and screwed around on my wife—I want to start over.*

He couldn't get those thoughts out of his mind. And when the police did go away, with their evidence from the boys' room in little plastic bags and their admonition that he was not to leave town, he muttered behind them, "Barring saving the world and other miracles, of course, I suppose I'll go nuts." He stared in the mirror of the finally empty house, and the only thing looking back at him was his own reflection.

The dragon came up behind him without warning and rested a taloned forefoot on his shoulder. "Give her a break," Birkwelch had said. "She has to sleep sometime."

Barney could see only darkness out the castle window. He was, he suspected, up past his bedtime. He wondered if any of the monsters were going to come in and tuck him in and turn off the light. Carol was already asleep on one of the three beds the monsters had given them. Jamie sat on the second, morosely replaying their defeat.

"Up the outside wall and in through a window. I can't believe it. They just climbed—and we didn't do any booby traps on the window—we didn't mine the floor underneath—nothin'. That's what we did. Nothin'. We were stupid!"

"I thought we did pretty good," Barney said.

Jamie flung himself backward and lay staring up at the ceiling. "We lost. It doesn't matter how good you do if you still lose."

Barney frowned. "But they didn't want to hurt us."

"Yeah. And *that* makes it worse." Jamie propped himself up on one elbow. "We should have been able to *cream* them."

"I'm glad we got caught," Barney said.

"Traitor."

"I am." He stuck out his lip and frowned at his big brother. "Ergrawll was really nice, even though we hit her on the head and tied her up. And the food was good."

"Listen, butthead. They're all monsters, and they swiped us from home."

Barney thought about that. "I know. But Mom is here now. She'll come get us."

Jamie sat up and stared at his brother. "Mom's *here*? You mean here, in the castle? Did you see her?"

"No. Not in the castle. Just . . . *here*." *He closed his eyes. When he thought very hard, he could feel her presence—but from far away.* "Wherever this place is."

"Oh, great." Jamie flopped on his back again. "More invisible mystery stuff."

Barney thought of something interesting. "Ergrawll said she and the rest of the monsters would have caught us with magic—but they were too tired from bringing us here."

"I'll bet. Monsters always tell stuff like that to little kids. That's cause only little kids are dumb enough to believe 'em."

"Nuh-uh!" Barney swung around and sat on the side of

his bed with his feet hanging over the edge. "I didn't believe her. So I made her show me. She really can do magic."

"What'd she do—pull a penny from your ear?"

"Nah. That's not real magic. She did real magic."

"Sure she did."

"She *did*. She made me some candy."

Jamie snorted. "I'll bet. She didn't make me any."

"It was chocolate. It was so-o-o-o good—"

"Prove it." Jamie sat up. "Give me some."

Barney smiled. "I ate it all."

"No you didn't. You're just lying."

"It was *really* good."

"Liar! Liar, liar, pants on fire!" Jamie yelled.

The door to the room opened, and Ergrawll stalked in. "That will be enough of that. Why is the light still on? Why are you children still awake? I want you to go to sleep right now."

Barney said, "You didn't tuck us in."

Jamie said, "Barney said you gave him some candy. You didn't give me any candy, and besides, it was just a trick. You can't really do magic, either."

Ergrawll looked from Jamie to Barney, then back to Jamie again. "Of course I can't do magic. No one can." She smiled, then turned her back on them and switched off the light. "You'll have to tuck yourselves in tonight. I don't tuck in."

"Can you sing bedtime songs?" Jamie asked.

"No. I don't do those either."

"What kind of baby-sitter are you?" Jamie demanded.

Ergrawll's shape filled the doorway. "A carnivorous one," she said. "Go to sleep." Then she closed the door and was gone.

Barney sat on the edge of the bed in the darkness, growing angry. "She lied to us." He stared at the shadowshapes of his feet, barely visible in the faint light cast by the tiny moons out the window. He kicked his feet and said it again, a bit louder.

Beside him, Jamie whispered soft, meaningless words. "Carnivorous," his brother said. "That's bad."

Barney didn't know what "craniferroots" were, and he didn't care. "She lied to us," he told his brother.

Jamie said, "Huh?"

"Ergrawll *lied* to us. About the magic. I *saw* her do it."

"You always fall for those stupid tricks." His brother's voice made fun of him.

"I saw *how* she did it. She made her hands into a circle, and did this funny, twisty thing in her head—" Barney acted out the monster's actions as he talked. "And then she thought 'candy,' and tasted it when she thought it . . . and smelled it, too."

Barney stared at the space between his hands, where thousands of tiny firefly lights suddenly shimmered and twinkled. His heart pounded as he watched. Beside him, he heard Jamie gasp. The firefly lights died, and something smooth and heavy and cool lay in the palm of his left hand— a block of something he just knew was wonderful. He tightened his grip around the firefly gift and lay back on the pillow. Slowly, he put the corner of the block into his mouth. He nibbled the tiniest piece of the corner away.

It was *good* chocolate. Better even than the monster's chocolate. Barney smiled into the darkness and waited.

"What happened?" Jamie finally asked. "What were those lights in your hands?"

Barney took a bigger bite of the chocolate. "Nuffing," he said around the mouthful of candy.

"What do you have in your mouth?" Jamie's voice was edged with deep suspicion. "Let me see." He got out of the bed and came over to look.

Barney shoved as much of the chocolate as would fit into his mouth. He wrapped his fingers tightly around what remained.

Jamie started prying his fingers apart. "Share," he hissed.

"You said there wasn't any magic. So there isn't any candy."

Somewhere in the castle, well away from their room, someone screamed—a piercing, anguished scream that went on and on, becoming gradually softer and more pleading, until at last it gurgled to a horrible stop.

Jamie froze at the sound of it, and Barney's fingers dropped the sticky remains of the chocolate to the castle's cold stone floor.

"What was that?" Jamie whispered.

In the hall, Barney could now hear the sounds of fighting—and of dying. He shivered. "You won't believe me."

"Yes, I will."

"You know the bad things that came after us before."

"Yeah. I know."

"Something's comin' after us again—and this one's worse."

Barney heard his brother suck in his breath. Then Jamie said, "You know how you kept the ghost away until you ran out of the closet?"

"*Batman* kept him away."

"Okay—yeah, I forgot. Batman. Okay. So—can you get Batman to keep this one away?"

Barney looked at the darker outline in the darkness that was his brother, and shook his head in disbelief. "Batman doesn't live here."

"I know. But couldn't you, like, make a Bat-signal or something to call him? Pretty fast?"

Barney sat silent, thinking.

"Isn't there something you can do? Barn? C'mon . . ." Jamie sounded scared.

Barney hopped down from the bed and felt his way across the room to Carol's bed. It was funny there were no monsters under the beds in the castle, he thought. He decided it was because they were all out in the halls, fighting off the thing that was coming.

He hopped onto Carol's bed, and Jamie imitated him.

Barney held out his hands and closed his eyes. He found what he needed in his imagination—felt the cool plastic, saw the bright green, the splashes of orange and red and blue and purple. The Turtles. In his mind's eye, he saw them bigger—giant-sized, grown-up sized, wielding their weapons.

Something began to shimmer in front of him. Outside the door—right outside the door—there was another of those horrible screams. Something scrabbled on the wood, thudded heavily. "No!" it howled—*she* howled. "You can't take them!"

The door blew open—splintered. Light rolled into the room, hazy and swirling, centered on the monster woman who fought to hold back something infinitely worse. The light rippled over her, licked along her body greasily, sucked her dry and devoured her. She threw a weapon at the horror in the hallway—a desperate move—then fell. The light that crawled over her flickered brighter, and her body withered, and her scream grew fainter and fainter, as if she were falling down a deep hole. The silence swallowed her scream. The smoky light licked along the stain on the floor where she had lain, then guttered out.

Jamie screamed. Carol woke up, opened her eyes, then buried her head under her pillow. Murp, curled up sleeping with Carol, woke, and arched his back and hissed.

Barney shuddered, his summoning of the Turtles forgotten.

Something stepped into the room—a blast of dank, stinking, freezing air; the rattle of bones; two gleaming blood-red eyes that glowed but threw no light.

The eyes stared at the spot where Ergrawll had fallen. Then slowly, slowly, the shadow of a head turned, and the eyes searched out the corner of the room where the children crouched, trapped. Barney wished himself invisible, or gone.

But the eyes found him—found them all. He felt the thing smile, though he could not see it.

"So here you are," it said. It looked at them, through them, and Barney, frightened, cried out. Its voice was soft, just a whisper, only the hint of a voice—more terrible for being so quiet. "Good. Now you will come with me."

CHAPTER 6

A man came to Minerva in her dream, walking along a dark and twisting tunnel, and he smiled. The smile seemed, in that darkness, bigger than the man.

He looks like Santa Claus, she thought. I wonder why I made him look like that.

She knew she was dreaming, and that surprised her. She decided to see what she could do while she slept. She reshaped the rotund, jovial man, stretching him long and thin and pulling his nose out until it could have put Cyrano de Bergerac's to shame. She giggled.

"Don't do that," the man snapped, and shifted himself back into his Santa Claus form. "It isn't dignified."

She made his ears large, huge, enorrrrrmous—she made them flap like Dumbo's.

"I said don't do that." He changed his ears back and sat on a rock in the tunnel—except it wasn't a rock in the tunnel. As soon as he sat on it, it became a white-painted cast-iron seat in a restaurant, and all the waiters were cheymats and blue dragons. She and Santa Claus were seated in a booth that was decorated with a red-and-green checked tablecloth, and the food was already on the table. The drinks were vivid blue, the vegetables gelatinous and purple. Little roast beasts lay on a huge china serving platter, singing. Their voices sounded like Alvin and the Chipmunks. When she listened closer, she realized the song they were singing was "White Christmas."

Santa picked up one of the beasts and took a bite out of it. It sang louder, its voice becoming a shrill squeal. Minerva stared, fascinated. It kept singing—and even when Santa had reduced it to a pile of bones, she could hear its piping little voice echoing from the man's belly.

"Ho! Ho! Ho!" Santa shouted, and his belly heaved and shuddered—and split apart, like a zipper unzipping.

"Surprise," a soft, hollow voice whispered. "It isn't Christmas after all." Santa's flesh peeled back like a coat flung to the floor, and a creature obscured by the deep folds of a cowled cloak pushed Santa's bleached white ribs apart and stepped out. From the shadowed depths of the black cowl, two red lights glowed like hellfires.

"Hello, Minerva," the Unweaver said. "Fancy meeting you in a place like this."

Minerva suddenly felt queasy.

The roast beasts were singing the helium-induced version of "Silent Night."

"What do you want?" she asked. Her voice quavered.

"I want nothing. In fact, I have several things I don't want. Perhaps you can take them off my hands." The Unweaver laughed and held out skeletal hands. Sitting astride the carpal bones were her three children, all the size of mice.

"Mom," they screamed, in tiny, squeaking voices that were almost drowned out by the roast beasts. "Mommy, save us!"

Minerva grabbed for her children. Her hands hit the Unweaver's, and his bones fell apart. Her children toppled to the floor of the restaurant.

The Unweaver fixed her in his burning gaze. "Naughty, naughty," he rasped. "Can't have them back now." He put his bones back on, caught her children without moving, and popped them into his cowl at the place where she guessed his mouth would be.

"No!" Minerva yelled, and reached across the table to strangle him. She wanted to rip him to shreds, to tear him bone from bone, until she found her children. But no matter how far she stretched, he was just beyond her reach. He *slipped away from her down a tunnel that suddenly appeared in the restaurant, streaming backward like a man falling down a hole. He faced her—not moving, but still becoming smaller and smaller—with her children screaming from somewhere inside his bones. Then the two red dots of his eyes winked out and he was gone.*

"Give me back my kids, you son of a bitch!" she roared.

"You better not pout, you better not cry, you better not shout," sang the roast beasts. "I'm tellin' you why. Santa Claus is coming to town."

She opened her eyes. *Wow! What a nightmare.*

Something smelled wonderful—and from down the hall she could hear hooves on hardwood. "He's makin' a list, and checking it twice," a pleasant baritone sang. Apparently Talleos was fixing breakfast. She sat up and took a deep breath.

"It is a stone bitch," she muttered, "when reality is just as bizarre as your dreams."

She got dressed. Talleos had given her another set of clothes—again a heavily embroidered long baggy tunic with embroidered belt, wrap-type leather pantaloons, and an embroidered vest in crayon colors. She was apparently stuck with the curly-toed purple boots.

They can't all dress like this, she thought. But then, they *didn't* all dress like that. At least one of them didn't dress at all. She winced and pulled on the loud clothes and the awful—but comfortable—purple boots, then went down the hall to breakfast.

He was grilling meat and eggs and big round slices of something maroon. "Healths of the day to you," he declared, and flipped the eggs in the air with a deft twist of his wrist. He crumbled green and red powder onto them, then tossed the maroon things. He seemed entirely too cheerful. "Grab a plate. Sleep well?"

"Good morning, I guess. Fine except for the nightmares." She grabbed one of the heavy blue stoneware plates and a fork—*looks like solid silver,* she mused—and he piled half of his feast onto it for her.

"Nightmares . . . hmmm—" He loaded up his own plate and trotted into the breakfast nook. "Sometimes nightmares can be very deep and meaningful—interpreted correctly, of course." Muted sunlight came through the oilskin coverings and burnished everything with its glow. She noticed that both his eyes were black where she'd tried to take them out with her thumbs, and he had a huge bruise on his throat. She decided it would be prudent not to mention this.

They sat, and at his urging she told him about her dream. When she'd finished, he sat quietly, staring off into space. She waited, trying to figure out what he was thinking from the expression on his face, and to see if he'd found any rich symbolism in her dream.

Finally he shook his head and looked into her eyes. "You ever do drugs?" he asked.

Caught off guard, she burst out laughing. "I've always had nightmares. I figured that was bad enough."

"Yeah. Dreams like that—drugs would be redundant." He shook his head again, chuckled, and dug into his breakfast.

She stuffed her face with the maroon slabs. They were wonderful, whatever they were. Rich and salty and starchy— crunchy on the outside, chewy on the inside. The exercise from the day before still seemed to be affecting her. She was starved. "So you don't think the dream had any deep significance?"

"Sure it did. You're worried about your kids. Doesn't take a master magician to figure that out."

Minerva was disappointed. She'd hoped Talleos would have some wondrous explanation for the dream—it was odd enough it seemed to call for one. And it had, at the time, seemed so *real*.

That was the end of conversation until they'd both finished eating. Then, however, Talleos said, "Speaking of master magicians—*you* have a lot to accomplish today. We're going to start your magic lessons."

They dumped their dishes on the kitchen counter; then he led her to a heavy, brass-bound door just off the library.

"The workroom," he said, and gave her a courtly, half-mocking bow. He opened the door for her, and she walked in.

Her first reaction was "You have to be kidding." The rest of the house had been so modern, so normal—that somehow she had expected the magic room to be more of the same. Pragmatic. Sensible.

It was anything but.

Huge, dusty tomes and scrolls and rolls of parchment bent the bookcase shelves along the far wall into inverted arches. Display cases along both side walls held bottles and jars and amphorae and phials, skulls and hides, half-melted candles, tiny figurines and nondescript bundles of dead plants and other scruffy things. She sidled leftward, edging cautiously past what she would have described as a stuffed devil. She wasn't entirely sure it was stuffed—hence the caution. She wanted a closer look at the jars and other paraphernalia. Talleos flipped a switch, and the interiors of the display cases lit up.

She turned one cork-stoppered jar so she could see past the label. The jar contained thick, gray, meaty things floating in a pale green solution.

"Tongue of the fabled flightless guerfowl—used in spells relating to speaking or singing." Talleos sounded disgustingly enthusiastic when he said that. She peeked back at him. He was grinning broadly.

Minerva wrinkled her nose. She couldn't imagine herself enthused about dead bird tongues. *But you never know*, she thought.

She moved another container and peered through the murky, colorless fluid to discover it was chock full of what looked like the body parts of small reptiles.

"Fetal dragon," the cheymat told her. "Already sectioned. It's powerful stuff—most spells won't call for more than a leg or an eye."

"Oh, yuck."

A third held long, thin, looping coils of something smooth and pale blue.

"Oh, that is *great* stuff," Talleos said, and sighed.

"Oh?" Minerva didn't trust Talleos for an assessment of what was great.

"Absolutely. It's an aphrodesiac. Penis of crested kirmin— a kirmin's penis grows from thirty to forty feet long. That one is a better than average specimen."

"Oh, *gross!*" She turned away, and almost ran into a little worktable upon which sat an alembic. The glass apparatus was full of noxious, gloppy green liquid on one side, and something brown covered with a coat of fuzzy mold on the other. "Eeeuw!" She looked back at Talleos, who wore a sweet smile.

The center of the room was clear. On the heavy wooden floor a circle had been painted with green, red, yellow, blue, and black paint. The geometric figure painted inside the circle had ten points, each of a different color.

"That's the decagram," Talleos said. "It will be your work center."

"I thought the pentagram was the magical symbol."

Talleos snorted. "A common but anthropocentric misconception. The pentagram became popular because a man, with arms and legs spread, could imitate one. Hermetic philosophers—who thought the universe circled Man the way the sun circled the earth—found this profound and significant."

"The sun doesn't circle the earth."

"So true. Nor the universe Man." Talleos clicked across the floor, his hooves tapping loudly. He pointed to the decagram. "The unicursal decagram, however, represents each of the possible emanations between the world of Knowledge and the world of the Unknowable Infinite."

Minerva twitched an eyebrow upward. "How fascinating that the Unknowable Infinite is reachable by such an easy number as ten."

Talleos frowned at her. "Even the Unknowable Infinite is within the reach of the true seeker. As you will discover."

He pulled a black robe off a coathook and handed it to Minerva. "Wear this. It is fitting garb for a seeker and future magus such as yourself."

She struggled her way into the garment with difficulty.

The robe draped down to the floor, the hem crumpled on the wood to form several folds of cloth around her feet. The sleeves enveloped her hands. They dangled well past her fingertips. The cowl hung over her face—hot and scratchy and uncomfortable. The robe must have been worn by a man seven feet tall, she thought.

"Don't you have one smaller?"

Talleos gaped at her as though she had suggested profaning a temple. "Have one smaller? Are you kidding? That is the Sacred Robe of Exarp. There aren't *two* of them."

The robe was wool—coarsely woven, scratchy, hot, and heavy. Minerva felt like she was wearing a bedspread—and not a good one, either. "How am I supposed to do magic with this on?" *How am I supposed to move with it on?* she wondered.

Talleos sighed. "You have to suffer a lot to do magic. That is just the way it works. If you want your kids back, you're going to have to wear the robe—unless . . ." He gave her a sideways glance and said, "No . . ."

Minerva hated games, and she had no time for coyness. "Unless *what*?" she snapped.

"Well, magic done skyclad is even more powerful than magic done wearing the mystical Robe of Exarp."

"Skyclad. *Sky*clad?" Minerva didn't recognize the term, but she didn't like the sound of it.

"Nude." Talleos gave her a hopeful little grin.

Her instincts were right on the money, she decided. "I'll suffer." She rolled the scratchy sleeves up all the way to her elbows, then reached down and tucked a portion of the front hem under the robe's heavy rope belt. She brushed the cowl back with a quick swipe of her hand.

"There. See? This will do just fine."

Talleos seemed to have been stricken by a fit of coughing. She watched him lean, shoulders heaving, against a rack of skulls. He gasped and choked, and his face turned duskier than usual.

"Are you all right?" she asked, concerned. She walked toward him, but he waved her off.

"Fine—" he croaked. "—Water—" and he clattered out of the room.

When he came back in, he looked much better. "Choked on some dust or something," he told her. His color was still high. "Okay!" He gave her a bright smile. "Let's get to work on the magic. Take a seat in the middle of the decagram."

While Minerva sat on the hard floor, Talleos pulled a huge book out of the bookcase, propped it on a carved bookstand, flipped to the first page, and began to read.

"'The beginning of magic is the beginning of the comprehension of the Manifest and the Unmanifest, the corporeal and the incorporeal, and the flow of the ions of time and not-time through the river of the Eternal Is. Within the spin of the single atom, the magus finds contained all secrets and all miracles of every facet of existence. And the harnessing of the powers of that atom is within the reach of the dedicated seeker. Above all, the seeker must strive for purity of intention, purity of thought, and purity of being.

"'To attain the purity required of the magus, the seeker must reach within and find a personal and internally consistent meaning for each of the thousand spoken names of God. The first of these names is Ke-Seh-Haveh-Kalla, which means . . .'"

Minerva felt her eyes beginning to glaze over. This was the way to do magic, was it? Oh, God. Her kids lives—and her own—depended on her ability to learn *this* stuff?

It felt like chemistry class all over again. She'd hated chemistry.

"'The second name of God is Gur-Gesh-Hegonokrisvedomio, which . . .'"

Darryl, you stinking pig, she thought, *I hope to hell you're as miserable and as scared as I am right now.*

"Geoff, I really don't know what happened. . . . No . . . No—some kids found her while they were out playing. . . . No, not *my* kids; the police are still looking for them. . . . Not yet. The police have tapped the phone lines—there weren't any ransom notes that anyone could find. . . . No, I guess they'll be doing the—ah—the au-au-autopsy— . . . today . . ."

"No . . . I'm all right now. . . . Thank you. I appreciate that—a leave of absence would help a lot. . . . I'd—I'd really rather not talk anymore right now."

All morning. The goddamned phone hadn't stopped. People telling him how sorry they were; people telling him he was a miserable bastard and the police were going to find out what he did; friends of Minerva's who wanted to commiserate with him; friends of his who didn't know what to say.

Minerva was right there in front of him, right on the other side of the fucking mirror. He couldn't touch her, he couldn't hear her, he couldn't actually see her—except once when *she* looked in a mirror. But, dammit, it was really her. Out of his reach.

He'd made the funeral arrangements. He'd sat on the other side of the funeral director's desk and picked out a casket and discussed the service. He'd cried. He couldn't help it. The funeral director had a mirror behind his desk. The whole time Darryl was discussing the details of the service, Minerva was standing behind the man, playing with powders and knives and wands and other weird shit. He wanted her back. No matter how hard he tried to convince himself otherwise, he couldn't believe she was coming back.

"If your face drags any lower, old pal, we can use it to sole your shoes." Birkwelch leaned along the back of the armchair and hung his head, upside down, in front of Darryl.

As a sight gag, it probably would have been pretty funny, but Darryl wasn't in the mood. "Go 'way," he snarled.

"No, man. I want to go to McDonald's and get some fish sandwiches and fries. They're my favorite."

"Good. Go."

The dragon did not get his face out of Darryl's way. "I want some company."

Darryl lost his grip on his calm. "You miserable son of a bitch," he yelled. He grabbed Birkwelch around the dragon's long, muscular neck and tried to strangle him—a feat he discovered was about as smart as trying to strangle a boa constrictor. One minute he had his hands around the dragon's neck; the next, he was lying on the floor on the other side of the room, watching lights going round and round on the ceiling, wishing he could remember how to breathe.

His mother stood over him, an unreadable expression on her face.

"How did you do that?"

He couldn't quite breathe yet. "Do what, Mom?" he wheezed.

"Jump across the room like that? And who were you yelling at?"

Yeah, Darryl, he thought, *how did you do that? Taken up flying in your spare time, have you?* "I don't know what you're talking about, Mom," he said. "I just fell down."

"Uh-*HUH.*" His mom looked, very slowly, from the armchair fifteen feet away to the place where Darryl lay and gave him the Fishy Mother Eye. He knew the look. It was the same look she'd given him when he came home at three A.M. from the party at Lisa Sherwood's house. It was the look that meant, "Don't give me that shit, dear. Mothers can read minds."

They could, too, he decided. He and Lisa Sherwood had been up to no good, all stories to the contrary aside.

He just shrugged his shoulders and sat up. "I didn't hear you knock."

She raised an eyebrow. "I didn't knock. I let myself in. I wasn't sure whether you would be answering the door today or not." Her face said the next time he planned on frolicking with Satan's minions, he needed to lock the door.

He thought that was a fine idea.

He stood. "Well—ah . . . Did you come over for any particular reason?"

She tipped her head to one side. She crossed her arms. Birkwelch, standing inches behind her, mimicked her every move. "I thought I'd stop over and see how you were holding up," she said.

"I wanted to make sure you weren't drinking yourself under the table or hanging yourself from the rafters," Birkwelch said in Darryl's mother's voice.

Birkwelch's imitiation was dead-on. Darryl, afraid he might laugh, tried hard not to look at the dragon, and ended up avoiding his mother's eyes, too. "I'm holding on," he said.

His mother glanced over at the armchair again. "You might want to hold on tighter," she said.

Birkwelch stopped his imitation in mid-move and stared at the woman. "She's pretty funny, you know?"

"I know," Darryl said, and as soon as the words were out of his mouth, realized he had answered the dragon out loud. He could feel the blood running to his feet. *We do not speak to our hallucinations when our mother is in the house. Do we, Darryl? No, we do not.*

"Well, I'm glad," his mother said.

Dumb luck. She thought he was talking to her. He might not be so lucky twice. He took his mother's elbow and guided her to the front door. "Mom—I'm really not feeling up to company right now." He reached for excuses. "And—I need to stay by the phone, in case the police call back with news about the kids."

"So you haven't heard anything?"

He shook his head. "I'll call you as soon as I do. I promise."

"I really think," she stopped on the steps and looked up at him, "you ought to come home with me. The police will be able to call you at our house—"

"The kids haven't memorized your phone number."

She stopped, and pursed her lips, and cocked her head to one side. "You're right. As soon as you hear anything, then."

"I promise."

He went back inside and looked at the mirror. He still couldn't figure out what Minerva was doing. Whatever it was, he wished she wasn't doing it with a naked creature out of Greek mythology who was hung like a bull.

The dragon came over and stood beside him.

"Who—and what—is that guy?"

"Talleos. My roommate. He's a cheymat."

"A cheymat." Darryl got a glimpse of the creature when Minverva turned her head. "He looks like one of those Greek things. Watchacallems. Satyrs."

The dragon grinned broadly. "If I tell you a secret, you have to promise not to tell."

Darryl shrugged.

"He *is* one of those satyrs. But it pisses him off no end that one of his ancestors got around so much—so he says Pan was just a myth. He's the last satyr. Who's going to argue with him?"

Darryl frowned. "Pan wasn't a myth?"

"He was a legend, man. He was *inspirational.*"

"You knew him?"

The dragon tipped his head back and sighed soulfully. "Oh, yeah. Now there was a guy who knew how to cruise chicks."

The phone rang. Darryl ran for it. It wasn't going to be the kids. Knowing what he knew, he didn't think the police were going to call with anything useful, either. It was more likely his mom, deciding he ought to get Call-Forwarding so he could go over and stay with her and dad. Nevertheless—

"Yeah," he said.

"Darryl. I heard about your wife. How awful." The voice was feminine, sweet, sexy—and he couldn't place it.

"Yes," he agreed.

"I baked something for you—I'll bring it over," the voice said.

Who is this? Who is it? he wondered. "Um, I'm not really feeling like company—"

The voice interrupted him. "I understand completely. I'll just drop this off and leave. But if you need to talk, you know I'll be there to listen. All you have to do is say the word."

Right. Say the word—and figure out who the hell you are. "I appreciate that." He hung up the phone, still not able to put a name or a face with the voice.

The dragon had stretched out in front of the French doors and was lolling on the kitchen floor in the sunshine like a cat. "Anything interesting?"

"Somebody from work bringing over food."

"That's good."

"I don't know. Can't quite place the voice." Darryl looked

at the beast on his floor. "Don't you have something useful to do?"

"I'm doing it."

"Working on your tan?"

"Keeping you alive. That useful enough for you?"

Darryl looked at Birkwelch to see if the dragon was trying to be funny. For once, the monster looked like he meant what he said. "It will do for a start." He looked around the kitchen, then out through the French doors into the side yard, overtaken by paranoia. "Um, should I, um, lay low or anything?"

The dragon snorted. Faint blue tendrils of smoke curled from his nostrils and circled around the dust motes in the sunlight. "Nah. The trouble is coming, but it isn't here yet."

"How do you know?"

"Dragons exist in five dimensions simultaneously, while humans only exist in four. We're superior. We *know* things."

The doorbell rang. "So if you know things, who's on the other side of the door?"

The dragon grinned, and closed his eyes, and started to speak. Then he stopped and his smile faded. "That's funny."

"Don't know, do you?"

"No. I don't."

Darryl went to answer the door. "Goddamned cocky dragons aren't as brilliant as they'd like to think," he muttered.

He opened the door, saw who was standing on the other side holding a bean dish, and slammed it.

"Internal Revenue Service?" the dragon asked.

"Cindy Morris."

The dragon cocked his head and studied Darryl like an entymologist with a new bug. "The name is unfamiliar, but the guilt certainly speaks volumes. Something about this is fascinating. Invite her in."

Darryl, speechless, nodded. He opened the door again. Cindy Morris still stood there, her expression bewildered. "Hi, Darryl," she said, and gave him a sweet, puzzled smile.

He couldn't think of anything he really wanted to say to

her—but the dragon wanted to get a look at her. "Won't you come in?"

Her smile grew. "I brought you a casserole. There aren't too many things I know how to cook, but—" Her voice trailed off, and she shrugged.

Darryl suspected the shrug was supposed to be cute. He took the casserole dish, and she followed him into the kitchen. The dragon was nowhere to be seen. *Interesting time to have to take a leak,* Darryl thought. He had no idea what to say to Cindy.

"Um," he said. "Ah."

"I know this probably seems awkward," Cindy said.

Darryl nodded. Awkward was the least of what it seemed.

"I didn't want you to feel guilty about the other night."

Darryl stared at her. *You have to be kidding,* he thought.

"No, really. I've been in love with you since I started at Phelps," she said. "I seduced you. I knew I shouldn't have at the time, but—I wanted you. I really came over to apologize for taking advantage of you." She smiled at him again.

She *still* had the greenest eyes he'd ever seen.

"Um, Cindy," Darryl finally managed, "I appreciate the apology. What happened—it wasn't all your fault. And I appreciate you bringing the casserole, and—um, and everything—" He stared at his feet. "I don't think we should see each other again, though."

"I wish you wouldn't say that. I know we started out badly, but I was hoping we could be friends."

"I'm sure you were," Birkwelch said. He walked up behind Cindy Morris and blew a tongue of flame at her.

She spun around, and her green eyes grew huge. She shrieked.

"She can see you," Darryl said.

"You bet your ass, she can. Why don't you make a pass at me, hey, sweetheart?" the dragon asked the woman.

Cindy hissed. Her skin melted and flowed; she became an animated Dali painting, stretching and deforming and changing into something other—something awful. Her body grew dark and leathery, gaunt and twisted. Her arms transformed into talon-tipped wings, and her face lengthened into a lipless muzzle, both jaws lined with hundreds of wicked, needlelike teeth. Only her eyes were the same—still wide and glittering, emerald green. She hissed again, and started to puff herself up.

The dragon snapped at her, his jaws only missing crushing her head because she darted out of the way.

The transformed Cindy lunged for the door, knocked it open clumsily, and launched herself into the air.

Through the entire exchange, Darryl had stared, rooted to the floor. He couldn't believe what he'd seen. "A-ha-ha-a," he gasped.

Birkwelch sauntered back into the kitchen. "Don't eat the casserole," he said.

"Okay." Darryl felt like sitting on the floor and gibbering for a while. He was willing to be meek. *What was that?*"

The dragon stretched back in front of the French doors again. "A Weird. They are bad, ba-a-a-a-ad news. So that was your one and only fling, huh?"

Darryl nodded, and shivered. Goosebumps rose on his arms and the hair stood up on the back of his neck. "'Weird' seems a pretty mild description," he whispered.

"No. *A* Weird. One of the magic-masters of Eyrith . . . the ones who want you dead. You're lucky, pal." The dragon chuckled softly. "If you weren't wearing that ring—or if you had taken it off for any reason while she was with you, she would have eaten you alive. Knowing her kind, she probably would have started with your dick."

Darryl closed his eyes and ran his hand over his forehead. He leaned weakly against the kitchen counter. The room looped and swayed around him, and his heart thudded desperately in his chest. *I could have lived forever without knowing that,* he thought.

Barney woke to find his sister's knee in his face, his brother's legs over his stomach, and Murp sitting on his chest licking his nose. He scratched the cat's head and looked around him. There wasn't much to see. All four of them were still trapped in the stone room, right where that terrible thing that stole them from the monsters had put them.

The room had no windows, and no doors, and no lights. The walls glowed faintly, and by the light of these Barney could see there was nothing in the room except for the children and the pile of filthy rags on which they lay.

Barney rubbed the sleep out of his eyes and frowned. He wasn't too hungry, but he had to go to the bathroom. Bad. He thought about this for a moment and decided it would be better if he didn't think about it. Instead, he tried to remember what he'd been dreaming. He vaguely remembered he and his brother and sister had been someplace with his mother, only the—the what? The Unweebil? Something like that—wouldn't let them go to her. They'd been in sort of a restaurant—but with singing food.

There were *bathrooms* in restaurants, Barney thought.

He *really* had to go.

He made himself a piece of chocolate, watching to see if the little firefly things would be there again. They were. He thought it was cool that he could see right through the chocolate at first, while the firefly lights swirled around—but as soon as they started to disappear, he couldn't. He wondered if maybe the lights were little tiny people, and they made the chocolate. It was all very interesting, and quite distracting—until his brother shifted and stuck a knee right into his belly.

Barney disentangled himself from his brother and sister and sat up. He ate the chocolate thoughtfully, then looked at the far wall of the room.

He was pretty sure he could have made the Turtles—if he hadn't gotten scared. They were pretty big. Maybe he could make a bathroom. He concentrated on it—thought of the upstairs bathroom back home, with its big, shiny sink and his footstool for washing his hands; with its bathtub big as an ocean, that sat up on shiny gold feet with claws on them—and its toilet with the wood seat and the bright blue water. If there were a door in his prison, it would lead to such a bathroom, he decided. The room needed a door anyway. He concentrated, and behind a shimmering square of firefly lights, the bathroom door from home appeared, fancy glass handle and all. It looked, he thought, kind of small. He was not in any mood to be critical, though. As long as there was a potty on the other side, he would be happy.

He opened the door and peeked in. Yep. There it was. He grinned. Mommy and Daddy sure would be surprised when they saw what he could do. He felt really tired all of a sudden. He guessed magic must be hard work, even if it didn't seem like it. He decided he would take a nap when he was done.

That would *really* surprise his mom. He hated naps.

His brother and sister were awake when he went back out. They sat there, looking all sad and scared, petting Murp. His brother looked surprised to see him.

"Where were you?"

"Goin' to the potty."

"There wasn't a potty in here last night," Carol said. "I looked."

"I know." Barney smiled. "There's one now."

Jamie and Carol looked at each other. For a moment, neither moved. Then both of them leapt to their feet and ran for it—Carol, who'd been sitting closer, arrived first. She darted in and slammed the door in Jamie's face. Barney heard the lock click.

"Oh, no," Jamie groaned. "She'll be in there forever."

"You take the longest," Barney said. "You always take books in with you."

"Well, I don't have any books, so I can't take longer— okay?" Jamie turned his back on Barney and pounded on the door. "I gotta go!" he yelled. "Hurry up!"

"I shoulda' made two," Barney muttered,

Jamie, catching his breath in between yells, evidently heard him. He turned back and stared at Barney. "You should have done *what?*"

"Made two. Bathrooms. Then I wouldn't hafta listen to you yell."

"You *made* the bathroom." Jamie frowned. "No. I don't think so. A little kid like you could not make a bathroom."

Barney was terribly sleepy. He didn't want to listen to his brother talk anymore. He made two books appear and carried them over. "Here. Read a book." He held them out, and when his brother didn't take them, dropped them at his feet.

Then he went back and curled up on the pile of rags and closed his eyes.

In the background, he heard his brother pounding on the bathroom door, yelling for Carol to get out of the bathroom—that they had an emergency. It sounded just like home, Barney thought.

The last thing he heard before he fell asleep was Jamie squawking, "Hey, these books don't have any words in 'em! They just have scribbles."

Let him make his own books, then, Barney thought.

Someone was shaking him.

"Quit!" Barney muttered, and rolled away from the hands on his arms and legs.

"Wake up."

He flailed out, kicking and hitting. His brother's voice, right in his ear, said, "If you don't wake up, I'm going to punch your lights out."

Barney squinted up at Jamie. "I'm sleepy."

"We figured how to get out of here," Carol said.

Barney sighed and sat up.

"You really made the bathroom, didn't you?" Jamie asked.

"Yes."

Murp yawned.

Barney followed suit.

"Then make us a door that goes out of here."

Barney looked from his brother to his sister. They were buttheads, he thought—but they were really smart buttheads. "Yes," he whispered. "I can do that." He walked to the nearest wall, and thought a door into it.

A very nice wood door just like the first one he'd made appeared in the stone.

Behind him, he heard Jamie and Carol gasp.

"I'll go first," Jamie said. He opened the door. He didn't say anything for an instant. Then he said, "There's a hall out here."

Murp brushed past Jamie's legs and ran out of the room. Jamie shrugged and followed him. Carol went next, and Barney brought up the rear. He was still terribly sleepy. He wanted somebody to carry him—or better yet, he wanted to go back to the rag pile and let his brother and sister come back and get him later. He only walked behind them because he was afraid they wouldn't.

Murp walked slowly—looking back at Jamie and yowling all the time.

"I'm coming," Jamie said. "We're all following you, Murp."

Murp kept up his chatter.

A cold wind whistled down the long stone hallway and blew past Barney. He shivered and woke up. "Oh, no!" he whispered. He yelled, "Run! Run!"

The children took off—but in front of their eyes, the walls grew together. A stream of gray smoke curled out of the floor and grew into a towering wraith in front of them.

"Going somewhere?" the thing asked in its horrible, whispery voice."

"Go away, Unweebil," Barney yelled. "We're going home."

"Yes. And I must say, I find it very impressive you got this far. I suppose I shall have to make a stronger cage for you."

He raised his smoky arms upward, and Carol shouted, "You're evil."

The creature lowered its arms and chuckled. "No. Not at all. Being evil is much too much work—especially when all of existence will wind down on its own. It's quite enough that I'm *not* good."

Then smoke billowed around the children, and Barney coughed, and choked, and his eyes watered. When it cleared, Carol, Jamie, and Barney were trapped on the inside of a giant, murky green ball. Murp was gone.

"He's *evil*," Carol repeated. "I hope he doesn't hurt Murp."

"Murp will be all right," Jamie said. "Us, too. We'll get out of here and go home. Barney can do some magic—"

Barney settled onto the rounded floor of the ball. It was soft and yielding. He lay back and closed his eyes. He would rescue all of them—he had no doubt about it. But he would do it *later*.

CHAPTER 7

"Talleos, I need a break." Minerva couldn't sit and listen to the cheymat drone on anymore. She stood and stretched, trying to get the kinks out. Sitting on the hardwood floor was killing her back—and her rear end, she suspected, would never be the same.

Talleos looked scandalized. "But you haven't started into the background for the subclasses of classes of spells based on the first and simplest name of God yet—you should at *least* get that far on your first day."

"My eyes are glazing over." She spread her feet apart and reached down to touch her toes, then pressed the palms of her hands flat against the floor. Minerva heard her vertebrae pop as she did. When she bobbed up, she told the cheymat, "Look, there has to be some other way to learn this stuff. I don't do well listening to lectures—never have—and having somebody read to me puts me to sleep. I'm a hands-on person."

"Hands on." The cheymat stared up and to his right, and his face became thoughtful. "Hands . . . on." He looked back at her and propped his elbows on his book and his chin in his cupped hands. "Yes. That we can do. Sex magic is relatively simple to learn and doesn't require the complex ingredients you appear to find so distasteful. And you don't have to memorize complicated spells or rules. Besides—it happens to be my specialty."

"I'm not surprised."

Talleos flashed a smug little grin. "Well, if it's going to be sex magic, I need to bring in the quilts."

"Don't bother. It isn't."

Minerva wondered if she could kill him and still save her children. Probably not. She paced over to one of the display cases, pretending the cheymat had ceased to exist. She'd spotted some creamy sheets of vellum on one of the shelves. She picked them up, then located a small case filled with charcoal sticks, some chalky crayons, and a few sharpened pencils lacking erasers. She took the case, too.

"Minerva, you're going to have to be flexible about things if you want your kids back," Talleos said, then noticed what she had in her hands. "What are you going to do with those?" His voice sounded suddenly nervous.

"I'm going to go sit outside in the fresh air and take some notes. I assume all the books are written in some script I can't read?"

"Absolutely. So there's no way you can take notes without my help."

Minerva took a deep breath, then let it out slowly. "There certainly is. I can write down what I remember, and then I can *think* about all this a bit."

The cheymat cast a covert glance up at a crystal sphere perched atop one of the bookcases. The sphere glowed with a soft, pale pink-white light. Minerva was surprised she hadn't noticed it before. She was pretty sure the entire room had been dark the first time she'd walked in—she should have seen something that glowed. Then Talleos frowned, and quickly turned back to her. "Why don't you just stay in here and I'll go over the material again with you—and you can take all the notes you like."

"I *need* to get out of this *house* for a while," Minerva snarled at him.

He assumed an air of indifference. "Fine. Ignore my help. Go take notes outside with the tourists if you want. It's your children that are missing, and I'm the only one who can help you get them back." He crossed his arms over his chest and glared at her. "Don't let the tourists take your holo, though, or—mind what I say—your presence here will get back to the Weirds. And if they find out you're here, you're doomed." He smiled again, then, tightlipped—as if that idea appealed to him. "Just a thought."

She clenched her teeth. "I'll keep it in mind."

Minerva stomped through the house and out the front door, walking as fast as she could without actually breaking into a run. She wanted to get as far away from the cheymat as she could, before she did or said something stupid, and he refused to help her. Still—*Sex magic, my ass*, she thought, furious. *He's just trying to take advantage of me because I'm desperate to get my kids back. And he's making up all the rest of this because I won't bump and grind with him.*

At least, she hoped that was the case.

The cheymat's house was surrounded by old-growth forest. Even in daylight, it was an eerie place. Huge, gnarled trees brooded beside the rustic log cabin, making way in spots for a narrow beam of sunlight to break through. One of the forest giants had fallen nearby. There, late afternoon sunlight streamed to the ground and illuminated the understory plants. Small conifers and frail-looking deciduous trees took advantage of the rare opportunity and grew with urgent profusion. The ground bloomed with a carpet of autumn flowers. Vines clambered up the trunks of the trees nearby, racing for the sun. Minerva knew the plants that reached the upper story first would crowd out the rest and kill them. Hard to think of such a pretty place being the site of life-and-death struggle.

She walked over to the fallen tree, picked up a stick, and smacked it on the trunk a few times. The she ran the stick under the trunk along the part of the tree where she intended to sit. She flushed out a little shiny blue birdlike creature, but no snakes. For Minerva, the snakes were the big thing. She knew intellectually that they weren't slimy— but they *looked* slimy—and they made her skin crawl. She didn't know if this world *had* snakes, but she didn't want to discover it did by sitting on one.

She perched on the rough trunk and looked around her. No tourists anywhere that she could see. Fine. So most likely Talleos was exaggerating the problem. She couldn't imagine tourists coming to such an out-of-the-way place, anyhow. She spread out a piece of the vellum, and one of the pencils, and started to take notes.

It seemed a shame to waste the smooth, creamy vellum on anything as dreary as notes. The material cried out for calligraphy, or an egg tempera illumination, or even a sketch of the woods. Not scrawled notes on the position in which one had to hold one's hands when invoking the first name of God.

Could all of that complicated rigmarole be necessary? And if it was, how could anyone have expected her to come across it herself? It wasn't the sort of thing that just sprang to mind fully formed, like Athena from the head of Zeus.

She wrote, *Magic Using The First Name Of God.*

She stared at the white sheet for a moment, then underlined her header.

Number 1—The first name of God is . . .

What *was* the first name of God? She couldn't remember. Something long and complicated—

She doodled along the edge of the paper, trying to think of it. Oh, well—on to the next point.

Ritual for invoking the name of God.

She could remember a bit more of that one. Something about *Face in the first direction, which is east, and cleanse the first direction—*

And then, she recalled, there had been some phrase in a foreign language, that had to be said exactly right—she couldn't remember it at all.

And after that, hadn't Talleos said something about doing a separate ritual for each of the four directions?

She doodled some more. She sketched one of the little flowers in front of her, filling in the delicate curves of the five petals with light strokes from a chalky, rust-colored crayon. She did an overlay of pink, then smudged the petals with her finger to try to match the texture. The vellum made a perfect surface; and under her steady hand, the flower seemed to burst into life on the page. Delighted, she laid down the background lines of the rest of the plant with nearly invisible pencil strokes, and sketched in some of the fallen leaves that formed its foreground. She didn't have any green with her—just the pink and the rust and a few other shades of browns and black. She chose a limited-palette approach. She'd always liked the feel of the world seen through a filtered lens—and to her, the limited palette created that effect.

The sunshine beat down on her shoulders, a delicious hot contrast to the cool breeze. The air smelled rich and pungent, redolent of rotting wood and leaves and fertile, dark, damp earth. She breathed deeply, and let the wind rustling through the forest canopy and the distant sounds of running water soothe her.

As the sketch progressed, she felt herself recapturing some of her self-confidence. Drawing had always done that for her. *Her* area of expertise, she thought, and grinned. The cheymat and his attempts to lure her into sex magic seemed less threatening at that moment. He was alone—the last of his kind, unless he should somehow find another cheymat. She tried to imagine being the last human—and decided if she found herself in such an awful predicament, she might be just as pushy and obnoxious and desperate as he was.

Not that she had any intention of doing what he hoped she would. She was willing to be understanding. And she would go a long way out of pity—but not that far.

Minerva kept drawing; and while she sketched, she considered what she knew of the nature of magic. Magic wasn't impossible. That she was in this bizarre situation was proof of that. Since it *was* possible, she would learn to use it. She would find a way to understand the forces she needed to control—if moving galaxies was what she had to do to save her children and get back home, then she would learn how to move galaxies. With a grin, Minerva reflected that she'd always believed she could do anything she put her mind to—the time had come to put her faith to the test. But no more letting Talleos upset her—no letting him get her goat, she thought, and giggled. She decided she'd use the "get her goat" line on him. That ought to annoy him.

The drawing seemed to take on form and design without

conscious effort on her part. For her, artwork had always been like that—a sort of communion between her and her materials; a joint effort to bring forth out of wood pulp and ground pigments and wax a new entity; an object able to convey an emotion, or a concept—or a sense of passion.

Minerva noted a space in the background of her picture that seemed to cry out for more detail. She studied the shadows and shapes already there, then sketched in a cat peering from beneath the vines—and wistfully, she made the cat into Murp. Broad-faced, round-eyed, and orange tabby-striped, with a white blaze down his nose, white bib and white feet, Barney's cat grew out of her memory until he stared back at her from the page.

She got a lump in her throat, and closed her eyes, and gripped the crayon so hard it snapped in her hand. She could see that horrible blue light again, and Barney with Murp tucked under his arm, running toward her—toward what he thought was safety. *I should have been able to save him,* she thought. Hot tears rolled down her cheeks. *A mom should be able to save her children, dammit. The universe shouldn't give you kids and then take them away.* She dropped the crayon fragments and her drawing and sobbed, burying her face in her hands.

"Mrrrrrrrp?"

A furry head shoved against the back of her arm and rubbed along her back. Her eyes flew open. *A cat,* she thought, while her heart raced. *Jesus Christ, what a weird coincidence.*

"Mrrrrrrrp?"

She turned around, and when she saw the cat on the log, began to shiver. Bizarre coincidence. It was a big orange beast with white markings—and bright yellow eyes . . .

. . . just like Murp.

Can't be. Murp vanished with Barney.

She reached out a trembling hand and scratched the cat under the chin. He butted his head against her hand and closed his eyes and purred like a chainsaw.

"Murp?" she whispered. The cat chirruped.

Cautiously, because Murp loved to be picked up and

cradled—but plenty of cats took offense at that sort of han-
dling—she picked the cat up. He flung his head back into
the crook of her arm and sprawled, all four legs sticking up
in the air, and the volume of his purring doubled.

Jesus Christ. She was shaking so badly she was afraid she
might drop him. She rolled him against her chest so she
could get a good look at his left hind leg. It couldn't be
Murp. But Minerva would be able to tell easily enough.
Murp had a white stripe that ran completely across his left
flank high up—sort of a racing stripe.

So did this cat.

"Murp!"

"Row-w-w-wr." Murp always spoke when spoken to.

She sat on the log, scratching the cat's belly, snuggling
him as close as she could. The questions raced through her
mind. Where had he come from? How? *How?*

She looked at the drawing, lying on the ground at her
feet—the drawing of Murp. Perhaps it was not a coincidence, after all. Still holding Murp close to her chest, she
walked to the bit of underbrush where she had drawn the
cat. Perhaps she could see pawprints—if Murp had walked
through that precise spot, she would write off chance occurrence completely.

But there were only more leaves under the vines. Not
pawprints—no conclusive proof.

And then she thought—*If I drew the kids, would they
come here?*

She ran back to the fallen tree, the cat still cradled in her
arms, and put him down to pick up the art supplies. "Oh,
Murp," she whispered, "could it be this simple?"

She sketched—closing her eyes from time to time to
bring each little face before her. It was so hard, so very, very
difficult, to get the features fixed in her mind—for she never
saw her children as faces with fixed features, as having noses
of a particular length, or eyes with the eyelid creased at a
specific angle, with the shadows falling just so over soft,
smooth, freckled skin. She thought of them as movement, as
voices, as personalities; fragile as sunbeams, transient as
hope, always changing. How could she draw that?

But she drove herself to remember the exact line of each jaw, the precise curve of each mouth—and she could hear their voices in her memory as she worked, and remember their hands in hers, slight and fragile.

"Mommy? . . ." a voice whispered into the gentle breeze, so faint Minerva first believed she'd imagined it.

"Barney?" she answered. Her voice caught in the lump in her throat. "Barney, where are you?" She looked around her wildly.

"The bad man has us," Carol said. "He won't let us go, Mommy." Her words were no louder than the rustling of leaves.

Then Minerva made out three faint shapes—ghosts standing in front of her in the clearing—and she fought to hold in a scream. Barney and Carol and Jamie stood only inches away, insubstantial as shadows. She reached out a hand to touch them, willing them to her with all her heart.

"Come get us, Mommy," Barney whispered.

"Please, Mom. Please don't let this guy have us," Jamie pleaded.

"I'll be there as fast as I can," Minerva said, and then the children were gone as if they'd been erased, and something dark and towering replaced them.

"So you *are* here," the huge shadow said. Its voice encompassed the horrors of her nightmares and made them all real. "How convenient."

Then it, too, vanished. Minerva became aware that beside her, Murp hissed, the fur on his back and tail standing straight out, his ears pressed flat against his skull.

The Unweaver.

She reached out and stroked the cat. "We're going to get them back, Murp," she said. Her voice trembled. "We're going to stop him, too. I'll figure out how this all works."

Darryl finished replacing the window in the boys' room and looked out across his backyard at the last scattered colors of sunset. Birkwelch sat on Jamie's bed, picking up and putting down toys. He was uncharacteristically quiet.

"I'm tired. I'll paint it later," Darryl said, and leaned

against the wall. "After I get Minerva and the kids back. I just wanted to get the hole fixed so the room would be ready for them."

The dragon stretched out on the bed and started running a toy truck up and down his scaled belly. "Things might not work out that way, Darryl, old pal."

"I'll get her back." Darryl tightened his grip on the putty knife. "She'll learn whatever she needs to know. You'd be surprised at how talented she is. She's a wonderful artist, and she's smart—"

The dragon put down the truck and picked up a G.I. Joe. "She's going up against the Unweaver. And you aren't doing anything to help her. She may not survive—and if she doesn't, you won't and your kids won't."

Darryl said, "What am I supposed to be doing to help her? What can I do from here?"

The dragon sat up again. "Where you are doesn't matter. The two of you are linked by the rings. You want to know what you can do? I'll tell you. You can believe in Minerva— and just as important, you can believe in yourself. What matters in this fight is your faith in the value of life, your conviction, your ability to carry on. You are fighting the master of chaos and discord and despair. You fight him with courage and determination, and by setting goals and winning through to them, no matter what the cost."

Be a Boy Scout, save all of space and time, Darryl thought. "That sounds very nonspecific. Can't I do magic, too?"

The dragon didn't meet his eyes. "There are complications. In life, you get to set your own goals. Your problem is you gave up on them when things got too hard." The dragon licked at his teeth with his forked tongue and blew a gentle puff of smoke into the cold room. "You didn't want them enough. You didn't care enough. And even that wouldn't have mattered—most people flush their dreams down the toilet when reality sets in. Except you and Minerva had the rings. When the two of you got disillusioned and gave up hope, bits and pieces of the Universes gave up with you— and the Unweaver got his edge. You sold your dreams for easy jobs you didn't care about. For a bigger house sooner. For safety. You sold your dreams far too cheaply."

"You're telling me time and space depended on whether I became a successful playwright? On whether Minerva sold her paintings? The survival of the Universes depended on two kids' ability to make their pie-in-the-sky daydreams come true?"

Birkwelch stared at him and said nothing.

"That's a stupid way to run things."

"Not when it works." Birkwelch put down the toy soldier and picked up a stuffed rabbit. He looked at Darryl and said softly, "If you *want* something—and *believe* in what you want—you can overcome every obstacle. You can do anything."

Darryl was surprised. Birkwelch, at that moment, was not his usual loutish self. He seemed to really believe in what he was saying. "Like getting my wife and kids back?" Darryl asked.

"That is what you now desire most of all? Your dreams have changed," the dragon murmured, almost to himself. "Ah, well."

Downstairs, someone knocked—a firm, authoritative knock. Darryl headed for the stairs.

"You don't want to get that," Birkwelch said.

"It can't be Cindy again."

"The Weird? No. Not so soon." The dragon watched him, eyes narrowed. "Worse than her, I'd guess."

Worse than Cindy, the cheap thrill from hell? He peeked out the window at the top of the stairs. He could see the landing below, stained yellow by the porch lamp. Two police officers stood in the puddle of light, one of them studying the line of footprints Birkwelch had left in the snow.

Darryl glared at the dragon. "So much for portents and mysteries," he snapped. He shouted, "Be right there," and ran down the stairs two at a time.

Believe and want, and the Weavers' rings will make it real, he thought. *Fine. I believe the police found the kids, and all three of them are all right, and will be home soon. I believe this whole disaster with Minerva was a mistake, and something will work out, and there won't be any funeral tomorrow.*

He threw the door open and stood panting. "Have you found them? Won't you come in?"

The police officers came in. Their faces were solemn.

The older officer said, "I'm Lieutenant Sandow. This is Sergeant Tomay. He asked to come along."

It's going to be okay, Darryl thought. *I believe. I believe. I can make it okay if I only believe.*

"Please have a seat, Mr. Kiakra," Lt. P. Sandow said.

The other man nodded. They waited until Darryl walked into the living room and sat in the big wing-backed chair.

"The news is bad. A couple on the other side of town found your children," Sandow rubbed the thumb of one hand against the index finger of the other. He looked miserable, Darryl thought. "When they arrived home from their vacation in Florida, they discovered a window in the top floor of their house had been blown in, but in exactly the same manner as yours was blown out."

Sandow stared off into the distance. Tomay studied his shoes.

Darryl gripped the arms of the chair. His heart thudded. *I believe they're safe. I believe they're alive. They're going to be coming home any time now.* "Where are my kids?" he asked.

"We found all three of them with a cat in the upstairs room." Sandow took a deep breath. Darryl could see the man swallow hard, could see the brightness of welling tears in his eyes. "None of them survived, sir," the officer said softly.

Darryl froze in the chair. *No,* he thought. *No. If I believe hard enough, they'll be fine.*

"That can't be," he said. "They have to be alive."

Tomay, who hadn't said anything until then, spoke. "I understand what you're feeling. I lost my little girl last year to cancer. When the doctor told me she was gone, I knew he had to be wrong. She was so young, and so brave—and I knew that she was going to get better. But she didn't. That's why I asked to come along to get you. I thought maybe it would help if you had someone with you who knew what it was like to lose a child."

Darryl's throat ached, and his eyes and nose burned. He couldn't breathe. "How can they all be gone? My wife, my kids—they're all I have. They can't be dead. I have to have something left. I have to." He gripped the arms of the chair so hard his fingers went numb. "This is a dream."

"I wish it were," Tomay said.

Sandow said, "We do need you to come to the hospital and identify them. I'm terribly sorry. I wish there were some other way—"

"I *want* to see them," Darryl said. "They're my children. Goddammit, I want to see them. I want to say goodbye." Tears ran down his cheeks. "Let me get my coat." He stopped in front of the coat closet. "I don't know that I can drive myself," he said.

"No, sir." Tomay went to the front door. "We wouldn't ask you to. We'll drive you there, and bring you back. Would you like to call your family before we leave?"

The family. Her parents. My parents. Oh, God, what am I going to tell them?

"No. I can't talk to them yet. Let's just go."

No one talked on the ride to the hospital. The officers didn't take him to the emergency room. This time the nursing supervisor met them at the back door of the hospital and led them all to the morgue.

Darryl dragged through the horror that followed as if someone else had control of his body. The calm other person answered questions and gave information, and all the while, the real Darryl inside wept and screamed and raged, and his heart shredded into ribbons. He could comprehend only pieces of the whole picture—the rows of aluminium refrigerators, the coldness of the room, and his children, slid out on flat aluminium trays and shown to him one by one. He felt himself fading inside, felt a part of himself dying—and when the three men walked away from the hospital to get into the police car, Darryl knew he'd left every bit of himself that mattered behind. The shreds of him that remained had no value, to himself or anyone else.

"You need to call your parents," Tomay said. "Have them stay with you tonight. I remember those first few days. You shouldn't be alone."

They went into the house with him. Darryl wanted them to leave. He had no intention of calling his parents. They would only try to stop him. He had decided on the way home that he knew what he had to do. It was the only solution, really.

But the officers weren't taking any chances. Sandow fixed him a cup of coffee. Tomay called his parents' house when he refused to do it and asked them to come over. Both waited until the older Kiakras arrived, gave them the news, and directed them to Darryl, who sat unmoving in his wingback chair.

Just like busybody small-town cops, he thought, *to keep a man from killing himself.* But his parents wouldn't be babysitting him forever.

He went into the bathroom. His father followed him to the door. "I'm going to take a leak," he told his dad, and his dad just nodded.

"That policeman told me what he went through. So I'm going to wait right here and break the door down if you aren't out of there in three minutes."

Darryl looked at his father's ashen, tearstained face. "Fine, Dad. I'll be out in three minutes."

He looked into the medicine cabinet when he was done—just a quick survey. But it was empty. No good.

Minerva was in the mirror. *You're dead,* he told her silently. *You are dead. Gone. They're going to bury you tomorrow, and the kids in a couple of days. And I'm coming with you. I'm not staying here by myself. I tried hope and faith and will, and they were all so much bullshit. So that's it. I quit.*

She couldn't hear him, even if he talked to her out loud. He couldn't touch her. She wasn't real. She was just a picture. He'd lost the real Minerva, and his kids, and his life, the moment he decided to walk away from what he knew was right. And not all the hope and faith and will and dreams in the world could make that kind of wrong right.

He came out of the bathroom and found his dad getting ready to kick the door down. "I forgot to synchronize my watch, Dad," Darryl snapped. He walked past his father, into the living room. His mother sat there, crying and carrying on. Darryl couldn't speak to her. He couldn't look at her, or at his father. He walked past them into the kitchen to get himself a beer, then stomped up the stairs, past the kids' rooms and into his own. He lay down on his bed, sipped his beer, and stared at the ceiling.

His father followed him into the room.

"I'm going to sleep, Dad."

His father nodded. "That isn't a bad idea. I'm going to sit here and keep you company."

"No!" Darryl clenched his fists. He wanted to scream. "I want to be alone."

His father sat in the chair next to the nightstand. "And I don't want to lose my son."

"Dad—" Darryl felt himself losing control. "I can't sleep with you staring at me. And I *have* to get some sleep."

Something of his desperation got through to his father. The older Kiakra stood, and took a pillow from Darryl's bed, and walked to the doorway. "Leave it open. I intend to sleep in the hall."

"Great," Darryl muttered. But that was better than having his father standing watch over him.

No sooner had his father moved out of sight than Birkwelch materialized. "It isn't over, Darryl," he said. "You haven't lost yet."

Darryl raised his head off the pillow and looked at the dragon in disbelief. He kept his voice low. "It's over, Mary Poppins. I'm just waiting for my parents to get out of my house so I can get the rope and hang myself from the balcony without interruption."

"You can't kill yourself," the dragon said.

"Why? Because the universe is counting on me?"

"Yes."

"Well, screw the universe." Darryl put his beer on the nightstand and turned his back to the dragon. "If the universe wanted my help, it shouldn't have killed my wife and kids."

"You can still get them back." The dragon moved around the bed to stand in front of Darryl again.

"Go screw yourself, dragon. I've listened to your stories long enough. I'm not listening anymore. This is the end. Game over. Find somebody else—or better yet, just let the whole universe go up in a puff of smoke."

"Let everybody cease to exist—husbands and wives and children, grandparents, newborn babies? All of them, Darryl? When you could save them all, and your own family, too?"

Darryl turned and glared at Birkwelch, then chugged the rest of his beer. Silently he lay back and closed his eyes and crossed his arms over his chest.

He wouldn't dignify the dragon's wheedling with an answer.

Barney glowered at his brother. "I don't *want* lasagna. I *want* a peanut butter and jelly sandwich. And I will *make* a peanut butter and jelly sandwich."

"That's stupid. You can have anything you want. *Anything.*"

"Yes. And I want a peanut butter and jelly sandwich."

"I want pizza," Carol said. "With pepperoni and black olives."

"Okay," Barney said. "How many slices?"

"Two. No—three. And Cheerwine."

Barney made them for her. He didn't get tired making food. Food was just little stuff, he thought. Bathrooms were much bigger. He was going to have to see about one of those pretty soon, too. But first, dinner.

For himself, he created a tall glass of very chocolatey chocolate milk, the way his mother would not let him have it—so much chocolate there was still a layer of syrup down at the bottom when he was done. Then a peanut butter and jelly sandwich—*smooth* peanut butter, so much grape jelly it squished out the sides when he picked it up, and *white* bread. The right way to make one, he thought.

He took a bite of it and closed his eyes. It was perfect.

"What about me?" Jamie said.

"You are mean and bossy," Barney answered.

"What are you going to make for me? I'm hungry, too."

Jamie might have been hungry, but he'd also yelled at Barney for creating the door so it opened where the Unweaver could get them. And Jamie had called him "stupid."

Jamie stunk like a skunk.

"I want lasagna," Jamie said. "And a banana split with three kinds of ice cream and hot fudge sauce and whipped cream. And nuts."

Barney nibbled his perfect sandwich, and sipped his perfect chocolate milk, and thought of appropriate foods for a stinky person. He considered that boiled cabbage stuff his mom made. It was pretty disgusting—kind of gray and slimy. It looked like the sort of thing that would glop out of the bowl when you weren't looking and come after you.

Or maybe liver. Liver would be good for a fink—it was fink food.

Then he thought of the perfect food. He'd never actually tasted them, but he'd seen them on a pizza his dad had eaten. They smelled *terrible* and they were gray and slimy like boiled cabbage, but they still had heads. Stinky fish. Yes. A big plateful of little stinky fish would be perfect.

He materialized them on the squishy floor of their cage, right in front of Jamie, then took another bite of his sandwich, and washed it down with his lovely milk.

"Hey!" Jamie yelled. "This isn't lasagna. This is— eeuwww! This is anchovies."

"Yes. Stinky fish."

"I don't want anchovies—"

"You have been mean to me. Mean and rotten and stinky—so that's what you get." He took the next to last bite of the perfect peanut butter and jelly sandwich, and considered what would make a lovely desert. Vanilla ice cream, he thought. Yes. That would be lovely. Perhaps with potato chips on top.

Jamie's face got red, and he started to yell. Then he stopped. He looked at Barney with a serious expression. He

studied the pile of dead fish in front of him, and watched
Barney eat his last bite of sandwich.

Barney smiled with his mouth open, displaying chewed
food.

"Oh, gross," Carol said, and turned away.

Jamie didn't say anything. He just sat there, looking from
Barney to the anchovies.

He took a deep breath. He let it out.

Barney waited.

Jamie squinched up his eyes like his stomach hurt. "I'm
sorry I was mean to you, and I'm sorry I yelled at you."

Barney kept waiting. He'd learned from his big brother
never to accept the first apology, or the first "uncle."

Jamie sat there for a long moment, eyeing the anchovies.
He sighed again. "And I won't yell at you anymore."

Barney nodded and crossed his arms over his chest.

Jamie's mouth opened to protest. He closed it again and
looked at the anchovies. "Okay. What else?"

"You won't call me names—"

"I won't call you names—"

"And you'll make my bed—"

"Make your bed!" He rolled his eyes. "Fine. I'll make
your bed."

Barney smiled, serene and content. "And you'll let me
play with your soldiers."

"No!" Jamie yelled. "No! I won't."

"Stinky fish," Barney said. He saw Jamie swallow. His big
brother closed his eyes and chewed his lower lip.

"Okay. You can play with my soldiers. As long as you don't
break 'em."

Barney made the anchovies go away. "What do you
want?"

"Lasagna."

He made the lasagna, and his own ice cream treat, and
leaned against the upcurving cage wall to eat it. He felt
deeply and wonderfully happy.

"We need to get out of here," Carol said.

Jamie wasn't talking. He ate his food in gloomy silence.
Served him right, Barney thought.

"The Unweebil's monsters are right outside of here," Barney said. "If I make a door, they'll come in and eat us."

"You're sure they're out there?" Carol asked.

"Yes." He nibbled on the ice cream. The potato chips were very nice, too—and his mother couldn't yell at him for putting them on top. "I can, um, hear them. They're hungry."

"Bet you could give *them* the anchovies," Jamie muttered.

Barney considered that. Anchovies were probably the sort of thing monsters liked. Well, monsters and fathers. He concentrated, and made a big pile of them where he sensed the monsters waiting. He made the dead fish as smelly and slimy as he could. Then he closed his eyes and listened.

He sensed the monsters' tremendous delight. Yep. It figured. "They do like stinky fish," he said.

"Then you can make them so much anchovies, they won't eat us when we go out," Carol said.

Barney thought that idea was unsound. He figured monsters would rather eat nice juicy little kids than stinky fish any day.

"Mommy and Murp are coming to get us," Barney said. "She told us she would."

"What if the Unweaver eats us first? Or kills us, and cuts our heads off and chops us into little tiny pieces?" Carol asked.

"Boy, you're cheerful," Jamie said. "But you're right. We should get out of here. You know what would be cool?" he continued. "I read this story where there was a house with doors that opened to all these different places. Like, one door opened in the mountains, and one opened at the beach, and one opened on a whole 'nother planet. It would be cool if you could make a door that took us home."

Barney thought about that, and concentrated on it. No matter how hard he squeezed his eyes closed, and how hard he thought about home, he could not make the magic in his head reach out to touch home. He tried nearer—tried to reach his mother. She was too far, too, though he could feel her coming. "No," he said at last. "I can't take us home. It's too far."

Jamie looked disappointed. "Too bad. I want to go home."

Carol nodded. "Me, too. But I want out of here, too. I'm afraid of the Unweaver."

"I can vision the door, though. I can take us toward Mommy."

"How far?"

"Pretty far."

"What about the Unweaver?" Jamie asked. "What's he doing?"

Barney reached out with his thoughts and felt around for the Unweebil's nasty, icky mind. He found it, and cautiously touched it.

The Unweebil's mind was lonely, and full of ugliness and hate. It was also concentrating on something besides children—something far away.

Barney pulled back. "He's busy right now. He's paying tension to something else."

"*Attention*," Carol corrected.

"That's what I said."

Jamie frowned at Carol. "If he's not watching us, we should go now."

"Okay." Barney thought for a moment. "I will vision a door, and the other side of the door will be far away."

"How far?" Jamie wanted to know.

"I don't know." Barney shrugged. "Far. Then I will vision locking all the doors here, so the Unweebil can't get out. And *then* I will vision a monster to eat the Unweebil."

Jamie said, "That's pretty good. But I think you should make armies to flank the Unweaver on both sides, and cut off his supply lines, and have a siege."

Barney glared at his brother. Easy for *him* to say—Jamie couldn't do any magic. "*You* can vision that. *I'll* vision the monster."

Jamie shut up.

Barney thought of one other thing he needed. He closed his eyes and saw a bright red, shiny wagon—a special wagon. It had a blanket and a fluffy pillow inside, and guns that stuck out from the side like the guns on his Turtle car. These guns, though, shot sleep darts. *So if I shoot them, the bad guys will sleep for twelve or four hours or years.*

The wagon appeared in front of him, built out of nothing by the tiny firefly lights.

"What's that for?" Carol asked.

"Because magic makes me sleepy. After I make the door, you guys can pull me."

Barney closed his eyes again for just an instant, to fix the special door in his mind. Then he looked at the squishy, curved wall of his cage and started the little magic fireflies to work on the door to someplace else.

CHAPTER 8

Murp was perfectly willing to be smuggled into Minerva's room inside her baggy peasant blouse—but then, Murp had always been amenable to weird and un-catlike games. *Thank God*, she thought. If the cat were any less mellow, the task would have been impossible.

Minerva didn't know why she felt it so important to sneak the animal past the cheymat. Probably paranoia, she thought. No doubt he would be delighted to discover she'd learned to use her magic.

Nevertheless, she didn't want to deal with his reactions at the moment, positive or otherwise.

She heard the cheymat banging around in the kitchen as soon as she entered the house. The smell of something wonderful filled the air. She trotted straight to her room, dumped Murp and the art supplies, and went out, carefully closing the door behind her. Then she went looking for her host.

Talleos' face, when he turned from the stove to greet her, displayed wariness for the briefest of instants—wariness covered over almost immediately by charm and a sort of amused superiority.

"You took your sweet time getting back. Those woods aren't safe at night, you know." He arched an eyebrow. "Wouldn't want anything happening to my prize pupil. So—how did the note-taking go?" he asked.

"Awful," she said with blunt honesty. "I couldn't remember a thing you said." She smiled at him. "I'm sorry I lost my temper with you. I did feel better, though, once I got out of the house for a while." *There. Not a single lie in the whole spiel.*

She caught just a glimpse of smugness in his smile before he turned away. "Magic can be a frustrating study—so complicated and full of rules and formulas." He speared the meat on the grill and flipped it deftly, then sprinkled bright red powder over it. "Anything interesting happen while you were out there?"

He asked offhandedly—but Minerva's nerves jangled.

"No," she lied, and smiled with the same easy cheerfulness Talleos displayed. "I didn't even see any tourists." She didn't understand why she was lying. If she told him she'd found her magic, maybe he could help her understand its use, or direct her in plotting against the Unweaver—after her dream, she felt sure it was the Unweaver who had her kids.

But something would not let her say.

"It isn't the tourists you see that you usually have to worry about. Oh, well." He shrugged, and smiled over his shoulder at her. "No matter. I didn't think the note-taking idea was very good anyway. You're just going to have to work with me, the way you did today. The master/apprentice relationship is the only one that really works with magic."

Minerva nodded, and kept her big news to herself. "How long do you think it will take before I'll be able to rescue my kids?"

The cheymat sighed, and tossed a few vegetable slices onto the grill, where they sizzled noisily. "Minerva, I understand your worry for your children—but in order to help them, you are going to have to focus on something else. If you're constantly worrying about them, how will you be able to achieve the level of concentration magic requires?"

Minerva shook her head slowly and let herself look distressed. *Play along with him. Find out what his goals are,* she told herself. "I don't know." She held out her hands, palms up. "I suppose you're right—so what do you suggest?"

He didn't answer immediately. Instead, he filled a plate and handed it to her. "We can talk better sitting down," he suggested. But once they were seated, he seemed more interested in eating than in talking.

Minerva let the subject drop until they'd both finished, then brought it up again.

"I hate to distress you, Minerva," the cheymat said. His expression became grave. "But from what I saw today, you have very little potential for magic at all. The Weirds might have been right in wanting to replace you with someone more talented. I won't let them now—I'm committed to helping you—besides, I *like* you. But I'm afraid this whole business is going to take a long time. It could be months— perhaps even years—before you're at a point where you will be able to take on the Unweaver."

Minerva made what she hoped was a chastened face, while inside she boiled. She hid her anger, and asked, "How can you tell? What do you look for?"

Talleos leaned back on his chair and laced his fingers behind his head. "Magic is an art," he said. "The ability to remember long, complex formulas and the sequence of body movements that go with them generally indicate one's predisposition to the craft. You couldn't even remember the first name of God—and that's the shortest and simplest of them."

"But you said none of that was necessary for sex magic. So why is it necessary at all? If magic is an art, why can't it *be* art? I'm an artist."

He frowned—then his face brightened again. "Ah. I see. I was unintentionally misleading. The only reason you wouldn't need to memorize the formulas and other details necessary would be because your partner, in this case *me*, would already know them." His smile became condescending. "And as for magic being art—how silly. That's just like saying music could be science, or mathematics could be botany."

"Of course," she said. "That makes sense."

He smiled. "That's just the way these things work." He shrugged gracefully. "We can really make some progress if you want to take that route. Of course," he arched an eyebrow, "I can understand your reasons for choosing not to."

Minerva pressed her hands in her lap and tried to look humble and penitent. "Let me think about all of this," she said. "I can't wait months or years to see my kids again." She closed her eyes and took a deep breath. "I'm going to go rest in my room. I'll see you tomorrow morning, okay?"

He nodded. "I don't see any problem with that."

Minerva went over to the stove and scooped a second helping from the pan onto her plate. She filled her glass with tap water. "Good night, then."

He watched her, eyes narrowed. "If you're still hungry, you can stay out here and keep me company."

"I'd rather not," she answered. "At least not until I've had a chance to think about things. I'll just take this into my room and eat it there. And then I'm going to sleep. I'm exhausted. It's been a long, awful day—and it sounds like there are going to be a lot more long, awful days."

Talleos stood, and walked toward her. "What *is* the matter, Minerva?"

Her eyes went round and she stared at him, this time with genuine disbelief. "You've got to be kidding." When he had the temerity to look puzzled, she said, "You figure it out." Then she hurried away before he could think of a reason to stop her.

In her room, she fed Murp the leftovers, then opened her window and lifted the oilskin so that he could go out when he needed to. The window was big enough for her to get through if need be, she noticed. A bit high, but—

She watched Murp inhaling his food and wondered how long it had been since he'd last eaten. She wondered if her kids had been with him, and if they were also hungry and uncared-for.

And she wondered why Talleos had lied to her. How did it benefit him that she not learn magic? Why pretend that he wanted her to learn? Was he really working for the Unweaver? That seemed likely—in which case everything he'd told her had been a lie. Her children were alive, though. She believed that—she'd seen them. And she would figure out how to get to them.

She retrieved the vellum and drawing implements, and tried to decide what she needed and how to go about getting it. She still wasn't entirely sure how the magic worked—but drawing what she wanted seemed integral to the process. She couldn't just draw her children and get them back, though. The Unweaver had blocked that.

She wondered if she could draw Darryl from memory—then wondered if she wanted to. She missed him. She wished he had been with her when the nightmare started. But he hadn't been, and she wasn't sure she could forgive him for that.

Besides, the idea of making a mistake worried her. She sat in the chair by the fireplace, her feet propped up on the hearth, trying to think of something to draw.

The sound of a slamming door woke her, and she realized she was still sitting by the fireplace, and that the fire had almost gone out.

"Talleos," a voice rumbled. "We need to talk."

Minerva heard the clatter of hooves on the hardwood floor, moving at high speed. Then she heard the cheymat whisper, "What do you think you're doing here?"

"I've got a problem."

"We've all got problems, pal. But if you don't get out of here, you might wake her up, and she'd hear you. And right now, everything is going just right."

"The hell you say," the stranger's voice growled. "The police found the kids' bodies today, her funeral is tomorow—and he is about this far from offing himself. And wouldn't that be a hell of a mess?"

"Good gods, Birkwelch, how could you let things get so out of hand?" The cheymat's whisper sounded desperate. "Come on in here if you have to talk. And keep your voice down."

Minerva held her breath, listening for more—but the only sounds were the cheymat and—Birkwelch . . . the dragon?—walking through the house, and another door opening and shutting.

They went into the magic room, she thought. With the

doors between her and the two of them closed, she could hear nothing.

So Talleos was hiding something. And the dragon was in on it—and it sounded like things were not going too well for Darryl, either. But what funeral was the dragon talking about?

She crept out the door and down the hall, noiseless. Her heart raced and her palms grew damp, but her mouth was desert-dry. She peeked around the end of the hall into the living room. Everything was dark. She slipped through the room, hugging the walls and staying in the deep shadows, and then went on through the foyer and into the library. The library fireplace threw darting shadows onto the books and made the room look uncomfortably alive. They'd closed the magic room door. She got right up to it, terrified she might be found out, and pressed her ear against smooth, cool wood. Still she could hear only the deep rumbling notes of the dragon's voice and nothing at all of Talleos.

She laid a finger along the doorframe and rolled it forward a millimeter at a time, pressing, hoping against all hope the latch had not caught. But it had.

She could have screamed with exasperation. Instead, she thought, *How could magic help me?*

She hurried back to her room, much less careful than she had been on her way out, closed the door behind her, and wedged a chair under the knob. Then she got out her paper.

She thought fast. If she drew the cheymat, perhaps she would be able to hear what he was saying, or perhaps he would appear in her room. Then the game would be up. If she drew the dragon, the same things might happen. Of course, she could do all that and have nothing at all occur. She wished she had a better idea of what she was doing.

But all she really wanted was to hear what they said—preferably without getting caught listening. *I need a big ear,* she thought. It seemed a bit stupid, but she drew one, then sketched it behind the jar of dragon bits on the shelf in the magic room.

Sudden conversation surrounded her—she felt as if she were right in the middle of it.

"—but you could screw up the whole show, here, Birk-welch," Talleos was saying. "She's bought it all—dammit, I even have her about ready to believe that crap about sex magic. She'll do anything if she thinks it will help her rescue her kids."

You miserable shit, she thought. *I should have known.*

"So I don't suppose you've told her that old Darryl is going to be burying her body tomorrow, or the bodies of her kids in a couple of days?"

Burying my body—the kids' bodies? But I'm alive—and they . . . well, they have to be alive, too. I saw them—they have to be.

"Hell, no, I haven't told her. She doesn't know how it works, and I don't *want* her to know. They're a lot stronger than we thought they'd be, you know. Look at the charge she put on that crystal. I sat her in the decagram and kept her concentrating for only a couple of hours—if I can keep her sitting in the middle of the decagram for another month or two, I'll be able to drain enough magic off her to make myself a few female cheymats. Then I'll be able to breed. There will be cheymats again—"

"What about her mate, and her young? You have it easy here, Talleos. You don't have to watch her suffering, because she doesn't know what's happening. But her husband's been watching her in mirrors. He knows she's here, but he still believes she's dead. I think Darryl would have killed himself tonight, except that I slipped nagral in his drink—it's the only way I dared come here."

"He can see her in mirrors?" The cheymat sounded worried. Then he sighed. "Oh, well—as long as she doesn't find out. Just handle things. Once I've got my cheymats—and a couple of female dragons for you, too—we'll let them go. We'll tell them how the magic really works, and they can get their kids back and go do something else."

She could hear the dragon snort. "You think the Unweaver is going to sit and wait after you've drained her dry? He's afraid to touch her children now—but if you drain her power off, you don't think he'll destroy them?"

"Human's aren't extinct," the cheymat snapped. "We are.

You are. Magic almost is—and it's the fault of these two people you feel so benevolent towards. Why should I feel guilty for saving my own kind?"

"They're not bad people. I still think if we taught them what they needed to know, then asked them, they would help us."

The cheymat made a growling noise, low in his throat. "I'll help myself."

That works both ways, Minerva thought. She raced around the room, throwing clothes into the duffel bag and looking for things she might need. She put all the pencils into the bag, and the vellum. She only had four plain sheets. She wished she'd taken more out of the magic room when she'd had the chance. Too late—she'd just have to draw small.

She had no idea what to do to locate her children. But now at least she knew what *not* to do.

She turned out the light and climbed out the window.

It was only when she was on the other side that she remembered Murp. She hadn't seen him—and she didn't dare go back in.

A furry form brushed against her leg. "Mrrrrrrrrp?" it chirruped.

She reached down and scratched Murp's chin. "Hi, guy," she whispered. "Let's get out of here while we still can."

They set off through the woods. Above the trees, a necklace of moons beamed softly, casting faint shadows.

"Wake up," someone whispered in his ear. "C'mon, wake up already. We need to get busy."

Darryl rose through layers of sleep, muzzy-headed and muddled. "Dad?" he said, and realized his father had never sounded like that. Darryl sat up slowly, and the room spun and dipped around him. The great god of headaches hammered through his skull with railroad-spike vehemence; he licked his lips and found them dry. In his mouth, foul and furry things grew.

"Your mom is asleep downstairs on the couch. Your dad is on the landing. I slipped them something to, ah, help them sleep. They should stay asleep—as long as we're quiet." The dragon sat on the side of the bed and it sagged under his weight.

"Oh. S'you." Darryl closed his eyes and fell back onto his pillow. "G'way."

"I lied to you," the dragon whispered. "There is something you can do to save your wife and your kids. Besides hoping and thinking good thoughts, I mean."

"Ri-i-i-i-ight. Lied t'me before, but now you're tellin' me truth." Darryl pressed his hands against his forehead. He wasn't going to have to kill himself, he thought. He was going to die any minute.

"Headache?" Birkwelch asked.

"Plague, more likely." Darryl tried rolling over and pressing his head against the cool pillow on the other side of the bed. It didn't help.

"That's because I gave you some of the same stuff I gave your mom and dad. I had to go someplace, and I didn't want you killing yourself before I got back."

Darryl rolled back and squinted at the dragon. "You gave me this headache? Lovely. Deciding, no doubt, that it would make me doubly sure to kill myself once you got back."

The dragon grinned at him. "Bitch, bitch, bitch. I did you a favor, man. Now I'm going to do you another."

"Oh, lucky me."

The dragon held out a glass. "Drink this."

"Decided to finish poisoning me? Let's hope you did it right this time." Darryl took the glass and got the liquid down in one swallow—which proved to be nothing more than good tactics on his part. It was unutterably vile. "Ha! Yeggh! Shit! What is that stuff? Jesus Chri—" And then the headache went away. It didn't fade, it didn't weaken. It just went.

"Better?" Birkwelch looked insufferably pleased with himself.

Darryl sat all the way up and swung his legs off the bed. "For the moment. Before it comes back, why don't you tell me the new lies you've thought up. Since you've apparently decided you didn't like the old ones."

The dragon's eyerilles flattened, and a tiny reddish light glowed from his nostrils. "I don't have to put up with that attitude from you, pal. I can leave your wife and kids stuck on the other side." His huge yellow eyes narrowed. "And without me, I don't think you'll figure out how to reach them."

Darryl crossed his arms over his chest. "The way I see it—*pal*—if you didn't need me, you would have been long gone. So cut the bullshit."

Birkwelch opened his mouth as if to speak, then closed it. Then he sighed. "Let's be honest. We both need each other. What I told you about the extinction of dragons was true. What I told you about magic and how it works was not." The dragon stopped and stared thoughtfully into space.

Darryl told him, "Go on. I'm listening."

"Real magic is extremely simple—but very hard to do well. When you pursue your dreams, your magic is positive. When you turn your back on them, your magic is negative."

Darryl snorted, and sang, " . . . So just follow that star, no matter how hopeless, no matter how far."

"That cynicism is bad juju, bud. Real black magic," the dragon snapped. "Lose it. If you had only pursued your dreams, if you had lived by your principles—if you hadn't stopped *caring*—we would never have had this mess. This is the thing you *must* remember—Weavers weave. They never unweave."

The dragon blew a cloud of noxious smoke into Darryl's face. Darryl coughed.

"I haven't done so badly with my life!"

"You've done *terribly*! The results suck." The dragon poked him in the chest with one huge talon.

Darryl was willing to admit his life wasn't turning out quite the way he'd hoped. He wasn't sure he was willing to take the blame for everyone else's problems. "Great. My fault. I didn't see anybody running along behind me, telling me I had to change jobs or the world would fall apart."

The dragon rolled his eyes and stared up at the ceiling. "Nobody told me . . ." he mimicked in a falsetto voice. "The universe doesn't work that way. Personal responsibility. You want your life to turn out good, you gotta *make* it turn out good. You don't work for what you want, you won't get it."

"So why are you telling me now?" Darryl leaned toward the dragon, frowning.

"Because sometimes—just *sometimes*, pal—the universe gives you a second chance."

Darryl clasped his hands together and stared down at them. Second chances, personal turning points, and starting over—starting from the bottom again. It would be easier to die, he thought, than to keep trying. Easier to give up than to go on. *Why is it*, he wondered, *that the easy choices are always the wrong ones?* He had no doubt that dying would be the wrong choice. Somehow, he had faith in the dragon—somehow he believed there was still hope. In spite of the lies, in spite of the pain, in spite of everything, he still wanted to believe.

He turned and faced Birkwelch. "There really is a way to get my family back?"

"Yes."

"What do I need to do?"

The dragon shrugged—or came as close to shrugging as its sloping shoulders and narrow, scale-plated chest would allow. "You're the one with the dreams. You tell me."

"My dreams." Darryl sighed and stared off into space. "I wanted to be a playwright. Broadway—maybe Europe. My name in lights . . ." He rubbed his chin, feeling the stubble with the back of his hand. "So that really was my destiny and I blew it, huh?"

The dragon sighed. "Who can say?"

"Well, that *was* my dream. To be a famous playwright. You said before that I was supposed to be a famous—"

The dragon stood up and stretched. "You said that. I didn't say anything. I just let you assume. The magic comes from pursuing your dreams. *Pursuing.* Nobody said a damn thing about succeeding."

Darryl stood, too. "You mean I might not make it as a playwright?"

"Yep."

"Yep?! *Yep?!* Is that all you have to say?"

The dragon gave him a hard look. "The magic is in the journey. Not the destination. You don't get guarantees."

It was four in the morning. Minerva's funeral would be at one that afternoon. Darryl wondered what people would say if they saw him rummaging through the junk piled in Minerva's art room, looking for his old Selectric typewriter—once upon a time the best machine money could buy, and a Christmas gift years ago from Minerva. He wondered if they would think him cold and heartless, or merely crazy, to be thinking about writing at a time like that.

He set the typewriter up in the art room. Then Birkwelch went slinking through the house, looking for typing paper. There wasn't any. The dragon finally ran out of the house and came back a few minutes later with a packet of the cheap flimsy stuff the convenience store had in stock. It wasn't twenty-pound bond—but Darryl wasn't typing submission copy, either.

He pulled up a chair, turned the machine on, and rolled the paper around the platen. The he glanced up at the dragon, who leaned against the doorframe, smoking.

He nodded toward the billows of smoke. "Do you mind?"

The dragon winced. "Can't help it. Indigestion. From nerves, I guess."

"Oh. Wonderful. You smell like a steel mill."

"Probably all the cans in my diet lately." The dragon left the room, still belching smoke, and came back carrying the bedroom mirror. "You might need this." He placed it so Darryl could see through Minerva's eyes, then closed the door to keep from waking his folks up.

It was dark in her world, too. She walked through a forest—huge, twisted trees leaned over her, their branches reaching for her. She seemed to be in a hurry. The satyr was nowhere to be seen. Every once in a while Minerva bent and touched something near the ground—Darryl strained to see what she was doing. Finally he realized she was petting a cat.

"That looks like our cat," he said.

Birkwelch belched out an especially large cloud of sulphurous smoke, and coughed. "Probably is," he said. "Eyrith doesn't have cats."

"But the cat was with the kids—the police found it. It was dead." He watched a bit longer and felt some of the pain recede from his soul. "If the cat's alive, surely the kids are, too."

"I told you they were."

"I didn't believe you." Darryl tore his attention away from the mirror and back to the typewriter humming quietly on Minerva's sewing table. He rested his fingers lightly on the home row—felt the keys smooth and cool beneath the pads of his fingertips. Once he'd had words that seemed to wait in those fingers, that would pour forth when he had a chance to put them down. Once—long ago. But no words waited to spill out as he sat in the art room, with the dragon breathing awful fumes over his shoulder.

"Write something," the dragon said.

"Write what? I don't know what to write anymore."

"Well . . ." The dragon sat on the thick forest-green carpet, so that his head was only a little higher than Darryl's. Absently, he scratched at the back of his neck with one hind leg, then fidgeted to reposition his tail. His wings opened partially, and Birkwelch shook them and settled them neatly across his spine. "Hmmmm. There are really two ways to go about this. The *right* way, of course, is just to write the stories that are important to you. That's the slow way, but the magic is safe when done that way."

Darryl nodded. "The other way—?"

"Is much riskier. You write the things you want to happen. No story. Just scenes, the way you want them to occur." The dragon sighed directly at him, and Darryl put his pajama sleeve to his nose and mouth.

Dragonbreath. Morning breath is a rose garden by comparison.

"That actually seems safer to me. More likely to get me what I want."

The dragon leered derisively at Darryl. "It only seems safer because you don't know what you're doing." The dragon laughed. "Direct meddling is always the shortcut to hell. On the other foot, I don't think you have time to do things right."

Darryl cracked his knuckles and looked at the blank sheet of paper. "So—how do I do them wrong?"

"Write what you want to happen—but don't get too far ahead of what is going on right now. You need to give yourself some space for damage control. And whatever you do, don't create any huge logic leaps."

"Damage control? I don't know what you mean."

"Let's just hope you don't find out."

Barney stepped through the door and out of the dimness of the cage into the darkness of true night. He locked the door behind him, then sent it back where it came from, and did the last bits of magic that trapped the Unweebil inside his castle and set a monster loose inside it to find and eat the fiend.

Barney had landed them on a rocky road—a darker strip of darkness that went straight on—seemingly toward nothing.

Jamie was a shadow in front of him, Carol a smaller one beside him. The stars were out, but they were dingy and dim and muddy-looking; the wind that blew against his cheeks was hot and full of sand.

He had no good idea of what he wanted to travel toward—but what he was fleeing was clear in his mind. He felt its terrible weight at his back; could see, in his mind's eye, its sharp-clawed fingers reaching out for him. He didn't want to turn around, but something compelled him.

A wall of clouds rose along the far horizon, stretching from the ground into the heavens, glowing with ugly, dirty yellow light. Lightning ripped from cloud to cloud and stabbed out toward him—reaching. It *was* reaching. Growing. Spreading. He could feel the hatred that came from the place, and he could sense what that wall of cloud meant, and what it did. It destroyed and devoured—it took things that were something and made them nothing. As he watched, a bulge grew in the wall, and the mass of clouds churned and heaved—and lurched forward.

Beside him, Jamie whispered, "Oh, man!"

"The bad place," Barney said.

"No joke. We need to keep moving," Jamie said. "We can use the darkness as cover and sleep during the day. That's what fugitives do."

Barney said, "I got to sleep now."

"That's okay. You get in the wagon. Carol and I will take turns pulling you."

Carol said, "I wish he could make us a car."

"You don't know how to drive," Barney muttered, and climbed into the wagon. "And Mommy said Jamie drives his bike so bad, he won't get to drive a car till he's thirty."

"Hah! That's what she thinks. Six years, man—just six years, and I'll be sixteen. Then I'll get my license, and look out world! *Vrrooooom! Squeek! Scrreeeech! Blam! Powie!*"

"I'm not makin' a car," Barney said.

Carol's voice was thoughtful. "That's prob'ly a good idea."

Barney's first indication that something was wrong came when he heard his brother whisper, "Quick! Off the road and hide!"

The wagon rumbled and bounced, and he hit his head on the metal rim. *I'll never let that butthead eat anything but stinky fish again*, he thought, but his brother started shaking him.

"Wake up," Jamie whispered. "There's something out there. It was following us, but now it's stopped."

Barney did wake up then. Jamie sounded really scared. He started to sit up, but Jamie said, "Keep down! Listen!"

Barney rolled out of the wagon and lay down in tall, dead, crunchy grass—and he listened. Out there in the darkness, something . . . slurped. He shivered, and goosebumps made all the hair on his arms stand up. He heard nothing at all for a long, tense moment, except for the hot, dry wind that blew through the darkness. Then he heard the same sound again, but from a different direction. Definitely a slurp.

He decided there were not many things a little kid hated as much as things that went slurp in the dark.

Jamie's and Carol's fear surrounded him like a blanket—and his own heart raced in tandem with theirs. Their terror nearly overwhelmed him; he couldn't think, he couldn't hear, he couldn't sense anything except the two of them hunkered down next to him, shivering.

He wished they would stop being so scared—wished it hard. To his surprise, their fear was almost completely washed away. The little bit left didn't affect him.

He closed his eyes tight and reached out for the slurping things; he tried to hear them thinking. He could sense them, but not well. Their minds were blurry and confused—and sort of washed out, he thought.

But the things weren't bad. They weren't scary. They just felt kind of . . . lost.

Barney stood up.

"Are you nuts?" Jamie hissed.

"No." Barney climbed up the grade, onto the road, and stood waiting. He heard a slurp, and a squish, and looked in the direction of the sound. He could make out the outline of a lumpy form that oozed from the berm onto the road. He walked toward it, and it stopped.

"Here," he said in his cat-calling voice. "Come here. Here, monster, monster, monster."

Behind him, he heard Carol start to cry. Just dumb, he thought. Anybody could feel that these things weren't bad like the Unweebil.

The thing on the road was afraid of him, but vaguely curious, too. It oozed toward him—*squish, slurp, squish, slurp*. He heard others like it crawling onto the road behind him, and saw that one which had climbed up from the side had gotten very close.

They were all afraid.

And they wanted something—but he wasn't sure what.

The first one reached him. He touched it—it was warm, but as slimy and sticky as it had sounded coming toward him. Kind of like a worm, he thought.

Barney liked worms a lot.

The worm-monster brushed against him. It smelled yucky—but everything smelled yucky since the Unweebil stole him and Jamie and Carol from the green-eyed monsters.

"Hi, little monster-monster," he said. It wasn't really little—it was shorter than he was, but lots and lots wider. He wanted it to like him, though. He patted the top of it, since it didn't have a head, and got sticky stuff all over his hands. "I won't hurt you," he told the worm-monster. "I'll call you Wormy."

Wormy had many relatives. Barney patted them all, and named them—Slimy and Squishy, Icky, Yucky, Stinky, and Booger. Booger was the littlest, so Barney liked him best. The monsters liked having names. They liked it when he patted them and talked to them, too. Barney could feel the beginnings of happiness in them. He still couldn't figure out what they wanted, though.

Jamie yelled at him from his hiding place. "Barney, if those monsters eat you, I'm gonna tell Mom it was all your fault. I'll tell her you were playing with them."

"No you won't," Barney yelled back. "I'll turn you into a frog. These are nice monsters." He patted Booger again and said, "Don't you have homes, little monsters? Is that why you're so sad?"

Home. The word stirred something in them, and one by one they began slurping down the road, away from him, and away from the lurking mass of the Unweebil's kingdom. Their wants became clearer to Barney—they wanted him to follow them.

"Come on," he called to his brother and sister. "They're going to take us to their home."

"I'm not going with monsters," Jamie yelled.

"Me either," Carol added. "I'm afraid of them."

"Then I'll leave you behind," Barney told them. "And you can make your own food." He marched after the monsters. *What poopyheads*, he thought. *Scared of nice monsters.*

Behind him, he heard the wagon start rattling, and the sounds of Jamie and Carol climbing the berm and following. *Uh-huh*, he thought. Even if he was the littlest, he could boss them now, because he could do magic and they couldn't. Just thinking about it made him smile. He liked magic.

He walked behind the worm-monsters, and Carol and Jamie walked behind him—they were mad at him. He could tell they were talking about him and calling him names. It was all right, though, because if they were mean to him, all they were going to get to eat was stinky fish and boiled cabbage.

They didn't have to go very far before the worm-monsters slurped off the road and into a stand of dead trees. Barney followed—then stopped, shocked. The monsters had taken him to their home—but it wasn't a monster home. It was a people home. It was falling down a little, and even in the dark he could tell it wasn't very nice. He had not expected a people house.

Jamie and Carol stopped beside him.

"Why did they come here?" Jamie wanted to know.

"I don't know. They were thinking of home. They don't think very well—all the pictures in their heads are fuzzy."

"You think they live here?"

Barney shrugged. "I don't know."

Carol said, "Ask them. And if they do, see if we can sleep in the house. I'm tired."

The monsters didn't scare Barney, and neither did the house—but there was something about both of them together he found very frightening. He stood, thinking. "Monsters, do you live in the house?" he asked them. They didn't know or understand. "Can we go in?" he asked. Again, he could only feel confusion from them.

He walked to the house and up the stairs and opened the door. Finally, he felt something from them. They were happy he was going in. They didn't seem to want to go in themselves.

"I guess it's okay if we go in," he told Jamie and Carol. "They like it."

The children found a bed already made and climbed in. None of them talked about the house or asked each other any questions. Barney felt something terribly sad about the place.

Lying between his brother and sister after both of them fell asleep, he thought about being mean to them. It was fun to make them do what he wanted, and fun to scare them— but he thought maybe he wouldn't do it anymore. At least not for a while. The sadness of the house made him glad he wasn't alone. He snuggled deeper under the covers, and finally fell asleep.

CHAPTER 9

Minerva pulled the cloak closed in the front and shifted the weight of the duffel bag so it rested higher against her hip. Murp trotted along at her side, yowling and bitching as he usually did when forced to exert himself. She'd carried him for a while, but fifteen pounds of cat—certainly a *lot* of cat—was just too much to carry.

She was glad he didn't show any inclination to wander off. The forest seemed to close in as she walked. Dark shapes loomed in front of her, then melted away as she moved nearer. She'd found a two-track path leading from Talleos' house. She had, of course, kept as far away from the path that she could. She expected pursuit. No sense, though, making her pursuer's job easy.

"I wish forests weren't such ominous places at night," she told Murp at one point. He chirped—neither agreement nor disagreement, simply acknowledgement that she was there and speaking to him. Minerva imagined that forests didn't worry Murp much—and unlike her, he could see well in the dark.

She had no idea how long they'd been walking. However long it had been, she couldn't tell any difference in the terrain. It was all trees covering gently rolling hills—with enough roots to trip her, enough holes in the ground left from rotted stumps for her to fall in, enough creaks and squawks and wavering, tenuous howls to scare the bejeezus out of her.

At her side, Murp hissed suddenly, then growled low in his throat. Minerva froze. She could hear, over the rustling of leaves and the steady scraping music of night insects, a ponderous, leathery flapping. It came from somewhere behind her and off to her left. A triad of slow wingbeats, a near-silent glide, another triad, another short glide—moving closer.

Murp flattened himself on a log, ears plastered against his skull, hackles raised. Minerva shivered, an atavistic fear of being prey fresh and new in her belly.

Flap . . . flap . . . flap . . . hiss-s-s-s-s.

Whatever it was, it was flying nearer, low. Just over the treetops. It sounded so—so *huge.* Minerva wanted to run—though surely she didn't need to run. Surely whatever the thing was, it wasn't after *her.*

Or had Talleos already discovered her missing? Had the dragon—Birkwelch—decided to fly after her? The thing that flapped nearer sounded big enough to be a dragon.

Run, panic urged. *Stay,* some primitive instinct demanded. Instinct overruled. She stood unmoving—even unbreathing—beneath the arching branches of a giant tree, her fingers wrapped around the hilt of the little silver knife. The creature flapped directly overhead, occluding much of the sky, looking big as a jumbo jet. Then it soared on past, and Minerva thought, *Oh, good. It wasn't looking for me after all.*

But it turned. Angled back around. She could see the emerald glow of its eyes far overhead. She'd never seen eyes that truly glowed before. She heard the steady flap of its wings—heard its softly muttered curse, heard it say, "She's here—I can feel her," in a voice that chilled Minerva to the bone. It was nothing she had seen before, no mostly-friendly dragon come to drag her back to Talleos' home, as she had thought.

No. In this world, where even her allies were against her, this thing was hunting for her—and it was truly her enemy. She could not doubt that.

Flap . . . flap . . . flap . . . hiss-s-s-s-s-s.

It flew past her, a bit to one side, canting into the breeze. She could see it as a darker shape against the night sky. It would come around again, Minerva knew. It would narrow its field of search, and it would find her. She did not want to know what it would do when it caught her.

She could not run away. The thing flew—it would outstrip whatever pace she set, and cut her off. And if she ran, she would betray her position. It would catch her all the faster.

At that moment, a gust of chill breeze blew past and rattled the leaves—and threw the flying monster off course. Minerva saw that giant, terrifying form slip sideways, lose altitude, and fight to regain it.

I need more wind. A hard wind. Maybe a tornado—or a hurricane. At very least, a gale. She wished she knew how well the monster saw in the dark. She was going to have to try for her paper and pencils—

She waited until it came around again—until she knew it was behind her—and hoped the tree blocked her from its line of sight. Then she made a fast grab for the art supplies. She waited motionless, with dry mouth and weak legs as it flapped right overhead.

While she shivered there, she tried to think of a drawing that would convey wind, but only where she wanted it. And she tried to figure out how she could draw with any accuracy in the dark. She decided to sketch a cloud with a face, its cheeks puffed out and straight lines representing wind blowing before it. She figured she could do that in the dark well enough—a few curves, a winged scratch to represent the creature hunting her.

Whether it would work or not—what factors might make her drawing, and her magic—succeed or fail, she didn't know. She had never gotten time to experiment. While she was being hunted did not seem to her a particularly good time to start.

The creature narrowed its circle, flapped behind her again.

She would only have one chance to get this right. One lousy chance.

The instant the flying nightmare was even with her position, heading behind her, she started her sketch. She spread one sheet of the vellum on her leg—so white it seemed to glow in the darkness—and scrawled her little glyphlike drawing, guessing at the shapes and drawing mostly by feel. She added every hope and prayer she could muster.

Flap . . . flap . . . flap . . . hiss-s-s-s-s-s—

The thing, directly above her, shrieked—a high-pitched nails-on-blackboard scream of triumph. "There you are!" it howled, and banked into a tight curve, and angled down.

The wind hit it at that moment—a wailing banshee gale that came out of nowhere and ripped branches off the tops of the trees over Minerva's head. The creature tumbled through the sky, end over end, up and out of sight in the blink of an eye. Minerva could track its progress by the noise of the storm which followed it.

When even the sounds of the instant gale finally receded, she dropped to her knees, shaking and nearly in tears. Murp crept over to her and butted his head into her stomach. She cuddled the cat, and shivered. "It isn't fair," she whispered. "I didn't ask for any of this. I wanted a normal life."

Well, no, that wasn't precisely true. She'd had a normal life, and she'd been bored out of her mind with that.

She'd wanted adventure—she really had. She'd wanted to matter in the scheme of things. She'd wanted to be someone of importance. She simply hadn't considered what it would mean to her life if she got what she wanted.

Now she had what she'd thought she wanted. And she was *stuck* with it.

"Murp," she said to the cat, "people can be really stupid sometimes."

Murp gave his usual reply, and flopped over so she could rub his belly. She did, then tugged a few times on his tail. "Come on. We need to keep moving, at least until daylight. Then we can find a hole to sleep in for the day. We'll go cross-country, maybe steal a horse—I wish I knew how to find the Unweaver. Talleos said he was here somewhere." She sighed. "Or do you suppose that was another of his lies?"

She stood and shouldered the duffel bag. Murp took off in pretty much the direction they'd been going before. Minerva followed. She didn't have any better ideas.

I miss Darryl, she thought. She wondered how he was and what he was doing. Birkwelch had said something about him being able to see through her eyes by looking in mirrors. She wondered if there were some way to bring him to her; she didn't think the woods would be so frightening with him along.

They'd gone camping back in the days when the two of them still had fun together. Not regularly, but often enough that they could put their tent up in the dark. They'd hiked into out-of-the-way places, set up camp, and vanished from the face of the earth on more than one weekend, to emerge tired, scratched up, and blissfully happy a couple of days later.

It's been years since we did anything like that. She and Darryl had taken Jamie camping when he was a baby, but the idea of taking two toddlers, once Carol came along, was more work than either of them could envision. And they'd started to get busier. Started to "need" that bigger house in that better neighborhood.

We gave up a lot for that house and that neighborhood. We gave up our time with each other—we had to have more money to feed our social standing. We turned out backs on the things that really mattered—and we didn't even notice we were doing it.

She remembered something—something ugly, something she'd pushed out of her mind long ago. She remembered looking at bigger houses with Darryl, back when the two of them just barely had a couple of dimes to rub together, back when there were three of them and Carol was on the way. Darryl had just moved to a part-time job at the ad agency. A real job—so they could qualify for a mortgage—but regular part-time so he could write, too. They were looking at cheap, ugly "older homes" and "handyman specials"—and Minerva, tired and angry—and jealous of a friend who'd just bought a wonderful new house—snapped that if Darryl would just live in the real world and support his family the way he ought to, they could afford a decent place to live.

Darryl didn't say anything, she remembered. He looked a bit hurt, but he didn't say a word. And he kept on writing for a few more months. They stayed in their apartment—Minerva couldn't find a house she liked that they could afford, and he said he couldn't, either. Then a full-time position opened up at the agency, and Darryl took it.

That was the end of his writing, though Minerva had not realized it until right then. Carol came along, and between moving into a nice, new house in a nice, middle-class neighborhood and a lot of bills they hadn't anticipated, she and Darryl had found their time tied up in separate directions.

Her painting had followed Darryl's writing into the abyss—though she still always thought of herself as an artist. She thought of herself as an artist/mommy/overworked-administrative-secretary/genius-waiting-to-be-set-free, she realized. A sort of martyr.

She cringed. Hard to imagine Darryl enjoying living with such a paragon of virtue. He never complained much. He did, however, stay gone a lot.

Minerva could have waited forever for that revelation. She'd liked the situation better when she was sure Darryl was at fault, and she was the wronged party. She was going to owe her husband an apology—if she ever saw him again.

Depression and exhaustion weighed her down. Guilt sat heavily on her shoulders, too—and fear and anger and loneliness came along for the ride. She had to sleep. She hadn't slept in so very, very long.

With Murp tagging along beside her, she searched through the darkness for someplace to hole up and rest.

Darryl's dad was still asleep. His mother was gone—no telling what she was doing. He kept his voice down. "I just want to know if that Weird who was after her *could* have been Cindy." Darryl had been arguing with Birkwelch ever since the mirror went dark, and he didn't think he was making much progress.

"And I've said I don't know. There aren't all that many

Weirds. Even so, I don't think it's likely the one would be chasing both of you—but I could be wrong. In any case, they'll be out in force trying to find her, I suspect."

"Why her? They *know* where I am."

Birkwelch had his back to Darryl. The dragon foraged through the fridge, not bothering to pull his nose out to answer questions. Darryl guessed from the vigor of the dragon's search he must be scrounging for beer. "Because—" *Thump! Thunk! Rattle!* "—she's in their world. Their power—" *Thump, crash, wham!* "Dammit, who drank the last beer?!"

"Keep it down. Dad's still asleep. And you did."

The dragon slammed the refrigerator door shut and turned to glare at him. "You sure?"

"Yes. Now you were saying . . . She's in their world and their power—"

"Oh, yeah. Their power is concentrated over there. They have allies. And they know the countryside. They can all shapeshift, you know. Makes it easy for them to get around—and for them to blend in."

Darryl remembered his meetings with Cindy, and shivered. "They can look like *anything?*"

The dragon's alligator grin spread wide. "Scary thought, isn't it? Well, they have some limits. They don't seem to imitate inanimate objects very well. And their appearances have to match their actual sizes fairly closely."

Darryl thought about that an instant. "So the cat with Minerva isn't a disguised Weird?"

"Not a chance." The dragon walked to the pantry and started digging through it. "A Weird can't make itself that small. Besides, the eyes aren't right."

"They all have those green eyes?"

The dragon shoved things around on the shelves and turned to Darryl with a disgusted snort. "You people don't have any Pop-Tarts or Twinkies or *anything.* Everything you've got in here has *fiber*—and *vitamins*—and shit like that."

"I was trying to lose weight. The eyes, Birkwelch."

"Yes. They all have green eyes. But they can hide them

behind sunglasses when they're dealing with anyone who knows what to look for."

"That seem's obvious."

"Nah. Eyrith's a pretty sunny place sometimes. Lots of the inhabitants wear sunglasses." He grinned again. "I do every once in a while."

Darryl closed his eyes and tried to keep from imagining the dragon wearing sunglasses. "The mind boggles."

"Let's go to Hardee's or McDonald's or someplace and get some high-fat, high-cholesterol food with flavor."

Darryl shook his head. "The funeral is today, and I don't want to go out. I want to watch the mirror so I can see when Minerva wakes up again."

The dragon propped his foreleg on the kitchen counter and drummed his talons on the imitation wood-grain surface. "She went through a lot last night. She probably won't wake up until after the funeral's over. You might as well eat breakfast." The dragon held out his other foreleg and jingled the keys to his Miata. Darryl realized he had no idea where the dragon was hiding the car. "I'll drive."

"No, thanks. I'm going to get some writing done, I think."

The dragon's yellow eyes went wide, and Darryl fancied the bright blue hide went a few shades toward the pastel. "On second thought, I think I'll wait around. I can get something to eat after the funeral."

"What?!" Darryl felt like hitting the dragon with a frying pan. "Don't you trust me?"

"No." The dragon skinned his muzzle back to expose sharp teeth. "I don't." Birkwelch looked agitated. His wings partially unfurled, and his rilles stuck straight out around his face. Darryl thought this made him look like a giant periwinkle.

"I'm just going to write her heading in the right direction to find our kids—the fastest way possible. What could go wrong with that?"

The dragon shuddered. "I don't know. Something."

Darryl wasn't going to let himself be deterred. He'd been stuck with passive watching too long—he refused to feel trapped and helpless anymore. He ran up the stairs to

Minerva's sewing room. First he checked the mirror, but obviously Minerva was still asleep. All he could see in it was himself. *I'll make things easier on her when she wakes up,* he decided. He sat down in front of the Selectric and typed:

```
   Minerva woke with warm sunlight on her
face, and the cat curled up beside her. She
felt well-rested, and good. Things were go-
ing to be all right--somehow she knew this.
Darryl loved her. She was sure of that.
   She hiked, going in the direction she
instinctively knew was right. The cat stayed
with her. The two of them came upon a road,
and a friendly native offered her a ride in
his truck. He was going in the direction she
needed to travel, and she knew without doubt
that he would not hurt her. She accepted the
ride.
```

Darryl looked at that passage. It didn't seem like much—the writing was stiff and dull. But this wasn't an attempt to be the next Neil Simon or Tennessee Williams. This was an attempt to save his wife and kids. The dragon said to keep it simple. And Darryl had seen the magical wind blow the Weird heaven only knew where. The magic worked.

One thing was missing, he noted. He read over the text again, just making sure, then added a final line.

```
   Murp went along for the ride.
```

The doorbell rang. He ran down the stairs, and unlocked and opened the door. His mother, brother, and sister-in-law waited on the other side.

"Morning," he said. "Um-m-m-m-m . . . I'm not really ready for company."

His mom didn't seem to have heard a word he said. She charged through the door and hugged him, then stepped back to look at him. "You have such dark circles under your eyes, sweetheart," she said. She stroked his face once, then stood on tiptoe and kissed him on the cheek. "You don't look like you slept a bit. I really think you would sleep better at our house."

Stan's wife, Paula, was staring at him. "You look awful," she said. "Your eyes are all baggy and bloodshot, and your skin is just so _waxy_."

Thanks, Paula, he thought. _You're still the sweetheart I always remembered._ "I woke up pretty early this morning," he said.

Stan said, "I hope you and Minerva had the sense to put wills together. If you didn't have a will, the state will take half of everything you have. You could end up losing this house if you didn't. And did you remember to get everything out of your safe deposit box before the people at the bank found out she was dead? Otherwise, all your assets are going to end up frozen and the government will _clean you out._"

"I had other things on my mind, Stan. But I'll manage."

"You can't afford to get sentimental at a time like this," his brother said. "You have to keep your head on straight . . . you have to be cold and efficient. I would be if Paula died."

"So would I," Darryl muttered, and walked away.

"Let me fix you something nice for breakfast. I'm sure you haven't eaten right this morning," his mom called. "I took one of your father's suits to the cleaners for you—they did it overnight for me and came in this morning just so I could pick it up." He could hear rattling sounds from his kitchen. "Don't you think that was thoughtful of them?"

"Yes, Mom," he agreed.

Stan and Paula had cruised out into the greatroom. His dad came down the stairs and wandered into the kitchen, holding his head.

"Give him some of this," Birkwelch said, and handed Darryl a one-ounce medicine cup filled to the brim with something green.

Darryl remembered his own headache, and handed his father the cup. "For the headache," he said. "Drink it fast— it's awful."

His father gulped it down, made a pained face—then suddenly smiled. "That's great stuff. What is it?"

"Peabody's Headache Elixer," Birkwelch said. "From *my* world."

Darryl gave him the name, then said, "It's an off brand. Kind of hard to find."

"Thanks." His father looked ten years older than he had a week ago. This business would kill him if Darryl couldn't make everything all right again.

He wanted to tell them, *She's still alive. The kids are still alive. I'm going to bring them back.* But he couldn't. There was absolutely nothing he could say that would help. He couldn't even tell them he believed things would get better. How could he say that to parents who thought they'd lost their daughter-in-law and their only grandchildren?

Minerva's parents must be even worse off than mine. They didn't lose an in-law. They lost their only daughter. And Keith, Minerva's brother, had to be devastated. He and Minerva had always been close.

I'll make it up to all of you, Darryl promised silently. *I'll find a way, and I'll bring them back. I won't screw up this time.*

He ate the breakfast his mother fixed. He understood she needed to do something for him—and there was so little she could do. He wore the suit they'd brought over. He let them drive him to the church when it was time. They needed to feel they were helping him, and after doing the magic and seeing there was something he could do to change things, he was stronger. He wasn't helpless anymore. He could allow them to feel needed.

He felt strong up until the moment he walked into the church and saw her there—lying in that damned casket with her eyes closed, and her hair soft and perfect, and her cheeks pink. He hadn't seen her since the emergency room—and in the ER, she'd looked like a stranger.

She didn't look like a stranger anymore.

He felt the shock of recognition slam into his belly—nausea and loss and anger at being abandoned. She was gone, the kids were gone, and he was alone. How could she do that to him?

At his side, the dragon said softly, "Steady, Darryl. This is the show for the family. It isn't the real thing, and don't you forget it."

Darryl inclined his head slightly—enough for the dragon to see and no more. Minerva was not the body in the casket. She wasn't.

He sat in the pew, forcing himself to remain detached, while the organ played, and the minister spoke, and various friends got up and talked about what a wonderful person Minerva had been. He did not let himself think of what was happening in front of him. Instead, he twisted his wedding band and thought about what he would write next—how he could phrase the words that would bring his family back.

In the limousine on the way to the interment, he rode alone. The dragon was, mercifully, absent. Both his family and Minerva's were in other vehicles. His brother and sister-in-law had offered to ride with him, but he'd quickly refused. Minerva's brother hadn't yet spoken to him.

At the grave site, he noticed that people seemed to split their attention between the casket and him. From time to time, he would catch someone glancing at him. The expressions were—educational. He saw pity, curiosity, and suspicion. The last from a number of the women who'd worked with Minerva.

They think I killed them, he realized.

The thought made him sick. He wasn't perfect. He'd screwed up his life all by himself. But he'd loved his family: all of them. He would have done anything to be on the other side of the mirror with them. He would have given anything to go back to the moment he decided it was more important to stay at work feeding his ego than to go home.

He refused to be led away when the minister finished the rites. He sat, watching two strangers winching the metal box that contained his wife's body down into the ground.

He cried in spite of himself—cried in complete silence, with his arms wrapped tightly across his chest and tears burning furrows in his cheeks. *She's alive*, he told himself. *That isn't her.*

He only wished he really believed himself.

His in-laws' house, when he got there, was already full of people. Minerva's mother spread trays of food on the kitchen table and along the counter. Neighbors came in a steady stream, carrying dishes covered with tinfoil or pots full of flowers. They hugged Mrs. Wilson, his parents, each other. They eyed him warily.

Minerva's father sat on the couch, trying to hold himself together in front of all the strangers. Minerva's brother's kid sat next to him, stolid and gloomy, kicking the couch rhythmically with his left foot. Minerva's brother watched Darryl, his face cold and distrustful. Along the far wall of the dining room next to the fireplace, the nurses and ward secretaries and office personnel who'd known Minerva gathered, eating off paper plates and discussing the latest hospital disasters; they fell silent as he moved in their direction, and watched him pass—still silent.

Then one of the ward secretaries, a large black woman named Margaret, broke from the group and came over and hugged him. "This is not the end for her, Darryl," she said. "You've got to believe she's on the other side now. She'll be all right—and you'll see her again some day."

Darryl nodded solemnly. "I know I will, Margaret. I couldn't live if I didn't believe that." He hugged the woman, and she returned to the circle of hospital employees.

He walked on. Behind him, he heard one of the women say, "I can't believe you talked to him, Margaret. I still say he murdered all of them."

Margaret said, "You can't judge people by appearances, and you can't decide about them by what you hear everybody else say. The good Lord will judge that man. It isn't your place."

He kept walking. He didn't want to hear more.

People patted him on the back. They said things, but nothing they said registered. He moved in a daze, speaking without knowing quite what he said. But he couldn't really hear them. The noise around him became like the rush of the ocean's waves—steady, pulsing white noise. He walked away from all of it. He needed to be alone.

He went into the bathroom and stared in the mirror.

Once again, he could see the world through Minerva's eyes. He pressed his face against the glass.

"I love you, Minerva," he whispered.

Barney climbed out of bed and peeked out a dirty window of the house. The sun was up and there were no clouds in the sky—but everything outside looked dull and hazy anyway. All the trees in the front yard were dead, the grass was brown and ugly; Barney couldn't see anything alive outside the window—except the worm-monsters.

They crowded around the steps, waiting. They were a lot uglier in the daylight than they had been in the dark. He wrinkled his nose; the worm-monsters were a gross gray-pink, and their tops gleamed with an oily sheen. Their bottom halves weren't shiny—they had pebbles and bits of grass and dead leaves stuck all over. In their blobby shapes he saw dark spots which he guessed might be eyes. The biggest one had a few mangy patches of red hair sticking out of its back. But they looked to Barney about as solid as Jello—and not nearly as pretty.

He felt sorry for them. He thought he wouldn't like to be a worm-monster.

"What are you doing?" Jamie asked.

Barney turned away from the window and looked at his brother. Jamie sat up in the bed, rubbing at his eye with a knuckle.

"Just looking," Barney said.

"They still out there?"

"Yep." Barney turned back to the window and watched the worm-monsters some more.

Jamie climbed out of the bed and walked around the room. He looked into the tall wardrobe, then walked into the main room, and found the bathroom. When he came back, he was staring into the center of a little clear ball.

"Look at this," he said, and handed the ball to Barney.

Carol rolled over. "Let me see, too."

Barney looked into it, and stared, fascinated. It was a living scene—a house, and a family of funny-looking people. They were running back and forth, tossing a white ball with a string on it to each other. The place in the picture was pretty—there were lots of flowers and the grass was green and the trees had lots of tiny leaves on them that trembled in the breeze.

And even though the people were funny-looking, Barney still thought they looked happy—they looked like a nice family. A mom, a dad, lots of kids. There were nine people in the scene.

"The ball they played with was right next to that," Jamie said. "I wonder why they left."

The scene finished playing, and the inside of the glass ball went dark for the briefest of instants. Then the moving picture began again.

Barney handed the ball to Carol and sat on the floor, thinking. The Unweebil had ruined this place—he could feel it. The same magic that built the towering clouds they were running away from also left the stink in the air here, and killed the trees, and wore out the ground.

Had it scared the people away?

Barney got up and went outside, out with the worm-monsters. He looked at them, and felt their sadness, and their confusion—and he felt their hope. They didn't know what they were, or who they were, but they saw something when they looked at him that triggered memories.

He looked at the awful blobs. There were only six of them. He wondered, with a sick feeling in his stomach, why there weren't nine. He sat on the bottom step and rested his hand on the slimy skin of the monster nearest him.

"You're people," he told it. "You have to 'member you're people. You forgot—but now you gotta 'member." He closed his eyes and pictured the scene he'd watched in the little ball, and he imprinted that clear, bright scene in the muddy mind of the worm-monster. "You're in there, aren't you? You're one of those people."

He felt its confusion, and then its sudden shock of recognition. Then he felt its shame, and its despair.

"Don't feel bad," he told it. "It's not your fault. The Unweebil did this—but he won't hurt you anymore. You remember who you are now, don't you?"

Yes, it thought. *I'm people. I remember.*

"Good. Now you gotta find all the rest and make them know they're people, too. We gotta go or the Unweebil will get us. But you do that, okay?" Barney concentrated on a little, tiny magic that would fix his order in the mind of the worm-monster. It *would* remember, and it would make the other worm-monsters remember, too.

He looked at it, surprised. He could see tiny changes in it as he sat there watching—its skin became drier; it made itself stretch tall instead of wide. It had a long way to go before it became people again, he thought. He hoped it found the rest of the family.

He went back inside. *I hope the rest of my family finds me*, he thought.

They spent all morning walking. Barney was hot and tired, and he wanted to make his brother and sister pull him in the wagon—but they were hot and tired, too. The children kept running across more beat-up houses, and more worm-monster people. Barney felt sad around the worm-monsters. He wanted to make them all better, but he couldn't. Instead, he kept reminding them they were people and doing the little magic that would keep them from forgetting. Even that little magic was tiring him, though, and the heat and the dust and the smell—and worse yet, the *feel* of the Unweebil's magic all around him—were getting to be too much for him.

They trudged along the road. Jamie worried while he walked. "This isn't good strategy, walkin' along the road in the daylight like this. We should have stayed in the house all day."

"He would'a found us if we stayed there." Carol fidgeted with the tassled belt of her shirt.

"He's lookin' for us now," Barney said. "He has been for a while—but I didn't want to say nothin.' "

"Anything," Carol corrected. "Didn't want to say *anything*."

"Me either," Barney agreed.

His sister looked at him, her face puzzled. Then she

decided it wasn't worth arguing about. She hooked her thumbs into her belt and plodded on.

The road curved to the right. Brush on either side blocked Barney's view, but he sensed a change in the air ahead. He walked slower, nervous, trying to decide whether the difference was good or bad.

All three of them reached the point in the road where they could see beyond the curve.

"Hey, look!" Jamie yelled. "There's another road!"

It was a good change, Barney realized—a very good change. He broke into a run, and his brother and sister came racing after him.

He felt the difference all over—as if he'd been on the inside of a bubble and had just broken through its skin to the outside. One instant, the weight of the Unweebil's magic sat on his shoulders, and in the next, it was gone.

"The grass is green," Carol whispered.

"It smells so *good* here," Jamie said.

Everything in front of Barney was pretty. The leaves on the trees were red and yellow, the sun was bright, the sky was blue. He could see animals around—birds and bugs and furry things.

When he looked back they way they'd come, everything was murky—hidden by a yellow haze. He wanted to get as far away from that place as he could.

"Well," Jamie said, "we can go straight, or right, or left. So which way is it going to be?"

Jamie and Carol both looked at Barney. Barney stared past them as three huge monsters flew into view over the treetops. Their giant wings flapped slowly, and their long, pointy heads swung from side to side.

"Monsters!" he yelled, and ran for the cover of the nearest trees. Jamie and Carol looked where he pointed, then scattered in opposite directions.

"No," one of the flying monsters screeched. "We've come to help you! We've been trying to find you since the Unweaver stole you from us!"

Barney stopped. Now that he thought about it, the monsters did feel familiar—and not threatening. He turned around, just in time to see the three of them land and change into the ugly, big-eared people he knew from the first castle. Watching them change was pretty gross, he thought. They were awfully ugly, and seeing them sort of melt from one thing to another didn't make them any prettier. But he was happy to see them. They could take care of him and Jamie and Carol until his mommy came to get them. Taking care of everybody made him tired.

"Hi," Barney said. "You gonna take us back to the castle and give us something to eat?"

The tall monster nodded solemnly. "Yes—we've been searching for you since the Unweaver kidnapped you—but we haven't found any sign of you at all, until suddenly you just appeared out of nowhere. Where were you?"

Barney pointed down the road they'd just left. "Up that road."

The green-eyed monster looked puzzled. "Road?"

Jamie rolled his eyes. "The road. The *road*. Right *there*."

All three monsters exchanged glances. Then they looked at the children. "You can all see a road there?"

"Of course," Carol said. "It's right there."

"For you, perhaps," the monster said. "Not for us. It may be that you must have a special kind of magic to see that road."

"I did some magic," Barney said. "That's how we got away from the Unweebil." All the monsters looked at him, astonished. Barney was tired, but not so tired he couldn't show off a *little*. "See—like this." He created a tiny piece of chocolate, and handed it to the monster closest to him, who sniffed it cautiously, then took a bite.

"Wonderful," the monster said, and shook his head. "Amazing. So small, and already a true Weaver. I wonder where we can find a partner for you, little one. You would solve our problems once the—other troubles—have passed."

A soft cackle behind Barney sent his heart racing.

"Oh, do tell the little beast what you mean by 'other troubles,' Weird," the whispery voice said.

The monster grabbed Barney and started backing away.

"Save the children," he told the other two monsters.

Barney wriggled around in the monster's arms until he could see the Unweebil. In the bright daylight, the Unweebil was nothing but a red-eyed shadow that crept across the green grass—but he left a trail of withered brown where he moved.

"Save the children," the Unweebil hissed. "Very sweet of you. Why don't you tell them you intend to murder their parents? See if they'll cling to you then."

"Liar!" Jamie yelled. "You're lying!" His face grew red. He glared at the Unweebil and tears streamed down his cheeks. Once again, Barney could feel his fear.

"Liar, liar!" Carol screamed. "*You're* the one who wants to hurt *us*!"

The Unweebil was telling the truth, though, Barney realized. He could feel it. The monsters wanted to help him and Carol and Jamie, but they wanted to kill Mommy and Daddy. Barney didn't understand—and he didn't want to. Nobody who wanted to hurt his parents was his friend. He bit the monster who held him—bit hard. The monster yelled, and held him with the other arm.

"Don't do that!" the monster shouted. "Let us save you. You can be angry later—but let us save you now!"

The monster was shifting, becoming the bird-shaped thing it had been when it found them. The other two monsters were doing the same.

The Unweebil just laughed at them. "Forget all this," he whispered. "Forget who you are, forget what you want. Just forget. It's very easy."

Barney thought of the people along the road who had forgotten they were people—how sad and lost they were. He thought of these monsters, who were trying to save him from the Unweebil, becoming like them. He could keep them from forgetting. He knew the magic—it was only a little magic. And they wouldn't forget.

But these monsters wanted to kill his parents. They wanted to—and he couldn't say the words that would save them.

He just couldn't.

We can get away from the Unweebil again, he thought.
We did before.

The monsters forgot. Their hands dropped to their sides,
and their faces became blank and confused. Jamie and Carol
and Barney slid to the ground.

The Unweebil chuckled again. "Very good, little Barney.
So nice to have you on my side. Standing by and doing nothing is always the best solution to a problem, I think."

Jamie and Carol started to run, but Barney stood his
ground.

"I can get away from you any time I want. I'm not afraid
of you," he said.

"You should be," the Unweebil whispered. He didn't
move. He didn't have to. He swallowed Jamie and Carol and
Barney without even trying—then Barney heard a terrible
sucking, tearing noise, and felt the awful weight of the
Unweebil's dirty magic surrounding him, and everything
went dark.

When it brightened again, he and his brother and sister
were in the Unweebil's stinking castle.

"The monster and the door locks were very unpleasant,"
the Unweebil told them. "You made me very angry when
you did your little tricks and caused me a bit of difficulty."
Barney was lying on cold stone, looking up. The Unweebil's
red eyes stared down at him. "Not a lot," the Unweebil
added, "but enough. I will have to make sure you don't
escape again."

"Hah!" Jamie snarled. "You think you're tough. You're
nothin'. You can't make us stay if we don't want to."

"You think not?"

One second Barney was on the floor—the very next
instant, he hung upside down in the air in front of the
Unweebil's glowing eyes. He tried to get away, tried all the
different magics he could think of, but the Unweebil undid
everything he did.

"Let me tell you how I will keep you here," he said. "In
just a moment, I am going to hurt Barney. This will be a
little lesson for all of you—every time you do something I
don't want you to do, I will hurt Barney some more.

Understand," he hissed, "it doesn't matter which of you makes me angry—Barney is the one I will hurt. And I will hurt him more, and more, and more, until there is nothing left of him to hurt."

Barney kicked at the Unweebil, and squirmed around to see his brother and sister. Jamie's face twisted with rage. "That's not fair," he shouted. "You can't hurt somebody who didn't do anything!"

"Yes, I can," the Unweebil whispered. "And, yes, I will. I don't care about being fair. All I care about is getting what I want."

And then he hurt Barney.

CHAPTER 10

Minerva flew over a bleak and featureless landscape, soaring like a bird. The world below her ʋas so devoid of detail she could not decide if she was five hundred feet above the ground, or only five. The gray plain spread to eternity, it seemed. Perhaps beyond. No breeze brushed past her, nor did the faintest whisper of sound reach her ears. She knew she was looking for something, but she could not remember what.

A twinkling light appeared below her—but no more had she seen the light and marked its location than the unending grayness snuffed it out. She dove toward the place where she thought it had been, spiraling downward.

Then she was upright, and without quite knowing how she came to be there she was inside a dingy, filthy stone building. She walked down a twisting passage, and on both sides of her were hundreds of doors. She knew she had to choose one. She didn't know why, only that she did. None of the doors meant anything to her.

She was very frightened.

In all that time she had heard no sound, but suddenly, the world filled with a slow, horrible pulsing. The noise did not come from any one place—instead, it came from all around her. And with the pulsing, she could see color for the first time. There were red footprints on the stone floor in front of her. She wanted to reach down to touch them; somehow, she understood, they were important. They were why she was . . . wherever she was. She tried to move her hand, to touch the little red footprints with one finger, but her body would not respond.

She did not understand, and she became even more frightened. She followed the footprints, and became aware that she was not actually walking. She was gliding forward, floating an inch or two above the ground.

The footprints turned toward one of the huge doors to her right, and vanished. Inside that door, she thought. The mystery is there. Minerva put her hand out and the huge doorknob turned into a lion's head with sharp fangs that tried to bite her. She knew this was the door she'd been looking for—that the secret she was keeping from herself was closed behind the massive barrier it made. Terrified, she gripped the lion's jaws with both hands, and twisted, and the door slowly glided open.

Her children stood on the other side, their arms reaching for her. She ran to them, and put her arms around them. They were so thin—almost wraithlike, and they were silent. She could feel the tears that rolled down their faces, though. She held them as close to her as she could; she wanted so much to tell them everything would be all right. But like them, she was mute.

The pulsing sound grew louder. It throbbed in her ears and shook the walls—and abruptly she realized that someone was behind her. Clutching her children to her, she turned.

A tall specter of a man stood in the doorway, wrapped in a deep-cowled cloak. She could see through him—he was nothing but mist. He flowed toward her, and said, "You have found them, but you cannot have them until you have beaten me." His voice, hollow and far, far away, blew like an ice storm around her and froze her heart. And though Minerva clung to her children, they became mist, like the man, and drifted out of her reach. Invisible weights pinned her in place, so that she could not move to go after them.

Mute, unable to cry out, she watched them leave.

Something began to scrape her nose off.

Minerva opened her eyes. Murp stood on her chest and licked her nose. Sunlight filtered through the canopy of leaves overhead; as the breeze blew the leaves, light flickered across her eyelids.

Another dream.

She rubbed the cat. "God, I'm glad you're here," she told him. "After nightmares like that one, I want to fling myself off a cliff." She sat, shivering in the warm puddle of sunlight, waiting for the nasty residue of the nightmare to leave her.

Murp shoved his head against her face and purred.

The horrible emptiness lifted slowly, and she began to feel better.

"Breakfast would be a real plus," she told the cat. She wished she had dared sneak to the kitchen to steal some food. All the running and adventuring the night before had given her an incredible appetite. She eyed Murp. "I read somewhere that cooked cat tastes lousy. Suppose raw cat would be any better?"

"Mrrrrrrp," Murp said.

"Never mind. Maybe we can swipe an apple pie off somebody's windowsill—or something."

Her intuition insisted she wanted to walk east, into the rising sun. She decided she was going to trust intuition about as far as she could walk on water. She needed magic.

She pulled out the same sheet of vellum she'd scribbled on the night before, and a pencil, and sketched a compass—a nice durable metal-looking one. Instead of drawing out the four compass directions, though, she noted only one—and that not truly a direction. "MY KIDS," she wrote; closed her eyes; concentrated until the paper abruptly became heavy.

A metal compass—her design—lay on top of the paper. "Shit," she whispered, impressed. The appearance of the cat, the transmission of sound that permitted her eavesdropping on Talleos, the wind that blew the airborne hunter away from her—all of those *could* have been coincidental. Not too likely that they were, she knew, but the possibility had existed. This latest occurrence could be nothing but the real thing, though. Magic.

Wow, she thought, staring at the compass. *I did that.*

She carefully lined up the arrow with the mark she'd used to indicate the location of her kids.

Straight east.

"Well, then . . ." she whispered. "East it is. Might be more to intuition than I thought."

She looked at her small supply of vellum, and then at Murp, sitting patiently by her side, waiting with the air of one who knows his god is about to drop something tasty at his feet. Her own stomach growled.

"I don't have much of this stuff," she said, eyeing the creamy parchment, "but breakfast *is* the most important meal of the day."

Murp waited in silence, apparently thinking that statement too obvious to require comment.

She looked at the vellum again. "I'll just draw small."

She sketched a bowl full of Tender Vittles, Murp's favorites, and an entire box of granola for herself. And a glass of orange juice. Then, as an afterthought, she drew a tube of toothpaste and a toothbrush—the angled kind.

She closed her eyes and concentrated—thinking big. Murp yowled. Minerva looked up, saw what she had done, and winced.

The bowl of cat food stood tall as a trashcan, and about twice as wide. Each Tender Vittle was the size of a large mouse. She'd made enough food there to feed a band of Bengal tigers. She picked Murp up and dumped him in the middle. After a moment of what looked like shock, he chirruped delightedly and burrowed into the food, then rolled on it, and then began to bat at the Tender Vittles and to nibble at various of the huge bits.

Her own box of granola would have made her a nice tent the night before. She glanced from that to the tube of toothpaste and the toothbrush, and shook her head. She wasn't sure she could tip the granola box—and even if she could, she doubted she'd be able to open it. She had a hard enough time opening the normal ones. She could have gone swimming in the glass of OJ.

Maybe she could reuse the same drawing, but concentrate on making the stuff the right size, not just bigger. She closed her eyes, concentrated, and opened them to see that nothing had happened. She took out the pencil and traced over the drawings, then repeated her previous steps.

This time, she got what she wanted, more or less. Things were still a bit off-size—the toothbrush was uncomfortably large, but would work, while the toothpaste was of the jumbo commune size. However, she had enough granola to last a while, and the OJ, she discovered to her delight, was freshly squeezed and delicious.

She and Murp finished their meals, she brushed her teeth—*A bit too much mint in the toothpaste*, she thought as her eyes watered and her mouth burned—and then they took off.

The two of them kept up a steady pace. They stopped once to drink out of a stream, and several times while Minerva double-checked her directions, then kept moving eastward.

Minerva guessed the time to be a bit shy of noon when she became aware of an intermittent hissing over the hill in front of her. She climbed the slope, wondering at the cause, and made sure she stayed well under the cover of the trees. When she crested the ridge, she was delighted to see a road, paved with blacktop (or something very like it), bisecting the ground in front of her. On that road, an occasional round-cornered and flared-finned six-wheeled vehicle gaudy as a Puerto Rican bus zipped past. These vehicles made no noise except for the sound of their tires on the road and the gusting breezes they left in their wakes.

At first she was startled. She hadn't expected automotive technology—she'd expected horses. "I should have known better," she told the cat.

I wonder, she thought, *if I dare hitch a ride. I don't imagine the general population will be up in arms looking for me—I'd think my presence here would be a secret.* She sat in the tall weeds that ran from the hilltop down to the road and watched the traffic. *Except, naturally, the road runs north and south, and I want to go east.* She double-checked her compass again, just to be sure.

That's odd. I thought I wanted to go east. The needle

seemed to have changed directions. She tapped it once, to see if it might be stuck. The needle swung freely, then reoriented itself—north by northeast, exactly paralleling the direction of the road.

Goosebumps rose on her arms as she looked from the needle down to the passing vehicles below. *How—how very . . . convenient.*

She'd wanted to find the fastest way to her kids. Perhaps the compass was showing her the fastest way—first straight to the road, then in somebody's vehicle heading north.

She would give hitchhiking a try. She put her hand on the hilt of her knife, just to make sure it was there. The very idea of taking a ride with a stranger scared her to death—but she wanted to get to her kids. For them, she'd take her chances. She needed to make sure, though, that the cat wouldn't get lost. "Murp," she said, "I don't imagine this will be your favorite game. Just stay put, though—okay?" She unzipped her duffel, picked up the cat, and dropped him inside. To her surprise, he curled into a ball on her spare set of clothes and after one giant yawn, fell asleep. "So maybe I was wrong," she remarked. "You don't look too put out." She zipped the duffel until the opening was too small for the cat to get out, but plenty large enough for him to get air. Then she stood and clambered down the steep shoulder to the pavement.

The compass needle swung around and began pointing south-southwest. Minerva stared at it, then swore and smacked the compass once with the flat of her hand. The needle spun crazily, then returned to its south-southwest orientation. "Dammit," she muttered. "This thing doesn't work after all. If that's the case, I don't have any idea which way to go. I might have been walking in the wrong direction all morning."

One of the gaudy local vehicles approached from the south. It was a truck of sorts, with a teardrop-shaped cab and a hinged cart on the back. Exotic livestock hung their curly-horned heads over the sides and cheeped. Minerva, suddenly suspicious, watched her compass. It followed the truck as if the point were attached to the vehicle by string.

So this is my ride, huh? Fastest way to my kids. Oh, well . . .

She stuck out a thumb, and the driver slowed and pulled off to the side.

"Need a ride?" the driver leaned out the window and yelled back at her.

"Desperately." She ran to the vehicle, then slowed as she got near enough to make out details.

The driver was a man—more or less. His face was weathered and browned; corners of eyes deeply creased; hair white and thin and wispy over his head. But his ears fanned out from either side of his skull in delicate, leaflike folds, and the tip of his bulbous nose curled over his mustache to touch his broad upper lip. His clothes matched hers—but they were faded and patched, and the cloth at elbows and wrists was thin and frayed.

Minerva took a deep breath, walked around to the passenger side of the vehicle, and got in. *Compass says this is the ride I'm supposed to take.*

The driver pulled a lever and stepped on a pedal, and the truck rolled forward soundlessly. He gripped a sort of ski-pole arrangement in either hand—Minerva thought the absence of a steering wheel made the interior of the cab look bizarre. She admired the embroidered seat-covers and the beadwork decorations.

"Yer one of them critters from the magical reservation, ain't yer?" the old man asked her.

Minerva winced. The old man, when he spoke, sounded exactly like Talleos' imitation of a tourist. "In a way, I suppose so."

"Yup—I figgered. None of you folks look *right*, y'know. I seen you suckers on the hollyvision bunch a times. My favert is that old-timey show, *MageWars.*" He grinned as he said it, so that his lips rolled back to his gums. Minerva caught an unnerving glimpse of his teeth. She noted with some discomfiture that his canines were almost an inch long. *This is the way the compass said to travel,* she reminded herself. *My ride.*

The old man suddenly turned and scrutinized her, though, and said, "I don' recollect ever havin' seen yer likes afore."

Minerva had the line for this one ready, thanks to the cheymat. "We're nearly extinct," she lied. "Very rare."

"Huh." The old man turned away from her, and she was surprised how relieved she was that those vivid green eyes were looking at something else. The corners of his mouth curled up in a smile, and he said, "I reckon that's it."

They rode in silence for a while. Minerva cast the occasional covert look at her compass, but it continued to line up exactly with the direction in which they moved. She settled back, determined to enjoy the ride.

The old man said, "So where yer heading for, you?"

"Don't know precisely," she told him. "I'm looking for something."

"Then, what yer lookin' for?"

Minerva shrugged. "I don't know that, yet, either. I guess I'll know it when I see it."

The old man scratched behind his ear, and Minerva was surprised at how big his hands were, and how sharp the claws that tipped them. Uneasiness settled around her like a cloak. It was all very well to think that the compass led her to this man, but she couldn't help but wish he looked less the part of the aging werewolf. She felt too much like Red Riding Hood for her own comfort. *What big eyes you have*, she thought. *And big ears, and sharp claws, and big teeth . . .*

He grinned over at her. Face on, it was not a delightful grin. Not charming. Somewhat less than utterly pleasing. She'd seen the likes on pictures of hyenas. "We'll be in Weezfield in just a few minutes," he said. "You see whatcher lookin' for there, you let me know. I stop for yer. Iffin not, I'm going all the way to Weirds' Hold today. Gotta drop off my kaldebeasts with the buyer up that way. Yer welcome to come along. I don't often get any company deliverin' stock. Not even critters such as yerself."

Minerva smiled—a strained smile, but the best she could manage at the moment. "Thank you. I do appreciate that." She took a deep breath. "I'm not actually a—ah, *critter*. My name's Min—er, Jean." She felt the sudden compulsion to keep some things secret.

"Minnerjean. Huh! Well, I'm Lorcus." The old man shrugged. "That's a right pretty name for a critter. But all you folks is so danged touchy about bein' called critters. What you want to be called then, Minnerjean?"

"People?"

"People. It figgers. You and danged dragons and lopers and kaldebeasts, too, more'n likely—everybody wants to be people. Well, Minnerjean, yer can't be born a critter and then turn *people*. You got to be *born* people." His smile when he looked at her that time was touched with condescension. "But there ain't nothing wrong with bein' a critter, honey. You just got to know your place is all."

Minerva bit her tongue. She would have loved to slap the old farmer down—but she didn't know the rules in this world, didn't know the place of women in general, or of female "critters" in particular. So she said nothing, and stewed.

They came into a village—evidently Weezfield, though she could not read the sign planted askew on the hillock before the village proper. The place was quaint, with single-story plaster houses painted in every conceivable pastel hue. Each house had a blue tile roof, and a bright red basket-weave fence about two feet high around the tiny yard. The houses were close together, with dirt paths beaten into the blue-gray earth between them.

The open market square in the center of town was busy—the inhabitants herded flocks of—well, of something. Minerva didn't have the foggiest idea what sorts of flocks those were. Girls chased after waddling four-legged duck-like beasts, while the curly-horned creatures Lorcus had earlier identified as kaldebeasts stood in the middle of the road, staring stupidly at hairy jade-green beasts which hopped past, kangaroo-like, on their hind legs.

She took an instant to check her direction on her compass, and shouted, "Oh, stop! Stop!"

The old man hit his brake, and Minerva nearly went through the windshield. "What's the matter, Minnerjean?"

Minerva pulled her duffel bag onto her lap, preparatory to jumping out of the truck. "I have to go that way," she said, and pointed to a cobbled road that twisted through the marketplace and off to the right.

"Well, that's the way I'm going, too. If yer'll just be patient—" He grinned straight at her again, and she tried to reconcile his cheery demeanor and friendliness with all those teeth. And claws. Mustn't forget the claws. "We'll get past the herds and the flocks soon enough. That's Old Stoneman's Road. Goes to Weirds' Hold. Bit of a ride, but I'm goin' that way. Yer sure welcome."

There didn't seem to be any reason to insist on walking. The man made her nervous, but not nervous in the way she would have equated with, for example, being around known sex offenders. There was nothing slimy about him. She came to the conclusion her anxiety was simply caused by being faced with someone so different. *He probably feels nervous around me, too.* She sighed. "Thanks. If you're sure you don't mind, then, I'll stick with you."

The cobblestone part of the road only lasted to the end of the town. Then it became flat cut paving stones laid out in a single raised lane. The shoulders widened at regular intervals to allow the larger vehicles to pass each other. Old Stoneman's Road, she discovered, was much more lightly traveled than the road she and Lorcas had just left. Her uneasy feeling got worse. Lorcas had grown silent as the village fell away behind them, and she didn't feel up to keeping a conversation going.

The terrain, which had been a steeply hilled and heavily farmed piedmont, became flatter, and the farms farther apart. Rolling meadows gave way to large marshy areas, and the road became a causeway for long stretches. She stared out at the countryside that flashed past her, at fens and bracken thickets and boggy lakes.

They rode over streams, and then two fair-sized rivers, and Minerva was glad she hadn't tried to walk. On foot, she would have made an easy target, if any of the flying things still hunted her. In the truck, she hoped such creatures would have a more difficult time tracking her. But still her disquiet grew.

As the ground below the causeway started to rise again,

the old man turned to her. Thoughtfully, he said, "Seems to me someone don't know where she's goin' but in as much of a hurry to get there as you are must be running away from something. That wouldn't be the case, would it?"

Minerva shook her head. "I'm running to something—I just don't know what yet. Really."

He tipped his head slowly to one side and rotated his ears up and a bit forward. His eyes narrowed. "Wouldn't be running toward the Veil of Illusion, would you?"

Minerva was nonplussed. "The what?"

He shrugged and smiled. "No, I guess not then." He seemed ready to drop the subject.

Minerva gathered up her courage. "What is the Veil of Illusion? If you don't mind?"

"No fit place for anyone—not even critters." And that was all Lorcus would say about it.

Minerva dropped the subject. They were coming into another village—more of a hamlet, really. A few shabby houses lined the road on both sides, and tiny, scruffy fields spread out behind them. She was having a hard time reconciling the cheymat's wealth and technological sophistication with the apparent poverty and backwardness of these other parts of Eyrith.

On earth, there are places this out of touch, she thought, *but not so close to civilization.* And then she reconsidered. Living in a middle-class neighborhood for most of her life, how did she know what the lives of the people around her were like? She saw the poverty and the squalor here because it was new to her eyes, and she hadn't yet learned to look past it.

She thought, if she made it back to her own world, she would pay more attention to other people. Maybe—if she really were a Weaver—she could do some good there.

"Old Stoneman," the farmer said, with a nod of his head back to the rapidly receding village. He then fell back to silence.

The duffel at Minerva's feet shifted—Murp had evidently awakened. She yawned and stretched, hoping to cover any noises the cat might make, but the farmer was not misled.

"What yer got in the bag?" he asked.

"Clothes and my lunch," she lied.

"Thought I smelled something fine in there—live meat, I reckoned, but didn't think yer the type to eat yer's live. 'S how I like mine, too." He gave the bag a wistful glance, and smiled hopefully at her. "Yer wouldn't like t'share, would yer? I've a bit of cheese and I'd planned t' kill one of the beasts in the back, mayhaps, if they didn't have something I liked in Weirds' Hold, but I've never smelled the likes of that."

Minerva tried not to let her dismay show. "Ah—" she said, and stared at the bag at her feet, which was now wriggling vigorously and would at any moment, she suspected, let out with an indignant yowl or two. "Um—" She gave the farmer an apologetic smile. "Really not even enough there for one, and I'd just brought this one along as a snack. If I'd known ahead of time, I could have grabbed another one, but . . ." Her voice trailed off into silence, and she gave him a helpless shrug.

His disappointment was evident. "Oh. Yes, I reckon the beast would have to be small to fit in there. Perhaps if you could tell me where you got it . . . ?"

Minerva brushed her hair out of her face and said, "Of course. I caught this one in the—ah—" *What did Talleos call the place? Oh, yes.* "In the Preserve."

Lorcus stared at her hand. Rather, she noted, he stared at her ring. And suddenly he smiled in a way she *did not like* at all. His attention snapped back to the road, and he said, "Then that would possibly be a magical creature, hmmm? I'd not want to eat that, anyway. Hard on the stomach, some of those."

"I imagine so," Minerva said, and edged farther toward the passenger door. The truck was moving awfully fast. The old man had decided to make some time, she could tell. Where before he had pulled onto the first shoulder he came to whenever another vehicle approached, now he just kept on driving, counting on the other drivers to make way for him.

Finally, she dared to say, "You seem in an awfully big hurry."

"Gettin' late," he replied, "and I'm gettin' hungry."

That was as much about that topic as Minerva cared to hear.

"Minnerjean," the old man said, "we're not far out of Weirds' Hold. Whyn't you let me buy yer a nice dinner 'fore you head on?" He smiled at her, keeping his teeth mostly hidden. "You've been fine company—and I'd like to treat you." He frowned a bit, and his huge ears flipped back. "They don't have real fresh meat in the big city—you'll have to eat killed-and-cooked. But it hain't bad. I've had it a time or two."

Minerva hated to appear rude—and as long as she didn't have to eat a live animal, or watch the old man eat one, she thought she could tolerate his company a while longer. He wasn't so terrible. He simply made her nervous. She smiled back at him. "Why, thank you, Lorcus. That's very kind of you."

His smile grew wider, so that she could see the fangs again. "Not a 'tall," he said. "Not a 'tall."

By the time Darryl got home from the family gathering after the funeral, it was close to four P.M., and he was exhausted. His mom and dad, refusing to be denied, were going to stop by in less than an hour. That didn't give him much time to write. He pushed open his front door and plodded toward the stairs.

The voice from the living room stopped him.

"I wish I could watch things in the mirror when you weren't here," Birkwelch called. "I read what you wrote while I was waiting for you, and I think you've created a recipe for disaster—but I couldn't see what was going on. There's no telling what might have happened to her by now."

"She's fine." Darryl started back toward the stairs again. "I only caught about two glimpses of her in mirrors the whole time I was at her folks' house. Those are people who don't believe in mirrors."

The dragon snickered. "Having now seen her mother, I can guess why."

Darryl laughed in spite of himself. "Minerva takes after her father."

"That hawk-nosed weasel? I don't think she was his off-spring, either. Minerva was a foundling is my guess," Birkwelch said, and followed Darryl up the stairs.

"Anyway, she was looking out the window of a bus or car or something—riding along at a pretty good clip. So you didn't need to worry."

Darryl noted the sudden silence behind him. He looked down the steps and saw the dragon standing halfway up, staring at him with a horrified expression. "Riding?" the dragon finally squeaked. "Sacred Karras protect us all!" The huge beast charged up the stairs at a speed Darryl found hard to believe, and dragged him down the hall and into the art room before he'd had a chance to realize it had happened.

The two of them studied the image in the mirror. The scenery whipped past. Darryl caught glimpses of verdant flatland, a built-up stone road, Minerva's feet and the duffel bag, and then a dizzying blur as she snapped from looking out the window to looking at the driver.

Darryl got a good look at the profile of the creature who was driving his way across the Eyrith countryside. He had huge, curly-edged ears, a flat, wrinkled face, and white lion's mane of hair. Darryl turned to Birkwelch.

"What is that thing?"

"That's one of Eyrith's highlanders—looks like a typical farmer taking his beasts to market." Birkwelch sighed and tapped the glass with one talon. "You might have been lucky this time. The Weirds will be using every means at their disposal to find Minerva—they will have sensed her presence in Eyrith the second she left the magic-shielded zone around Talleos' cabin. But the highlanders don't go in much for anything the Weirds want."

Birkwelch glared at Darryl and added, "Even so, let me make a suggestion. Never write for the 'fastest' anything. Write for the 'safest'—or there's no telling what sort of trouble you'll write everybody into."

Darryl looked at the ugly farmer uneasily. Every time the man opened his mouth, two sets of long yellowed fangs glinted in his mouth. Minerva glanced from the man's face

to his hands, and Darryl saw sharp claws instead of finger-
nails tipping his fingers. "I can't believe she accepted a ride
from something like that," he finally muttered. "I wouldn't
have."

"If she'd stayed on the road, the Weirds would have had
an easy time catching her."

Birkwelch suddenly sucked in a breath and stared at the
mirror. Minerva and the farmer were coming into a town,
and Minerva's glance moved from indecipherable signs to
some attractive wattle-and-daub houses, and then to a huge
dark stone fortress that stood off in the distance on a giant
artificial mound.

"What?" Darryl asked when the dragon didn't say
anything.

"They're going right into Weirds' Hold." The dragon
appeared to be unable to believe what he was seeing.

Darryl studied the bouncing view of the approaching
town and shrugged. "So?"

"Those walls on the mound . . ." The dragon pointed to
the fortress again.

"I see them."

"That *is* Weirds' Hold."

Darryl glowered at the dragon and growled, "So . . . what?
Get to the point!"

"Think, man, think! Nobody would call a place Weirds'
Hold unless it had Weirds in it, would they? Weirds' Hold is
the Weirds' keep. That bastard farmer is taking her right to
them."

Darryl leaned heavily against the sewing table that acted
as his desk. "This could just be coincidence."

The dragon scratched between his scales and looked at
Eyrith in the mirror. The farmer parked his vehicle in front
of a large windowless building on a back street. "Could be."
The dragon looked at the sign, and shook his head. "Don't
think it is, though. That's the Sacred Brethren Waystation.
The Weirds run it."

"They're going to get her?"

Minerva grabbed her duffel, got out of the vehicle, and
walked around to the old farmer's side. Darryl got his first

look at the man's face from the front. The farmer's eyes were the same vivid, glowing emerald Cindy's had been.

The dragon saw those eyes, too. "They've already got her," he said.

Barney's feet still bled a little. They hurt so bad where the Unweebil had cut them that Barney didn't want to move ever again. He curled in a ball on the mattress he'd made for himself, and faced the stone wall of the cage.

Jamie patted him on the back, "You can make it all better, Barney. Don't let that stinking Unweaver make you quit. You can get better."

"Mommy didn't save us," Barney said. "She was right here—and she didn't save us."

"That was a dream," Carol said. "It wasn't real. You know that."

"We were *all* there. You saw her, too."

"Well," Jamie said, "yeah—we *saw* her . . . but she wasn't really here. I mean, all that stuff was just a dream."

"She can't beat him," Barney whispered. "She can't. We're gonna be stuck here with the Unweebil forever, and we're gonna die."

Barney lay curled on the little mattress, staring at his hands. They looked thinner, he thought, and paler. He almost imagined he could see through them.

The Unweebil was going to win, and that was going to be the end of everything.

CHAPTER 11

As Minerva stepped into the restaurant, the feeling of vague disquiet that had grown in her over the two hours of riding became full-fledged panic. She could see nothing ominous or out of place about the restaurant; it was clean and well lit and pleasantly decorated in a sort of faux-rustic fashion. The chandelier was made of old pikes, with electric lights in the shape of burning candles affixed to the weapon points. The tile floors and tabletops gleamed, and the waitresses, in outfits that made Minerva's seem drab by comparison, were neat and cheerful. The two sturdy young women—creatures of the same species as Lorcas—welcomed Minerva and the farmer, seated them at a table, and brought water and a dark red wine, all the while keeping their curiosity politely in check.

And still, she worried. "Where's the, ah—the ladies' room?" She lifted her duffel onto her lap.

"The privacy rooms?" The farmer pointed toward the back, toward two doors, marked with swirls and circles and little hatches.

Minerva winced, and said, "I can't read what they say. Which one is for women?"

The old farmer laughed and pointed to the one on the right.

Minerva thanked him and quickly excused herself.

Once on the other side of the restroom door, she locked

it, and knelt, and peered under the door. She could see a thin sliver of the dining room, including the farmer's boots, and the waitress's boots right next to him.

I'm being paranoid, she thought. *She's just taking his order*. Even so, Minerva brought out her paper and a pencil. Murp popped out of the bag, too, and stretched and yawned. Then he sat next to her, and watched while she drew a tiny ear, and concentrated on hearing.

". . . three eggs, and the chorgin, and slab kaldebeast. Rare. No—I get kaldebeast ever' day. I think I'd like the morlu. Cut me a piece about two-three fingers thick . . ."

Minerva quit listening. *That was certainly silly of me. He is just ordering*. She went to the bathroom, and let Murp use the trash basket as a litter box. When they were both through, she popped him back in her duffel and washed her hands. Murp seemed less thrilled about taking up residence in the duffel the second time, but she bribed him by sketching some Tender Vittles and Pounce cat treats, and tossing them in with him.

When she got out, the waitress hurried over to the table, smiling. The farmer was gone.

"Take your order?"

"I don't know what I'd like. What do you recommend?"

The waitress listed a few things, and Minerva picked from names she thought she recognized. Then she asked, "Where did Lorcas go?"

The girl gave her a vacant grin and shrugged. "Don't rightly know," she said, "but he ordered a meal would choke a grevvil. He'll be back any time."

Minerva grinned. *More paranoia*, she decided.

Her meal and Lorcas' arrived—huge platefuls of sizzling meat and dark vegetables in thick sauces—and an instant later, Lorcas returned as well. He hurried in from outside, looking rather flustered, but he smiled when he saw her. "Had to water the beasts in the truck, and then I thought I ought to call the mate and tell her I got here all of one piece. "

Minerva grinned. She wished she could call her husband and tell him she was safe and on her way to find the children. "No problem," she said. "I just figured if you didn't hurry back, I'd finish my meal and eat yours."

Lorcas eyed her heaped plate with some doubt, then laughed. "I woulda' paid to see that."

They dug into their food. "Thank you," Minerva told him between bites. "Thanks for the ride, and for the meal, and everything. You've been very kind."

The farmer smiled over at her, his green eyes almost glowing. "My pleasure." His voice sounded oddly hollow. For an instant she fancied his features shifted—they seemed almost to run and blur—but when she rubbed her eyes and looked at him again, nothing of the kind recurred.

I don't feel tired, she thought. *Must be a trick of the light. The lighting in here does seem a little bizarre.*

And indeed, as she thought that, the lighting in the restaurant briefly dimmed to brown, then came back up again. Lorcas cocked his head to one side and his ears swiveled. "Reckon I'll go check on the animals. Right back."

Minerva nodded and continued eating. No sooner was Lorcas outside, though, than she rethought his actions. *Damn, but I wish this place had a window,* she said.

And at that moment, pale glowing black letters ghosted in a transparent stream across her plate. They looked like they'd been typed—Courier typeface—complete with a typo that the invisible typist struck out and retyped.

```
Minerva, (they said) get ixi out of there
while you can. The old man was a plant, and
the restaurant is a trap. I love you. Darryl
```

She looked around, trying to appear casual. The waitresses were watching her. She smiled, and picked up her bag, and walked back to the women's restroom. No sense tipping them off, just in case they were in on things.

How did Darryl get that message to me? she wondered. She hid in the restroom, scared stiff. Minerva locked the door—though if anyone really wanted her, the door was thin and the lock flimsy. A good kick would open it. What could she do to get herself out of trouble?

She got out her vellum. She had two completely clean sheets left. Not much ammunition.

First things first. She drew a heavy oak beam set through two massive metal rings to bar the door. This time, she concentrated on the image and kept her eyes open, watching the door to make sure the magic worked.

She saw a shadow form along the place where the beam would be, and faint sparkling shimmers of light—the sort of effect she would have imagined pixies dancing in a fairy ring would create. The light coalesced into a solid, rainbow-colored glow, then flickered out.

Oh! Magic is just like sex, she thought. *It works better with your eyes open.*

She heard a commotion out in the dining room. The restaurant's front door slammed, and heavy-booted feet marched in. Deep, threatening voices shouted, "Where is she? You were supposed to keep her here!"

One of the waitresses yelled back, "She went in there! We didn't let her get away! She's trapped!"

The next instant, the door rattled from a vicious kick.

"Come out now and we won't hurt you!" the voice from the other side of the door demanded.

I bet. Just kill me, disintegrate me, and turn me into dust motes.

"Eat shit and die, scum-sucking maggot!" Minerva yelled back. It was sort of cliché, but she'd always wanted to say that. She'd just never had the chance before.

The restroom had no window, no other doors, and solid walls. Minerva tried scraping her way through what she had hoped would be dried mud. But the walls, under a thin wattle-and-daub coating, were solid stone masonry. The building, which had looked primitive and not terribly durable, was in fact a disguised fort.

The door shuddered with repeated kicks. Her huge beam, its bolts sunk into solid stone, would hold against almost anything. But the door itself wasn't very sturdy. The instant one of her pursuers took an ax to it, he'd be through. She thought desperately, then drew a bolt running vertically through the door into the floor below and the huge lintel above. As an afterthought, she sketched what she imagined as two-inch-thick metal cladding to line the back of the door.

It shimmered into existence.

The next kick, when it came, was muffled, but the swearing wasn't. *Hope he broke his leg*, Minerva thought. The door wouldn't hold forever, she thought with some amusement, but it would give her a little time.

What she was going to do with that time was another matter entirely.

Darryl had found a way to communicate with her. She wondered if she could communicate back. Minerva recalled the dragon Birkwelch saying something about Darryl watching things through her eyes—seeing everything she saw in the mirror back home. If that were the case, Darryl would be able to read notes she wrote to him, if she just looked at them. And whatever trick he had discovered for writing to her, perhaps he could perform again.

She wrote, *Darryl, can you read this?*

After an instant, glowing print appeared in the air in front of her.

Yes.

How do I get out of here? she scribbled.

The machine characters scrolled through the air. Dragon says draw a door.

She stared at the solution for an instant. "Shit," she muttered. "Of course." Behind her, the things that were after her began to batter the door with something heavier than their boots. A felled tree, she guessed. Or maybe the old man's truck. They wanted her pretty badly.

She wondered what was on the other side of the wall—and wished she had some weapon besides the little silver knife. What she knew about the functionings and operations of weapons, however, she could stuff into the point of a bullet with room left over.

And then Minerva remembered Mrs. Mindley that day at FoodLion—the day the whole mess started. She remembered wishing her grocery cart had sported front-mounted machine guns and a flamethrower, so she could blow the wicked witch of Data Processing away. And Minerva smiled.

"Yeah. That's what I need. The shopping cart from hell. But motorized."

With the rattling and clanging and shouting behind her, and the first tendrils of smoke curling under the door, it was hard to concentrate, but she forced herself. She needed to get the design right. She settled on a wide-tread four-wheeled vehicle with large tires. She hurried the artwork, and the thing came out looking like a demented moon rover. *Live with it*, she thought. She drew her best guess for a flamethrower mounted on a swivel stand on the left side of the dash, and a few lines suggesting a machine gun on the right. Big seat with harness seatbelts, rollbar over the top, glass bubble half-shell cover designed to give her two-hundred degrees of field of fire. Then the operating details—steering wheel, ignition key, accelerator pedal, brake, and speedometer with the top speed—actually the only speed—marked at one hundred miles per hour.

Detroit would laugh itself sick.

The hinges on the door behind her gave with a sickening crack. Minerva stared at her sketch and concentrated. Metal screeched against stone, and the smoke grew thicker and more acrid. And Murp yowled in terror. In the midst of the turmoil, the light of her magic coalesced slowly. She controlled the size and shape of her evolving vehicle, and watched with pleasure as it became solid beneath her hands.

Now the door out of here.

She belted herself into the buggy with the duffel strapped around her waist, pressed her foot on the brake, then turned the key which grew out of the ignition. *Shit*, she thought, noticing an omission in her vehicle's design. *Forgot a gear shift. Bet it doesn't do reverse.* The motor made no noise, but she could feel it vibrate and pull against the brake. *Good enough.* She spread the vellum on her knee, and with charcoal drew a long, smooth arch. She focused on the wall she hoped led out of the building entirely and concentrated on making it go away.

It did.

Water sprayed out of the hole in the wall—gushing out of plumbing no longer connected to anything. Voices on the other side of the wall shouted. Minerva couldn't tell what was out there. *Oh, well.*

She took her foot off the brake and pressed the accelerator, and the buggy launched itself from the restroom into the great unknown like a thoroughbred from a starting gate. Her drawing flew from her lap and fluttered behind her. People welled up in front of her and dove to either side, screaming. A flock of winged nightmares—toothy man-sized horrors—flapped into the air at the sight of her and flew her way. She'd come out on a cobblestoned street, a busy one, full of late-afternoon shoppers carrying home their treasures, and farmers with their beasts and their carts nearly empty of produce, and an entire herd of small children, perched safely out of the way, who shouted and laughed as she rocketed by.

The buggy was still accelerating. She lifted her foot from the accelerator pedal, but the infernal thing seemed to have a mind of its own. It bounded down the street, caroming off the uneven road surface. The grips of both the flamethrower and the machine gun swung and bucked. The machine gun butt hit her in the face so hard she saw stars. She didn't dare take her hands off the wheel to see if it had done any damage, but from the pain and the feeling of wet warmth on her right cheek, she was pretty sure it had opened the side of her face.

Bad design, she thought. *Fucking awful design.*

She pushed on the brake and slowed. Immediately one of the huge winged things passed her, wheeled around, and dove. She hit the brake harder, grabbed the flamethrower grip with her left hand, and pulled the trigger.

This turned out to be a tactical error. Flame shot out and roasted the diving monster—but it also washed back at her. She jerked her hand away from that weapon and gunned the buggy again. The falling monster hit the glass dome over her head with a solid thud and slid off behind her.

One down. She tried to be enthusiastic about her first kill, but a quick look over her shoulder showed there were entirely too many where that came from.

All she could smell was singed hair and blood. She felt

like she had the worst sunburn of her life, and if what she knew of burns was correct, that pain was only going to get worse. She needed to look at the compass to see which way she had to go, and she couldn't slow down enough to pull it out of her bag. The damned buggy had two speeds; stop and one-hundred miles-per-hour.

On the other hand, she thought, brightening a little, *I'm not stuck in the bathroom anymore, and now I don't have to walk.*

"She shouldn't have a flamethrower or a machine gun," Birkwelch said.

Darryl ignored the dragon. "All right!" he screamed. "Good save, Minerva! Way to go." He typed furiously:

    Miraculously, Minerva didn't run over
    anyone. She got out of town without crash-
    ing, and raced toward the place where her
    children were being held hostage.

"Does she always drive like that?" Birkwelch interrupted.

Darryl looked closer at the mirror. For the briefest of instants at a time, he would get a glimpse of the speedometer. The needle looked like it was glued at one hundred. He thought about it for an instant, then nodded and laughed. "Yeah. Usually worse."

"Eeep!" The dragon rubbed his long muzzle thoughtfully. "She was driving a station wagon and nearly ran me down— guess I should have known." He watched a little longer. "I wish she'd look behind her. I'd like to know how many of the Weirds are keeping up with her."

"You don't think she lost them?"

"Not a chance." The dragon sighed. "Their magic doesn't compare to hers while she's wearing a Ring, but flying is one of their specialties. She won't evade them just by driving fast."

Darryl felt confident. He'd figured out the trick of making messages appear in the air. He'd gotten her safely away from the disguised Weird who'd caught her. And she was out of the town and hadn't flattened a single pedestrian. He was getting the hang of magic.

"So what does she need? What could get rid of flying Weirds?"

The dragon gave him a sidelong glance and said, "Well, I could, if I were there. But I'm not."

"Can you get there?"

"Not in time. I'd have to go through the gate—which would dump me at the Hallyehenge, and *that* is a couple hours from where she is, flying fast."

Darryl nodded. "I see." He studied his typewritten page, with its cryptic descriptions of the events he'd made happen in Eyrith, and nibbled on the skin on the inside of his lower lip. "Yeah. Birkwelch—do dragons come in flocks—or what?"

"Only during orgies."

Darryl gave the blue dragon a nasty glare—and the beast grinned.

"The term for large groups of dragons is a thunder. A thunder of dragons." Birkwelch sighed and said wistfully, "There haven't been enough dragons to make up a decent thunder in more than a century."

"A thunder." Darryl nodded thoughtfully. "Okay. Thanks."

Darryl began typing again.

```
    Out of nowhere, a thunder of dragons
darkened the sky. They plummeted into the
center of the Weirds, and drove them from
the air. The Weirds fled into the woods, and
the dragons hunted them down to devour them.
```

He looked up at the mirror, eager to see his next miracle take place. Immediately the fact occurred to him that it took a hell of a lot of dragons to darken a sky. A whole hell of a lot. He hadn't seen so many flying things since he watched Hitchcock's *The Birds*.

A second fact followed right behind that first one. Birkwelch had fainted. At least Darryl assumed he had only fainted. He was sprawled out beside and behind Darryl, his eyes partly open and rolled back so only the whites were showing. The dragon's mouth gaped, and his tongue lolled out to one side.

Birkwelch looked disgusting, Darryl decided.

He checked the mirror. Minerva had come to a complete halt. She was firing the flamethrower with one hand and the machine gun with the other. She was shooting indiscriminately, he noted—and hitting more of his dragons than she was the Weirds he'd sent the dragons to get rid of. Then he saw why. One of the dragons came in at her—low, fast, and from the side. Minerva caught the movement out of the corner of her eye, and turned in time to lay down a steady pattern of machine gun fire. The big beast went down, crashing into the side of her buggy. Then he saw the world lurch, as Minerva turned to face another monster that had attacked from the other side.

"Dammit, dammit, dammit!" Darryl yelled, and ran back to the typewriter. He sat down and wrote—

    The dragons quit attacking Minerva and
    concentrated exclusively on the Weirds. They
    did not bother the little buggy as it drove
    off to safety.

"That ought to fix it," he muttered.

He watched the mirror. Minerva was in the middle of a flame duel. A dragon on her left belched huge gouts of fire at her. One on her right was keeping low and just out of range of her machine gun. Others hovered in front . . . waiting. The Weirds were nowhere around, but that seemed less comforting than it would have seconds earlier.

"So leave her alone already!" he yelled. "Leave her alone, dammit!"

His hands pounded the keyboard.

    The dragons are her friends. They will
    not hurt Minerva. They are good, friendly
    dragons who eat Weirds but **will not touch
    Minerva!!!**

"That won't work." Birkwelch had come around, and was staring over his shoulder. "Dragons are like people. We're creatures of free will. You can set us up to fit into a scenario, but once the scenario is set, you cannot change the natures of dragons on a whim." The dragon shook his head slowly. "You've established your characters. You created man-eaters there. They aren't going to turn all nice and cozy for you after they've done your dirty work."

Darryl stared at the dragon, and his mouth fell open. "You mean I'm stuck with them like that? I can't fix them?" He stared at the mirror in horror. Minerva was fighting for her life on the other side of it, and she looked like she was losing. "I thought I could do anything."

"Everything has rules. You can do anything, as long as you work within the rules."

Darryl wrapped his arms around himself and looked through his wife's eyes at the steady stream of oncoming horrors.

"What can I do?"

Beside him, the dragon sighed. "I don't know. Maybe she knows."

Darryl rested his fingers on the keyboard. *Don't fuck it up this time*, he told himself. Minerva couldn't survive too many more of his mistakes. He had another idea. This one, at least, seemed harmless. He took a deep breath, then typed—

```
Darryl  spoke  to  Minerva,  and  for  the
first  time  his  voice  carried  to  her,  and
when  she  spoke  to  him,  he  could  hear  her.
```

"Minerva?" Darryl said softly. He became aware that he could hear a thread of conversation in the back of his mind. It went, " . . . goddamned sonovabitching luck to get run over by dragons how the hell am I going to get myself out of this one; I can't even take the time to draw anything . . ."

That was Minerva. Evidently she was talking too loud to hear him. He yelled, "Minerva! Listen! Just tell me what you need, and I'll do it."

The steady stream of profanity died, cut off in mid-verb.
"Darryl?"

"Yes, baby. It's me. What do you need?"

Minerva had her answer ready. "I need to get rid of these
dragons."

"I know that," he shouted. "I can see that. But what do
you need to get rid of the dragons?"

"It would be nice if they could just disappear the way they
appeared. The machine gun and the flamethrower seem to
have an unlimited supply of ammo, but they're both getting
too hot to handle."

"Can I make the dragons disappear?" Darryl asked Birkwelch.

"You can." Birkwelch looked grim. "That's Unweaving—
and every time you do it, you hand the Unweaver some of
your magic. But I don't see any other alternative this time.
Just promise to replace them when you can—maybe that
will repair the Unweaving."

"Fine," Darryl said. "Someday I'll make you some more
dragons."

He typed—

    As abruptly as they'd arrived, the drag-
ons vanished.

This time his magic worked. The dragons melted away
without a trace. He could tell Minerva had dropped into the
seat of her buggy.

"Are you okay?" he asked her.

"I've been better. I've got some bad burns, and I'm cut
up. And I'm tired." She sounded damn near dead.

"The Weirds are gone. With any luck, you won't have any
more of those to bother you. But watch for the green eyes,
okay? That's your tip-off." Darryl couldn't help but be happy.
The two of them could talk to each other again. He'd missed
her—missed her touch and her presence and her warmth,
but hearing her made her seem not so far away. It was easier
to believe she really was alive somewhere when she talked
to him.

"The Weirds—the big flying things . . . and the farmer, too?"

"Yes. They can change shapes—look like anything they want. They're the ones who want us dead."

"Figures." Minerva opened her duffel bag. Darryl could see her pulling Murp out of it and stroking the cat. "It's going to be okay now," she crooned. "We're going to get the kids."

Darryl noticed Minerva's vision becoming blurry in spite of her glasses. He saw a slight edge of gray around her field of vision.

She's about to faint, he thought. "Minerva," he shouted, "lie down. I'm going to send you a first aid kit and some Gatorade. Drink as much of it as you can and keep your feet up."

Minerva lay her head on the back of the seat and stared up at the darkening sky. "Okey-doke," she agreed.

Minerva never said "Okey-doke."

```
     A gallon of Gatorade and an incredibly
complete first aid kit that contained a
handy field guide to first aid appeared on
the floorboard of the buggy next to Minerva.
```

Minerva looked down, and saw the rucksack in the floor-board. "Thanks, Darryl," she said.

"I love you, baby," he told her.

Darryl heard an ambulance siren screaming up the street. "I love you, too," Minerva told him. It felt good to hear her say that—

Boy, that ambulance is loud, he thought. *It sounds like it's right outside the house.* "Min—I'll talk to you later. Find someplace safe, and get some rest." He heard her muffled reply as he headed for the door.

He opened it.

His mother stood on the other side.

Darryl yelped, and said, "Mom!"

The ambulance *was* outside his house. The siren quit howling. The ambulance doors slammed. *Oh, God,* he thought, *something's happened to Dad.* His mother's face was ash-gray, and she wrung her hands. She looked like she's been dancing with the dead. "Mom . . . is Dad okay?"

Downstairs, he heard people talking—voices he didn't recognize. His mother nodded vigorously, but didn't say anything.

She watched him as though she thought he might suddenly sprout wings and fly; it was only when he realized she was worried for—or about—him that it occurred to him she might have overheard him in the art room.

"Mom," he said, trying hard to sound calm, "when did you get here?"

She gnawed on her bottom lip and frowned. "About ten or fifteen minutes ago," she admitted.

Best case, ten minutes. What had he said and done in the last ten minutes? He'd shouted at his dead wife. He'd talked to an invisible dragon. He'd typed lots of oddball stuff on the typewriter that, if taken seriously by anyone, would certainly seem to indicate he was nuts. Not good. Not at all good. He took a deep breath. Smiled.

"Mom," he said, "there are a lot of things going on you're going to have to trust me about. It will all make sense soon," he promised. *I hope,* he added silently.

His mother pressed her hand to her cheek. She looked ready to cry. "Oh, sweetheart, you've been under so much pressure—"

"He's upstairs right now," Darryl heard his father say. The tread of heavy feet echoed in the entryway, and two burly EMTs came around the corner of the stairwell.

Thanks, Dad. Darryl looked down at them, they looked up at him—the whole scene reminded him of a shootout at high noon. Any second one of them was going to say, "Are you going to come quietly or do we have to shoot you?"— Darryl could feel it coming. His mom said, "Darryl, we called the ambulance. These nice men are here to help you."

Birkwelch peeked out the art room door. *"Nice men?* Now she's talking baby talk, no less," the dragon said. "If I were you, I'd pretend to be sane."

Pretend? I am sane. I hope. Darryl wanted to tell the

damned dragon off, or at least give him a dirty look—but he didn't dare. All those people were watching.

"Mr. Kiakra," one of the EMTs said, "we really think you ought to come to the hospital with us. The doctor can help you, and you will feel better."

"I don't need a doctor," Darryl said, backing up. "I feel just fine already—all things considered."

His mother stage-whispered, "Darryl, you were talking to Minerva. And saying things about making dragons disappear—" She seemed to don resolution before his eyes. Her hands went to her hips and her voice grew firm and sure. "I want you to go to the hospital and let them check you out. Maybe the doctor can give you a prescription that will help you. *Everybody* needs help sometimes, and we all understand how terrible all of this has been."

Then her eyes filled with tears. He hated it when she cried. "Darryl," she whispered, "I've lost my grandchildren and my daughter-in-law. I don't want to lose my son, too. Please . . . for me . . ."

Darryl knew when he was beat.

"I'll go," he told her. "For you. But I'm not crazy, Mom. I'm really not."

He walked down the stairs to meet the two EMTs and said he could drive himself. They told him that was all right, and they were sure he could, but since they'd come all the way out and had to go to the hospital anyway, there wasn't any need. They were giving him the kid-gloves treatment, but he didn't protest. *Protesting your sanity to people who've already decided you're nuts,* he thought, *is a sure way to convince them you're nuts.*

Birkwelch rode with him to the hospital, sitting primly in the shotgun seat of the ambulance, leaning around the corner from time to time to make faces at the driver. Darryl pretended not to notice.

"I don't know where we'll get food now," Jamie complained.

Carol shook Barney again. "He won't even move. Jamie, I'm really scared."

Barney listened to her, but he didn't respond. He wished she would go away. He wished *everything* would go away.

"The Unweaver isn't going to give us food or water," Jamie said. "He wants us to starve."

"Barney doesn't care anymore."

"I care." Barney could hear Jamie pacing back and forth in the tiny cell. "The monsters—didn't they say something about how they couldn't see the road because you had to have the right kind of magic to see it?"

"Well, yeah," Carol agreed. "But they musta' been wrong, 'cause we could see it."

"What if they were right, though? Would that mean we could do magic, too?"

Barney began to take a slight interest in the proceedings. Could they do magic? he wondered. No—they just hoped they could.

"How did he do it—do you know?" Jamie asked.

They couldn't do magic. Only he could. He'd show them.

Barney sat up. At first, he felt weak and floaty, almost like his body was mostly air. As he sat, though, he began to feel more solid—and as he felt more solid, his feet started hurting again.

He whimpered from the pain.

"He's awake!" Carol said, and ran over and hugged him.

"No mushy stuff," Barney growled—but he was secretly pleased with the attention.

"Okay." Jamie sat down and looked at the cut places on Barney's feet. "Those are getting kind of bad, Barney," he said. "If you know how to make them better, you ought to do it."

Barney smiled a little smile. "I know how to do magic."

"Then do it. Don't leave your feet like that."

Barney nodded. His big brother made sense, he thought. He stared at his feet. They were all red and swollen, and the bottoms were all slashed up, and had yellow stuff running out of them. He felt a little sick. He tried to do something to make them okay—but the more he tried, the more he couldn't do anything.

He sat back, feeling maybe he ought to just curl up in the corner again.

"Can't you fix them?" Carol asked.

"No."

"Why not?"

Barney yelled, "I don't know! Okay? I don't know!" He started to cry.

His brother sat down on the mattress beside him. "Can you do other magic?"

Barney sniffled. "I . . . I don't know."

"Try something," Carol whispered. "Try some chocolate. That would be nice."

Chocolate, Barney thought. Even through the haze of pain, with his feet throbbing and burning and hurting so bad, he could think *chocolate*. The taste, the smell, the feel—Barney could make chocolate real. He held out his hand, and the candy shimmered to life in his palm.

"Here," he said, and handed it to Carol. "You can have it."

Jamie grinned broadly. "See? You can do it. You really can. So do some magic, and make your feet better."

"I—I can't."

Jamie snorted with frustration. "Tell me how you make chocolate. What makes the magic work? 'Cause if it works for chocolate, it will work for your feet, too."

Barney didn't want to be stubborn, but he couldn't seem to help it. "It won't."

"Bar-r-r-ney . . . this is important."

Barney tried to figure it out. "I can think about the chocolate," he said. "Even when it isn't here, I know just what it's like. So I can make it. But I guess—I guess my feet hurt so bad I don't remember what they felt like when they didn't. So I can't fix them."

"That's magic?" Jamie sounded disappointed, almost like that wasn't good enough.

"You can't do it."

"Maybe I can. I was trying to remember magic spells, like 'hocus-pocus,' but those didn't work." Jamie frowned. "I'd like a hot dog, I think." He sat cross-legged on the mattress beside Barney, and squinched his face all up, and knotted his fists into tight little balls. "Hotdog," he muttered. "Hotdog. I want a hotdog."

Barney watched him with interest. He didn't think he looked anywhere near so silly when he did magic.

No hotdogs appeared.

Barney grinned. "You have to smell it cooking—and you have to taste how it tastes when you bite it. You have to feel the hot in your mouth. You have to vision biting it so much you think you already have it—"

Jamie yelped, and spit something brown and round out of his mouth. "Too *hot!*" he yelped, and sat there panting with his tongue hanging out like a dog's.

Barney laughed. "You got to vision it in your hand, dummyhead—not your mouth." And then he realized his big, poophead brother had done magic, and he grew quiet. It wasn't fair—after all, he was the littlest. He needed magic. Jamie didn't.

"Let me practice," Jamie said, and sat on the bed for a while, making ice cream and chocolate and cake and icy cold cans of Coca Cola that turned out to be impossible to open because Jamie had never paid very close attention to how those pop-tops worked.

And then Jamie bent over and looked at Barney's feet. "I know what they're supposed to look like," he said. "Maybe I can fix 'em." He stared, and his face grew thoughtful, and suddenly Barney felt warm, wonderful tingling where before there had only been pain.

Jamie stopped after a minute. "I'm tired," he said. "Do they feel better?"

"Lots." Barney bent his leg to look at the sole of one foot. It had interesting scars on it—but the red and the bleeding and the gross yellow stuff were all gone.

"I'm gonna quit, then," Jamie said. "I need a nap."

In the far corner of the room, Carol suddenly shrieked. "I did it!" A butterfly, bright orange and purple, like nothing Barney had ever seen before, fluttered around her head.

Barney eyed her, disgusted. *She* could do magic, too? It just wasn't fair.

Nothing was fair, he thought darkly.

"You know what I want more than anything in the world?" Carol whispered.

"You want to go home," Barney growled.

"That we could have, I mean."

"No. What do you want?"

"You know the crystal ball in *The Wizard of Oz*? The one Dorothy sees Aunt Em in?"

Barney nodded.

"I want one of those. So we can see Mommy."

Barney was still grouchy. "Then make one. *I'm* not going to."

She glared at him. "Stinky boy." she said. "If I have to make it by myself, I won't let you look in it."

Barney wanted to see Mommy, too. He sighed, and got carefully to his feet, and gently stepped on them. They worked okay, he thought. Suddenly he was a little bit glad Jamie could do magic. And Carol, too, he decided. He guessed he could be generous—and besides, Carol had the good idea about the crystal ball.

Barney and Carol sat beside each other. "We should hold hands," Carol said.

Barney shrugged. "Okay."

"We have to both tell this so it will work. I think it's a big ball—"

"—big as a basketball—"

"—okay—and the glass is real green an' shiny—"

—and all you have to do to make it work is look in it and say what you want to see—"

"—and it's on a pretty stand, so it won't roll, or break—"

"There it is!" Barney whispered. "There it comes!"

Carol dropped his hand and hugged herself. "Oh, yes! Isn't it beautiful?"

The magic crystal ball grew in front of them, shimmering into existence beneath the busy glow of the tiny firefly lights. And when the firefly lights vanished, it glowed anyway— beautiful, beautiful.

Barney and Carol looked from the ball to each other.

"You first," Carol said.

"That's okay. I've done lots of magic. You can go first."

Carol smiled. "Okay," she whispered, "I want to see Mommy."

The inside of the ball grew brighter and brighter. Then a picture grew in the middle of the green fire, and some of the brightness died down so the two of them could stand to look.

Barney could see her. Mommy. She was coming for them—and she had guns.

"All right, Mommy!" he said under his breath. "Get 'em."

CHAPTER 12

Minerva dreamed of her children, and her husband, and her home; of her life before it fell apart, or more correctly was ripped apart—but when she woke, nothing remained of the dream but the tattered ghosts of voices crying, "Mommy, come get us."

Minerva uncurled from her place on the seat of her buggy and stretched. Her entire body ached. The burned places on her skin were little islands of terrible pain in a sea of duller hurts. Her right cheek felt hot and swollen—she had discovered an antiseptic cream in Darryl's emergency kit and used that, but it didn't seem to have helped much.

I must have passed out after I applied the goop, she thought. She wondered how long she'd been out.

Her clothes were damp, the faintest of lights pinked the horizon in front of her. She had been, she thought, traveling east. Which would make that faint light sunrise . . . and that would mean she had survived a night sleeping in the open. Lucky. Getting underway as soon as possible seemed a prudent idea. Luck had a nasty way of running out when counted on.

Murp, of course, wasn't in the bag anymore.

"Murp," she called softly. She heard no catlike sounds. If Murp were around and safe, she should have no difficulty bringing him to her. The cat was fond of his stomach and had formed an almost spiritual attachment to Tender Vittles.

The sound of one of those paper wrappers tearing ought to bring him on the run.

She magicked up a couple packets of the cat food, and while she was at it, a sizzling hot plate of steak and eggs for herself, and some classy silverware to eat it with. *Might as well live a little,* she couldn't keep herself from thinking. *No telling how much longer I'll have the opportunity.*

A bathtub would have been her next creation—she felt scrungy and disreputable. She suspected she smelled. But the idea of submerging her burned skin in water made her stomach twist into knots; and, too, the faster she got underway, the sooner she'd reach the children.

Murp appeared at her side before she'd even torn the first wrapper. He leapt onto the seat of the buggy next to her and studied her steak with a gimlet eye. She opened the cat food and waved the paper packet under his nose, but he remained unswayed. Murp had apparently decided after what he'd been through, he deserved to live a little, too.

Minerva scratched him between the ears and conjured him up a nice little steak—raw—and sliced it into tiny pieces. He gave her a grateful look before he inhaled the meat, and she felt gratified.

She decided to plan ahead a bit. No one was on the road near her—she could detect no signs of danger. She had no intention of making another roaring-across-the-country-out-of-control joyride. The previous day's sketch of her vehicle was long gone, of course. She sketched another on her final sheet of vellum, and added an automatic gearshift that included reverse and additional markings on the speedometer, in ten-mile-per-hour increments. "No sense making that same mistake twice." She also added a dash mount for the compass, so she could see where she was going and where she needed to be at the same time. The improved buggy appeared behind the first.

"Let's get a move on," she told the cat. In front of her the sky had pinked up, and the scars on the earth around her were becoming visible. She stared at the black, burned gashes and torn ground that formed a perimeter around her buggy, and shivered. "We made a mess last night, cat. We are damned lucky to still be here." Murp looked up at her, round-eyed and unconcerned, and *mrrrped*. *God, I'm glad the cat's here. If I didn't have him, I wouldn't have anyone at all to talk to—*

That wasn't quite right anymore, though, was it? Hadn't Darryl found some way of speaking with her? She seemed to remember that, although the memories might have been false, created by her distress and her wish that such a thing were possible.

"Darryl? Are you there?" she asked. She got no response. She took a deep breath, and said loudly, "Darryl, if you can hear me, say something!"

"Sh-h-h-h-h-h!" She heard him plainly. She nodded thoughtfully. He was there—but this was evidently not a good time. She considered for a moment that he did not have her luxury of being alone in the wilderness—some luxury. Hah! Nevertheless, she could talk to him anytime, whereas she could see he would have to watch his moments.

"Talk to me when you get the chance then," she said. And added as a wistful afterthought, "I wish you were here."

He didn't reply.

She started the buggy and followed the arrow back out to the main road, then east and south. She kept the buggy at about sixty miles per hour, and within a half hour was at a crossroads of sorts. The road she was on continued steadily southeast, its tarmac gleaming in the bright sunshine. Another road crossed it, an overgrown cobblestone-paved track that ran southwest and northeast. To the southwest it didn't look too bad—not kept up, but there was nothing about it that worried Minerva. To the northeast, the road vanished into weeds and a copse of mangled trees, and the sky above the track hung low and glowering, shimmering with heatwaves and crackling with energy. Thunderheads piled on top of each other, their bellies full and dark and angry.

The compass pointed northeast. Minerva drove tentatively past the intersection, and the needle whipped backwards, almost with angry emphasis, to point at the road she was trying to leave behind.

Of course. It can never be the nice white house with the picket fence, can it? It always has to be the castle ruins on the hill with the booming door knocker and things in the dungeon.

She turned back, reluctance dragging at her gut, and steered the buggy onto the track. She crossed a line there; no sooner had the back tires left the main road that she felt as if she'd walked open-eyed through an enormous spiderweb. Beside her, Murp arched his back and hissed and spat at nothing. Minerva whimpered quietly in the back of her throat and rested one hand on the grip of the flamethrower.

She drove carefully, but as fast as she dared. She felt eyes watching her from the close overgrowth on either side of the road. From time to time as she came around a curve, she would catch sight of something shambling across the track ahead of her. Brush cracked around her, shadows lurked—and the spiderwebby feel of the air became thicker and more pronounced the further into the wasteland she penetrated.

The trees shrank, and became warped and hideous; tumored, gray-leaved. Bare patches of ground appeared— not rich dark earth, but hardscrabble, bleachbone white. Something had sucked the life out of this land and left its wraiths sobbing in the air. Minerva drove by an abandoned cottage, its hipped roof swaybacked, its windows empty and dark; shadows clung to the house like spanish moss. A bit further on she passed another just like it, and then a clump of them all together; dead places, full of palpable ghosts even in daylight. Her skin crawled. She constantly felt unseen things that touched her, licked at her skin with damp, slippery tongues, poked and pinched with invisible fingers.

The needle on her compass pointed onward—into worse. Barney and Carol and Jamie were somewhere ahead—and though she yearned with her whole heart to retreat, to find someplace safe to hide, there was no one else who could do what had to be done. *Courage isn't feeling brave,* she thought. *It's going on when you're scared shitless.* She kept going.

Murp growled suddenly, stiffened on the seat beside her, and all his fur stood straight out. Then he streaked down to the floor of the buggy and squeezed himself into the duffel bag. This did not seem a cheerful omen to Minerva. She sensed nothing different in the air around her—the place was increasingly awful, but seemed to be growing worse at a steady pace, without anything that would suddenly spook the cat. Still, cats *sensed* things. She kept driving, trying to look over her shoulder and to both sides at the same time, goosing the acclerator at every straight stretch.

A low, shuddering wail reached out of the ghastly trees to her right and tore straight through her, into her bones. She had never heard a sound like it—and hoped she never would again. She wished for engine noise or road noise— anything to cover it. It went on and on, then died in an awful gurgling sob. That wail seemed to be a signal. From the dying lands to either side of her, shambling two-legged monsters from a demented artist's post-holocaust nightmare dragged themselves forth. They stared at her, glared at her, while their hands reached out in threat or supplication, and their ragged, sloppy mouths emitted nerve-scraping keening wails.

Oh, no! Her heart pounded up into her throat. There seemed to be hundreds of them moving onto the narrow, weed-choked road. He finger twitched on the trigger of the flamethrower, but stopped. Dead, dry grass and weeds surrounded her. The flamethrower might clear those hideous shambling things out of her way, but would give her an obstacle that was potentially worse.

She reached for the machine gun—and a sight caught her eye that left her stunned. One of the things held a bundle in its arm—a baby. Its other hand held the hand of a smaller creature. Mother and children. She took her hand from the weapon, and yelled, "Get out of the way!" She slowed just a bit, and the things cleared passage for her, though they still reached out to touch the buggy as it passed and left smears of themselves on the glass.

What happened to the people who had once lived in those desolate houses? Where they killed? Unwoven? Or were they the creatures who stood by the road, awaiting hope and salvation from any source?

"I'm going after the Unweaver!" she yelled. "I'm going to make things right!"

The gurgling wails and the hideous keening rose in pitch and volume. Minerva felt sick.

The nightmare creatures fell behind her, as did the last signs of life. She entered onto a sere and inclement plain where nothing grew, and the air, oppressive before, became parched and sand-laden. The road ran on, a cobblestone ribbon between two seas of dried mudflats; gray earth touched gray sky along a ribbon of billowing, seething black that ran from one edge of the horizon to the other. Minerva had never seen anyplace in her life she wanted to go less. But the compass pointed on, so she went on.

Then the voices started.

"Mommy," Carol whispered, "the crazy man says he'll hurt us if you come here."

"Mommy, Mommy, Mommy! I'm so scared! Come get me!" Barney wailed, then screamed—in terror or pain, Minerva couldn't tell.

"Mom, this guy says you gave us to him because you didn't want us anymore. He's lying, isn't he?" Jamie sounded weary, and hopeless.

Her children, her babies—that bastard was trying to destroy her by hurting them. But he could see her coming, knew where she was every second—and he could hurt them, she suspected. She was afraid the threat wasn't an empty one.

She stopped the buggy, turned it off, and stared ahead of her. What could she do? She would have paid good money for an easy answer.

Murp poked his head out of the duffel and yowled. He looked around him and sniffed the air, and his ears plastered themselves flat against his skull. He retreated to the inner world of the bag again. Minerva could feel for him. She wished she could retreat to a nice safe cocoon and still do what had to be done. She wished she could be invisible, or two places at once—

An idea occurred to her. "Darryl," she said softly, "I need help."

Darryl didn't answer. *He could still be in an awkward spot and not able to talk*, she reasoned. *Maybe if I just tell him what I need, and let him know I need it fast, he can get to someplace private.*

If the Unweaver could hear her whispered requests, she was doomed. Of course, if she couldn't get through to Darryl, she was probably doomed anyway—and the kids, too.

Sitting in a parked buggy at the edge of a desert, with a hellish storm brewing, Minerva outlined her plan to an absent husband she only hoped could hear her.

Darryl heard her, all right. Her timing sucked. From what he could tell, there didn't seem to be much she could do about that, though.

Dr. Folchek settled back into his seat, and scratched something on his notepad. "I see. So you were merely writing fiction, and reading the bits of it out loud to yourself. You did *not* hear voices speaking to you? That's what you're saying?"

"That's what I'm saying. Look, Doctor. I was at my wife's funeral yesterday. I know the score. We don't have to keep dancing around this, while you act like I'm telling you deeply significant stuff."

"But you are telling me 'deeply significant stuff,' Darryl. Do you realize in the hour we've talked, you have used all sorts of vague euphemisms relating to your wife and children, but not once have you come out and said the word 'dead'? Your guilt over not having been at home during this tragedy is evident, as is your denial that they are all, in fact, gone." The scrawny little bastard smiled slightly, and said, "There. You even have me doing it. I said 'gone' when I meant to say 'dead.'" Folchek steepled his fingers and sighed. "Your reponses evidence poor coping mechanisms, some neurotic tendencies, and grave instability. You are aware of the world around you, but you are not, for the moment, living in it." He picked up his pen and tapped it on the pad. "I'll point out to you, since you don't seem to realize it—that writing fiction starring your dead wife is not an appropriate response to day-of-the-funeral stress. It smacks of denial."

"Dr. Folchek, you'll pardon me for saying so, but you are full of shit." Darryl crossed his arms over his chest. "There is no 'appropriate' thing to do on the day of your wife's funeral. Now, I have to go take a leak. You mind?"

"Denial *and* hostility . . ." He shook his head sadly. "Of course you may use the restroom, Darryl. Please, be my guest. The door is right behind you."

Darryl wished the door were down the hall somewhere, but he could hardly ask for a restroom further from the office. Maybe the doctor would have a nice, noisy ventilation fan. Darryl snagged a pencil from the top of a file cabinet on his way in, but Dr. Folchek caught him.

"Please leave the pencils out here, Darryl." The man's voice chased after him. "If you wish to write something, you are welcome to write it out here."

Darryl put the pencil back on the cabinet and swore vehemently under his breath. He went into the bathroom, flipped on the light, and looked for the doorlock. There wasn't one. There wasn't a ventilation fan, either. He'd have to keep it quiet. Of course, without a pencil, his plan to write down the things Minerva needed to happen and flush the evidence once he'd written it was, well, down the toilet.

Darryl sat on the commode and looked around the bathroom. There was nothing—*nothing*—in there he could use to write . . . or scratch in wood . . . or smear on the floor.

There was a mirror, placed by someone who apparently enjoyed watching himself crap. Darryl wondered if the shrink himself couldn't have stood a bit of therapy. Still, it was the first one he'd seen since the day before, when the EMTs brought him to the hospital, and his parents and the ER doctor insisted he stay at least until the shrink could do his evaluation. He'd shared a ward with a real wacko, and the room had not contained anything potentially dangerous.

Darryl looked through Minerva's eyes at the grim terrain

she faced, and at that boiling wall of cloud. "Minerva," he whispered, as softly as he could, "sweetheart—I'm here. Give me a minute to figure out how to do this, and I'll have you ready to go."

He could tell she started at the sound of his voice—his view of the world in front of her jumped, then steadied again. And her voice reached him, calm and practical. "I'll be right here."

Darryl scrutinized the bathroom. A sink in a cheap wood cabinet, recessed fluorescent ceiling lighting with a bolted-down wire mesh over it, the toilet, a standard medical-facility hand-soap dispenser, an industrial toilet paper dispenser. The ugly mirror.

He needed to think fast. He could fake constipation if necessary, but even that would only buy him a short time.

He looked at the soap dispenser again. He could hear Folchek rummaging around in the other room. *Good—keep the little bastard busy,* he thought. He stood and got a good glop of soap on his finger, and with it, began to write on the mirror the things Minerva said she needed.

Minerva, her belongings and the cat became invisible—except to her husband—at the exact instant a double of each of these appeared. The double took the armed buggy, turned around, and retreated back the way Minerva had come. Meanwhile, Minerva, with her cat, her supplies, and a flying carpet that appeared in front of her, and which was also invisible, continued toward the children.

He waited a moment and watched the mirror. A tacky Persian rug with seatbelts appeared in his field of vision. "You got everything you need, Min?" he asked finally.

The scene in the mirror bounced wildly. He caught glimpses of Minerva in the weird peasant clothes he'd seen earlier, sitting in the hell-buggy she'd made, while her hands attached to a different body picked up the duffel, petted the cat, and strapped everything onto the rug. The sensation of viewing two of her was too uncomfortable to be believed. But when she glanced at herself, he looked wistfully. Even burned and filthy and ragged, she was beautiful and wonderful, and he missed the hell out of her.

"Okay," she told him. "The kid's voices are staying around the buggy. I suppose that means the Unweaver can't see me. I wish I knew that for sure. It's the sort of thing I would rather be very sure of." Her voice wobbled slightly, and she said, "Can't you come with me? I wish you were here. I'm so scared."

"I'm scared, too," he told her. "The dragon said the only gate is the one you came through, and I could go through it, but I'd end up the same place you started out."

"The Stonehenge place?"

"Yes."

He heard her sigh across worlds. "No good, then. You can probably help me more where you are."

"I know," he said. "At least, I can if I can get back home."

She paused, as if thinking over the implications of that. "What do you mean, *if* you can get home?"

"I'm in a bit of trouble over here. But I think I can convince the twit who's trying to lock me up that I'm sane."

The bathroom door opened. "I'd say your chances of that were fairly slim, actually, Darryl."

Darryl jerked around, and met Dr. Folchek's eyes. "This isn't what it looks like . . ." he started.

Dr. Folchek smiled a benign smile and nodded politely. "It never is. The mirror is two-way, you see. I apologize for the invasion of privacy, but I once had a lad kill himself in my bathroom. I've taken special precautions to make sure it never happened again."

Dr. Folchek shook his head sadly. "I confess you came very close to convincing me you were sane. Stressed, but sane. Your sort of psychotic break is frightening, though, Darryl. To be able to keep your personal demons under such control in public, and to give in to them so totally in private—"

"You don't understand. I'm just as sane as you are."

"Oh, I'm certain to you everything seems that way. Neurotics worry constantly about how crazy they are; psychotics don't. They are always certain they're sane. But Darryl, you must understand that talking to your dead wife and attempting this sort of—er, magical—yes, magical communication with her through writing proves you have suffered a break with the real world. Please understand that a high percentage of people who suffer traumatically induced psychotic breaks recover eventually. And, God knows, the trauma you've suffered is enough to induce . . ."

Darryl tuned him out. Behind him stood Birkwelch. "So much for making 'em believe you were normal, eh?"

"Yep," Darryl said.

"Yep?" Dr. Folchek stopped in mid-harangue and stared at Darryl. "Yep, what?"

"Let's have some fun. Wiggle your fingers at him," Birkwelch suggested. "Something magical-looking."

Darryl grinned, and made a few mystic passes with his hands, and uttered a couple of nonsense syllables. "Hod kahooda, nokooda noo," he intoned—and just for fun, crossed his eyes.

The dragon slowly lifted the doctor off the floor. The doctor began to shout, and then to scream. "Do a circle," Birkwelch said next.

Darryl slowly traced a circle in the air with his finger, and Birkwelch turned the doctor upside down.

Darryl made shooing motions with his hands, and Birkwelch backed the inverted doctor out into the main office. "They have this all on tape, you know," Birkwelch said.

"No shit?" Darryl grinned. "That ought to be good for another psychotic break or two."

"Darryl," the doctor said, "you must realize that these paranormal abilities are an outgrowth of your psychotic break from reality, and terribly dangerous. Please let me help you."

Darryl ignored him. He glared at the dragon, who had deposited the screaming doctor, still upside down, into his office chair. "Where the hell were you?"

"Waiting back at the house for you. I *did* think you would be able to convince these yo-yo's you were sane without help from me—probably a lot better than you could with my help." The dragon snorted a thin puff of smoke into the doctor's face, and the man began to cough. "Obviously I had too much faith in you."

"Fuck off," Darryl said, then grinned. "You can only convince them you're sane if they want to believe it. This turkey didn't." He looked toward the office door. "I imagine all hell is breaking loose out there. How do you propose we get out of here?"

"In the time-honored manner." The dragon pointed to the doctor's closet, and Darryl walked over and pulled out a set of scrubs.

"Wear those," the dragon suggested.

Darryl laughed. "Sure. Why not?" He quickly stripped off his patient gown and put on the scrubs. Birkwelch held the doctor's feet; Darryl removed his sneakers while the man struggled and screamed. Darryl put them on. "Shit," he said. "Minerva has feet this size." He let his heels hang out the back. "Car?"

"I brought mine."

"That mean you're driving?"

"I don't intend to let *you* drive my car."

The office door flew open, and several men dressed like Darryl ran in. They stopped when they saw the doctor upside down in his chair.

"I found him like that," Darryl said. "Babbling about flying. You got him?"

The doctor was screaming, "Stop him! Stop him!"

One of the orderlies nodded and started over to help Folchek, but the other stared at him suspiciously. "And who the hell are you?"

Darryl, primed by years of Minerva's hospital stories, sighed. "New radiologist. Willy Hill. I need to get back to work." He nodded to both men, and eased out the door.

"He's a patient," Folchek screeched.

Darryl and the dragon darted into the fire escape, and once hidden in the closed stairway, ran like hell.

"Be glad," the dragon said, "they didn't stick you on the locked ward. I would have had to take out a wall, and that would have been very hard to explain."

Darryl concentrated on running. He didn't bother answering.

They'd made it from the fifth floor down to the second when Darryl heard sirens.

"Ambulance?" he asked Birkwelch.

"Police." The dragon sounded certain.

Darryl wished there were some sort of window in the stairwell. He wanted to look out into the parking lot and see where the police cars were stopping. "Maybe they're going to the Emergency Room," he suggested. "Minerva says the police end up in the ER a lot."

"That's on the other side of the building from here."

"Don't suppose they're after us, do you?" Darryl said, though he figured they probably were.

"Nope." The dragon's voice was cheerful, and he glanced back at Darryl and grinned. "Not after us at all."

"Well, good."

"After *you*. They can't see me."

"I hate dragons," Darryl muttered.

They hit the bottom landing and charged into the hall. Two police officers stood there, waiting. As Darryl careened into view, they both pulled weapons and aimed them at him.

"He went that way!" Darryl yelled, and pointed down the hall.

"Don't even try it," the police officer said. "You're going to have to go back upstairs with us. If you go without any trouble, we won't have to put handcuffs on you."

"Birkwelch!" Darryl looked past the police officers to the dragon, who shrugged his wings.

"I can't stop bullets for you, pal. You'd better go with them for now." His face rilles flicked up and down. "I'll see if I can't figure out a way to spring you."

Darryl felt bitterness in his heart. "Oh, thanks," he snarled back at the dragon, as the policemen led him to the elevator. "Thanks just tons."

Barney, Jamie, and Carol sat around the crystal ball and watched Mommy coming to rescue them.

"She looks like Sigourney Weaver in *Alien*," Jamie said.

"She looks like Rambo," Barney added. Then he thought about that a second. "Except pretty," he added.

They cheered her on. Barney yelled and screamed as she'd passed the worm-monsters—who were looking pretty good, he thought. Jamie raised his fists in the air—his victory sign. Carol hugged herself and laughed and shouted.

Mommy was coming. This time, she was going to get them.

In the middle of the picture, a shadow suddenly twisted like smoke. It crowded out the picture of Mommy—and it looked at them with glowing red eyes.

It started to laugh.

"She won't be coming, children. She isn't strong enough—and she isn't brave enough." The Unweaver kept laughing. "And besides, you're going to tell her to go back."

"No, we aren't," Jamie said.

"Yes, you are. Would you like to hear?"

The children froze. Suddenly, they heard Carol's voice.

"Mommy, the crazy man says he'll hurt us if you come here."

"That wasn't me, Mommy," Carol yelled, but Barney knew it didn't matter. The Unweebil wouldn't let her hear the real kid voices. Unless . . .

Barney did a magic, and yelled, "Mommy, Mommy, Mommy! I'm so scared! Come get me!" but the Unweebil shot fire out of the crystal and burned him, and he screamed.

"No more of that," the Unweebil said. "I'll say what I want said, thank you very much."

Then Jamie's voice started without him.

"Mom, this guy says you gave us to him because you didn't want us anymore. He's lying, isn't he?"

"I never said that!" Jamie shrieked.

"Mommy," Barney's voice begged, *"go back. Or he's gonna kill us. You gotta go back."*

"No, Mommy. Don't listen to the Unweebil," Barney begged. "Please, please, please don't listen."

Their voices went on and on without them, saying things they would never have said.

Barney, Carol, and Jamie sat and watched in silence. Their mother parked her buggy on the road and waited. She listened, and from time to time, her mouth moved, but she didn't really say anything out loud—except to Murp.

And then, as all three of them looked on, she turned around and drove back the way she'd come.

They screamed and pleaded and begged and made every promise they could think of—but finally Carol couldn't stand it anymore. She stared at the crystal ball and screamed, "Break! Break!"

Barney joined in the chant with her. Then Jamie did, too.

"Break!" they all screamed at the crystal ball. "Break! Break! Break!"

The glass shattered, and the picture of their mother's retreating back vanished in the shards of broken glass.

"I hate you, Mommy," Barney whispered.

Carol bit her lip. "I hate you, too."

"I will never forgive you, and I will never love you again," Jamie said.

All around him, Barney could hear the Unweebil's soft, snakey laugh. It didn't matter anymore, he thought. Nothing mattered.

He started to cry, and threw himself down on the mattress. Jamie and Carol did the same.

"We're never gonna get out of here now," Jamie said between sobs. "Never. Never, ever, ever. We're gonna die here."

"I know," Barney said.

CHAPTER 13

The flying carpet had lifted off the ground the instant Minerva uttered the word "go" and tore off toward the Unweaver's domain. The carpet had seemed simple enough—in fact, *nothing* she'd thought of could have seemed simpler. Sit on a flying rug and go where you want to go.

In practice, flying a carpet turned out to be rife with unexpected problems.

The carpet wriggled and swayed beneath her. Minerva hadn't felt so green since the time she went sailing with friends and found out she was, in fact, the type of person who got sick while sailing in small vessels—even in very, very calm seas. She hadn't thought she would be; she had always believed people who got seasick were sissies or hysterics. She'd assumed that she, who had been a tomboy as a child and who still wasn't afraid of much of anything, would take to the sea like a fish.

Camels, ships of the desert, had more business in the ocean than she.

Sailing the high seas, though, was a pleasure jaunt compared to this ordeal. Minerva fought to keep the carpet level. She leaned forward, trying to hold the front straight to keep it from shimmying in the wind; but she overbalanced, and she and the carpet and everything on it went into a forward roll that left her flying while hanging upside down. She was strapped on—thank heavens for safety belts and the common sense to wear them. She gripped her glasses with one hand and watched the ground rushing under her, very far away. Even in her nightmares, she'd never experienced anything like this.

Help! she thought. She would have welcomed rescue from the Unweaver. Barring that, she would have welcomed a single glimmering of inspiration.

Kayaks, she suddenly thought. *People who ride in kayaks go upside down.*

Minerva swung her upper body from side to side in a move she hoped approximated a kayak roll. She wanted with all her heart and soul to be upright again. After dangling far too long swinging back and forth like the clapper of a bell, she built up enough speed to flip upright—and enough speed, unfortunately, to go right on over and down the other side. She managed to stay calm, kept rolling, and swung up again.

She flung out her arms and stopped her roll while she was still upright that time, but the left edge of the rug curled under when she did. The carpet side-slipped in a maneuver guaranteed to thrill a fighter pilot.

"A-a-a-yyyygh!" Minerva swore, yanked frantically at the carpet side, and nearly flung her hands over her face as the flying rug skimmed the top of the mud flats before gaining altitude again. Slowly it came back under control. When she was fairly certain she wasn't going to die in the next instant, she cautiously inched her hands forward along the edges of the rug until she held the corners, then spread them as straight and tight as she could. The carpet wallowed like a pig, but did not roll or dive or flip over again.

Minerva became aware of Murp protesting bitterly in the tongue of cats from inside the strapped-down duffel bag—and of a steady stream of profanity which issued from her own mouth, as well.

" . . . gave me the idea I'd rather have a goddamn flying carpet than a nice four-wheel drive, anyway?" she snarled into the breeze. "The shithead who invented the *idea* of flying carpets spent too much time smoking dope from a hookah! Sumbitches are unstable! They *flip!*"

Murp, inside the duffel bag, yowled plaintive agreement every time the damned carpet hit an air pocket and bucked. Minerva would have thrown up if she could have done it without tipping herself over.

The sun beat down with merciless intensity. The wind whipping past her could have been heated in an oven. Her mouth was parched and full of sand, her eyes gritty. Dust caked on her skin, clogging the creases. Dust turned her clothing gray.

Ahead, the Unweaver's domain loomed. All sunlight died at that border; the Unweaver's wall was oily, creeping smoke held back by an invisible membrane. Minerva tried to suppress a shudder. The compass pointed straight into the center of that greasy, hellish maelstrom—she gripped her compass like a lifeline and thought of her kids.

"I—can—do—this," she said through clenched teeth. "I can. I will."

She wished Darryl were with her. It was odd—she felt closer to him at that moment, though he was a universe away, than she had in years. Knowing he cared helped. Knowing a lot of the distance between them the past few years had been her fault helped, too. She could remember why she had once loved him—and finally she began to think she still did. *There are a few facts in life a woman really needs to be sure of,* she thought. *One is that she loves her husband. That isn't always as easy to know as it ought to be. The other is that he still honestly loves her—and that can be even harder.*

The flying carpet was nearly to the smoke-walled domain of the Unweaver when it began to lose altitude. Thunderheads piled higher as she approached; lightning flashed between the towering clouds. A quiet moan of dismay escaped Minerva. Then the carpet pitched through the smoke wall and tumbled to the ground.

Minerva unstrapped the duffel bag and let Murp out first. Then she released herself from the carpet belts, and stood, and rummaged through the duffel for something to tie over her face. The air in the Unweaver's demesne—well, *wasn't*. The place stank of sulphur and rotting fish and unwashed bodies in a crowded room. She couldn't see much. The dense gray haze and the clouds overhead blocked out most of the light.

She felt a sudden blaze of hatred for Talleos. He would have left her children trapped in this place, while he got whatever it was he was after—no matter how long it took. Trapped in this stinking darkness, this hot hell—

For an instant, her anguished longing for her children nearly overwhelmed her. She could feel their cheeks, soft as rose petals, pressed against her face, their arms wrapped around her neck as they hugged her good-night. She could feel their hands, soft and fragile and tiny, clasped in her own. She could feel their weight in her arms and on her hip, the weight of a procession of babies grown bigger, who still wanted to be picked up and held and kissed "to make it better"—her children. Hers. For whom she would move heaven and earth.

For whom she was going to have to.

So be it.

The magic animating the flying carpet had failed within the borders of the Unweaver's domain. That had been Darryl's magic—but the fact that it ceased working was a mystery that needed to be solved before she dared go on. Did *no* magic work within this place? Was there something about just the flying spell that didn't work? Or—had something happened to Darryl?

She rummaged through her duffel bag again, this time looking for vellum and pencils. She was almost out. She frowned. Somehow, she had forgotten she was so near the end of her supply.

Now what?

Minerva considered, then got out the last scrap of vellum and the last pencil. In an unused space, she sketched a good paint box and a thick sketchpad, all the while concentrating on supplies—like the energy source in her armored buggy—that could not be depleted. She watched as a closed paintbox and a luminous sketchpad shimmered into existence before her like fireflies in formation.

So magic works. I can't think of any way to test specific

problems with the carpet. I guess that means I need to figure out a way to see if something has happened to Darryl.

She sat in the the hot, stinking darkness and considered. *He's managed to see what I've been doing,* she finally decided. *Perhaps I can use a magic mirror to check on him.* She could draw herself a little hand mirror, something portable.

She opened the paintbox—and a rainbow streamed out, washing against the ugliness around her like a tide of hope. Tinkerbell and all her friends in party getup couldn't have been more beautiful, nor could they have appeared at a better time. She peered down into the surprising depths of the little paint box, and found several good mohair brushes and pots of light in every possible color.

Bewildered, she pulled out one of the little glass pots and unscrewed the lid. Ruby light, rich and deep as the heart of good red wine held up to sunlight, bright as the soul of a gemstone, glowed in the pot. A radiant overflow spilled up and out, and streaked the greasy gray air around her with one thin line of pure loveliness. She took up a mohair brush, and dipped it into the center of the glowing stuff, and lifted it out. The bristles, coated in light, shimmered and flashed like living things. Minerva waved the tip of the brush through the air once, fascinated, and the brush left a solid trail of fire hanging in the air. Mesmerized, she formed another line, and then another, fashioning them into a mirror of light. She covered the red pot, and opened one of silver— and filled the center of her mirror with glimmering fairy dust.

The mirror, completed, hung before her in the air, too beautiful to be believed. Minerva reached out a trembling finger to touch it, and it slipped into her hand, radiantly warm. She stared into glowing surface, and first she saw a ghost of her own reflection; but that fell away in an instant to reveal a dark scar on the surface of a planet, then the whole of the planet spinning in space, then all of space . . . and then, with terrifying speed, another planet, a continent, a building, and a man.

Darryl. Lying tied, straight-jacketed, seemingly unconscious, with policemen and orderlies and a shrink she knew
and despised standing over him.

"Son of a bitch," she muttered.

He hadn't been able to come to her. There was no gate
near where she was. She looked from the box of paints to
the reflection of her husband, held prisoner. If he were with
her, he could help her save the kids. She didn't think he
would be able to help her, or himself, straightjacketed in the
psych ward of the hospital.

A gate between the universes; she'd traveled on such a
thing coming to Eyrith. It hadn't seemed like much at the
time. Could she make a gate?

She took out the biggest paintpot, full of white light. In
the air she painted a circle that began above her head and
stretched to her feet, as wide as her arms would stretch to
either side. She completed the perimeter, then spiraled the
line inward, seeing herself at one end of the coil of light and
Darryl at the other. With a sucking sound, the murk cleared
from her tunnel. The darkness was held back by the glowing
spiral, and the tunnel terminated in a bright light on the
other end.

She stuffed the drawing pad into the duffel bag and slung
both duffel and paintbox over her right shoulder. Then, still
armed with her paintbrush and her container of white light,
she stepped into the tunnel. "C'mon, Murp," she said.

The cat *mrrrped*, and trotted at her heels.

She walked, until it seemed she was making no progress.
Then she began to trot. The far end of the tunnel, still
bright, seemed no nearer. She ran. Murp, bitching heartily,
fell behind. She stopped and looked back, he ran to catch
up, and when she turned again, she was at the other end.

Magic, she thought. *Arrrgh!*

She did a quick bit of magic to make sure she would be
visible to the people in the room. Then she stepped out of
the tunnel, and the blue dragon who'd been standing by the
door saw her first. "Well, goddamn," he said, and gifted her
with a crocodile grin. "Nice timing."

"Hi," she answered, and pushed a policeman out of her

way to get to her husband. "Darryl," she said, "can you hear me?"

"Ma'am," the police officer said, "how did you get in here? You aren't supposed to be in here."

The shrink puffed up and said to the orderlies, "Get her out—right now." Then he looked at her more closely, and grew pale.

Minerva pointed a finger at the doctor. "Look, asshole," she snarled. "You know damn well he's my husband. I've come to get him."

"His wife is dead," Dr. Folchek said. His voice wavered.

The police looked from Darryl to Folchek to Minerva, faces showing bewilderment.

"Scary thought, isn't it?" Minerva grinned at them, and shook Darryl. "Babe, wake up," she said.

One of the policemen tried to grab her, but his hands went right through her. His scream cut into the air, high-pitched and wavering. It ended abruptly when he fainted and collapsed to the floor.

"Anyone else want to try?" Minerva was in a bit of a Clint Eastwood mood. She wanted to urge them to make her day. She wanted to wreak havoc. The simple fact of her presence, though, would probably be enough for that.

"She's a hallucination," Folchek said, at the same moment Darryl sat up out of his body and looked around the room.

"Minerva," he yelled, and flung his arms around her.

He felt warm and wonderful. She hugged him close, trying not to look too hard at the other Darryl, the one who lay on the table, not breathing, beginning to turn a waxy, ashy gray. "Babe," she said, "we've got to get moving. We've got to get the kids."

Folchek twitched, staring between the dying Darryl on the table and the living one that walked toward the tunnel of light with his wife. "No," the man said. "This is a form of mass hypnosis. A hysteria-induced hallucination. None of you are seeing what you think you see."

"Wait up," Birkwelch said. "I can see I don't need to hang around here anymore."

Minerva laughed, and all of them ran for the tunnel.

"No!" Minerva heard Folchek wail as they passed into the suspended link between the Universes. "No! Call a code, for godsakes! Quick! He isn't breathing!"

She didn't look back. She couldn't. Darryl was with her—the part of him that she could bring was right beside her . . . alive and breathing and real. What had just happened in the universe she left behind, she wasn't ready to think about.

Not yet.

The hot wind gusted and spiraled around Darryl, Minerva, Birkwelch, and the cat.

"Can it possibly all be like this?" Darryl's feet dragged; the clothes Minerva had magicked up for him clung to his skin. He plodded unthinkingly. The ground shifted and bubbled under him, while in front of him landmarks appeared and disappeared with terrible regularity.

"No," Birkwelch said. The dragon favored Darryl with a slit-eyed grimace. "It's bound to get worse."

"Thanks, dragon." Minerva, a few steps ahead, didn't bother turning around. Darryl could tell by the set of her shoulders she was pissed off—probably because of Birkwelch's big mouth, but not necessarily. He slogged faster and caught up with her.

He kissed her. "Babe, something's wrong. Anything I can fix?"

She turned a tired, sweaty face to him and pushed her slipping glasses up her nose. "There has to be a faster way to find him than this. Has to be. We're wearing ourselves out before we even get where we're going. How the hell can we win our kids back if we're too tired to fight him?" She looked away, and her shoulders sagged. "But I guess I'm too tired to think. I haven't come up with anything that could work."

Darryl pulled her against him and stared past her, into the endless fog-shrouded gloom. While he watched, a hulking rock plinth heaved itself up out of the quaggy ground a few feet away, towered upward until its top vanished, stories above him, in the gray haze, then sank into the ground again.

Nothing of it remained. It carried out the entire cycle in utter silence.

"She's right," Birkwelch said softly. "Wandering around in his murk like this, you're playing his game. You might wander forever without finding him, following your little compass the way you are."

Minerva pushed herself away from Darryl's chest and looked at the dragon, surprise evident on her face. "How can that be?"

Birkwelch sat cautiously on the shifting ground and blew a short, blue-white blast of fire into the air. Even he looked tired and cranky and disgusted, Darryl noticed. "I don't imagine the Unweaver's home, or fortress, or whatever he occupies, has any fixed location within this place. I suspect his place is wandering around in this goddamned soup, and we're chasing after it." The dragon sprawled on his belly in a graceless flop, and snorted.

"Why didn't you say something, if that's what you thought?" Minerva snapped.

"Lady, I figured if you could have done something about it, you would have. And you just said you couldn't think of anything to do—so my bitching would have been pretty pointless, wouldn't it?" The dragon closed his eyes, and dozed.

Darryl noted with alarm that the instant the dragon drifted off to sleep, his color bleached from blue to gray, and he began to sink into the muck.

"Birkwelch!" he and Minerva yelled at the same time.

The dragon's eyes flew open, and he heaved himself upright. Some of his color came back. The tips of his wings and the tip of his tail looked hazy for an instant, then solidified. His head snapped from side to side, looking for danger. When he didn't see anything, he stared at Darryl. "I wanted to take a nap. Just a little nap. Couldn't let me have a few minutes of peace, could you?"

He glared at the two of them.

"Look at yourself," Darryl whispered. "You nearly disappeared."

The dragon stretched out one taloned foreleg and gaped

in horror at the gunmetal gray color it had become. "Shit!" he whispered. "This place started to unweave me." The dragon shivered violently and stared into the gloom around him with horrified eyes.

Darryl said, "I might have an idea of how to get ourselves to the Unweaver's door. Minerva, you have a pencil and paper in that paintbox?"

"I have some paper." She pulled out the sketchpad she'd created for herself before she discovered her paints worked on air. "And a pencil or two in the duffel, I think."

She shuffled through the contents of the duffel bag and came up with the required pencil.

Darryl held the sketchpad in his hands, noting the ordinariness of the rust-red Bienfang cover and the extraordinary glow that emanated from the edges of the paper beneath it. *Radioactive art pad*, he thought, and gingerly opened the cover.

White light streamed off the first blank page and burned a tunnel upward through the gloom. "Wow!" Darryl flipped the cover shut as fast as he could, afraid something in that murk might notice. "What the hell kind of paper is that?"

"Um—" Minerva managed half a grin. "Haven't the faintest. I wanted something that wouldn't run out. I would assume that's it."

Darryl crossed his ankles and dropped to the ground; he rested the tablet on one thigh, and began to write.

Out— he scratched, but though he pressed hard on the surface of the paper, no letters appeared. He traced the shapes of the letters again, and swore. "This pencil doesn't write."

Minerva and Birkwelch pointed at the air in front of them. Glowing letters burned there with the same brilliant, cool white as the "paper" on which they had been written.

Out Out, Darryl read.

"Damned spot?" Minerva asked.

"Er—no. Not what I was going to say."

"Thought not," the dragon muttered.

"Well, I guess it does work after all." Darryl put pencil to paper again, and wrote:

> *Out of the mist, born from the formless ground, a road arose. It was carved of a single piece of stone, raised high above the murk—beautiful, indestructible, and unsinkable. It glowed with a radiance that burned away the sullen fogs and unending gloom. And it led straight to the Unweaver in his lair.*

"Yes!" Minerva said.

Birkwelch, too, seemed impressed. "Nice piece of rock, fella. I wouldn't have thought you had anything that pretty in your imagination."

The road was raised like an ancient Roman aqueduct, delicate arches holding up a span of stone strung over them like glowing white ribbon. "Really," the dragon continued, "I don't think I've ever seen such a pretty piece of engineering work."

"Thanks," Darryl said. He was pretty impressed, too.

"Only two problems that I see," Birkwelch added. "First, you didn't make any way to get up there."

Darryl sighed. "Yeah. I'll have to fix that. What was the second problem?"

"The Unweaver knows for sure now that at least one of you is here."

Darryl and Minerva exchanged glances. "That's very bad, isn't it?" Minerva asked.

Birkwelch said, "You'd think so, wouldn't you?"

I hate dragons, Darryl thought.

He focused on his paper, and wrote another line:

> *A ramp curved up from the ground at Darryl's feet to the road high overhead.*

Darryl pictured the curving beauty of the white stone ramp; the elegant, simple bellied sweep of upreaching path. His words burned themselves into the sky; his thoughts transformed to solid form: the ramp, seamless and perfect, lay before him.

The dragon, with a sly grin, spread his wings and flew up to the road above. From overhead, he called down, "Hurry up already."

Minerva turned to Darryl. "Gets on your nerves a bit, doesn't he?"

"You haven't even heard him sing. Of course, it would be worse if there were hundreds just like him."

Minvera frowned. "I was meaning to talk to you about that—"

"Later." Darryl sprinted up the ramp. The last thing he felt like hearing about was the Great Dragon Fiasco, and his failure to be a brilliant magician.

The day brightened, and Darryl's mood lifted. The bridge shed enough light to banish the gloom around it, but the fogs and clouds were blowing away, too.

The dragon cocked an eye heavenward and said, "So much for our cover."

"Shut up, Birkwelch." Minerva reached the top of the ramp and looked down the road in both directions. She smiled suddenly. "Hey, look! A city." She pointed to her right and consulted her compass. "Yesss! That's the way!"

It wasn't far. The place looked to Darryl like an exercise in ugly—a city that had not so much survived floods, famines, and fires as one which had gone down beneath their weight . . . while still retaining upright walls.

"What a dump," the dragon muttered.

Darryl found himself agreeing.

At his side, Minerva whispered, "Oh, no!"

"What?" He looked at her with alarm.

"Murp's gone."

Darryl tried not to snap at Minerva. "Maybe the cat will show up. But Murp is the least of our worries right now."

Minerva started toward the city, hurrying, Darryl suspected, so he couldn't see her cry. "I know that," she said, "but it seems like a bad omen."

"It isn't like you could eat the damned thing," Birkwelch said. "Cats taste worse than Wheaties."

"Shut up, Birkwelch," Darryl said, and hurried after his wife.

Barney saw his mother and father coming for him in his dream. They were with a dragon, and with Murp.

But this time, Barney knew better. His parents weren't ever coming for him. They didn't really want him.

So he turned his back on the dream, and drifted into the darker gray places of sleep, where nothing bothered him at all. And finally, in his dream, a voice offered him rest, and peace. The voice offered him an escape from all the hurt. He listened to the voice, and let go of himself completely. He joined with the nothingness, and forgot the pain.

CHAPTER 14

Minerva stepped off the bright, shining road into the battle-broken ruins of the Unweaver's city. She wished the cat were with her; conversely, she wished the dragon weren't. She discovered herself incapable of appreciating witty remarks made while walking into the jaws of death. She would have preferred the dragon to act as afraid as she felt, but barring that, she would have found silence acceptable. Instead—

"Ho, puny godling! We three mortals have come to beard you in your lair!" the dragon bellowed. "Come out, puling fiend, and show your scabby visage!"

"Shut up, shut up, SHUT UP!" Darryl hissed.

The dragon turned to Darryl in apparent surprise. "He *knows* we're here. The least we can do is go into this massacre looking like heroes." Birkwelch appealed to Minerva. "Look, if we're going to be stripped atom from atom and fed into the bonfires of eternity, I at least want it said that we went with a bit of style. Don't you?"

"No!" Minerva and Darryl said together.

The dragon gave each of them a hurt look and retreated into silence.

Darryl turned to Minerva. "Which way?"

She held the compass in her hand. It pointed down a twisting alley filled with rubble and overshadowed by shattered, tilted walls. "That way." She frowned. Right at the point where the alley twisted, she could have sworn she saw something move. Its shadow smeared across one whole wall, grotesque and undefinable. She glanced at Birkwelch. "If what you said before still stands, how are we supposed to protect ourselves?"

"Think happy thoughts?" The dragon acted like he'd seen that hulking shadow lurking in the alley, too. He puffed a flame experimentally, then sighed. "I don't know. I'm not a Weaver. I do know that it's harder to create than destroy, which is why there are so many destroyers and so few creators." The dragon moved into the street, in the direction Minerva had indicated. "I'll do what I can to protect you."

Minerva and Darryl followed. The stink of filth and sulphur was worse in the ruins, the air closer and damper and hotter. The ground rumbled intermittently, and Minerva became aware of a grinding sound, very low—she could not pinpoint its location. Sometimes it seemed nearby, sometimes it came from a point far away. The sound made her uneasy—there was about it something of the giant's rhyme in the Beanstalk fairy tale: "I'll grind your bones to make my bread."

The alley twisted hard to the left and split into a T. Minerva consulted the compass. "Right," she said. The right road was narrower than the left. The bombed-out buildings overhung it further. It figured.

The three of them moved warily onto the new road. Something keened, off in the distance—a shrill, heartrending, animal cry of anguish.

"Ugh!" Darryl whispered. "I could have done without that."

Shapes and shadows moved near the corners. Minerva pointed to them, and Darryl nodded.

Birkwelch's ears swiveled, and he stopped. "Listen," he said.

The grinding sound grew louder and moved closer. Minerva shivered in spite of the heat and checked the compass again. The three of them reached the next intersection: a Y. Minerva checked the compass. It wavered back and forth between the two possible roads, spun once in a complete circle, then settled into place, pointing to the left branch. Minerva frowned—she hadn't seen any sort of uncertainty in the compass's directions before.

Then the grinding grew louder, and this time it seemed to come from the place the trio had just left. Birkwelch bounced from one hind leg to another, and the tip of his tail whipped back and forth like an angry cat's. "Can't you do that any faster?" he asked.

Minerva pointed down the dark, narrow, twisting left alley. The rumbling began up ahead—horrible crushing stone-on-stone noise. They seemed to be heading straight into it—but the arrow on Minerva's kid-compass was unwavering.

Then, from the air around them, Jamie yelled, "Mom! Mommy! Daddy! Go back! Please go back! Don't let him hurt us!" The child-voice echoed and re-echoed through the twisting ruins, punctuated at the end by a scream that left Minerva's heart in her throat. She broke out in a cold sweat. Beside her, Darryl went ghost-white.

Carol shrieked, "Mommy, Daddy! No! If you come here, the Unweaver will kill us"

"Don't hurt me, monster! Don't—!" Barney's cry dissolved into a bubbling, wordless howl.

Birkwelch snarled and all of them began to run. They came to another intersection. "Which way?"

The grinding and the rumbling was all around them, constantly growing louder—Minerva had to yell to be heard over the steady, subterranean roar. "The needle's still spinning," she shouted. "Wait a second!"

The needle twirled around, while the roar grew thunderous and the ground beneath her feet began to shudder. From the gutted windows of the broken buildings around them, Minerva saw eyes looking down at her, glowing dully in the shadows. Then the needle settled on a direction—back the way the trio had just come.

Minerva's head snapped up, and she spun around and stared back the way they'd just come. The alley deformed before her eyes, the buildings shifting and moving closer. The noise—

"Oh, God! Run!!" she yelled, and charged toward the place they'd left. The buildings slid together faster the closer she got to the escape, the alley grew narrower, and suddenly she saw the end pinch off before her eyes.

"Retreat!" Birkwelch shouted, and darted back. Minerva and Darryl followed, racing as fast as they could, while the rest of the alley crushed together behind them.

The four-way intersection became a courtyard before their eyes, the alleys wiped out of existence by the moving bank of solid, blank walls. And when the last of the alleys closed off, the buildings advanced toward Minerva, Darryl, and the dragon, slowly but steadily. As the ruins advanced, they also grew taller, so that the gutted windows towered high out of reach before any of the trio had a chance to use them as a means of escape.

Minerva looked up. "Another magic carpet?" she yelled to Darryl. The two of them, she thought, were the only ones who really had to worry. Birkwelch could fly.

Darryl nodded.

Minerva opened her paintbox, grabbed a brush and light-paint—and the buildings arced toward each other over her head, grew into a solid ceiling, and swallowed the light.

The grinding stopped. In the unexpected silence, Minerva could hear her own harsh breathing and that of her companions.

"Trapped!" Darryl shouted. "We need a tank!"

"No!" Birkwelch yelled. "I already told you—no destruction! Everything you unweave makes him stronger."

Minerva painted a sphere of light that hung in the air between them, driving out the darkness and casting weird shadows on the walls behind them. "Turn the other cheek, then?" she asked.

"Too passive." The dragon leaned near enough that she could smell his breath—even in the stink of the city, this was unfortunate. "It is not enough that you refrain from unweaving; you must also weave. 'He who does no evil, but neither does good, is still evil by default.'"

"Who said that—Buddha?" Darryl asked.

Birkwelch wrinkled his muzzle and snorted. "The Worm

Kiffaulter. Draconic philosopher. It's from a long parable about the munching of babes and woofers and the aquisition of treasures great and small—but I figured the parable was probably a species thing." The dragon's toothy grin only emphasized the direness of the situation. "I skipped to the moral at the end."

"Good." Minerva stared into the glowing light-paints in her box. "So we have to *create* our way out of here?"

Her question was punctuated by a soft plop.

Minerva pushed the light-sphere upward—it floated toward the ceiling and threw its light into the farthest corners of the unnatural cavern. In the last pool of shadow, something moved.

"Yes," Birkwelch said, stepping toward the hulking shadow. "And now would be a good time."

The shadow-shape welled up and oozed moistly toward the dragon, making long, sucking, slurping sounds as it progressed. It was not large, but what it lacked in size, it made up for in gruesomeness. The dragon shot a blast of flame toward it, but did not touch it. It retreated, bubbling and wailing.

There was another plop, from the other side of the cavern. The rainbow paints glowed softly. Minerva clutched the first pot she touched. Darryl leaned over and kissed her.

She kissed him as hard as she could, and when she pulled back, brushed tears from her face with a backhanded swipe. "In case it's good-bye," she whispered.

He had a pencil in one hand, the paper pad in the other. "I won't let it be good-bye," he promised. "Not again. Never again."

Minerva heard a third squishing plop. All three of the creatures oozed toward her and Darryl. They had dagger-lined maws and horrible eyes. They advanced, and the dragon laid down lines of flame on the earth in front of them, galloping in circles around the cavern, racing from one monstrosity to the next, renewing each line of fire as it flickered out. "You're running out of time," Birkwelch bellowed. "I can't keep this up forever."

Minerva dipped the brush into the paint—she'd come up

with green. *Green,* she thought. *Green as meadows, green as fields, green as forests.* She flung up a horizontal line in the air, undulant, a rolling hill. "Wide-open meadow," she yelled to Darryl.

He pressed his back to hers and began to write. She read his words in the glowing air around her while she painted:

> *The field was peaceful. Short grass ruffled in waves at Minerva's feet. Three gentle horses cropped the grass, while a cool breeze blew past, and—*

The writing stopped unfolding in front of her. Minerva, madly brushing in hints of blue sky and wispy white clouds, said, "—and on the front porch of the house on the hill . . ."

"Yes," Darryl said.

> *—on the front porch of the house on the hill, the Unweaver sat, smiling politely, drinking lemonade.*

"I HATE LEMONADE!" an unfamiliar voice shrieked.

The closed-in labyrinthine ruins were gone. The oozing monsters were transformed into miniature ponies that nibbled at the lovely green meadow grass and plucked the rainbow-hued flowers, tails flicking lazily. On the front porch of a lovely white antebellum mansion, a plump little man sat, lemonade glass in his hand—at least for an instant. Then the lemonade glass deformed into a thing of leprous ugliness, and the paint on the house began to peel. Layers of the plump little man stripped themselves away into a cloud of dark smoke that formed over his head—skin and flesh, sinew and bone feeding into the wraith; man devolving into fog.

The ponies lifted their heads and laid their ears back. They, too, began to shift and change—not so much to become something else as to melt away into less than they had been before.

"Don't let him spoil it!" Minerva yelled at Darryl. She kept painting—retouching the house and the little horses to keep them firmly grounded in reality, adding fences and an orange tabby cat on one fencepost—and then painting in the Unweaver—painting a woman, a grandmother—kindly, sweetfaced, the sort of woman who would yearn to dandle her daughter's babies on her knee, who would bake bread. Darryl's followed Minerva's lead. His words glowed in the air.

The Unweaver, who had loved nothing, believed nothing, embraced nothing, in that moment became something—became human, learned to care—and in that becoming, embraced and affirmed life.

Nice, Minerva thought. *Nice touch, Darryl. Conquer by creation, leave something good in the place of all the evil and destruction.*

Minerva looked up at the woman—for indeed it was a woman who stood on the veranda of that plantation house. The tired Weaver walked up the hill toward her and reached out her hand to touch her—to touch the creature who had once been the Unweaver, and who was redeemed.

The woman watched Minerva's hand come toward her, and her mouth opened, as if she were about to say something—

But the mouth kept opening, and opening, and the flesh of the face peeled back and fell away, and a scream—rage, or terror, or pain—rent the air. Then the Unweaver ripped itself to shreds before Minerva's eyes, almost beneath her fingers, and the last remnants—two burning glowing sockets that might have been eyes, suspended in a cloud of gray haze—sucked down into a crack between the floorboards of the veranda and were gone.

"Er, nice try," Birkwelch said. He'd just finished reading Darryl's words, which were fading quickly into nothingness. "Nice concept, anyway." He flipped the rilles of his face backward and sighed. "But pointless. You cannot change the essential nature of the Unweaver. He's a primal force."

"In other words—'a valiant effort, but to no avail,'" Darryl muttered, and kicked the bottom step of the veranda.

"Don't take it so hard," the dragon said, and patted Darryl

on the back. "You've got him on the run. You've probably chased him out of this universe entirely."

"He's probably hiding under the floorboards of the house, plotting revenge," Minerva said.

The dragon looked around him. Minerva saw him studying the big white house, the rolling hills, the manicured pastures, the horses, and the lovely picket fences. Birkwelch shook his head vehemently. "Not his kind of place. Hanging around now would drive him nuts. He tried to tear your Weaving down, and failed. I don't think he's here anymore."

"Great. Wonderful." Minerva studied the house and frowned. "I don't care whether he's still here or not. I just want to find the kids."

Birkwelch stood on the veranda. "About the kids—they could be in anything," the dragon said. "They could *be* anything. Everything that was here before is still here—but it's all been transformed. Since none of the little dears have come bounding out the door yet, I'm assuming there might be a problem."

Darryl gripped the porch rail. He and Minvera had crossed universes to get their kids back. They'd beaten the Unweaver. They couldn't have come all that way, done all the things they had done—conquered entropy personified, for crissakes—to lose at the last minute.

"In the house somewhere, then?" Minerva looked worn and scared to Darryl. Her eyes were huge and shadowed, her skin pale.

"Let's go," Darryl said, and walked up the steps and onto the porch. He didn't want to wait any longer—didn't want to talk about finding the kids, or talk about possible problems, or *talk* about anything. He just wanted to get in, get them, and get the hell out. The idea of home seemed dearer to him than it ever had.

He swung the door open and walked in. And stopped. What had been a Southern plantation on the outside . . . well, *wasn't* on the inside. The walls were stone, pale gray. The front door opened into a hallway, with doors on either side. The hallway inside the house extended much farther than the walls outside the house.

"I've been here before," Minerva whispered.

Birkwelch and Darryl looked at her with, Darryl suspected, nearly identical expressions of disbelief.

"In a nightmare," she added. "There were bloody footprints on the floor, and a door with a lion's head—it was all very vivid." She closed her eyes. "Also, I was flying," she said.

Darryl was willing to give consideration to the concept that Minerva's dreams might have some validity. He never had before— *But*, he thought, *just living from day to day can give you reason to reconsider the possibility of most anything.*

They walked down the hall, opening each stone door. All the doors opened easily, but all the rooms were empty. "If this place looks the same as it did in my dream, does that mean we didn't succeed in defeating the Unweaver after all?" Minerva asked.

Birkwelch dismissed that out of hand. "You beat him, fair and square. Rearranged him, completely overturned his own private hideaway— No, babe. The Unweaver is history around here."

Darryl said, "Now all we have to do is keep in mind the fact that dragons are basically full of shit." He stepped ahead of Birkwelch, and smiled just a bit as he heard the dragon protest.

"I saved your ass from the Cindy-monster, pal. It wouldn't hurt you to remember that."

Minerva turned to him, curious. "The Cindy-monster?"

Darryl, who had managed to forget, due to the press of events, the precise details of his culpability and moral failings, remembered them again in sudden, horrifyingly vivid detail.

"Ah, yes," he said, struggling for detachment, "ah, the Cindy-monster was one of the Weirds, like the ones who went after you. Green-eyed monsters . . ." He should have found a better way to phrase that, he decided.

Minerva gave him a penetrating look, and he thought he

would be certain to kill the dragon at his earliest opportunity. But at that moment, they came to a place where the long hall crossed another long hall—and at the intersection, they found small, red footprints running along the floor to the left.

Minerva spotted the footprints and took off in a flat-out run. Darryl galloped after her, with the dragon bringing up the rear.

Minerva skidded to a stop at the point where the footsteps turned and led beneath a closed door. "We're coming, kids," she shouted. Darryl heard no response from the kids, but all the doors were solid stone. He imagined they were fairly soundproof.

Minerva stopped. She pointed to the lion's-head doorknob and said, "Watch that. It came to life in the dream and nearly bit my hand off." She removed her vest and wrapped it around the doorknob—but no amazing transformation took place. The doorknob stayed a doorknob. Darryl grabbed it, turned it, and shoved the door open; Minerva brushed past him yelling, "We're here—"

The room, like all the other rooms, was empty. Well, not precisely empty. Darryl noted the child's bloody footprints going across the floor to a thin blanket laid out on the stone—and the meager remains of several meals. He reached down and touched one of the footprints—the blood was dry. The prints were very small. *Probably Barney's,* he thought, feeling rage build inside himself. *And we let that bastard get away—we should have annihilated him, no matter what the fucking dragon said.*

"They were here," Minerva whispered. "They were. Where are they now?"

"Not likely he took them with him," the dragon said. "I don't think he was in good enough shape to do anything requiring that much effort."

Minerva was on her knees, tracing one of the tiny footprints with a finger. "We don't even know that they're still alive."

The dragon looked from Darryl to Minerva, then back to Darryl. Darryl saw his expression grow more and more

exasperated. "Well, you're Weavers, dammit. Weave yourselves a way to find out."

Minerva looked up at Darryl, but stayed on the floor. "I
have the compass, but that turned out not to be very
reliable."

"I have an idea." Darryl took the pad and pencil and got
ready to write.

"I do hope you've thought this out fairly well," Birkwelch
said. "More carefully than your evil dragon fiasco, in any
case."

"Shut up, Birkwelch," Darryl and Minerva said in
tandem.

Darryl wrote:

> One moment, Darryl, Minerva, and the dragon Birk-
> welch were standing in an empty room of the
> Unweaver's lair. The next instant, they were magically
> transported to their children, who were safe and healthy
> and happy to see them.

The last glowing letter scrawled itself into the air a few
inches in front of one of the room's blank stone walls. Then,
as the three comrades-in-arms looked at each other, the
room dissolved into a swirling, shimmering rainbow of light.
Darryl hung, suspended in weightless, timeless nothingness
for what could have been a second or an eternity—and then
the world reformed itself, this time in vivid emerald greens
and sunset oranges.

The three of them were standing out in the pasture again.

"No," Minerva wailed. "It didn't work."

The horses looked up at them, ears flicked forward in
curiosity. The orange tabby cat leapt down from the fence in
one fluid movement and launched himself onto the back of
the smallest horse. He yawned and settled himself into a
crouch on the horse's rump.

"Mrrrrp?" he asked.

The grass was sweet, and the creature perched on his
back was companionable. The creatures who stood around

him making so much noise were very familiar. Their presence was somehow reassuring. The little horse did not know why. It wan't important. He enjoyed the warmth of the sun, and the pasture, and the quiet.

The little horse couldn't seem to remember many pleasant things from before. It remembered fear and pain—

But that was over. Gone.

And the horse, being a horse, did not let itself be bothered by the past.

CHAPTER 15

The three miniature horses trotted up to Minerva and Darryl, whickering. *No*, Minerva thought, remembering how she and Darryl had *created* those horses—had changed them from malformed nightmares into something better—

—Remembering how close she had come to destroying the monsters—

Not monsters. Her children. The Unweaver, that misbegotten fiend, had twisted her children—made them into monsters. His idea of a joke, no doubt.

The sky and the earth seemed to spin—Minerva felt faint. She sat on the grass, and rested her head in her hands, and shivered. The littlest horse walked behind her and nuzzled her on the neck, and she started to cry.

She let herself—let the fear and the tension flow out of her. Just bawled, until she ran out of tears. It was what she needed right then. When she'd cried herself out, she brushed the hair away from her face and looked up.

"When we were in the Unweaver's trap, he sent the kids to us, counting on us not knowing them—and destroying them," she said. "That would have been the ultimate irony, wouldn't it? The Weavers unweave their own children."

Darryl knelt between the other two horses, an arm around each of their necks, a look of mingled shock and horror on his face. "They were running toward us . . . Not attacking us—running toward us. Wanting our help. We would have killed them," he said, "if it hadn't been for the dragon."

Birkwelch smiled a broad alligator smile and flopped back in the grass. "No flowers, no parades, no ticker tape—nothing like that," the dragon said. "Just throw food and women."

"Shut up, Birkwelch," Minerva said. "Let us be grateful to you. Let us say thanks without you making a big joke out of it." She managed to stand again, though she still felt sick and weak. "We owe you."

"And I'll make sure you pay." The dragon looked up at her, and his grin stretched wider. "Darryl's already promised to make a whole harem of girl-dragons for me."

Minerva glared at Birkwelch, and he sighed.

"Look, I appreciate your gratitude, but I only did what I came along to do. All this mushy stuff makes me uncomfortable."

It figures. Dragons aren't the mushy sort. She gave the dragon a hug around the neck and dropped the subject.

Darryl had sat on the ground, pad and pencil in hand. He wrote:

> *All three children were returned from horse-form to their human forms, healthy and whole and uninjured.*

Minerva watched millions of tiny lights spring to life around and through the horses. The lights glowed brighter, compressed tighter, and squeezed and twisted her children from horse-shapes into child-shapes. And then Barney and Carol and Jamie stood in front of her—naked and emaciated and filthy, but smiling.

"Mom—"

"Daddy!—"

"Who's the dragon?—"

"You saved us!—"

"I *missed* you!—"

It took a while to get everything sorted out, to get hugs and kisses, to get the kids clothed—to discover her nightmares had actually happened.

Birkwelch, still sprawled in the grass looking pleased with

himself, said, "Dreams are the secret battlefield of the soul. And they're real—the big dreams are anyway. For every battle you fight in your dreams and win, you gain something you didn't have before. And every battle you lose, you lose for real."

The children curled up against her and Darryl, uninterested in dreams or magic. They wanted only hugs and kisses; the simple reassurances of their parents' touch.

Minerva needed reassurance, too, but hers could only come from knowing.

"Where did the bloody footprints come from?" she asked.

Barney, who had flatly refused to put shoes or socks on, looked down at his feet. "The Unweebil cut my feet," he said, "because I ran away with Murp once. He made me walk on them. He was mad."

His feet were healed—but she could see the scars. Horrible scars.

"He said you didn't love us," Carol added, "but you kept coming to see us, so we knew he was lying—and that made him even madder. He was really afraid of you."

"But then you turned around and went back," Jamie said. "And the Unweaver made us forget," he added.

"I didn't, though," she told them. "I never went back. I never stopped coming for you."

Minerva took it all in. She had her kids back. She had her husband back, in a way she hadn't had him for years. Her life had meaning again. All that was left was going home.

But that could wait. Night was falling on Eyrith, and the day had been long, and terrible, and exhausting, and had come at the end of a chain of long, terrible, exhausting days. With her family safe around her, she wanted to sleep.

Darryl created a house for them in the middle of the pasture—no one wanted to sleep in the mansion. Darryl wrote the house into being complete with a fully stocked refrigerator, three bathtubs with endless hot water, and one huge bed for the whole family to sleep in. There would be a time for separate beds, he'd said, but the time hadn't come yet.

The dragon settled in with beer and television, the kids ate, bathed, and crawled into bed, and after a good long soak in the tub, Minerva followed them. Darryl curled up next to her on the bed, and the two of them hugged and spooned together, too weary to talk.

Minerva was asleep almost the instant her head settled onto the pillow.

She walked through the darkness, painting light—gifting the universe with luminous flowers, emerald cliffs, rainbow-bedecked waterfalls. She created an Eden, in which beautiful beasts of every imaginable type cavorted, and her children laughed and ran and played.

She walked through that wonderland, knowing it was of her own making. She felt wonderful—magical—godlike—

She waved her hand, and in the distance, a shimmering alabaster city grew out of the rolling hills. Nearer, she created hummingbirds that flitted, gemlike, in the cool, radiant morning.

All this is my handiwork, she thought. I can do anything.

But then she noticed her alabaster city was graying and crumbling. Trees browned. The waterfall dried up, and the earth grew parched and sandy. One of the hummingbirds died in midair and toppled at her feet. Before her eyes, it decomposed. A mushroom grew out of the body, and stretched taller and wider, becoming huge—the mushroom towered over her. It split from bottom to top, and the cloak-garbed Unweaver stepped out of it.

"I am the canker at the heart of the world," he said. "There is nothing you can create that I cannot destroy. Even time, your greatest enemy, is on my side."

"You are nothing." She rested her hand on the hilt of the silver dagger in her belt, and laughed. "You don't frighten me. I beat you."

"You don't frighten me," the Unweaver mimicked, falsetto. "Give you a magic ring, and you can save the universe." He laughed. His laughter was hollow, and horrible, and ringing. "You win a minor skirmish—but only with the help of your husband and a dragon, and as a result you think yourself master of the universe. Very well, little master of the universe—can you fight me alone and win? I am immortal. Entropy cannot be destroyed. But

you are mortal, and someday must lose." His hood fell back, and Minerva saw there was nothing beneath it but two glowing eyes. "The universe will wind itself down to nothing, and I will be triumphant—now or later . . . with you or without you. You cannot win this war—yet because of someone else's error, you are destined to fight it."

The Unweaver laughed. "Puny creature of flesh, whether you die tomorrow or today is all the same to me. You will still die, and all your works will come at last to nothing."

Minerva would have argued the point with him, but what he said was true. In her heart, in her soul, in her bones, she could feel its truth, no matter how much she tried to deny it. Death would some day meet her and win.

In the short run, her fight with the Unweaver was brave and glorious: her victories bright to behold. But in the eternal measure, her fight would only last a moment, no matter how long that moment might be—and the outcome was preordained. She and her world and her universe would all wind down to chaos.

She stared at the ring on her hand—the Weaver's ring. Its perfection mocked her. Who am I? she wondered. Who do I think I am, to confront the eternal and triumph? I failed as an artist—I gave up. Quit. I was chosen as a Weaver by mistake. I'm no hero. I'm nobody special at all. If my kids hadn't been kidnapped, I wouldn't even have fought.

She sank to her knees, while the Unweaver towered over her. How silly, to think one person could really matter in the scheme of things. One person—one average, normal, nobody of a person—can't really make a difference. The universe is too vast, and eternity too incomprehensible, and people too unimportant.

But a small voice in the back of her mind screamed, So WHAT! In spite of everything, you won, dammit! If it was a little victory, so what? You won it. You saved your kids, you rescued your husband, you saved the universe. So what if you were the wrong person, and nobody special. You cared, and you fought, and goddammit, you won anyway! Everyone was against you, no one believed in you, and you still won!

Minerva looked up into the face of the Unweaver, and

suddenly smiled. "That's right," she whispered, and her smile grew broader. "I did win. I won now . . . today . . . this fight."

She stood and walked toward the Unweaver, gripping the knife, and this time there was no uncertainty in her. "I won this time. I won because I cared. Because I loved. So what if I didn't fight you alone? Love and caring make allies. People who care never have to fight alone for long."

She drew the knife and her smile grew fierce.

The Unweaver backed up a step, his cloak swirling around him. He seemed to Minerva to shrink the tiniest bit.

Minerva took another step forward. "And if I can't fight you forever . . . so what? When I fall, when I can't fight you anymore, someone else will be standing behind me to take my place. Maybe that someone won't be anyone special, either. But it won't matter.

"Don't you see that?" she asked. "It won't matter, because the person who comes behind me will care, too.

"You can't even lay claim to the end of the universe. Chaos may just curl itself into a ball of fire at the end of time, and fling out a new universe, like a phoenix rising from the ashes. Life will be born anew, and love will be waiting for it. And you will be as lonely and loveless and empty then as you are now."

The Unweaver shriveled under Minerva's attack. He collapsed in on himself, and his fear and his emptiness radiated from him in waves.

Minerva looked from him to the silver blade in her hand, and was surprised to feel a sudden rush of pity for the creature. To embrace nothingness, to choose emptiness, to desire grief and despair, to face an eternity in which nothing good could ever happen—

She threw the knife away from her. It soared in a high arc, glittering in the sunlight, and vanished over the edge of the cliff.

Minerva could suddenly see it all—her place in the universe, Darryl's . . . the Unweaver's. "You're a part of the creative process," she whispered. "Without you, there would be no ashes for the phoenix to rise from."

The Unweaver shrieked, "No! Not so! I am the antithesis

*of creation!! I destroy! I destro-o-o-oy!" His smoky form
ripped itself to shreds, and vanished.*

And Minerva woke.

"It was real," she whispered, and sat up.

Beside her, Darryl was rubbing sleep from his eyes. "I
had a dream about the Unweaver," he began.

She interrupted him. "It wasn't a dream, Darryl. It was
real. We fought him again, and we won again.

"As long as we care," she said, staring at her three children, who slept in the bed beside her, "and as long as we
never give up, I don't think we can lose."

They stood at the top of a gently rolling hill—Darryl,
Minerva, the blue dragon Birkwelch, three small children.
The land which fell away beneath their feet had been baked
mudflats only moments before. The inhabitants of the beautiful little cottages, people who were almost, but not quite,
human, had been nothing so lovely or so fine when Minerva
had first crossed their path.

"It's back the way it was before the Unweaver came?"
Darryl asked.

"Maybe even better." Birkwelch shielded his eyes and
stared almost into the sun. A shadow passed over it, and as
he studied that shadow, his face lit up. "There's one now."

"There should be a lot," Minerva said.

"Thanks for bringing them back," Birkwelch said. "And
the satyrs—er, cheymats—too. I know Talleos would thank
you if he were here."

"Probably not." Minerva snapped the words out; Darryl
noted surprising depths of bitterness in her voice. "'Thank
you' didn't seem to be the sort of thing that would occur to
him."

"He was always awfully self-centered," Birkwelch agreed.
Then the dragon stiffened and pointed toward the newly
green horizon. "Shit, shit, shit," he snarled. "Weirds."

Darryl looked where the dragon pointed and froze, his
heart pounding. Five winged forms alternately flapped and
soared toward the hill. Darryl wondered if the Weird who
had also been Cindy would be among them—or if she had

died trying to save his kids from the Unweaver, or in Minerva's firefight. He could imagine recriminations, anger, or even further disaster as the fallout of the Weirds' arrival—but he could not think of anything good that could come of a meeting with them. So he waited, pad and pencil in hand, trying to think of magic he could do quickly that would control them without destroying them, should the need arise.

The Weirds circled slowly and landed one by one; and one by one they transformed—melting from huge, ugly flying monstrosities to the quasi-human creatures which were native to Eyrith.

None of them looked like Cindy, though they all had the same glowing green eyes.

When the last of them finished their transformation, the first, a brawny man, stepped forward and dropped to one knee, and hung his head. Behind him, the other four Weirds followed his lead.

"We beg your forgiveness, Weavers," the man said, "for betraying you, for stealing your children, for plotting against you, and for failing to guide you. We made errors, and compounded the errors by betraying the principle that should have guided us—never unweave, never destroy."

Darryl took a moment to make the transition from expecting disaster to figuring out something gracious to say. He would have loved roasting the sons of bitches who kidnapped his kids and trashed his life, but the Weirds were right. "Never unweave, never destroy" was a good rule. He wouldn't have had his kids without it.

"You are forgiven," he said. He thought of adding something sort of flowery and formal, but decided against it. He was stretching the truth as it was.

Minerva evidently thought so, too. She looked at him out of the corners of her eyes and arched an eyebrow in disbelief. Then she shrugged. "There is no anger between us."

I wouldn't bet on that, Darryl thought, eyeing his wife. *You toasted a bunch of their folks. And I fed a bunch more to dragons. I'd be willing to bet there'd be plenty of anger— if they didn't think showing it would get the rest of them cooked as Birkwelch's dinner.*

"You are truly gracious," the big guy said, and stood. An awkward silence followed, until one of the women at his side gave him a surreptitious jab in the ribs with her elbow. He dissembled well, turning the *woof* of pain into an almost natural-sounding cough. "Because of the hardship we have caused you, and the disorder we have wreaked in your life, we hereby offer Eyrith as home for you and your family for however long you choose to stay here."

"You are generous and kind," Minerva said, "but we have other plans." She gave them a nice little bow, and in the smoothest brush-off Darryl had ever seen from her, she added, "Which we really must be attending to now. If you will excuse us—"

The Weirds' relief was so evident it was comical—and they were perfectly willing to take a hint. They reformed into "fly-ugly" mode, and within an instant were launched and winging their way home.

Birkwelch cocked an eye-ridge and looked from Minerva to Darryl. "That seems sort of premature. I'd have thought you would at least have considered staying here. Eyrith is about as much like your homeworld as anyplace you're going to find."

"We're going *home*," Darryl said.

Minerva nodded.

"Ah, guys," the dragon said, "I hate to be the party-pooper, but back home, you folks are *dead*. Don't you think that might make things difficult? Just a little? Eh?"

"We've already figured that out," Minerva said. "We're going to go back in time to the point where all this mess started. Only this time, we're going to do things differently."

"Ah, no—" Birkwelch, shook his head with such vehemence Darryl almost expected him to dislocate his neck.

"Why not?" Darryl asked. "We've learned our lesson. When we go back, we'll do things the way we should have done them the first time."

The dragon kept swinging his head back and forth. "No, you won't. Or rather, no, you didn't. You've learned better *now*, but back then, you made your choices. And the past does not come with an eraser. You go back, and all you'll do is form a loop in time, so that you get to relive this little adventure over and over and over."

Darryl and Minerva exchanged glances. Darryl said, "What do we do, then? I want to go home."

Minerva sat and stared off into the distance. "We can't change the past." She looked up at him and grinned suddenly. "But we ought to be able to play merry hell with the present."

The whole family sat on the grassy hill in Eyrith, getting ready to go home. Daddy wrote the story of the way it was going to be. Mommy painted the pictures.

"I think you ought to magic us rich," Jamie said.

Carol said, "Magic me as the most beautiful, smartest girl in the world."

Mommy sighed. "You are already smart, and already beautiful. And, Carol—if we make you different, how will your grandma and grandpa know you?"

"Could you at least magic me better grades in Language Arts?" Jamie asked.

"We'll see."

Barney knew what that meant. It meant "No—but I don't want to argue anymore." He grinned. Jamie was such a butthead sometimes.

"What about you?" Mommy and Daddy asked him. "Do you have any special requests?"

Barney could think of a million neat things that he could have asked for—but he couldn't think of one that was important. "No," he said. "I just want to go home."

And anyway, he thought, *even if Birkwelch says magic doesn't work the same back home . . . I bet I can still do some stuff.* He intended to try.

Minerva pushed the doorbell and listened to the familiar ring. She heard footsteps clicking on the flagstones in the entryway. Her mother opened the door.

"Mom—" Minerva managed to say before her mother screamed. It was quite a scream.

To her credit, Mrs. Wilson didn't faint. She leaned against

the doorway, breathing heavily, and she did turn whiter than the paint on the doorframe—but she didn't faint. "You're dead," she said.

"No, Mom, I'm not. Darryl isn't, the kids aren't. Everybody's fine."

"You aren't going to believe this," she told her mother, and even as she said it, she knew they would believe. Darryl had written it that way. "We were kidnapped by . . . um . . ." She winced, and gave her mother what she hoped was a sheepish grin. " . . . by space aliens." She took a deep breath. "The FBI and the CIA are doing everything they can to cover it up."

They were, too, she thought. She and Darryl had stuck an alien theme a mile wide into their story. The whole thing was going to wreak havoc with the US defense budget for the next few years. She hated that, but . . .

Her mother hugged her, and cried, and dragged her into the house, and laughed, and screamed some more, and called her brother and her father and all the neighbors—

It was worth it. It was worth the confusion, worth the deceptions, worth everything she and Darryl had done just to see her parents coming back to life. She suspected Darryl, at his house with his folks at that moment, felt the same way.

Not until quite a bit later did her dad ask the second big question.

"Minerva," her father asked, "why in heaven's name would aliens kidnap you?"

Minerva twisted the Weaver's ring on her finger, and shook her head sadly. "They thought we were somebody else," she said.

Minerva noticed that both she and Darryl had gotten quieter and quieter as the day progressed. Their story, at least temporarily, seemed to be holding. The presence of the CIA agent parked in the drive kept the neighbor's questions in check. Her friends were thrilled to hear from her—after the initial shock, at least—and the same went for Darryl's. The hospital still had her job open, and Geoff Forest offered Darryl his back—with a raise, even.

With nightfall, she and Darryl settled down at last. The

kids were asleep, the house was quiet, and the two of them sat side by side in the loveseat, staring into the crackling flames that leapt and danced in the fireplace.

Things were more or less back to normal—and Minerva knew they would get more normal as the days went on. She believed this—but her pulse pounded in her ears, and she felt as if at any instant, she would leap out of the seat, jump out of her skin—explode.

"Darryl?" she said. Then she paused, uncertain.

He looked over at her, and she noticed the crease between his eyebrows, and that he'd been biting the skin on his lower lip. "You're thinking it too, aren't you?" he asked.

She sighed. "Probably."

"We can't stay here." He looked back at the fire.

He'd said it first. Thank God, he'd said it first. She agreed. "We can't. I can't go back to the hospital. I can't *do* that anymore." She stared down at her hands, surprised to see they were trembling. She realized just the thought of trying to be what she'd once been had left her shaking.

"I told Geoff I'd think about my old job—but I won't." He leaned over and looked into her eyes. "There are universes out there waiting for us. We have things to do."

"But not here." Minerva grew more certain of that with every passing instant. "They know us here. They won't be able to let us be what we have to be."

"We'll go . . . somewhere—maybe travel." Darryl leaned back and stared into the flames. "I'll write, you'll paint—" He nodded, and the worry lines vanished from his forehead. "We'll do what we should have done all along."

Minerva felt light and full of energy. Yes, she thought. She'd been dreaming of this moment all her life. "We can visit from time to time, maybe—now they know we're all right—" She closed her eyes and thought out loud. "We'll need to call our folks, give them some story—probably blame it on the CIA or the FBI—a witness protection program—something like that. . . . We need to tell the kids—"

Darryl chuckled. "Barney will be happy, at least. He was pretty upset about not being able to make chocolate out of thin air."

Minerva glanced over at him. "So you want to go to one of the magic universes?"

Darryl arched an eyebrow. "They're fun."

"Yeah. They are." She nodded. "And we have to take Murp."

"Yes," Darryl agreed. "Definitely. The little guy deserves to come along."

"We won't need much more than that." Minerva couldn't really think of anything they'd need except each other.

"We have to get past the CIA guy out front."

"No problem." Minerva smiled and drew an imaginary spiral in the air with her finger. "We'll just walk through the wall," she said. "That'll drive 'em nuts."

"When do we leave?" Darryl asked.

Minerva closed her eyes and thought. They'd wasted so much time already. They didn't know how much time they had—but they knew it wasn't forever. "Tonight," she said.

Darryl hugged her and grinned. "It'll be an adventure," he whispered.

She laughed, feeling better the instant the decision was made. "In that case, we'd better find Birkwelch."

THE END

MERCEDES LACKEY:
Hot! Hot! Hot!

Whether it's elves at the racetrack, bards battling evil mages or brainships fighting planet pirates, Mercedes Lackey is always compelling, always fun, always a great read. Complete your collection today!

Paksenarrion, a simple sheepfarmer's daughter, yearns for a life of adventure and glory, such as the heroes in songs and story. At age seventeen she runs away from home to join a mercenary company, and begins her epic life . . .

ELIZABETH MOON

THE DEED OF PAKSENARRION

"This is the first work of high heroic fantasy I've seen, that has taken the work of Tolkien, assimilated it totally and deeply and absolutely, and produced something altogether new and yet incontestably based on the master. . . . This is the real thing. Worldbuilding in the grand tradition, background thought out to the last detail, by someone who knows absolutely whereof she speaks. . . . Her military knowledge is impressive, her picture of life in a mercenary company most convincing."—**Judith Tarr**

About the author: Elizabeth Moon joined the U.S. Marine Corps in 1968 and completed both Officers Candidate School and Basic School, reaching the rank of 1st Lieutenant during active duty. Her background in military training and discipline imbue The Deed of Paksenarrion *with a gritty realism that is all too rare in most current fantasy.*

"I thoroughly enjoyed *Deed of Paksenarrion*. A most engrossing highly readable work."

—**Anne McCaffrey**

"For once the promises are borne out. *Sheepfarmer's Daughter* is an advance in realism. . . . I can only say that I eagerly await whatever Elizabeth Moon chooses to write next."

—*Taras Wolansky, Lan's Lantern*

*   *   *   *   *

Volume One: Sheepfarmer's Daughter—Paks is trained as a mercenary, blooded, and introduced to the life of a soldier . . . and to the followers of Gird, the soldier's god.

Volume Two: Divided Allegiance—Paks leaves the Duke's company to follow the path of Gird alone—and on her lonely quests encounters the other sentient races of her world.

Volume Three: Oath of Gold—Paks the warrior must learn to live with Paks the human. She undertakes a holy quest for a lost elven prince that brings the gods' wrath down on her and tests her very limits.

*   *   *   *   *

These books are available at your local bookstore, or you can fill out the coupon and return it to Baen Books, at the address below.

PUBLISH IT AND THEY WILL COME

At Baen we believe there is only one road to success: Define a market, and then serve that market with unswerving devotion. We have chosen those sf readers who demand sf of the really, truly kind, and who want to have some fun. Have we succeeded? Judge us on the merits of the titles listed below.

Free Poster!

If your local bookstore doesn't stock these titles, it should. If you special order any of these titles from your bookstore, send us a copy of the special order form and this coupon with the title ordered checked, and we'll send you a free poster!

Available at your local bookstore. If not, special order it, then fill out this coupon to get your free poster and send to: Baen Books, Dept. BA, P.O. Box 1403, Riverdale, NY 10471.

Name: _____

Address: _____

_____